I0760644

BOOKS BY TIM MCBAIN & L.T. VARGUS

The Shadows of Love series

The Violet Darger series

The Victor Loshak series

The Charlotte Winters series

Casting Shadows Everywhere

The Scattered and the Dead series

The Clowns

LOVE HER DARKLY

LOVE HER DARKLY

A SHADOWS OF LOVE NOVEL

L.T. VARGUS & TIM MCBAIN

SMARMY PRESS

LOVE HER DARKLY

PROLOGUE

Jimmy Maddox tongues the roof of his mouth. Flexes his knuckles on the steering wheel. Feels the rumble of the engine thrumming through the car and into his hands.

Waiting. Waiting for the witness to leave.

No. Make that *witnesses*. Plural.

His eyes latch onto the moving objects in the motel parking lot. Two figures doing a dance he has seen before — the fighting couple on vacation.

Man and wife cast mostly in silhouette under the streetlights. Backs rigid. Arms windmilling angry gestures.

After a flurry of insults, the bride retreats into the rows of parked cars, and the groom follows.

To Jimmy, it seems like something they should talk about on the Discovery Channel. The domestic dispute ritual of the homo sapiens.

Jimmy just needs them to leave. Needs to get the fuck out of here himself, as a matter of fact.

But there's just one little thing he has to take care of first.

His hand slides down into his lap at the thought.

He fingers the grip of the gun there. Feels the surface gone cold in the air-conditioning.

After a second, he puts his hand back on the wheel.

His eyes stay locked on the altercation framed in the windshield.

The couple have now backpedaled to the far edge of the lot, where the fight continues.

They'd probably come here to sunny Florida looking for their little slice of paradise. The perfect vacation — a kind of suburban birthright in the eyes of the masses.

But life doesn't work the way people think it does.

Jimmy squirms a little in the driver's seat. After so much

time on the road, it feels wrong to hold still, to keep motionless. To wait.

Even the Charger's engine seems unhappy about it. Grumbling under the hood. Impatient.

Her voice comes from just next to his ear.

"What do you think they're fighting about?"

Scarlet. Of course.

She'd held so quiet in the shadows of the passenger seat that he'd thought she might be asleep.

"I dunno," he says after a second. "Vacation drama. Being miserable and hating each other is all part of the fun, I think."

"Not like us," Scarlet says.

"No. Not like us."

She leans in. Kisses his ear.

Soft lips brush against that seashell of flesh attached to his head. It makes his skin ripple.

And he loves her so much it makes him sick. He loves her so much he wants to explode into a fiery spray.

It's a bodily feeling for him, love. An electric current that spirals in his gut and tries to burst out of the top of his skull.

"Wait," he whispers. "I think they're going."

Scarlet's lips retract from his ear.

They both watch as the two figures move toward the mouth of the lot. The street is there, and the beach lies just beyond it.

Jimmy leans forward. Adjusts his hands on the wheel again. Feels his heart glugging in his chest.

The couple starts down the slope of the beach, sinking out of view. In the dark, it almost looks like the surf is engulfing them.

Jimmy makes himself wait a few more seconds. Every follicle on his body pricks up as the moment of action draws near.

The air-conditioning hisses. Soft wind rasping out of the vents to brush over his forearms and slide over his chest in an icy sheet.

"OK. We're good," he says finally. "You think?"

Scarlet nods once.

Jimmy yanks the gearshift, and the Charger starts forward. Creeps over the blacktop.

He finally flicks on the headlights as they reach the edge of the lot, but then he stops. The brakes squeal faintly.

"Here," he says, handing over the gun.

Scarlet tucks the weapon into the duffel bag between her feet. It disappears into the mess of dollar bills piled within, and then the zipper closes over all of it.

"OK," Jimmy says again, as much to himself as her.

They pull out into the street and sidle up to the well of darkness just there on the left. A ravine runs off to one side of the motel parking lot. A vine-covered slope leading down into a gully.

Jimmy puts the Charger in park. Takes a breath.

And then he shoulders through the door and ducks into the night. Loops around to open the rear door.

It's there in the backseat.

The corpse.

Seeing it in the weak glow of the dome light makes Jimmy's breath hitch in his throat.

Jesus.

The body lies flat on its back. Khakied legs tucked down into the footwell at an odd angle. Dead eyes staring up at nothing.

The gas station logo marks the chest of the navy blue polo with an orange splotch. The nametag there says Justin.

And something about that, the name, shifts the body from an "it" into a "him." A real person.

Jimmy leans in and hovers over him, over Justin. Watches the way his shadow spreads over this stranger and engulfs him.

A big boy, Justin had been. Tall and broad.

Maybe 6'4", 230. A little soft around the edges.

Still is pretty big, Jimmy supposes.

Just dead now.

Jimmy hooks his hands into the armpits and heaves, but the

weight seems to stick there like a magnet.

He shimmies it back and forth. Works it loose. The shoulder blades scooting over the upholstery as he drags it backward.

Once the bottom is free, gravity rips the head and shoulders over the fulcrum and down to the asphalt. The skull thuds into the ground, and the sound of it reminds him of a dropped melon. Makes him suck his teeth.

He changes his grip then. One hand on a shoulder and one hand on a hip.

Lifting the dead weight is like trying to finagle some beached sea cow back into the ocean.

He staggers. Rolls the body up to the lip of the ravine.

When it reaches the tipping point, the momentum wants to keep going, wants to hurl both of them over the edge. But Jimmy catches himself.

And then it's gone.

The bulk. The heaviness. It glides down into the dark. Makes a swishing sound on the wet grass.

Jimmy can only stand there and stare into the void, eyes twitching over the nothingness at his feet. He blinks, his gaze drawn deeper into the abyss that just devoured the body. Sucked it down into a black hole.

And now "he" is an "it" once more.

It seems wrong somehow to not be able to see the body. A couple hundred pounds of person just gone.

Like this guy, Justin, never existed. Like none of this is even real.

The emptiness of it wants to hold Jimmy there. Wants to keep him still, pull him under.

He twists his head. Wrenches his vision away from the black hole at last. Breaks the spell.

And then he walks back to the car. Climbs in.

Scarlet moves for him again. Soft kisses climbing down the line of his jaw.

He tries to swallow, and the spittle goes down funny. Makes

him cough a few times.

His head feels light.

For a second, he can't remember how he got to this moment — throwing a dead body down into a ditch in the middle of the night — but then he does.

He loves her, he knows. That's the how and why that led to this, to all of this.

He would do anything for her.

Anything.

That sensation of love wanting to rip its way through the walls of his chest comes over him once more. A violent feeling. Red and overwhelming.

But the dome light dims to black after a few heartbeats. And the dark inside the Charger comes as a comfort, a relief.

He finds Scarlet's hand with his. Squeezes.

Maybe they can disappear, too. They can drive out of here and melt into the darkness.

Like sliding down that slope into oblivion.

He shifts into gear. His foot finds the accelerator.

And finally Jimmy and Scarlet are moving again.

CHAPTER 1

The sun wasn't even up yet when Detective Avery Stinson parked near the far end of the motel parking lot. She chugged down the last of her Sumatran and snugged her travel mug in the cup holder.

Then she flipped down the visor and checked her hair in the mirror, though she wasn't sure why. The messy bird's nest on her head suggested she'd just rolled out of bed, which she had. She clacked the visor back up, not bothering to fuss much with her bedhead. No one here to impress, was there?

Finally, she climbed out to start the trek across the blacktop on foot.

As she walked, the faint morning twilight illuminated details of the motel itself — the Sea Spray. First she saw the two rows of aqua doors, brighter than the rest of the building, an upstairs and a down, all of the panels facing out toward the lot.

It was only after a moment that the rest of the image came clear. Peeling paint surrounded those doors, an off-white coating on the wooden siding the shade of a discolored tooth.

Off to the left, cars choked the lot, as she'd noticed when looking for a parking spot. That made sense. Tourist season was already ramping toward its apex. Between the spring breakers and the various members of law enforcement flooding the crime scene, she felt lucky to have found a spot at all.

The ocean flopped and rolled in the distance, a subtle white noise like radio static underlying everything here. The sea was having one of its potent days, it seemed, like the air here had been liberally seasoned with brine.

At the front of the lot, she closed in on the perimeter of police tape flapping in the breeze. The line of yellow plastic snapped and popped against the posts it was tethered to. Something ominous about that noise.

She couldn't see any of the techs or detectives within the demarcated area yet. The grass sloped down and out of sight, and she figured they must all be huddled closer to the bottom of the gully.

As she got to the edge, she looked down, and there it was. The techs swirling, the cameras flashing and clicking.

The dead man lay in the center of it all. Motionless.

He looked pale and small lying there in the ditch. She noticed that, first and foremost: how small he seemed despite his height. Fragile. Insubstantial, even. Then she paused to catalog the finer details.

He lay on his side in a semi-fetal position, the arrangement of the limbs awkward in a way that somehow communicated quite clearly how lifeless he was. Arms splayed. Lower legs jackknifed.

Right away she got a flash of what had happened. He'd slid or rolled into this spot. Dead weight pulled down the slope by the simple force of gravity. He'd reached this strange final resting pose like someone had hit the pause button mid-tumble.

The dead man's face had ended up mashed into the grass. A head of dark hair stared back at Stinson instead, thinning a bit so the stark white scalp was oddly visible through it.

A dark polo shirt, navy blue with a white collar, swaddled the round belly and gentle bulges of the love handles. Looked like a uniform to her, the shirt. Maybe a fast-food joint or a convenience store or something. Could be that he'd just gotten off work before it all went down — whatever had landed him here.

She imagined a car pulling to the shoulder just about where she stood now — a muscle car, the 9-1-1 caller had said, mid-aughts model. She imagined it stopping there in the deep hours of the night. Headlights gleaming in the dark. The body unceremoniously shoved over the breach. Flopping down the hill. The door slamming shut, and the car tearing off into the night.

She blinked, and her mind-movie dissolved back into reality. Back to the dead body laid out in the grassy thicket and the techs circling around it.

She ducked under the tape and made her way down the slope to get a closer look. Baby steps the whole way, and still the soles of her shoes slid against that carpet of grass slick with dew.

The ground leveled out at the bottom, and she came to an unsteady stop a few yards shy of the corpse just as two of the techs rolled him onto his back. The head held oddly rigid on the neck, and his face stayed contorted like it was still pancaked flat against the ground.

So rigor mortis has set in, she thought. *Dead at least four hours, less than twelve.*

The jaw was locked open in a gape. Purple bags bulged under the eyes. Every other feature looked droopy, pulled like taffy. The dead always looked sad, Stinson thought. Every corpse vaguely somber, like a lost child.

A voice said something unintelligible above her, and she glanced up.

Her partner, Detective Brant Taft, perched at the top of the ravine, hugged up against the fluttering police tape. Looking at him from this lower vantage point somehow made him look about a man-and-a-half wide.

His body seemed to be fighting his white dress shirt, which looked to have been purchased a few sizes ago. Taft had plumped steadily since she'd joined the Durango Beach PD six years ago, her partner going from a stick-thin guy to something more in the portly range. "Run to fat" was how he often phrased it, constantly joking about how alarmed his doctor was about the weight gain.

"What?" Stinson said, thinking he might repeat whatever he'd said.

Instead, he held up an index finger. He continued to eat a cheese Danish the size of a medium pizza, crammed his mustache right into the pastry and cream cheese like he was making out with it, and Stinson realized that he was waiting outside the tape to finish the thing. It made her shudder. How could someone eat this close to a dead body?

She looked down at the bloated corpse and then up at the eating cop. Shook her head.

"Not very respectful. Chowing down at a crime scene."

His thick salt and pepper eyebrows bounced around before he answered, jumping, crunching, dancing — wildly expressive caterpillars.

"Eh… I somehow doubt our deceased friend here gives a rip. Hell, I'd offer him a bite if it'd do him any good."

She shook her head again.

"Heart disease is a real thing. You know that, right, Taft?"

He chewed and swallowed.

"Nobody lives forever. I'mma enjoy life while I'm here, and then I'm gonna die when I die. That's the plan."

He finished the pastry, licked each finger on that hand individually, ending with his thumb, and then he ducked under the tape and skidded down the hill. His dress shoes somehow looked like hooves as they slid. He continued his thought on the way down.

"When I was like forty or so, I realized something about life. Something big. See, even if you eat nothin' but kale salad and avocados or something, and you exercise, and you live to be 96? What good are those years after, say 80, really? I mean, maybe if you're extremely lucky, a few of 'em are OK, but… you can't work. You're pretty limited in how you can play. No sex life to speak of. Your hearing and eyesight start going, so reading and music are kinda limited as sources of joy. If you're still eating like a damn rabbit, you're not enjoying that aspect of life so much. So what do you do? You watch TV, and that's about it, right? Shoot, I'd rather live right here and now."

He'd reached the bottom of the hill by the time his monologue was done.

"My grandparents were big on game shows," Stinson said, picturing the two of them reclining in matching La-Z-Boys while families feuded and the big wheel handed out fortunes.

Taft's face screwed up like he'd tasted ass.

"Game shows? Christ. I'd take a crib death over that. Better to die as a small boy than to go out on that grim note."

Stinson clicked her tongue.

"Oof. I'm afraid you missed your chance to die a small boy decades ago."

Taft squinted at her.

"Funny."

One of the techs closest to the corpse stood from a kneeling position, a black man with neatly cropped hair and glasses. It wasn't until he was fully standing that Stinson realized it was the medical examiner, Dr. Michael Wheatley. He almost never beat them to a scene.

"Early for once, huh, Doc? Just wanted to see what it felt like, I bet," Taft said.

Wheatley smiled. He, at least, found Taft amusing, always laughing and grinning at the big lug's jokes.

The M.E. held up a black bifold wallet.

"Got the victim's ID here—"

"Wait, wait!" Taft interrupted. "You know I've always felt that I'm a little bit psychic. Watch."

He put two fingers to his temple and squinted, as if concentrating on something.

"Yeah… yeah, I think I'm getting something. I'm seeing the letter J. Jerry? Jason? No… Justin. Yes. Our vic's name is Justin… Higgins."

He blinked his eyes open, looking pleased with himself.

Dr. Wheatley flipped the wallet open to reveal the driver's license for one Justin Higgins, 38 years old.

"Very impressive, Detective," he said with a smirk.

Stinson wasn't in the mood for Taft's games. She stared her partner down.

"Are you done?"

"What?" Taft played innocent. "I can't help it if I get these premonitions sometimes. It just happens."

"Will you get on with it already? What else do we know?"

"Alright, alright. The first unis on the scene clocked the deceased's shirt. Has a Citgo logo on it, so it wasn't a huge leap to figure out he worked at one of the local gas stations."

Taft bobbed his head as he continued the narrative.

"Sure enough, our Mr. Higgins went missing from his shift last night over in Peachtree. Taken during a robbery, presumably to keep him from calling it in. We're in the process of getting the surveillance footage sent over now."

Stinson blinked as she processed the information.

"Robbery. Do we think it could be related to this crime spree we keep hearing about?"

Taft's eyes lit up, and his eyebrows did another little hop.

"Could be. Yeah. For sure, it could be."

The scene fell quiet for a few seconds.

They'd all seen the stories on the news. The spree of armed robberies ripping down the coast. North Carolina. South Carolina. Georgia. The mayhem seemed to follow that long strip of beach.

The grainy footage of a hooded man with sunglasses looking like the Unabomber committing armed robberies. No clerks had been harmed. Not even so much as a scratch.

Until now.

Stinson gazed down at the dead body again. The somber face stared up at nothing. She called his name to mind. Justin Higgins. Thirty-eight years old and working the late shift at the gas station. Wrong place at the wrong time, and now he was gone.

The techs started loading his stiff form into a body bag. She wondered a moment how they'd get him up the hill to take him away, but her mind didn't dwell on it long.

She turned her attention back to Wheatley.

"Anything on a cause of death at this point?"

The doctor shook his head.

"Don't know yet. No visible wounds. No signs of blunt force trauma or strangulation."

She blinked again. Pondered this. It didn't fit.

"So… what happened then? I don't get it."

"Like I said, there's no obvious sign of foul play," the ME said with a shrug. "But we won't know anything for sure until after the autopsy. I'll be in touch this afternoon with the preliminary results. Tox screen will take longer."

She nodded, but her focus had already turned inward, working at the edges of the puzzle placed before her.

Armed robbery.

No obvious foul play.

But someone dumped the body.

She fixed her gaze on the sloped spot where the corpse had tumbled from the road down into the ditch.

What the hell happened here?

CHAPTER 2

Ellie grasped the edge of the curtain and nudged it aside, producing a five-inch gap to peek through. She pressed her face to the glass of the motel room window and squinted at the scene across the way.

Her pulse quickened when she saw that the police cars were still there, hunkered under the Sea Spray Motel sign. Worse, there were more of them now.

That couldn't be good. That many police cars could only mean something bad had happened.

She tried not to imagine the awful possibilities, but she'd watched too many true crime documentaries for that. Her mind went straight to "dead body" and "murder" and then a list of appropriate adjectives to describe the crime scene: bloody, gory, disturbing, gruesome.

All the things one usually associates with a relaxing spring break vacation, she thought, and then felt a twinge of unease.

No. Not unease.

Guilt.

She felt guilty.

And maybe she should. She had lied, after all.

The lie hardly seemed worth it now. Especially if she were to get caught…

Her stomach flip-flopped at the mere thought, and she realized she was gripping the drapes so tightly that her knuckles were turning white.

She closed her eyes.

Breathe.

Stop freaking out.

Everything is fine.

When her eyelids fluttered open, she spotted another police car rolling up to the scene.

"Five police cars now," she said.

"No shit?" Courtney said from somewhere behind her.

There was a rustle and the faint squeak of bed springs, and then Courtney was beside her, thrusting the curtains wide open with a swishing sound.

Ellie lurched for the two flaps of fabric and whisked them closed again.

"What are you doing?"

"Uh, trying to get a look at what's happening."

"They might see us," Ellie said, her voice somewhere between a hiss and a whisper.

Courtney chuckled.

"The police? What, did you rob a bank or something? Are you on the lam?"

"No, it just seems like we should be, I don't know… discreet."

"Uh-huh." Courtney still sounded amused. "Is that what you call all those murder podcasts you listen to? Discreet?"

"That's different," Ellie said, and she was poised to argue further, but Courtney gasped and jabbed a finger at the thin slice of window not covered by the curtains.

"Check it out! I totally called it."

Ellie had to adjust her angle to see what it was that Courtney was so excited about. At first she thought it was the sixth police car now pulling to the curb, but then she saw the bulky vehicle behind that.

An ambulance.

"A meatwagon with no lights? No siren?" Courtney said, the pitch of her voice rising in excitement. "You know what that means. There's *totally* a dead body down there."

Ellie realized she was shaking her head, unable to stop herself from objecting even though she'd had the same thought herself. As though she believed she could make it all go away if she summoned enough denial.

"Just because there's an ambulance doesn't necessarily mean…"

She didn't want to finish the sentence. Speaking it aloud would make it more real.

"...doesn't necessarily mean that someone didn't just get totally *murdered* right outside our motel room?" Courtney asked.

Ellie was still trying to come up with another feasible explanation when Courtney gasped again and shoved at the curtains to widen the gap.

"Is that those guys from earlier?"

Ellie moved closer to the glass. She didn't have her contacts in, and all she could really see were two blurry-faced silhouettes approaching from the sidewalk.

"What guys?"

"The ones staying in the next room over. From Detroit. John and Wes." Courtney's nose was actually touching the glass now, and her breath clouded the surface. "It *is* them. And it looks like they're coming from the crime scene."

She pulled back from the window.

"Let's go ask them what they saw," she said, already heading for the door.

"What?"

Courtney paused with her hand on the doorknob.

"They got up close and personal, and I want the tea. Plus, John is super hot."

Courtney snatched up the little kimono she'd been wearing as a bathing suit cover-up from the peg next to the door and shrugged it on over her skimpy pajama set. Despite adding more layers, it made the cropped camisole and short-shorts look even sexier. Then she whipped the door open and strode out into the early morning gray.

Ellie glanced down at her baggy flannel pants featuring characters from Winnie the Pooh. Once upon a time, the background had been bright bubblegum pink, but the last ten years had faded it to a dingy peach.

Then there was her shirt. Two sizes too big, printed with a series of anthropomorphic teeth marching in a line, and branded with the logo of her middle school orthodontist.

The giant letters spelling out "MEOW" across Courtney's butt seemed to mock Ellie's own choice of frumpy sleepwear.

Ellie blew out a breath. A mirror was mounted on the back of the door, and she paused in front of it. She tucked the front of her huge t-shirt in. Studied her reflection. Grimaced and untucked the shirt again.

Can't polish a turd, she thought as she grabbed her key card from the top of the dresser and chased Courtney outside.

A cold feeling that had nothing to do with the temperature outside ran through her as soon as she stepped through the doorway. She couldn't see it yet, but she knew. Across the lot, encircled by all those cop cars, a body lay dead in the grass.

Courtney was already halfway across the parking lot, standing with the two guys. When the motel room door *thunked* closed, she turned back.

"I called it, El. I told you it was a body!"

Ellie couldn't stop her gaze from sliding over to where police tape now cordoned off the edges of the ravine.

A body. A dead body. Right over there. Not a hundred yards from where she stood. Goose bumps sprang to life on her arms, and she rubbed at the bare skin.

Her flip flops scuffed over the ground as she approached the group.

"So what happened?" she asked, even though she was fairly certain she didn't want to know.

It was the broad, muscular one with all the tattoos who answered. The one who, thus far, they had never seen wearing a shirt — like maybe his body rejected fabric.

"Cops wouldn't say, exactly," John said. "Only would confirm it was a DB — dead body — but wouldn't specify one way or the other whether it was foul play or not."

He inhaled deeply.

"So it was *definitely* murder."

Muscular, tattooed, and melodramatic. He was exactly Courtney's type.

Ellie squinted.

"What makes you so sure?"

"These tourist towns like to keep a squeaky-clean image. If it was any kind of accident, they'd be out here with bullhorns trying to reassure everyone. A grisly murder kinda ruins the vibe, you know?"

"I mean, what else could it be anyway?" Courtney asked. "Does anyone die of natural causes at the bottom of a ditch?"

Now the other guy spoke up. Wes. Unlike his friend, he was fully clothed. His build was also more wiry, and Ellie had to admit that his shaggy brown hair and stubble was 100% *her* type. Which was sort of a moot point, since Ellie didn't really date.

"I don't know." Wes pointed at the sprawling complex of buildings situated on the far side of the ravine. "There's that nursing home down the street. Maybe one of the olds wandered outside and fell."

On the one hand, Ellie appreciated that Wes wasn't going along with the sensationalist instincts that Courtney and John seemed to share. On the other, his alternate suggestion was unsettling in its own right.

"That's… bleak," she said.

Wes thrust his hands into the pockets of his jeans.

"I mean, it happened to my great aunt. Dementia. She was on a locked ward and everything. There was supposed to be no way for the residents to get out. But she did. Spent a whole night roaming the woods nearby. They finally found her the next morning, but by then, she'd caught pneumonia. She died like a month later."

"Wes, my man," John said, clapping him on the shoulder. "You always know exactly what to say to lighten the mood."

"What are the odds that it's someone from the motel?" Courtney asked.

Ellie wasn't following the question.

"Who?"

"The victim. The body. What if it was, like, someone staying right here?"

Ellie blinked. A little moan started deep in her throat, but she cut it off before anyone might notice.

"Hell, what if the *murderer* is staying here?" John said. "Could be peeking out one of those windows right now. Watching us."

"Uh… holy shit," Wes said.

He lifted his arm, and all their heads turned to follow the trajectory of his pointing finger.

The ravine.

A flurry of movement roiled along the rim of the gully. Paramedics jockeyed for position and yelled back and forth over the whir of a machine — a crane, Ellie realized. The black line of its cable stretched down into the pit and out of view.

The whir changed pitch. Something gravelly joining in. And then she saw the cable pull taut.

The payload lifted into view slowly, steadily.

A body bag strapped to a backboard. The bulge beneath the vinyl shifted, the shape of the body within vaguely discernible. The bulk jiggled just a little as it floated higher and higher.

Ellie couldn't stop the words from entering her skull.

Dead weight.

The man operating the crane pulled a lever, and the ascension cut off. Now the body hovered before them, suspended over the gulf of the ravine. It twirled a little at the end of the cable, and the breeze made the vinyl ripple.

The crane arm swung it in then, pulled the bulk over the land where the paramedics could secure it. They fanned around it, gripped it, muscled it into the back of the waiting ambulance.

It was another minute before the vehicle moved. Rolling slowly away.

No lights.

CHAPTER 3

Stinson and Taft strode across the blacktop of the motel parking lot. It was barely after sunrise, and the sun was already bringing the heat, coils of it reflecting off the asphalt and winding around the detectives' ankles.

Stinson couldn't believe that it would only get hotter for the next several hours. At least the humidity would also be terrible.

Taft had somehow acquired another pastry — a bear claw with impressive height to it. Did he have a box somewhere he wasn't sharing?

"You know, you talk like you're seizing the day," Stinson said. "But it mostly seems like you're seizing the donut."

Taft chuckled and ripped off another hunk of fried dough with his teeth.

Looking closer, Stinson recognized the pastry as something prepackaged. Processed junk food.

"I can't believe you eat that hydrogenated crap."

He looked down at the swollen dough in his hand.

"Huh?"

"Trans fats, dude. It's like the single worst thing you can do for your heart. You've never heard of that?"

"Yeah. Of course I've heard of it. I mean… not really."

Stinson tilted her head before she went on.

"Well, they process these fats, right? Kind of turn 'em into a substance the consistency of melted plastic. It makes 'em shelf stable for months. And the problem is that once you eat it, this altered fat, it never really leaves your system. You've got this semi-gelatinous goop in your bloodstream, damaging your veins. That leads to biofilms collecting there. Basically gross gunk and bacteria and cholesterol clotting your arteries."

"Shit," he said, still staring at the thing. After a second, he took a small nibble.

"So the FDA issued a regulation. Anything over half a gram, you have to list it on the ingredients. Anything less can be rounded down on the nutritional information to 0 trans fats. Except it's bullshit."

"How so?"

"The companies figured out that they can mix a small amount of this hyper-processed fat — the most plasticky of them, even worse than the standard trans fats — and it kind of converts the other oil into a trans fat. It's technically less than half a gram, but it fucks your heart just the same."

"Christ."

"I just picture that all the time. The liquid plastic sludge flowing through my veins. Weird goo coating my insides like that fake butter they squirt on popcorn at the movie theater."

"Well… I guess I'll picture it now, too. So… cool. Thanks."

Stinson hooked a thumb back toward the ravine behind them.

"So what do you think happened back there?"

"What do you mean? Robbery. Murder. They dumped the body out the vehicle, down in the death pit back there. Two plus two equals four, no?"

"A murder with no wounds? No marks? It doesn't make sense."

Taft took a slow-motion bite of donut. Chewed.

"They coulda smothered him. Asphyxiation without the, you know…"

He held the donut in his mouth a second to pantomime a strangulation motion with his hands. Made a sharp little *crick* sound deep in his throat.

Stinson tilted her head again.

"Maybe."

"Hey, that kind of thing can be hard to detect. Given we're talking, you know, a cursory exam."

"Stop trying to convince me. I said maybe."

"Who's trying to convince anyone? You asked me what I thought happened, and I answered."

His cell blipped then, just as he took the last bite of bear claw. He fished the iPhone out, swiped the screen.

"Got the security footage here. Wanna take a look?"

Together they watched a pair of twenty-seven-second videos. The same chunk of time shown from two angles.

The first camera looked down from the far side of the potato chip aisle, pointed straight at the door with the top of a bag of Ruffles in the foreground.

A ski-masked figure entered the convenience store, sort of shuffling funny like Quasimodo and then jumping into some kind of karate stance on the red rubber floor mat. His arm extended before him, gun pointed at the guy behind the counter from some ten or twelve feet out. Everything about his body language seemed playful to her. Overly dramatic on purpose.

Stinson cataloged his dress. Plain black t-shirt. Blue jeans, maybe wide-legged. A pair of Ray-Ban knockoffs hugged around the top half of the ski mask and covered his eyes, but a big smile showed through the mouth hole. He kept licking his teeth, too.

Could that be a drug thing?

She didn't know.

The lips moved then. Gliding over the teeth. Speaking. Soundless for them, since they had no audio feed. He dipped the gun toward the cash register a couple times.

On the far-left edge of the screen, Justin Higgins moved his hands toward the register, and then he hesitated. It looked to Stinson like he just froze. She even wondered if the video file might have lagged.

Ski Mask turned the gun toward the window and blasted three times, the muzzle flares flickering so fast it looked like stop-motion animation. The glass exploded, bits raining everywhere.

Higgins opened the register real quick then. The clerk worked his way from left to right, pulling out stacks of bills and cramming them into a small paper bag.

The gunman strode closer while the money got loaded. He grabbed something off the counter — a packet of beef jerky according to the report.

Higgins paused for a second before he thrust the bag of cash toward the robber. When the perp took it, he then gestured with the gun again, looping motions with his wrist.

Higgins hesitated again, and then he hopped over the counter and followed the gunman outside.

The second clip showed the same thing from a camera angled downward from behind the counter. This emphasized the robber's feet as he shuffled into that awkward position just inside the door.

Stinson thought the same thing she'd thought the first time.

He's playing. It's like a kid pretending to rob a store more than the real thing.

Next they got a quick shot of the car rolling by the parking lot cam — a third video, briefer than the others. For just a second the driver's hand was visible on the steering wheel in a patch of light shining down from one of the lamps out there. Then the car glided out of the frame.

"So they parked in the camera's blind spot before the guy got out," Taft said. "No look at the driver, beyond that sliver of hand we saw. Never got a look at the plate, either. Figures, right?"

Stinson shrugged.

"Not much to go on."

"Same thing in the footage from the Dairy Mart up in Savannah. They kept in the blind spot. Nothing to really identify 'em. Makes me think it's them — Jimmy and Scarlet — and they learned from their first few jobs. But how can we really say?"

"Ski mask fits the stuff I saw about the spree," Stinson said.

"Lotta armed robberies with ski masks."

"Guy looks the right height, too."

Taft bounced his head back and forth like he was weighing it, and then he nodded once.

They ran through all three videos again.

"Why the small bag?" Taft asked, as they got to that part of the video.

Higgins had loaded the money in an almost comically small paper bag, given the options. It looked like it'd barely fit a pint bottle of Jack Daniel's.

"He was probably in shock. Gun in his face, you know," Stinson said. "I read this article about how people in shock can often not concentrate enough to dial 9-1-1. They dial 9-9-1 or sometimes just press 9. They say you should practice dialing it, actually, so that if you're in an emergency and panicking that sort of muscle memory will kick in, and you'll do it right."

Taft straightened up, and he pursed his lips.

"Practice dialing 9-1-1? I'll be sure to get right on that. Heavy reps. Maybe I'll put on a helmet first."

When they watched a third time, something new stuck out to Stinson.

She reached over to Taft's phone and paused the video, and the ski-masked figure froze with one hand closing around the bag. She tapped her finger at the screen.

"Here's my question," Stinson said. "If they planned to kill him, why not just shoot him right there?"

Taft got a faraway look as he thought about it. Then he muttered softly enough that it was probably to himself.

"As soon as he has the bag of money. *Pop-pop.*"

"You think?"

He blinked. Swiveled his eyes to meet hers. Then he nodded slowly.

"So maybe they didn't plan to kill him," he said. "Maybe they wanted to take him down the road, prevent him from calling it in. Buy some time, right? But once they're on the road, something goes wrong. The guy starts freaking out or something. They panic and smother him."

Now it was Stinson's turn to hesitate.

"Why not use the gun? If they're panicking, I mean."

"No mess in the car, maybe. Blood everywhere if they shoot

him."

"Yeah, maybe."

Taft killed the image on the screen and put the phone away.

"So you talked to the lady who found the body this morning?" Stinson asked.

"Yeah. Took a brief statement. A vacationer in from Idaho or maybe it was Montana. Seems like a piece of work, too. She was quiet, but you could feel the psycho rolling off her in waves. Probably keeps her husband's nuts in a vice grip."

Stinson looked up at all the aqua motel doors facing them in the parking lot.

"We'll have to canvas. Talk to all the guests."

Then she turned to face the building off the other way, a stark gray-looking box across another parking lot on the other side of the ravine.

"We should talk to the people at the nursing home across the way, too. Someone might have seen something, heard something."

Taft made that ass-taste face again.

"Shit. I don't want to go over there. The old folk's home? Nasty place. I don't know what those people did that their families would want to stick them in the worst nursing home in the state, but it had to be something awful."

"Well… we'll flip a coin. Winner canvases the motel. Loser goes over to Brookville."

Taft got sweatier all of a sudden. He looked frightened, Stinson thought.

"Wait. No way. Do me a solid, Stinson. You know I can't stand the smell of those places. Old piss and industrial disinfectant. My old man died in a place like that and just thinking about the smell and all those old people stewing in their own juices makes me want to puke."

Stinson dug a quarter out of her pocket. Poised it on her thumb, ready to flip.

"Aw, Christ. You know I'm going to lose. We both know it."

"It's a coin flip, Taft. It's fifty-fifty."

He shuddered.

"There's a motel right here full of vacationing babes in bikinis, and I'm going to get stuck talking to a bunch of grannies in peepee diapers?"

"You call it in the air."

She went to flip, but he held up both hands and stopped her again.

"Wait! NFL style. You let it fall to the ground. None of this catch the coin in your hand shit. Those kinds of things can be manipulated."

She glared at him.

"Fine. You call it in the air."

Then she flicked her thumb. The coin tumbled skyward, flipped end over end.

"Tails. No! Heads! I meant heads!"

The silver blur started its descent. Flipping, flipping.

It jangled down onto the asphalt. Bounced twice. Rolled to a stop between Stinson's shoes.

Tails.

Stinson smiled to herself.

Taft lost.

CHAPTER 4

Stinson crossed the parking lot of the Sea Spray Motel, narrowly avoiding a puddle of vomit buzzing with flies.

Lovely, she thought. *Nothing says spring break like binge drinking until you puke.*

She scanned the row of doors on the first floor, zeroing in on number 17. She double-checked the room number in her notes and reminded herself of the names of the witnesses.

Dan and Tanya Palmer.

She strode up to room 17 and raised her fist, poised to knock. But the sound of voices inside made her pause. They were arguing, by the sound of it.

"Saved up for months."

A woman's voice. This had to be Tanya.

"I know."

A man this time. Dan.

"Looked forward to this for longer than that. Over a year, Dan. We'd been planning this vacation for over a year."

"I know, hon."

The shades over the window were partially drawn, and Stinson could see some of what was going on inside from her vantage point. Tanya, pacing from one end of the room to the other. Dan, perched on the end of the bed, smoking a cigarette.

"We drove 16 hours straight through the night to get here. Drove right through a thunderstorm and everything."

"I know. I mean, hell, I'm the one who did the driving."

Tanya glared at him for a full second before she went on.

"All that planning. All that effort. And what do we get? Relaxation? Rejuvenation? Fun in the frickin' sun?"

She smiled in a way that made her look wolfish before she went on.

"Hell no. We get a bunch of gloomy shit. A dead body laid

out at our feet. A chubby corpse face down in the grass. Morbid. As morbid as it gets. A real-life nightmare scenario. Some fucking vacation."

In the middle of Tanya's rant, Dan dropped his cigarette on the motel bedspread. Stinson watched him snatch it up and brush furiously at the puckered burn mark on the blanket.

She could see him doing the mental math.

Shit. Are we going to get charged for that?

Tanya's voice somehow grew more shrill.

"Are you even listening?"

"Yeah. Yep. I just said, 'I know,' didn't I?"

She squinted at him like she was scanning his face for any sign of deceit, any hint of weakness.

Dan kept his expression blank. Hit his cigarette. Blew smoke up toward the ceiling tiles.

The spat between the couple was bringing back unpleasant memories of the time when Stinson had been married. All the stupid nothingburger fights with her ex-husband. All that time and effort wasted. She didn't want to hear any more.

She banged her fist on the door and watched Dan almost drop his cigarette again.

The door opened a crack and brightness flooded into the gap. Orangey Florida sunshine. Tanya's sour face appeared in the opening.

"Dan and Tanya Palmer?"

"Yes?"

Stinson held up her badge.

"Sorry to bother y'all. I'm Detective Stinson with the Durango Beach PD. I know you had an awful morning, but I was hoping to go over a few things with you again if I could."

Tanya's scowl deepened.

"We already talked to the police. First thing this morning. Gave a statement to a Detective Taft. Big fella. You can refer to that."

Stinson blinked in the doorway, holding back a smile. She always liked the ones who showed a little backbone.

"I reviewed your statement, as a matter of fact. That's why I'm here. I have a few follow-up questions if that's OK."

Tanya let out a breath. It sounded like a hissing semi-truck stopped at an intersection.

"Look, we're here on vacation. Supposed to be, anyway. We paid a lot of money to be here. And all this morbid crap is really ruining the vibe, you know?"

Detective Stinson allowed her face to soften a little. Her gaze locked onto Tanya's.

"I know it's a hard thing, getting mixed up in something like this. I know it's not fair, and I wish it didn't happen to you. But the fact is, we've got a man dead, and it's my job to figure out what happened. For him. For his family. I'm only asking for a few minutes of your time."

Tanya blinked hard. Then she pointed a finger in Stinson's face. Her words came out through clenched teeth.

"Lady, your job ain't my concern. I don't gotta tell you anything."

There was a limit to Stinson's amusement, of course. She wasn't about to allow someone to impede her investigation.

She stiffened her jaw and arched her brow and gave Tanya what Taft called "The Look."

"Ma'am, it's hard for me to understand you being so defensive about something like this. It raises questions, OK? If I have to dig into your background, treat you like a suspect, we can do it that way, too."

The air seemed to go out of the other woman all at once.

Her shoulders sagged. That hardness drained from her face. She let her chin dip almost all the way to her sternum and took a deep breath before she spoke.

"I'm sorry. It was a long night, and finding a corpse wasn't on our vacation to-do list, like I said. I guess I can go back over the story one more time."

Tanya opened the door the rest of the way, that brilliant glow lurching over the carpet and spreading to touch all corners of the room. Stinson entered.

For the next several minutes, Tanya went through it again, more or less repeating what was already in Taft's notes. Walking on the beach. The car pulling up. Crossing the street and finding the body.

Stinson nodded to herself as she jotted down a fresh detail here and there.

While his wife talked, Dan ran his fingers back and forth over the scorched spot on the blanket where he'd dropped the cigarette. He covered the blemish with a pillow, holding it there for a moment and then pulling it away.

Pillow on. Pillow off. Like he was trying to decide how noticeable it was.

Lucky for him, Stinson didn't think this place looked like the type to wash the outer bed linens more than once a decade.

When Stinson asked if it was usual for the couple to be up so late, Dan explained that between the time change and the long drive here from Montana, their body clocks were off. That's why they'd been up so late.

"So take me back to the time before the car stopped at the ravine. The vehicle came out of the motel parking lot. Is that right?"

Both Tanya and Dan bobbed their heads.

"Yeah. We watched the headlights flick on, and it pulled out of the lot and stopped by the ditch."

"OK. So had you seen the car prior to that? When you came out of your room, was it there?"

Dan shook his head.

"I don't remember."

Tanya blinked a few times.

"I remember hearing it. It was running. Idling, you know?"

She wheeled her head around to look at her husband.

"Do you remember that?"

He nodded slowly.

"Yeah. Now that you mention it, I remember. That low grumble was there — I think the whole time we were out there."

"It was settin' there when we walked out," Tanya said. "At probably like 3 or something close to that. And it set there for probably twenty minutes or so before it actually moved."

Stinson's pen scribbled furiously over the noise from the window unit in the corner of the room. It grated out an awful sound like it had something caught deep in its throat.

"Is that… ya know, relevant?" Dan asked.

Stinson didn't look up from the page as she answered. "The timeline is getting clearer. It's something."

CHAPTER 5

Ellie stared at her reflection in the bathroom mirror as she brushed her teeth, unable to get the image of the body bag out of her mind.

It was strange. She hadn't actually seen anything all that disturbing. No blood or gore or anything. Just rumpled blue plastic in the vague shape of a person.

Maybe that made it worse. Now, the whole thing was left to her imagination. And her brain couldn't help but fill in the blanks with the most shocking possibilities. Gaping wounds. Missing limbs.

Are we nuts to stay here? she asked herself.

If the universe really went around giving signs to people, surely a dead body being found a few hundred feet from where one had chosen to lay their head was the kind in big, glowing neon letters that read, "GET OUT."

A hundred little beach towns just like this one stood along the coast. It wasn't like Durango Beach was all that special. It might be hard to find a room right in the midst of spring break, but it wasn't like they were all that picky. They couldn't afford to be.

There was an argument to be made that there was no good reason *not* to move on to the next little beach town down the road. And a body-bag-sized reason in favor of moving.

Quickly she realized the flaw in this plan. If they found a hotel somewhere else, Ellie would have to use her own credit card to book the room, since Courtney had already maxed hers out getting this one.

If her parents saw a charge for a Florida hotel on her credit card bill, they'd know she'd lied to them.

She dribbled minty foam into the sink and filled a small plastic cup from the tap. As she rinsed her mouth with the water, the sharp cold of it seemed to spread through her.

She never should have lied. The guilt she felt over it… the worry? Not worth it. But telling them the truth about how she was taking off for spring break was hardly an option either.

She remembered the blow-up over the whole Europe thing and winced.

It was back when she'd graduated with her bachelor's degree. Between her undergrad GPA and her LSAT score, she'd pretty much had her choice of law schools. It was her parents' dream come true.

And so, Ellie had thought maybe she'd earned a break. Just a small one. Courtney was deferring her first semester of grad school to travel around Europe, and she'd been begging Ellie to come with her. A lot of people waited a little while before starting their J.D. Putting it off for one semester didn't seem like a big deal.

She'd planned for it. Waiting for the right moment. The days following her graduation seemed like the perfect time. Her parents were still gushing about how proud of her they were. How she'd worked so hard, and look how it had paid off, what a bright future she had in store. She thought they'd be primed to agree that she deserved this small reward.

Oh, how wrong she had been.

And really, she should have known. That her father would dismiss the idea outright. That he'd give one of his impassioned speeches about how critical this period of her life was. How competitive law school would be. That having a singular focus on her education would make or break her future career. That right now was the least appropriate time to be thinking about gallivanting from one bar to another and lazing around on beaches.

Then he'd finished with his patented mantra: "There will be time for all of that later."

And so while Courtney "gallivanted," Ellie found herself in a lecture hall that September.

Was that why she'd lied to her parents and snuck down

here for spring break? Was she bitter about how they'd vetoed the Europe trip and was trying to get some kind of revenge? Prove a point?

Part of her still couldn't believe she'd done it. And yet here she was. Somehow, with her strange powers of persuasion, Courtney had managed to convince her to slip away to Florida for the week.

"Don't think I haven't noticed how that little muscle under your eye is twitching again. Remember what the campus doctor said? It's caused by *stress.* Stress kills, Ellie. So if you think about it, I'm basically saving your life by making you go on this trip."

Ellie peered at her face in the mirror. She hadn't thought about it until now, but her eye had stopped twitching at some point since they'd been here. Courtney had been right. She really had needed this. And if not for the dead body, this place would be the stress-free paradise she'd been dreaming of.

She tilted her head toward the ceiling and popped one contact in and then the other. At the same time, she nudged the bathroom door open with her knee.

"What do you think about finding a hotel somewhere else?" she asked.

She froze there on the threshold, blinking her contacts into place and squinting into the eerily still room.

"Courtney?"

She didn't know why she said it. It was obvious the room was empty.

Movement outside the window caught her eye. She stepped closer and saw that Courtney was back out on the sidewalk, talking to John and Wes.

But mostly John.

Ellie watched Courtney lean forward and brush her hand against John's bare chest, laughing at something he'd said.

Ellie sighed.

That settled it. She could forget leaving Durango Beach for somewhere a little less murdery now. Because Ellie had seen that look on her friend's face enough times to know what it meant. Infatuation. There was no way she'd be able to drag Courtney away from John at this point.

I just need to put it out of my mind, she thought. *No more thinking about dead bodies.*

She closed her eyes and took a breath, trying to clear her head. But the image of the body bag was still there. Hovering over the ravine. Waiting.

It was too big. Too profound. The kind of thing that would probably be etched in her brain forever.

CHAPTER 6

Detective Stinson paused outside of the couple's room, jotting a few notes. The heat of the early morning sun felt good on her face. It wasn't the blazing fireball it would be in a few hours, so she might as well enjoy it while she could.

She rolled her neck to one side and then the other, eliciting a series of pops and cracks. This was what she got for not going to bed early when she was on call. But Tess, her eleven-year-old daughter, had begged her to stay up a little late so they could watch the extended edition of *The Fellowship of the Ring*. And how could she say no to that?

In a year, Tessie probably wouldn't want anything to do with her. She'd be too busy with friends and boys. Which was how it was supposed to be, as far as Stinson was concerned. That didn't make watching Tess grow up any less bittersweet.

She thought, again, about the job she'd turned down last year — an intelligence analyst gig up in Deerfield. Careerwise, it would have been something more challenging than what she was doing now, maybe even something fulfilling, and there was even a really good school district there for Tessie. For some reason, she'd said no anyway, and she found herself coming back to the decision often of late.

When she looked back at it honestly, she thought maybe it was the idea of all that change that had scared her. Things had gotten stale in Durango Beach in the years since her divorce, but she'd settled into it, gotten comfortable with the stasis. Maybe it was underrated in some ways, comfort. Everybody else seemed to be chasing something, desperate for everything to be new and exciting all the time.

Stinson checked her watch. It was going to be a long ass day, and she was already tired and starving. There wasn't much she could do about the lack of sleep, but the hunger?

She got out her phone, poised to text Taft to see if he was almost finished at the nursing home. They could take a quick breakfast break and then get back to it.

Stinson had managed to tap out the first half of the message when she heard voices nearby. The scrape of footsteps on the pavement. The clip clop of a pair of heeled sandals.

A group of four huddled outside one of the doors some thirty or forty feet down the row. All four were college-aged, maybe a little older. Definitely tourists. She could always tell.

As she looked closer, she realized she'd already seen the two men. They'd been sniffing around the crime scene, asking one of the unis what was going on. Sometimes that was suspicious, but Stinson's gut told her this was just your garden-variety curiosity.

She didn't remember seeing the two women, though. One was taller, with honey-colored hair that fell in loose waves. The kind of hairstyle that looked effortless but had probably taken an hour to get just right. The other was average height, curvy, with olive skin and a tangle of brown hair just past her shoulders.

Stinson's stomach gurgled, reminding her of the breakfast she'd already promised it. Urging her to put the canvassing on hold for the moment.

But no. It'd be better to talk to these people now. A place like this, no one came here to hang out in their motel room. Once the sun was fully up, the guests would scatter to the winds: sunbathing, scuba diving, jet skiing.

Stinson swiveled on her heel and strode toward the group.

"Good morning," she said, pulling out her badge. "My name is Detective Stinson. Are you folks staying here at the motel?"

The bigger of the two men stepped forward, apparently nominating himself the de facto leader.

"Sure are. Is this about what happened this morning? The dead body in the ravine?"

Stinson noted his forwardness. A lot of people got shy or a

little wary around cops, even if they had nothing to hide. This guy wasn't one of those. He struck her as the kind who didn't do timid. Didn't do a whole lot of thinking before he opened his mouth, as a matter of fact.

"It is," Stinson said with a solemn nod. "Do you have a minute to answer a few questions?"

"Of course," the bigmouth said.

Stinson clicked her pen.

"Why don't we start with your names and what room you're staying in."

Bigmouth's name was John Henza. The other male was Wesley Forester. They were in room fifteen.

Stinson pointed her pen at the blonde.

"Courtney Peterson. Room sixteen," the girl said, twirling a strand of hair and blinking with eyes as wide and innocent as a cartoon baby deer.

It was a convincing act, but Stinson wasn't buying. The detective wondered what she was hiding, but she doubted it was anything worth pursuing. Standard college kid stuff, probably. Some pot or maybe an outstanding speeding ticket.

Now that they were up close, she saw the girl had a smattering of freckles over her nose. She suddenly reminded Stinson of a Midge doll she'd gotten for her seventh birthday. Everyone used to fight over that doll, even though she and her friends had dozens of Barbies between them. After so many incarnations of Barbie, though, having one doll who looked a little different had seemed novel, apparently.

The dark-haired girl beside the Midge lookalike seemed to shrink when Stinson turned her gaze in that direction.

"And you, miss?"

The girl swallowed.

"I'm Eleanor Levine. Ellie. Same room." She gulped. "Err, sixteen. Is the room number, I mean."

Stinson took all this down, observing as she did how Ellie stammered out her response. Again, it didn't arouse any suspicion in the detective. The girl didn't look the type to have so much as a parking ticket on her record. There were some civilians who just reacted this way to cops. Worried they'd somehow get in trouble for merely existing, it seemed.

When she'd first noticed them, Ellie had been trailing behind the others. Had they been a pack of gazelles, the predators would have zeroed in on her as one of the weak ones. An easy target. And once Stinson had started talking to them, the girl had frozen and gone quiet. Like maybe if she held still enough, she might simply disappear. Classic prey behavior.

Stinson finished writing down their information and moved on to the questions. Now wasn't the time to get distracted by her "little observations," as Taft loved to call them.

She asked a few more icebreaker, background-type questions first. Where they were from (Detroit and Chicago, respectively), how long they'd been in town (just got here a couple days back), what they were doing here (spring break). Then she got to the red meat.

"Did any of you see or hear anything unusual early this morning between, say, two and four A.M.?"

Stinson wasn't surprised when John had something to volunteer.

"Ma'am, I got up to take a leak around three, and I saw a car idling in the parking lot. A muscle car, I think. Older. Like early 2000s or something?" He scratched under his chin. "Couldn't tell the color in the dark. Really only noticed it because the rumble of the exhaust was so loud. Sounded like the muffler was fuc— er… messed up."

Stinson scribbled down the approximate time and a description of the car. She didn't have high hopes, but it was something.

"Did you see the driver of the vehicle or notice anything else?"

"Well, a while later, I heard a door slam."

"A car door?" Stinson asked.

"No, one of the motel rooms. It, like, rattled the window in our room, so I figure it had to be close. Then there was some kind of commotion. Yelling. Sounded like a… what do you call it… a domestic thing? A squabble. Two people, yelling back and forth. A man and a woman. I got up again and looked out the window, but I couldn't see anybody. Not too much later is when I first saw the police lights."

Stinson was pretty sure the "squabble" would be Dan and Tanya just before they discovered the body. Still, she made note of it. She glanced up at the rest of them, hanging on the girls in particular. Women were, in general, more observant about certain things, at least in Stinson's experience.

"Anybody else?"

Midge — Courtney — shrugged.

"By the time we woke up, the police were already outside," she said.

This was what Stinson had been afraid of. In a dinky tourist trap like Durango Beach, the whole town was dead between one and seven A.M. Hopeless when it came to finding a good crop of eyewitnesses.

"Can you tell us if the victim was staying at the motel?" Ellie asked.

Stinson clicked and unclicked her pen.

"I'm not really supposed to give details, but… no. He lived in the next town over. No relation to the motel that we've found so far. And this area is generally safe. There's no need for you to worry."

John stepped forward again, like he was cutting in front of the others in line.

"Ma'am. Would this be connected to the crime spree on the news? The Bonnie and Clyde thing?"

"I'm not going to comment on the particulars of an ongoing case. But from what we know about those two, they don't tend to stick around in one place for too long. Again, I don't see any reason for you to worry."

Stinson could see lingering apprehension on Ellie's face.

"Look, you stick near the beach and the main strip, and

you're going to be fine. There's no reason for ordinary folk like you to give any of it one more thought," she said, tucking her pen back into her pocket. "Now you folks go on and enjoy your vacation. Thank you for your time."

And even though the words coming out of Stinson's mouth sounded confident enough, they felt wrong.

After so many years on the job, she knew that safety was never guaranteed.

CHAPTER 7

An orderly led Detective Taft through the elongated lobby of Brookville Nursing Home. Scrubs the color of a dolphin cinched tight around the big guy's shoulders, and a patchy beard adorned his jaw with a vaguely orange hue to it. His hair was darker than his beard but just as curly.

"Unit B is just through here," the orderly said over his shoulder. "My name is Pete, by the way. Pete Murphy."

They shook hands and then walked toward a barrier — a glass door threaded with chicken wire — and Pete plucked the ID card from where it hung around his neck and swiped it over some black electronic sensor. The machine chirped, the door clicked and opened, and they passed through.

The rest of the building looked dated, something nineties purple and turquoise about it all, like a hospital trapped in the Clinton era. This was a little disappointing to Taft after the high-tech door.

Well, it's probably one of the worst nursing homes in the state, he told himself. *You knew that. Shouldn't have got your hopes up.*

The glossy tile floor clapped out their footsteps, beige as a pair of Dockers. Long fluorescent bulbs buzzed overhead, and the ceiling tiles around them were yellowing like old newspapers.

"We've got one lady who might have seen something, but..." Pete trailed off there.

"You have doubts?" Taft asked.

Pete's mouth clicked.

"Let's just say she has her good days and bad days and leave it at that."

They kept going. A faintly chemical smell seemed to swell as they trod deeper into the building, probably a cleaner though

Detective Taft couldn't help but think of embalming fluid.

They walked past a lot of closed doors. Heavy wooden things with windowpanes, more of that chicken wire cutting the glass into little panels.

Taft scratched the back of his neck. Uncomfortable. Everything here looked, smelled, sounded like an old hospital in some small town.

Like the one his dad had died in.

Don't go there, he told himself. *Think about something else. Think about… Jesus. Anything! Sing a song.*

Mary had a little lamb, little lamb…

But it was no use. The surroundings thrust him back into the memory like a bad dream.

Drifting through that harsh fluorescent light down an endless hallway. Death surrounding him, enveloping him.

Cirrhosis. Stage five. His dad had started drinking at six years old, or so he claimed. Taft wondered if perhaps that was a bit of exaggeration on the old man's part, now that he thought of it. But whether he was a bona fide alcoholic or not was never up for debate. He supposed it didn't matter when it had started.

Bourbon and gin for decades, and then he switched to beer and wine in his later years — maybe that was supposed to help, Taft didn't know.

Even after the old man had been hospitalized, he kept drinking. Sneaking bottles into his room. Back to bourbon by then. He must have had help with it, with smuggling it in. Someone who didn't know better, maybe. Someone who thought they were helping.

He drank right up until about two weeks before the end.

And then he couldn't anymore. Couldn't drink. Couldn't get up. Couldn't even talk.

He was as yellow as a butternut squash when he died. Something beyond jaundice. It glowed under his skin, that golden shade. Almost looked radioactive in some way. Cartoonish. Like Homer fuckin' Simpson.

He hadn't spoken in nine days by then. But he seemed to be

trying to. He'd look at you, maintain eye contact, move his head, move his hands. His lips would part but nothing would come out. In a way, it was like when he was really drunk. Maybe that fit.

The body looked smaller right away once he was gone. Shriveled on the slab at the mortuary. One amber hand stuck a few inches above his chest, fingers parted slightly, rigor mortis holding them there like a statue.

Taft shuddered at the memory. All the old pain roiled anew in his gut, in his chest, in that vault behind his eyes.

"Here we go," Pete said, as they rounded a corner. "This is Unit B, which has the clearest view of the ravine."

They passed through another keycard door and entered a lobby-looking area with a couple of robed elderly people lounging in it. It reminded Taft of a waiting room at a dentist's office. A flat screen played Food Network on one wall, and magazines fanned over a coffee table in another corner. A stack of board games cluttered a shelf not far from that. Based on some of the signage, and the glazed look in the eyes of those robed residents, he gathered that this was the psych ward.

They crossed the space, took a right turn, and now they plodded down the long hall. A window to the left gave a nice view of the ravine, and then two more rows of doorways occupied the rest of the corridor.

"The folks in these rooms might have gotten a pretty good look, if any of them were awake," Pete said, pointing a thumb at the doorways on the left.

The clear view looking right down on the ravine had raised Taft's hopes of something here turning up, but he reassessed now.

Maybe someone saw something, he thought. *Maybe. But it's old folks — the psych ward, even — and the crime happened in the middle of the night. So… probably not.*

Yep. Probably just wasting my damn time here, but what the hell. Gotta chase down all the info we can get. That's part of the job.

"And how likely do you think that is?" Taft asked. "That any of them were up, I mean."

Pete's lip curled on one side.

"I'm not sure. The bulk of the residents are medicated at night, especially here on Unit B. Some are on sedatives. A few others go the supplemental route with melatonin or valerian root. What time did you say this was? Like one in the morning?"

That wasn't quite right, but some gut instinct told Taft to guard the exact timeline, to leave his answer murky.

"Around then, we think, yeah."

"Well… we're talking about lights out at nine P.M. throughout the facility, and all of the residents have generally already turned in by then, so… I don't know what to tell you, man. I guess you never know."

Neither of them spoke for a few seconds.

"Can't hurt to ask, can it," Taft said finally.

The big detective sighed and started working his way up the left side of the hall. Pete led him from room to room, sort of an uninvited chaperone, but Taft liked the idea of someone on the staff being present as a way of perhaps loosening some tongues. Some people, even old folks, clammed up when it came to talking to the police.

The first six residents Taft talked to — four old ladies and two old men — hadn't seen anything, though they seemed eager enough to talk anyway.

A couple of the women went on about their grandkids acing standardized tests and getting into Yale and the like. The first old man had a granddaughter who had made Honorable Mention All-District in tennis. Thrilling conversation.

Another old lady, Phyllis Lumley, wanted to file a formal complaint about how they used to have tapioca pudding here at Brookville that was "divine," and now the residents were stuck with this "vanella shit." Her face scrunched into a few thousand wrinkles as she repeated it in disgust, "vanella." She seemed convinced the police could do something about this no matter how much Taft protested. He didn't mention that he found tapioca appallingly booger-like in texture, but he really wanted to.

When they finally disentangled themselves from Mrs. Lumley and hurried to the next room, the orderly stopped Taft shy of the door with a grave look on his face.

"Little warning about the next resident here," Pete said. "Mr. Tessier — Walter Tessier — is what we call a, uh, spontaneous defecator."

Taft squinted.

"Spontaneous..."

Pete bobbed his head twice.

"About once every other month, he squats and dukes. Sometimes in his room. Sometimes in the common area. Once out in the yard. Then he usually smears it all on his chest. Sometimes he throws it around. No one wants to touch him, after that, of course. So it's... you know... a whole deal."

Taft was speechless.

"I think it's a territorial thing," Pete went on. "I mean, when you watch him do that... there's something deeply hostile about it, you know? An anger rising to the surface. Like something a captive chimp would do, maybe."

Mr. Tessier was, mercifully, napping. Taft left his card with a note asking him to get in touch if he had seen anything, and they moved on to the next room with no threat of fecal smearing hanging over their heads.

The rest of the hall held no help. Just more stories about grandkids excelling academically, and one rambling anecdote about a boy with a "withered, little arm" who got stung by a bee. Taft didn't really follow that one and just nodded politely and said, "Oh yeah?"

At the end of the hall, Taft entered the final room. Pete informed him that this was the one who'd told the staff she'd seen something, but the detective remained doubtful.

The little old lady sitting there in her bed shot a beaming smile at him, eyes glowing. She looked more alert than most, he had to give her that.

Taft introduced himself, shook her frail hand which somehow made him think of gripping a baby bird. Her grin only intensified as she told him her name: Nancy Lasseter.

"I knew the police would come. I knew!"

Taft smiled back, kept his voice light.

"Did you now, Nancy?"

"I saw. I saw the whole thing. Now, I wasn't completely sure what I was seeing at the time — it was awfully late, and I was still half-asleep — but I've put two and two together in the time since then. And I knew the authorities would come snooping around sooner or later, that they would want to know."

Taft chewed his lip. Some defense mechanism didn't want to let him believe that this might actually pan out into something useful. A lead. A clue. Anything they might be able to match up with the vacationing couple's story.

He looked her over again. Clear enough eyes. She'd also seemed to have used fairly sophisticated syntax when she spoke. Clauses and all that.

"And, uh, what was it that you saw?"

She blinked. Smiled now as hard as she could.

"You know."

Taft swallowed.

"Yeah? Well, you better just say it out loud, right? For the official record."

She tilted her head to the side like a cocker spaniel before she spoke.

"The UFO, of course."

Taft stared at her. Felt like a deflating balloon inside. He said nothing.

"Three lights zipping around the sky. Then they cohered into a silvery disc hovering just above the ravine outside the window. Aliens. Definitely aliens. Oh, I know they want to probe me, but I won't allow it."

"Nah," Taft said, before he could stop himself. "Not on the first date, anyhow."

CHAPTER 8

Stinson sat with Taft in the conference room, the gloss of the tabletop shimmering between them where the reflection from the overhead bulbs touched it. Oblong shards of light glowing on the wood.

A few uniformed officers likewise huddled around the table. Papers shuffled among them, bleached pages riffling as they changed hands — the FBI profiles that had been sent in from Quantico just minutes ago, emailed and printed.

Stinson had looked the psychological report over. She wasn't sure how much it would help them.

The chief of police, Bill Bannon, stood in front of the small room, scribbling on the whiteboard, his black marker squeaking faintly. Even at 59, he was a well-muscled slab of masculinity with hairy arms and a flawlessly groomed crew cut the almost-white shade of birch bark. He capped the marker with a flourish of his hands and turned to face the semicircle of law enforcement gawking at him.

His voice boomed over the room, deep and confident. His way of speaking had always reminded Stinson of a high school wrestling coach, though the crew cut may have biased her on that.

"Here's the deal, gang. Most of you already know, but at this point we believe we are indeed looking at part of the Jimmy and Scarlet spree."

Whispers fluttered among the uniformed officers, but Chief Bannon put his hand up, and the chatter cut out.

"Given the interstate nature of their crimes, we've been in touch with the feds. A consultant from the BAU quickly sent along a psychological profile. Seems like a bunch of psychobabble to me, frankly, but they say it could help us pin down these scumbags, and I'm all for that. Think of it sort of like a scouting report to let us know what we're up against, right? Might just help us predict their behavior, give us an edge. So everyone get a look at it today. That's an order."

He pumped his right arm then, bicep jumping, his thumb gesturing at the whiteboard behind him.

"Now there's a chance our criminals blew through town and are already long gone. Sure. That could be. But there's also a chance they're still in the area. They struck twice in a fourteen-hour period on the outskirts of Greensboro before they moved on, so there's a, you know, precedent, OK?

"In the meantime, we'll do what we do around here. We'll work. We'll hustle. Hard-nosed police work is what solves crimes, people. So let's talk about what we know about our perps at this point."

From there, the chief went over some of what he'd highlighted on the whiteboard, giving biographical backgrounds of the fugitives. He punched buttons on a laptop, which brought up photos on a large projector screen as he talked.

"Let's start with our Clyde: James Franklin Maddox. Jimmy. Twenty-six years old. From the Lincoln Heights neighborhood of Charlotte, which I'm told is on the rough side."

Maddox's face glowed on the projector screen. Hollow cheeks. Chiseled, bony details. Dead eyes. His hair swept up from his forehead like James Dean's.

"Looking at the mugshot here, you're probably thinking he's a Rhodes Scholar. An artist in residence at Georgetown or something. Gifted and deeply sensitive. But no. I'm afraid he's a run-of-the-mill dirtbag. Eighteen arrests and counting. Mostly burglary-related. Home invasions. Smash-and-grab type-a deals. I guess he leveled up to armed robbery here just recently. And they say people can't change and grow."

Bannon ran through a few more mugshots. Maddox's stubble grew and shrank in the various photos, but his eyes stayed dead, and his hair never changed. Stinson would have considered him kind of handsome if it weren't for those cold eyes.

"By all accounts, Jimmy here had a tough upbringing. Watched his dad get shot dead on the street when he was six. Drug-related. His mom was in and out of mental institutions after that. He got shuffled around. Stayed with aunts, grandparents. His first legal trouble happened when he was twelve. Burglary gone wrong. He busted some poor homeowner in the face with a crowbar, knocked out nine of his teeth. He also knifed a kid in juvie, though that was officially self-defense. Still, a history of violence worth noting."

The photos clicked by on the overhead screen, moving from mugshots to images culled from Maddox's various social media accounts. Maddox held a beer in quite a few of the personal shots — always Pabst Blue Ribbon in a tall boy can, from the looks of it.

"Next up, we've got Jimmy's partner in crime: Scarlet Burlew. Twenty-two years old. She was originally raised in Levittown, Pennsylvania — another fairly rough place to grow up. She moved to North Carolina when she was sixteen. Linked up with Mr. Maddox sometime in the last few years, and the result is playing out in gas stations and convenience stores, a path of destruction coming right down the eastern seaboard and into our backyard.

"The info I can dig up, be it from the media or other law enforcement agencies, doesn't fill in Ms. Burlew's background or history in any detail like the rich tapestry of arrests and violent incidents we have with Jimmy Maddox. She had no criminal record prior to this. She got good grades in school. Played volleyball and ran track. That kind of stuff. No college. She'd been working as a clerk at a chain pharmacy for the nine months prior to the crime spree."

Up on the screen, photos flipped past of Scarlet Burlew. Pale and freckled, she always wore big sunglasses that covered her eyes and much of her face, something wicked in the smile curving under the dark lenses. Her crinkly hair seemed to be dyed a different shade in quite a few of the shots, though it appeared that auburn was the natural shade. In the older photos, she looked so skinny that Detective Stinson wondered if the girl might have had an eating disorder, but she'd looked healthier of late. Maybe some trouble in the past. Maybe the kind of trouble that'd pushed her into the arms of a walking rap sheet like Jimmy Maddox.

The chief clicked and clacked on the laptop again. Then he lowered the lights in the room, so the projector beam became the lone glowing shape.

"OK, that's kind of the bird's-eye view of our two perps. Now let's run through some of the footage real quick, see 'em in action."

Surveillance footage rolled on the screen where the pictures had been. Not the clips Stinson and Taft had watched earlier, though they were familiar enough to her from cable news.

"This was one of the first crimes — the second, as far as we know," the chief said. "At an Exxon station in rural South Carolina, not far from Columbia. You can see that Jimmy hadn't adopted his signature ski mask yet."

Jimmy Maddox's tall frame stepped through the doorway and moved toward the counter. A hood and some aviators mostly covered his face, but it was him alright. Stubbly chin. Bony shoulders looking sharp through his sweatshirt, showing how skinny he was underneath.

One of those wiry types who swayed a little when he walked, Jimmy swaggered up to the counter. The gun dangled funny at the end of his arm, an awkwardness Stinson hadn't remembered seeing in the more recent robbery footage, like maybe he wasn't comfortable with it yet. It was a .38 snub nose. Looked tiny in his long fingers.

"What's with that grip?" Taft asked just above a whisper. "It's like he's holding the gun weird or something."

So he was noticing the same thing as her. The rap sheet may have suggested a hardened criminal, but Jimmy Maddox didn't look the part here.

There was no sound on the footage, but Jimmy's head

swayed back and forth and Stinson could imagine him delivering the "give me all the cash out of the register" with some 'tude. He got the money in a small paper bag that seemed about the right size for a 40-ounce of Schlitz.

Then he ran out the door. The camera angle shifted to the outdoor view on the projector screen, and a smaller version of Maddox rushed across the parking lot, jumped into the passenger seat of a Honda, and they tore off.

In another video, Maddox repeated the process in a different gas station, a different town. His body language read a little more nervous, at least in Stinson's view. Maybe due to the cashier being a big dude, broad shoulders, tattoos spiderwebbed over most of his neck.

Still, Jimmy went through the motions, swaggered, waved the gun, got the money, got out of there.

"Different car," one of the uniformed cops said, as they raced away in a little Nissan on-screen. "That's a different escape car."

"Yeah, they've been dumping the cars shortly after the jobs," Chief Bannon said. "They're all stolen, from what we know at this point anyway."

Stinson grimaced at that, thankful that the low light in the room would cover it. Tracing a make and model down could have been a promising avenue, and a license plate even more so. Now all of that was out the window.

Two more clips played. They looked, more or less, identical to the first two except Jimmy had a ski mask on now.

"We don't have footage of a couple of the gas stations they hit in rural Georgia," the chief said.

"No camera or what?" another uniformed officer asked.

"Negatory. But I think you get the gist. Stickup jobs. Nothing fancy. You'll want to take a look at this footage just here."

The screen cut away from the glowing interior of gas station to the darkness out in the lot. The car, a Ford Focus, rolled slowly into the frame.

"This is the only footage we have of Scarlet Burlew at any of the crime scenes."

The car crept forward into the lacework of light shining down on the lot, and there she was behind the steering wheel.

The crinkled hair surrounded her face. She looked more angular here than she had in the most recent photos — dimpled cheeks and thin cords of muscles at the crook of her jaw, which made Stinson think of the "heroin chic" super models of the 1990s. She didn't have the sunglasses on, so Stinson could finally see her eyes.

Scarlet craned her neck and stared straight into the camera. For a second, there was something soft in her eyes. A flash of fear or vulnerability, maybe. But then she smiled, just faintly, and Stinson saw a darkness filter into her expression, a hollowness, a death behind the eyes that gave the detective a chill.

The car tore away a second later, taillights flaring red as they fishtailed out of the lot, and then the screen went dark. The conference room felt heavy with quiet.

Bannon's gorilla-esque silhouette drifted toward the door and snapped the lights on. Everyone seemed to fidget once that harsh glare hit them.

"Look, we're still waiting on the full medical report for the details, but let's not get this twisted. These two animals killed that boy from Peachtree and dumped his corpse in a ditch in our jurisdiction.

"Coming on our turf? Big mistake. Big mistake.

"Because I know the men and women in this room will not rest until we've brought Jimmy and Scarlet to heel."

The room held still for a beat, and a mix of feelings pulsed inside Stinson. She'd found Chief Bannon's words stirring enough, felt a spike of adrenaline as he motivated the troops, stoked their pride.

But the truth was that they were up against a bunch of dead ends. There was no clear course forward, was there?

The flash of pride soured in full, and Stinson gritted her

teeth instead.

Something about this case had crawled under her skin and settled in as an itch.

She wanted answers. She wanted to find the fugitives and bring them in. She didn't know what had changed, what had hooked her emotionally.

Maybe it was the challenge of stopping a pair that had eluded authorities in multiple states already.

Maybe it was something about that smile on Scarlet Burlew's lips as she stared into the security cam.

Maybe the two of them rampaging down the coast with their smug body language just rubbed her the wrong way.

They'd looked gleeful in the surveillance footage, and now a man was dead. Dumped in a ditch like a bag of trash.

Whatever the reason, the case felt personal now.

Still, hours had passed since they'd dumped the body. They could be hundreds of miles away by now.

She clenched her molars harder. Felt the muscles in her jaw quiver and jump.

Just then, the door to the conference room burst open. Every head in the room snapped in that direction.

Sergeant Booth stood there, chest heaving as though winded from running across the small building. The desk sergeant had always reminded her somewhat of a walrus. Maybe it was the thick mustache, which happened to be trembling just now.

"We just got a call. Guy found it. The vehicle," Booth said, still standing in the half-open doorway. "They ditched the Charger from last night out in farm country."

The chief smacked his fist into his hand.

"Damn! I was hoping we might have more time before they switched vehicles again."

Booth's mustache twitched. He looked flustered with himself, like he was forcing the words out.

"No. Wait. I didn't… Jimmy and Scarlet? The guy says they're still here."

CHAPTER 9

Courtney set a breakneck pace across the parking lot, her sandals snapping a frenzied rhythm against the pavement.

"What's the rush?" Ellie asked, hurrying after her.

"Well, when I woke up from my nap, I saw the guys heading down to the beach. And those three skanks from Louisville stopped and talked to them."

"John and Wes?"

"Yes!" Courtney's tone indicated this was supposed to be obvious. "We have to get down there and stake our claim before those Kentucky whores get any ideas."

Ellie paused when they reached the sand. She kicked off her sandals and went the rest of the way barefoot.

"You realize how insane you sound, right?"

"Hey, it's like they say." Courtney pulled a tube of lip balm from her bag and smeared it over her lips. "The early bird gets the worm."

"More like the crazy bird gets the worm," Ellie said. "And just so we're clear, the 'worm' in this scenario is definitely a penis, right?"

Courtney snorted and cupped a hand over her eyes, scanning the crowded beach.

"Do you see them?"

Ellie squinted over at her.

"Don't you worry that we might be… imposing? We were just with them most of the morning. Maybe now they just want to hang out together."

Courtney threw back her head and cackled.

"Why is that funny?"

"Ellie! Guys don't come to spring break to hang out with each other. They come to spring break to find hot girls. Well, the straight ones do, anyway." She stopped and gestured at herself and then Ellie. "And if you haven't noticed, we are a couple of total babes."

Courtney pointed at the cluster of cabana tents and beach umbrellas arranged on the sand.

"Oh! I think I see them!"

The clopping sound of Courtney's footsteps slowed now. Ellie supposed that since she'd spotted her quarry, there was no rush.

"You know what your problem is?" Courtney asked.

"No, and I can't wait for you to tell me."

"You worry too much."

"Oh, well, in that case… yes, I know exactly what my problem is."

"At some point, you just have to say, 'Fuck it.' Push all the doubts and worries aside. Stand tall. Look in the mirror, and tell yourself, 'I'm a hot piece of ass, and every guy is dying to hook up with me.'"

Ellie laughed.

"I'm serious. It works."

"You look in the mirror and say you're a hot piece of ass and every guy is dying to hook up with you?"

"You're goddamned right I do. Every day. Even when I look and feel like shit. Sometimes you gotta fake it 'til you make it."

A seagull swooped over their heads with some kind of food wrapper clutched in its beak.

"Seriously though… You act like if you worry about all the bad things that *might* happen enough, you'll figure it all out and not have to go through it or something. But that's not how it works. Because when the bad thing *does* happen, your only real choice is to deal with it as it comes. You don't have a choice, at that point. You have to do it, so you do."

For several seconds, Ellie was silenced by the profundity of this statement.

"That might be the smartest thing you've ever said," she said, finally.

Courtney's eyebrows appeared over the top edge of the

sunglasses.

"Don't sound so surprised. I'm a hot piece of ass, but I'm not *just* a hot piece of ass."

Ellie laughed.

From his position under the shade of a cabana tent, John turned. His expression changed when he spied them drawing near. He smiled and waved them over.

"Ladies! I was just telling Wes, I hope we see the girls here."

Courtney didn't miss the opportunity to shoot a glance at Ellie that contained a crystal-clear message despite there being no words spoken aloud: *I told you so.*

Ellie helped Courtney spread out their beach blanket so it was part in and out of the shade. Courtney was the type who liked to roast herself for several hours a day. Ellie was the type who started to wither if she spent longer than twenty minutes in full sun.

The beach was already packed with people. Plenty of other college-aged spring breakers were strewn across the shore, but Ellie noted several families with young children and a handful of retirees as well.

The sand felt almost silky on her feet, and she liked smushing through the top inch or so that had been warmed by the sun to the layer underneath that was still cool.

She closed her eyes and listened to the ambient noise surrounding them. The *shush-shush* of the water lapping against the beach. Gulls screeching as they hovered in the air, waiting for someone to drop a morsel of food. The hollow *pong*ing sound of someone hitting a volleyball.

A new sound crept in, decidedly less pleasant than the rest. It was a woman's voice, sharp and ringing with bitterness.

Ellie's eyelids fluttered open. There was a couple passing in front of their spot. A bit older than their group. Married, if the way they were nagging at one another was any indication.

"See? I told you we should have come down earlier," the woman complained. "All the cabanas are taken."

"I'm not the one who took forever in the bathroom plucking my mustache hairs."

The woman took the tote bag from her shoulder and swung it at her husband, and a bottle of something flew out and landed with a soft *thud* in the sand in front of where Ellie was sitting.

"You're such a pig! I don't know why I even put up with you!"

Ellie waited for one of them to notice that they'd dropped something. When they didn't, she scrambled to her feet and scooped up the tanning oil.

"Excuse me," she said.

The couple were so immersed in their argument, they didn't seem to hear her.

"Look, here's a spot with an umbrella. Real close to the food stalls, too. Primo real estate."

"Yeah, that's just perfect," the woman said, her tone indicating it was anything but. "If I want my hair to smell like French fries for the rest of the day."

"Excuse me," Ellie said, louder this time.

The woman spun around, already glaring daggers.

"What?"

The way her jaw snapped open and closed reminded Ellie of a yapping chihuahua.

Ellie held out the bottle.

"You dropped this."

"Oh," the woman said. She stalked over and snatched it from Ellie's fingers. "Thanks."

Her tone was icy, as if it were somehow Ellie's fault the tanning oil had fallen out of the bag.

Ellie imagined some people might have some snappy response to this kind of rude, antisocial behavior, but she just smiled and said, "You're welcome."

Like an idiot.

She scuttled back to her spot in the shade.

"Oh my God." Courtney snickered. "What a complete bitch! You know, they were at the breakfast buffet in the motel yesterday, and it was the exact same thing. I think their life might be one long, nonstop argument."

"Sounds like my parents," Wes muttered.

"I'm pretty sure they're the ones who found the body this morning," John said. "They were being interviewed by the police when we walked over to the crime scene."

"No way!" Courtney said. "You know what? When we talked to that detective this morning, I'm pretty sure she was coming out of their room! Freaky."

The couple was setting up their gear beneath an umbrella now and debating how they should angle it to get the most shade.

"Why do people like that even get married?" Courtney asked.

"Right?" John said. "Imagine waking up to that resting bitch face every morning."

"More like resting succubus face. I mean, Jesus. She almost took El's head off for picking up the crap she dropped. Total psycho."

John suddenly swung around to face Wes.

"Aww shoot. I was supposed to remind you to charge the spare batteries for the cameras."

Wes nodded.

"It's all good. I charged them last night."

"Cameras?" Courtney asked. "For what?"

John glanced left and right, as if he was worried someone might be listening in, then leaned toward her.

"Have you ever heard of 'urban spelunking'?"

Courtney's eyes went wide.

"No. What is that?"

"Isn't spelunking where you go into caves?" Ellie asked, flicking a fly from her leg.

John aimed a finger at her.

"That's exactly what spelunking is."

"So *urban* spelunking would be…" Ellie paused, trying to imagine something cave-like in a city. "…exploring sewers?"

"Eww," Courtney said.

John laughed.

"We actually have done a few sewers and drains. Mostly around Minnesota, which is kind of the mecca of 'draining' in the US."

"Shut up," Courtney said. "You're telling me you voluntarily went into a sewer and trudged around in poo?"

"Most sewers are a lot cleaner than you'd think. It's mostly water, and it rarely smells worse than pond scum," John said.

"We mostly do aboveground exploration anyway. Old factories. Abandoned amusement parks. Stuff like that," Wes explained.

"That's kind of cool," Ellie said.

"Yeah, but why?" Courtney asked.

"Well, at first we were doing it just for fun, but then we started documenting it on social media, and now we kind of have a following."

"Really?" Courtney got out her phone. "What's your username?"

"OK, check this out," John said, reaching for the black baseball hat perched backward on his head.

He spun it around to reveal a logo with two cartoon monkeys and text that read "The Spelunking Monkeys."

Courtney read the name out loud and tapped at her phone screen with her thumbs.

"What do you think of the hat? Keep in mind, this is just a prototype," John asked, zeroing in on Ellie, for some reason.

"Very slick," she said.

He pumped his fist.

"Yes! I don't mean to brag, but this was my first time designing merch, and I think it turned out pretty fire."

Courtney gasped.

"Look at this, Ellie. They have like 150,000 followers on

Insta!"

She held out the screen and used her thumb to scroll through some of the posts. Ellie had taken a photography class in high school and vaguely remembered some of the principles and techniques. The rule of thirds. The golden ratio. The pictures were expertly composed from what she could see.

"These are really cool," Ellie said.

"That's all the work of my man, Wes. He's the one with the artistic vision. I'm the guy with the big mouth."

"OK, so what does this have to do with charging spare batteries?" Courtney asked. "You're going to one of those abandoned places today?"

John stretched and yawned, and something about the sound reminded Ellie of a bear.

"That's the plan."

"Can we come?" Courtney asked, without missing a beat.

Ellie cringed at her friend's willingness to so blatantly invite herself. And then she realized Courtney hadn't only invited herself…

"Wait, what?" Ellie said.

But John was already nodding.

"Sure. If you don't get too scared once you hear where we're going."

Naturally, this only increased Courtney's curiosity.

"Where are we going?" she whispered.

John waggled his fingers dramatically.

"The Burdick Murder House."

Courtney's eyelids fluttered. The look on her face reminded Ellie of a kid listening to a ghost story.

"What is that?"

John's mouth tightened into a smug little smirk.

"Ah, but that would be telling. You're just going to have to wait until tonight to find out. If you dare."

CHAPTER 10

Detective Stinson rode shotgun in Taft's SUV. They wove through a few city blocks, hit one of the main roads, and then rocketed out away from the concrete into rural nothingness.

The green crush of semi-tropical foliage choked both sides of the road here. Palms and vines and creeper-type thickness crawling up over telephone poles and road signs. Soon enough the chaotic tangle of the wild land gave way to the orderly rows of orange groves as far as the eye could see. More oranges than people out this way.

"What the hell road was it again?" Taft said, his eyes shifting around in his head like marbles.

He looked frazzled. Maybe everyone was. For all they knew, they were about to chase down the 21st century's equivalent of Bonnie and Clyde.

"Highmore Road," she said.

"Wanna punch the address into the GPS?"

She did.

After gathering himself, Sergeant Booth had gotten the story out straight, his voice shaking a little with adrenaline. The 9-1-1 caller had not only found Jimmy and Scarlet's ditched Dodge Charger on their property, he'd found Jimmy and Scarlet, the actual people. They'd taken off on foot immediately, but they'd apparently been hunkered down in his barn for at least part of the morning. Couldn't have gotten far, either.

Stinson pulled out her phone and read the call transcript again while the GPS voice rattled off the next step in the directions for Taft's benefit.

DISPATCHER: 9-1-1, where's your emergency?

CALLER: Can you hear me?

DISPATCHER: Yes, I can.

CALLER: Hello?

DISPATCHER: 9-1-1, this is Shae. Where's your emergency?

CALLER: Hi, uh, Shae. This is Elmer Ferguson. I got this is, uh… Got them killers, Jimmy and Scarlet. Them what killed the cashier last night, from that Citgo over in Peachtree? I found 'em on my property here just a minute ago. Uh… they was sleeping in my barn here last night, I expect.

DISPATCHER: What's your address?

CALLER: 3011 Highmore Road.

DISPATCHER: And you say that the fugitives are in your barn?

CALLER: No. They *was* in my barn as of a few minutes ago. I spooked 'em when I went out there to gas up my tractor. I come back in the house to get a shotgun, and when I went back out there, they was gone. Took off into the woods off the western edge of my property. Land belongs to Bob Howard on the next farm over from mine. Big chunk of wooded acreage there.

DISPATCHER: OK. I'll send someone immediately. Let me get you mapped real quick. Do you know the address of the farm next door?

CALLER: Yes, ma'am. It's 3303 Highmore Road. It's a scoot. Lotta acreage between here and there, like I said.

DISPATCHER: Thank you. Let me pull that up.

CALLER: OK. Oh, and I found their car, the Charger they was driving last night when they dumped the, uh… body. They parked it out in the weeds just off my driveway. Prolly ran out of gas, way I figure it. Decided to hole up for the night.

DISPATCHER: (Unintelligible.)

CALLER: Can you speak up, um, Shae?

DISPATCHER: We've got someone on the way now. What did you say your name was, sir?

CALLER: Elmer Ferguson.

DISPATCHER: Perfect. Thank you.

CALLER: How long, do ya think?
DISPATCHER: How long?
CALLER: How long do ya figure it'll be before the po-lice get here?
DISPATCHER: Soon. They'll be there soon.
CALLER: Uh-hah. But how long do ya think? Like five minutes? Cause these sons a bitches are getting away presently.
DISPATCHER: The police will be there very soon, Mr. Ferguson.
CALLER: If they're comin' in from town, it'll be a while. Twenty minutes or something at a minimum. That's too long.
DISPATCHER: Please stay on the line with me here, Mr. Ferguson.
CALLER: Hell, I could get the dogs after 'em now. Hunt the two of 'em just like raccoons. Have 'em secured before the cops even show.
DISPATCHER: No. Mr. Ferguson. Elmer. These are armed and dangerous fugitives. Please stay in your home with the doors locked.
(The sound of a door slams in the background quickly followed by a metallic screech that must be the opening of a dog pen.)
CALLER: Come on, pups. We got us a little huntin' to do.
DISPATCHER: Elmer.
CALLER: Listen, cell reception gets spotty once I get toward the back of the property and beyond, so I figure I'll lose ya at some point. I just wanted to apologize for it in advance.
DISPATCHER: Elmer, please remain in your home until you are contacted by the officers reporting to the scene.
(Static hisses over the line.)
DISPATCHER: Mr. Ferguson?
(Static continues.)
DISPATCHER: Hello? Are you there?
End of call.

By the time they pulled onto Highmore Road, Detective

Stinson's palms were slick with sweat. For a second, she wondered why she was nervous, then she sniffed a little laugh at herself.

Why am I nervous?

I don't know. A civilian with a loaded shotgun and a pack of dogs is going after two wanted criminals. What is there to be nervous about?

She watched the trees whip past out the window again. The orange groves had been replaced by fields of corn, punctuated by a haphazard row of oaks along the perimeter that made this section of Florida look more like the Midwest to Stinson's eye.

"Hope Elmer Ferguson didn't already perforate our criminal lovebirds with a few loads of buckshot," Taft said. "He can be a mean son of a bitch, that's for sure."

Stinson turned to face her partner.

"Wait. You know the 9-1-1 caller?"

Taft grinned and nodded, those caterpillar eyebrows wriggling above his crinkling eyelids.

"Oh yeah. Me and Elmer became good buddies when he got into a land dispute with one of his neighbors. Let's just say Elmer hadn't felt the other fellow's lawn hygiene was up to snuff. The neighbor had let it get a little scruffy. Crab grass, too. After a few heated exchanges about it, Elmer went over and mowed the guy's yard himself. Naturally that violation of boundaries led to a fist fight, and that fist fight escalated to the both of them pointing guns at each other amidst a screaming match. It's a tale as old as time. I got there in time to de-escalate the whole thing, but…"

Stinson gaped at him.

"What part of that is natural to you?"

"You haven't lived in the south your whole life, Stinson, and it shows. You do not. *Ever*. Mess with another man's lawn. It may as well be punishable by death. Almost was for Elmer Ferguson."

Stinson thought about it. Then she shrugged.

"It's just grass, though."

Taft chuckled at that.

"Just grass," he repeated. "Southerners, by and large, are descended from honor-based societies. You defend what's yours to the death, and no one thing you can defend is more important than your land. A lot of it dates back to the sheep herders in the hills of Scotland and Ireland. Back then, you let someone or something infringe on your land, on your flock, your whole family might not make it through the winter as a result. You had to be real hard-nosed to ensure your tribe's survival. And those values, that attitude, they're alive and well here in Durango Beach. Fuck around with some guy's lawn and find out."

They drove in silence for a while after that. Stinson looked out over a sea of corn that sprawled into the horizon.

"Anyway, like I said, I hope Elmer hasn't shot Jimmy and Scarlet. It'd be a shame," Taft said. "Lotta paperwork on our end of things, you know?"

Stinson put the two ideas together for the first time. The crime spree had rolled right up onto Elmer Ferguson's property. Jimmy and Scarlet had ditched the car in the weeds, probably slept in his barn, and then cut out into the woods. That'd be a lot of violations of his honor, wouldn't it? Maybe he really had hunted them down and shot them.

More woods flitted against the sides of the road. Stinson caught a flash of a white Camaro parked in the roughage just off the shoulder. She found it striking for reasons she didn't understand, but it whooshed past quickly.

"Here we go," Taft muttered.

The GPS computer voice started squawking again. Taft slowed the SUV as they passed a small farm stand with a sign that read, "FERGUSON'S FARM FRESH PRODUCE." They wheeled into a gravel driveway that gently curved as it carried them deeper onto the lot.

Techs already worked around the abandoned Charger just off the driveway. The muscle car had blazed a trail into the weeds, knocking a bunch of dried-out thistle stalks flat. The passenger side door hung wide open, and the techs still looked to be documenting the exterior of the car, meaning Jimmy or Scarlet had left the door that way.

Stinson pictured the scene.

The car rolling in here in the black of night.

The door left open.

Wait.

Something struck her as wrong about the image. Something didn't fit.

The car door hung open in her mind's eye, and the interior light spilled out of the open doorway and lit up a big slice of the night.

Would they have been able to kill the dome light?

Or could they have parked here shortly after dawn, when the light wouldn't have mattered?

Either possibility was plausible enough, she supposed.

The SUV zoomed past the Charger and left the image behind. In the rearview, Stinson could only see the tops of the techs' heads hovering above the weeds.

Beyond that, red and blue lights twirled up by Elmer Ferguson's farmhouse. A cruiser sat at an angle between the barn and the house with the lights still spinning on top.

The SUV crunched over another stretch of gravel and finally pulled to a stop just behind the angled cruiser. Taft put it in park, and they climbed out.

A thrum of electricity had entered Stinson's limbs at some point, though she hadn't fully felt it until she stepped off the rugged driveway and onto the soft grass of Elmer Ferguson's meticulously maintained yard. Adrenaline flowing. Heart beating.

Even with the humidity pinning its warm, wet blanket around everything, the country air smelled fresh and green and clean in Stinson's nostrils. The descending cloud of mosquitoes quickly erased any sense of the scene being idyllic, however.

She swatted at the bloodsuckers and followed Taft as he trudged toward the barn.

"So who do you think will find something first," the big detective said. "Us or the team next door?"

While they searched the Ferguson farm, the chief and a couple of other units had headed over to Bob Howard's neighboring property to begin the search from that side of the woods. A phrase Elmer Ferguson had used on the call replayed in Stinson's head: *Lotta acreage, like I said.*

She made a *hm* sound in her closed mouth as she pondered Taft's question. Her eyes swept out over the woods beyond the barn.

"Just looking at how dense those woods are, I'd think it'll be us. Can't see anybody getting far in that kind of thicket, especially a couple of city kids from a thousand miles north of here."

Taft sighed.

"Dang it."

"What?"

"The way you said that… I guess it just seems like the dogs would get 'em, ya know? Some hunting hounds on their home turf will tear through those woods a lot faster than any human, ya know?" Taft shuddered before he went on. "I can't stop picturing those two kids with ragged shotgun wounds in their chests. They're felons, sure, but they don't deserve that fate, do they?"

Taft's words painted a picture in Stinson's head. Jimmy and Scarlet laid out in the ferns. Sheets of red coating their torsos.

Taft poked his head in the barn door. Looked both ways.

"Nobody in there," he said.

But Stinson's eyes had already slid past him, past the barn. She stared into the wall of green beyond both.

Branches stirred at the edge of the woods, leaves vibrating along one cleft in the foliage. The wagging of the sticks and stalks intensified.

Taft followed her gaze. They both locked onto that point of agitation.

Sergeant Booth appeared in the shadowy spot between the

branches, that silver mustache just about glowing from the patch of sunlight touching the bottom half of his face. He stepped into the opening, and then he stopped. Chest heaving. Face pale.

His gaze shifted from Stinson to Taft and back again. The grave expression spoke volumes, at least to Stinson.

Christ.

That farmer and his dogs killed those kids.

Booth waved them over, something soft in the gesture. His lips moved but no words came out for a second. When they did, he stammered, voice gone thick with emotion.

"I… uh… cuh-called it in already. Uh. I think you two just need to see this for yourselves."

Then he turned and strode back into that narrow fissure in the green, disappeared into the shadows under the canopy. It looked like the woods just swallowed him up.

Stinson hustled to catch up, some part of her afraid maybe she'd lose him in that forested gloom, though she knew the impulse was irrational. She could hear Taft's footsteps quickening to keep pace with hers. For a big guy, he was light on his feet.

She stomped through growth that quickly went from knee-high to waist-high, crossed that dark borderline at the edge of the woods. Her heart slammed against her rib cage.

The ground opened up again as soon as she got under the trees. Crushed leaves the shade of Earl Gray tea coated the soil here, replacing the tangled green thicket she'd just waded through.

She scanned the way ahead. At first, she saw only the black of the tree trunks forming bars in the endless gray of the open spaces between them. Her eyes took a few seconds to adjust to the shade.

Then movement pulled her gaze. Booth's back tottered in the distance. He'd somehow pulled away from them, though his pace looked plodding from back here.

She darted forward. Speed-walking. Then picking up into a

jog.

The dead leaves crunched underfoot. Laid a papery drumbeat beneath the scene.

Booth stopped in the distance, drawing up on a low spot in the land. He stood still. Head down. Thumbs hooked around his belt loops. Elbows out in a relaxed pose.

Stinson raced for him. That scared part of her frantic now. Something freshly urgent about all of this.

Again, she pictured the two "criminal lovebirds," as Taft had called them. Down in the weeds. Chests punctured by buckshot. Sheets of blood flowing out of them.

But something wasn't right with that image. She knew that now.

It was too still here. Too quiet. Even Booth looked like he was standing at a funeral procession, staring down into the grave as they lowered the casket.

Something is up there. Something important.

But where are the dogs?

Her head snapped to the left and then to the right. Eyes pivoting in their sockets. Surveying all.

The woods held empty in all directions. Silent. Sleepy and serene.

She rushed up on Booth, took those last few paces to pull alongside him. Slammed both of her heels into the soft earth to stop all at once.

And then she saw.

Elmer Ferguson lay belly down in a patch of black muck. His face was submerged in the mud, nose pressed straight down into it, the black smears crawling up over his cheeks on both sides.

The exit wound had left a red crater where the small of his back had been. A canyon of wet red. That sheet of blood just like she'd pictured, but turned around in all ways.

Naked bone — whiter than bleached teeth — stood out from the ruddy mess around it. A few vertebrae. Part of a hip bone.

She couldn't breathe. Couldn't think.

Could only stare into that red hole. Her gaze digging deeper and deeper.

Taft whispered next to her.

"Aw, Jesus."

Stinson blinked. Blinked again.

Suddenly she was able to break her gaze from the wound. Eyes sliding over the green around the dead body instead. The afterimage of the wound persisted for a moment, still glowing red in her retinas. And then it was gone, and she could see the whole scene again, could breathe again.

Elmer's three dogs lay dead in a haphazard spread around the fallen farmer. Something wrenching and sad and final in their flat dark eyes. They'd died alongside their master.

Movement drew her eye back to the corpse. A dark speck zipped by, just above Elmer's open back.

They all tracked it, heads moving in unison like they were riding together in a car, centrifugal force pulling as they rounded a corner.

Then Stinson could see it.

A black fly twirled down into the wound. It looked like an image from a family reunion, except this was a man's insides instead of a potato salad.

None of them moved. None of them spoke.

They watched the fly happily rub its feet together as it prepared to feast.

CHAPTER 11

After an hour or so of baking in the sun, Wes felt like a hot dog on a roller grill at a gas station.

He finally clambered to his feet, tugging off his shirt.

"Anyone else up for a swim?"

Everyone else agreed and set about disrobing as necessary to get down to their bathing suits. He happened to glance over at Ellie just as she was sliding her t-shirt over her head, his eyes falling on the place where the tank-style top of her suit stopped to reveal a narrow slice of stomach.

By comparison, Courtney's tiny bikini was much more revealing. And yet there was something about that sliver of skin just below Ellie's navel that drove him a little crazy. He forced himself to look away so it didn't seem like he was ogling.

They splashed around in the waves and dug out handfuls of sand from the bottom, looking for shells. Courtney found a conch bigger than her fist, but dropped it when a wave splashed saltwater in her mouth.

The sun dried them off quickly after they returned to the cabana. Courtney was in the middle of braiding Ellie's hair when they heard a distant whizzing hum coming from the water. Two jet skis crashing through the surf.

Courtney sucked in a breath.

"I want to do that."

"What?" John asked. "The jet skis?"

Courtney nodded.

"Let's go, then."

Her face went full pout, and she crossed her arms.

"I tried. They said I have to take a test to get my temporary boating license. A test! The whole point of coming here is to get away from exams and grades and all that crap."

"You don't need a boating license, because I already have

one," John said, pulling the card from his wallet and holding it out with a flourish.

Courtney actually gasped.

"You would take me?"

"Hell yeah," John said. "Who else wants to go?"

Ellie shook her head.

"Pass." She turned to a new page in her book. "I'll stay here and watch our stuff."

John turned his gaze on Wes.

"Wes, my man. You want in on this jet ski action?"

Wes grabbed a drink from the cooler and shook icy water from his fingers.

"I don't really get jet skis. You sit on it. It moves forward. It's fun for about ten seconds, and then it's like, 'OK. Now what?'"

Ellie chuckled at his description.

"What are you talking about?" John's voice was incredulous. "It's like… a four-wheeler on the water. It's the best."

"Four-wheelers are even stupider," Wes said.

John's nose wrinkled up.

"You're crazy," he said, and he and Courtney walked off, heading for the rental place.

The pair of jet skis they'd been watching earlier continued to buzz around, throwing out rooster tails of water. Wes watched the contraptions zig and zag for a moment before turning to Ellie.

"I'm not crazy though, right?" he asked. "Jet skis are dumb."

"I've only ridden one once, when I was like eight. But yeah, the novelty wears off pretty quick." She squinted over to where John and Courtney were moving down the beach. Her friend had an excited bounce in her step. "For some people, at least."

"'Novelty' is the perfect word for it," Wes said. "It's like… you ever ride around in a Jeep with the top off?"

"No, but my uncle had a convertible for a while."

Wes raised his eyebrows.

"Miserable, right?"

"Awful," Ellie agreed. "You see them on TV, and somehow it seems like it's the coolest thing ever. But in reality, it's cold and windy and your hair gets all tangled up. That was when I realized there's a reason most cars have, you know… roofs."

Wes laughed. He was about to ask Ellie if she wanted to go grab some food from one of the nearby stands when an older woman — Wes guessed she was probably in her sixties — waved from the cabana next to them.

"Yoo-hoo! Excuse me!"

Her hair was dyed an unnatural shade of dark purple-red that Wes imagined was probably called something like Brandywine or Cherry Cola.

"Would you happen to know what time it is? My phone is dead, and this one doesn't believe in technology." She smacked the bare back of the man lying on a towel beside her. "Isn't that right, Gerald?"

The man grunted and lifted his head. He was so deeply tanned, his skin was the color of an old baseball mitt.

"Huh?"

"I said we don't know what time it is because *someone* refuses to join the twenty-first century and get a cell phone."

Gerald squinted over at them before letting his head flop back down to the towel.

"Uh-huh. Sure. Whatever."

The woman rolled her eyes *and* her head.

"Mr. Personality, here."

"Not a problem," Wes said, swiping at his phone. "It's—"

He stared down at the date on the screen, and his mind went entirely blank for a moment. No thoughts. No feelings. It was like existence just glitched out for a beat.

And then a jolt of blinding anger hit. Lightning flashed behind his eyes, between his teeth. Cold current surging through his skull.

Memories overtook his vision. A montage of images, tinged

red around the edges.

A dirt track winding up a mountainside.

Police dogs pulling their leads taut.

All the people fanning through the brush, poking sticks into it.

When his awareness came back to the present, he was vaguely aware of Ellie beside him, asking if he was OK. A distant part of him knew he should respond, should reassure her, but he couldn't. Not yet.

He was lost in it. Drowning in it.

He glared out at the ocean, at the empty spot of water past all the swimming tourists and boats. Not really seeing any of it.

Ellie sounded miles away when she read the woman the time from her own phone screen.

And Wes was still stuck. Stuck in the anger. And guilt. And sadness. But mostly anger. Which was strange. It had never quite felt like this before.

Finally, he saw the stricken look on Ellie's face.

Shit. I'm making her uncomfortable. I'm sitting here with this cute girl, acting like a goddamn weirdo.

He closed his eyes. Took a breath.

"Sorry about that." He swallowed. "I just realized it's the anniversary of my brother disappearing. Kind of caught me off guard."

"Oh my God," Ellie said, looking horrified. "What happened?"

Wes shrugged.

"He went on a hike out near Mount Rainier with his dog and… that was it. Never seen again. We did the whole search thing. Helicopters and scent hounds and all that for over a week. Nothing."

"That's so awful. I'm sorry, Wes."

He rubbed a hand along his cheek, the stubble tickling his palm like Velcro.

"Yeah, it's pretty fucked up," he agreed and heaved out a sigh.

He was quiet for a second. A wave slapped at the beach.

"Not knowing what happened. That's the hardest part, I think. You can't stop thinking that maybe he's out there somewhere. You think maybe one of these days, Jason's going to come jogging out of those woods.

"But as time passes, it becomes more and more clear that's not going to happen. Like, I know he's dead. I know it. But it can never quite be all the way real inside, like a wound that won't quite mend."

He was pretty sure he should stop talking now. Change the subject to something less depressing. But now that he'd started, the words kept coming.

"It's impossible not to obsess over it. So eventually I started finding ways to distract myself. That's how our Instagram first started. Well, John originally made the account a while back, but we'd barely done anything with it. So I went through all the photos and videos I'd taken during our explorations and started uploading them. It got a little traction, and suddenly I had something else to focus on. Something I could actually control. Work, you know.

"Making it a success became my new obsession. And it felt good to be getting so much positive attention. Especially for my art, which I'd never thought would be anything more than a hobby. But these past couple months, it's been starting to feel kind of… empty. It feels insane to say that, because we're basically making a living off the ad revenue at this point. How can I possibly complain about that?

"But it doesn't mean anything. Not really. And now I guess I need something to change, you know? Sometimes I think you need to change to survive."

He fell quiet for a second. Eyes spearing empty space.

"Life seems like this story that accumulates. Like all the hours, all the things you do have to add up to something. A grand finale. A happy ending. Something. But for a lot of people, maybe most people, it just cuts off, you know? It was never building to anything. It all lead to nothing."

"Like your brother?" Ellie asked, her voice quiet.

"Yeah," he said.

In the silence that followed, it occurred to Wes that Ellie was probably regretting not opting for the jet ski ride after all. He couldn't be worse company if he tried.

"Sorry. Again. I swear I'm not usually such a downer."

"I don't think that," Ellie said.

"Yeah, but come on. We just met, and here I am launching into all the miserable shit that's going on in my life. I mean, I generally try to wait until at least the second date for the really grim stuff. That's just common courtesy."

Ellie chuckled a little at that, and Wes joined in after a second.

They looked out at the ocean together.

CHAPTER 12

Stinson and Taft crunched back over Elmer Ferguson's property. The gravel driveway stabbed at the soles of Stinson's shoes, unforgiving underfoot after so long squishing around on a carpet of dead leaves with a padding of rich black soil beneath.

Still, it felt good to get out from under that darkness stretching over the woods, to step back into the sunlight. It felt, Stinson thought, like waking from a nightmare, going back into the normal world, into real life.

But even daylight couldn't erase what had been done in those woods, couldn't heal the wounds, couldn't bring the dead back to life. For the people who loved Elmer Ferguson or those dogs, this nightmare was only beginning. It would never go away.

"He have a wife?" Stinson asked.

Taft bobbed his head.

"Helen. Nice lady. She's out of town from what I overheard. Guess I'll probably be the one to tell her."

He blinked and looked like he was staring at something far away.

They trudged on. Stinson waved another cloud of mosquitoes away and gazed over her shoulder into the darkened woods behind them.

A whole mess of techs tore through the crime scene now, stomping out over the dead leaves. Setting up lights. Documenting. Swabbing. Bagging. Photographing the dead. The process would take hours, still going as the sun went down and carrying on deep into the night, most likely.

Stinson shivered at the thought. She was glad she didn't have to spend that kind of time at the worst scenes. She saw her share of the aftermath, but her job typically involved a lot of interviews, reviewing case files, chasing down any and all leads. It was grim in its way, nobody would question that, and she'd learned to harden herself to it over time.

But to spend so much time in the place where the trauma had occurred, where the violence had played out, to dwell there for hour after hour the way the techs did, would be too much for her.

That kind of darkness marked a place, she thought. It left a negative energy a sensitive person could feel. If you stayed with it too long, if you let it get under your skin, it marked you, too.

The darkness stayed with you.

CHAPTER 13

Ellie felt her cheeks go red, warmth flushing the skin. She was glad her sunglasses were big enough that they covered half of her face.

I generally try to wait until at least the second date for the really miserable stuff.

That had just been a joke, right? Wes had been joking. This wasn't a date. She knew that. So it had to be a joke.

So why was she blushing?

She fiddled with the cooler, hunting around for a Coke more to look busy than out of thirst.

Geez, why was she being so neurotic?

Courtney, she thought. *This is Courtney's fault.*

When they'd returned to their room after talking with the guys, Courtney had started playing matchmaker.

"You should totally hook up with Wes," she'd said.

Ellie raised her eyebrows.

"Uhh… random."

"No, it isn't. I see the way he looks at you. Plus, you guys laugh at the same dumb stuff. He's perfect for you."

"Courtney, laughing at the same stuff doesn't make us soul mates."

"Who said anything about soul mates? I'm saying you should bounce on it, not get married."

Ellie shook her head.

"He lives in Detroit."

"So?"

"So at the end of the week, I'll never see him again."

"So? Sometimes that's a good thing," Courtney said with a chuckle. "El, I say this out of love. But you are too serious for your own good. You need to learn how to loosen up and have fun. You act like a one-night stand would kill you or something."

Ellie scoffed.

"I don't think it would *kill* me," she said. "I just don't see the point."

Ever since the day in first grade that Ellie had come home from school and told her mother about the boy in class she had a crush on, her parents had made it clear that dating was another item that fell under "there will be time for that later."

Despite that, she'd had boyfriends. And she'd had sex.

OK, so maybe it was just the *one* boyfriend, but still. She'd gotten the gist. A few pumps under Ted's Spider-Verse poster while both of them were buzzed on Boone's Farm. Big whoop.

Ellie had mentioned all of this to Courtney once. Told her she thought the whole thing was overrated. And Courtney had cackled and said, "That's what every girl thinks until they do it with someone who knows what they're doing."

She finally fished a can from the cooler and sat back, glancing over at Wes. He hadn't seemed to notice her blushing, so at least there was that.

Her eyes went to the sea then. Spotted a shape moving across the turquoise water. A jet ski with a tall person driving and a smaller person in back with golden hair fanning out in the wind.

"Hey look," she said, pointing. "I think that's John and Courtney."

Wes trained his gaze on the water and nodded.

"You're right."

They watched the jet ski zip across the surface, hooking a hard turn into a wave and then tipping sideways, dumping both riders into the ocean.

"Wipe out," Wes chuckled.

Ellie ran her thumb through the condensation on the icy can.

"Oof. I'm not sure Courtney was expecting to get wet. She won't usually go past like knee-deep water, because she's afraid of sharks."

Wes breathed out a laugh.

Both riders climbed back on and took off again. Looping donuts into their own wake. Crashing in the surf. Courtney apparently hadn't demanded John take her back to dry land yet, so that was something.

When the pair returned a while later, Courtney literally skipped over to the cabana.

"You had fun, I take it?" Ellie asked.

Courtney knelt in front of her and clasped her hands together.

"It was uh-mazing!"

"And are you cured of your shark phobia now?"

Courtney tilted her head to one side.

"What do you mean?"

"Well, we saw you guys wipe out, but you don't seem too upset about going into the water."

"Oh *that*!" Courtney plucked at one of the sodden strands of her hair and clicked her tongue. "You know he threw us off on purpose? And I completely freaked out, to be honest. But then John told me about the sonic shark deterrents they put on all the jet skis and boats around here."

Ellie's eyes narrowed.

"The what now?"

"It makes a sound the sharks don't like and keeps them from coming near the jet ski," Courtney explained.

Ellie locked eyes with Wes.

"What an interesting piece of technology I've never heard of," she said.

Wes nodded along with her.

"Yeah, that sounds, uh… not real."

"What? No. It's real," Courtney said, looking to John to back her up. "Tell them, John."

His mouth stretched into something between a grimace and a smile.

"Busted."

"You made it up?" Courtney slapped his arm. "Why would

you do that?"

"I could see how panicked you were getting when we went in the water. I was just trying to calm you down."

"I'm never riding on a jet ski with you again!" Courtney said, like it was an actual threat with teeth.

She pretended to be angry with John for a whole two minutes before she fell right back into flirting with him.

When they got too hot, everyone took another swim. John kept hoisting Courtney in a fireman's carry and pretending to carry her out into deeper water while he called out, "Here, sharky, sharky, sharky! Time for a snack!" Courtney played along, gleefully kicking and screaming until he tossed her into the waves.

Watching their antics, Ellie couldn't help but smile. Courtney was probably right. She *was* too serious.

Because it was spring break, damn it. She was here on this beach in Florida. She might as well make the most of it.

CHAPTER 14

When they reached Taft's SUV, the big detective kept going, lumbering down the driveway toward the edge of the property. At first Stinson thought he might be in some kind of trance, obeying that gritty drumbeat of the gravel against the soles of his shoes. Then they strode up on the abandoned Charger, and it made sense to her. He wanted a closer look.

The muscle car had been driven into the drainage ditch on a diagonal. The front end tilted into the muck, and the whole thing looked twisted so the driver's side was lower. It reminded Stinson of a listing ship.

Taft toed up to the edge of the gravel and stopped. He stood and watched from about twelve feet out. Now it was Stinson who couldn't help but walk closer.

She stepped off the driveway into the raspy thistle stalks. The dry broken things felt like stepping on brittle bones.

A few techs still swirled around the car. Once Stinson got a glimpse inside, she could see why.

Balled-up fast-food wrappers formed one solid pile on the floor. Some bottles and cans stuck out of the papers printed with various chain logos — Taco Bell, Arby's, Bojangles. A lot of Diet Coke cans, it looked like. Maybe six or so tall boy cans of Pabst Blue Ribbon strategically scattered throughout.

One of the CSIs carefully bagged a foil burrito wrapper. She sighed a little to herself as she sealed the plastic.

Stinson took a stab at the math. Probably at least fifty pieces of garbage there, she thought. Maybe as many as a couple hundred. And the techs had to document them all.

She shook her head, took another step closer, and leaned toward the passenger side window. There was one more thing she wanted to see.

It took her eyes a second to adjust to the gloom inside the

vehicle. At first the dash held dark, shadowed. But then the instrument panel sharpened into focus, and she could see it.

The needle on the gas gauge touched the red line next to the E. Out of gas, like they'd thought. It still didn't make much sense to hide out in a barn like they had, but at least one piece of the puzzle fit.

She shook her head again and backed away. Climbed the sloping land and stepped up onto the gravel.

"You think it was just luck?" Taft asked as she got back. He kept his voice low.

"What do you mean?"

"I mean, these two have eluded state police and local departments across four states and counting. Makes you think maybe they know what they're doing. But then you see how they're living. Like dirtbags. Slobs. Leaving piles of potential evidence everywhere in the car. Dumping the vehicle in a ditch and going to sleep in a barn some 150 feet away? That seem like the work of criminal masterminds to you?"

For some reason, while her partner spoke, Stinson thought only of Elmer Ferguson face down in that black clay back there in the woods. The image was already burned into her memory, would stay with her for the rest of her life. It ranked right up there with the worst of the horrors she'd seen on the job. All of them ready to be spooled up and projected onto that screen inside her skull without warning, without notice.

"It is pretty chaotic," she said after a while. "The whole thing."

"Psh. Chaotic is being generous. Sloppy is what this is. Really, really sloppy. Freakin' amateur hour. Still… why haven't they been caught yet?"

She shrugged. Thought about it, still picturing Elmer Ferguson's corpse all the while. She made a clicking sound with her tongue before she spoke.

"Here's my question. Elmer took a load of buckshot pretty much point blank, center mass. His dogs, too."

"Right."

"But Ferguson's gun wasn't fired. It wound up pinned under his body. He basically fell on it without getting a shot off, probably already dead by the time he hit the ground. So… did Jimmy and Scarlet have a shotgun with them this whole time? And if so, why not use it in the barn when Elmer first confronted them? Why run out into the woods and then shoot the guy?"

Now it was Taft's turn to shrug and think.

"Way I figure it, they were happy enough to get outta dodge, right? Live and let live. Kumbaya. All that. But once Elmer sicced his damn hounds on 'em, it kinda forced their hands. I ain't sayin' they shoulda killed the farmer or his animals, but… they were kinda backed into a corner, weren't they? I can understand that." He shrugged again, harder this time. "Dispatcher told him not to do it. Told him to lock his door, and stay home. Dumb son of a bitch."

Stinson only realized a second later that Taft had been wiping his eyes as he said that last part. He sniffed once before he went on.

"Anyway, as far as them having a shotgun… Hell, we saw the damage up close. No question about what did that."

Stinson tilted her head one way and then the other. She decided not to express any of the doubts welling in her. Instead she said:

"Makes you wonder what else they might have."

Just then, Chief Bannon gave one of his loud whistles somewhere up by the barn. Stinson turned in time to see the big guy with his thumb and index finger still hooked into his lip.

"Bring it in, gang," the chief hollered. He was looking at the two detectives.

Stinson and Taft hustled that way, the gravel digging at their feet again.

"Look, this will hit the media shortly and be everywhere, but I wanted you two to be the first to know," Bannon said, his voice a little hoarse. "We just got word from the medical examiner. Our death this morning? Justin Higgins? The preliminary exam points to it being a medical event."

Stinson blinked. Taft opened his mouth, but he didn't say anything.

"The gas station attendant had a heart attack," Bannon continued. "Or at least that's how it looks for the moment. Still waiting on the tox screen stuff, I believe. But unless they poisoned him…"

Again, they were quiet. After a second, Taft voiced aloud what Stinson was thinking.

"This doesn't make any sense."

CHAPTER 15

Ellie watched a gull swoop down and snatch up the small piece of pizza crust John had tossed for it.

They'd covered a wide range of topics while they lazed on the sand that afternoon. The time Courtney had asked for a unicorn for her birthday, and her parents had gotten her a pony with a fake horn. John's fascination with exotic reptiles and insects. But no matter where the conversation strayed, it always seemed to lead back to the dead body from that morning.

"The mistake most people make is thinking a murder is a *who*dunit when it's really a *why*dunit," Wes said. "You gotta find the motive."

Ellie nodded in agreement.

"Money, jealousy, or revenge. If you throw serial killers into the mix, then you add a whole slew of other motives. Lust, control, 'the devil made me do it.'"

"Pretty sure the victim was male, so that probably rules out a serial killer," John said.

"So you're gonna write off another Jeffrey Dahmer, just like that?" Ellie asked.

Courtney peeled a piece of pepperoni from her slice of pizza and popped it in her mouth.

"Just because you've watched like ten thousand hours of true crime documentaries doesn't make you an expert," Courtney said.

Ellie tapped the side of her head.

"That doesn't stop me from thinking I am."

"Aren't you going to be a lawyer? I'd say that makes you kind of an expert," John said.

"Oh, well… I'm probably going to end up doing corporate law, not criminal. Sounds boring, but it pays well," Ellie said, not sure why she felt the need to justify it.

Courtney rolled her eyes.

"Ellie still thinks she has to do whatever her parents say."

Ellie shot her a look.

"What?"

"It's true," Courtney said, pursing her lips. "If you actually did what you wanted, you *would* go into criminal law. Admit it."

"When have I ever said that?"

"You're the one who wanted to volunteer at the public defender's office until your dad told you he wasn't sending you to law school to waste your time on poor criminals. And you always talk about how you'd love to do pro bono work for the Innocence Project and stuff like that. Things that actually help people."

Ellie squirmed a little and dug her toes deeper into the sand.

"Corporate attorneys help people… in a way."

She was thankful when John spoke up then, changing the subject.

"You know, I'm taking this film class, and we just watched *The Godfather*. Now I'm thinking… what if it was a professional hit? I mean, all those old mob guys retire in Florida, right?"

"Doesn't the mob usually try to hide their hits?" Wes asked. "Jimmy Hoffa style."

Courtney frowned and ate another piece of pepperoni.

"The sausage guy?"

Ellie chuckled.

"That's Jimmy Dean."

"You kids talkin' about the stiff they found over yonder?"

All heads turned to a man standing near one corner of their cabana.

He was of indeterminate age — he looked maybe sixty to Ellie, but his skin was so wrinkled from the sun that he might have been younger. His pompadour was a shade of deep black that she suspected came from a box, especially given the flecks of white in his stubble. The coif looked like it had been shellacked in place with an entire tube of hair gel. Mutton chops rounded out the look.

His bowling shirt, black jeans, and boots looked decidedly out of place on the beach.

"Yeah, man," John said. "Pretty crazy."

The man made a clicking sound with his tongue.

"I guess that depends. Way I heard it from a friend I got who works at the dispatch, there were no wounds or nothing on the corpse. Could be it was some kind of, whadyacallit… medical episode? Hell, that's how my daddy went out. Was walking his dogs on the back forty and just keeled over on the trail. Massive stroke. Dead before he hit the ground, or so they say. Dogs both took off into the brush. Bolted. Took me hours to find 'em. Probably seemed like quite an adventure to the pups, I expect. Free at last, you know?"

"If it was a medical event, why would somebody dump the body in the ravine?" Ellie asked.

"Well, it wasn't 'somebody' that dumped him. It was that Bonnie and Clyde couple that's been all over the news. Jimmy Maddox and Scarlet Burlew."

"See?" John said. "I knew it!"

"The dead body was a clerk from a gas station in Peachtree, the one that got robbed by none other than Jimmy and Scarlet last night. They snatched him during the robbery is what happened. Body turned up in the ravine a few hours later."

"Oh yeah," Wes said. "We've been seeing them on cable news all week."

The greasy black pompadour bobbed up and down.

"I'm sure you have. Been the lead story just about every night, and everybody'll be talking about it now. Place like Durango County doesn't get that kind of excitement very often, unless you count the time them Hendrix boys blew up a bunch of mailboxes over in the rich part of town a few years back."

He laughed a little, and it sounded like, *Heh, heh, heh.*

"Still gives me a chuckle to think about that one. Mailboxes all blown to hell. Shredded copies of *Good Housekeeping* and *Redbook* all tattered to pieces, blowin' across people's lawns. The more uppity folks were hollerin' about juvenile detention and no leniency, but I figure everyone's got a wild heart when they're young. Don't necessarily mean you're a bad seed. Though it's probably best to get it out of your system before you turn eighteen. Nothing on the permanent record that way, you know?"

John leaned over and flipped open the cooler. Got a beer for himself and offered one to the man.

"Don't mind if I do," he said with a smirk, leaning closer to grab the can.

Ellie got a big whiff of cologne that reminded her of sweaty old men playing bocce ball.

"Much obliged." He popped the top, took a long swig, and sighed. "Name's Duke, by the way."

John raised his beer and introduced the group.

"So you live around here?"

"Sure do. In fact, you can see my humble abode from here," Duke said and then pointed at the sea.

At first Ellie thought it was some kind of joke, but then she spied something bobbing in the waves in that direction. A boat.

"You live on a boat?" Courtney asked.

"Only way to have a piece of oceanfront if you're not a millionaire," Duke explained. He smeared the heel of his hand under his bottom lip. "And with the way them scientists are always talkin' about the sea levels rising, I figure I'm all set."

Ellie squinted at the vessel swaying on top of the water.

"What's it like, living on a boat?"

"What's it like, you ask? Well, shit. It's like *freedom*. I am beholden to no one. No property taxes. No mortgage. No landlord. Just the word makes me sick. Land*lord*, like they're royalty or something?" He made a spitting sound. "I, for one, refuse to submit myself to serfdom. A peon, I am not."

"Landlords are the worst, man," John said.

"Amen, brother."

"Don't boats like that usually have names?" Courtney asked.

"They sure do, darling," Duke said, beaming down at her. "I call her *The Problem Child*. Fits her, too. She's a temperamental creature. I swear she's got a mind of her own sometimes."

He took another long pull from his beer.

"If you've got time while you're here, I could take you out. I know some good spots for snorkeling. Less crowded than any of the places here on the mainland. If we're lucky, we might see some dolphins."

Courtney gasped.

"I love dolphins!"

"I also dabble a bit in photography. Portraiture and the like." He lowered his sunglasses and looked Courtney up and down. "You look like you might've done some modeling in the past, am I right?"

Ellie wrinkled her nose. Now *that* was creepy.

Courtney giggled and opened her mouth to speak, but before she could answer, a shrill voice cut through the air. The couple under the umbrella were at it again.

"What do you mean you're going back to the room? We just got here!"

The man uttered something unintelligible.

"The public bathrooms are right over there," his wife said, even louder now. "Use those."

"I can't," the man whined. He was still keeping his voice low, but the wind seemed to be carrying the conversation their direction. "Dammit, Tanya, you know I can't poop in public restrooms."

"I really think there's something wrong with you."

"Why? Lots of people don't like going in public bathrooms."

"I'm not talking about that. I know for a fact you already took one of your disgusting shits this morning." Her voice was full of contempt. "I almost gagged when I walked into the bathroom after you were done! You need to see a doctor, because I can't take it anymore."

"I'll be back," the man said as he crawled out from under the umbrella.

A moment later he crossed in front of their cabana, his mouth twisted into a grimace. Duke watched him go by, waiting for him to pass out of earshot before speaking again.

"Now I was taught to never raise my hand against a lady," he said, shaking his head. "But some women… well, they ain't ladies."

From beside Ellie, Wes whispered, "Yiiiiiiikes."

She snorted quietly.

"Well, I thank you again for the beer, and I hope you'll take me up on my offer," he said, starting to walk away. "If so, just tell Marco that you're looking for Duke, and he'll get word to me."

When he'd drifted a fair way down the beach, Wes looked around at them.

"Who the fuck is Marco?"

"No idea, dude," John said, laughing. "I think old Duke might be a little nuts."

"And a lot creepy."

"I don't know" Courtney said. "He mostly seemed nice to me."

Ellie was taking a drink of soda and almost choked on it.

"Uh, would that be when he suggested that some women deserve to be hit? Or when he asked if you'd ever done any modeling, which, by the way, is serial rapist code for *I want to get you alone so I can make you my next victim.*"

Courtney pointed her nose in the air and sniffed.

"You're obviously jealous."

Ellie let out a bark of laughter, but the encounter with Duke had left her feeling a bit uneasy.

It hadn't just been what he'd said, either. The guy's overall vibe had been off. She ran back through the interaction, noting that he'd first jumped into the conversation when they'd been discussing the dead body. And she couldn't help but think about the notion that some killers apparently liked to insert themselves in the investigation of their own crimes.

The thought made a chill run up her spine.

She told herself she was being silly. If what Duke had heard was true, that it was a medical episode, then there'd been no murder at all.

But even if there had been, what were the odds that they'd randomly end up conversing with the killer? Highly unlikely.

Still, the guy had been undeniably weird. Ellie was glad he was gone.

CHAPTER 16

Jimmy Maddox turns himself sideways. Jams his body between a pair of tightly packed trees. Feels the wood snug around him.

The trunks compress his ribcage from both sides, rough bark scraping against his chest, grating at his back, the pressure seeming to mount and mount.

That helpless feeling of being trapped clamps around his ribcage. And then the bark's grip releases all at once, and he is through.

Standing. Breathing. Basking a moment in that sense of relief.

Scarlet presses herself through the same gap a beat later, but she has no trouble fitting.

He holds her hand for a second. Helps her keep her balance as she steps through a mess of knotty roots.

The crushing woods are going dark around them. A quickly descending gloom, the shade thickening like bean soup.

Some panicked part of Jimmy keeps thinking that night must be falling already, that they'll get trapped out here in the dark with the police hunting them down.

But when he looks into the open spots to the west, he can still see the sun. It's fallen behind the tree line, hence the bean soup, but they still have a couple hours of daylight left. Maybe more.

Just gotta get out of these woods before dark.

Stay one step ahead of the police if we can.

He ducks under a pine bough. Walks like a hunchback for a few paces. Pops back up in a small clearing.

He moves into the center of the glade. Feels like he can finally breathe again. Even the humidity seems softer here, merely awful instead of unbearable.

He stops and looks around. Foliage clogs his view in all

directions beyond the treeless patch. An impossible tangle of creeper, fire bush, magnolias, and scrubby pine growth.

Scarlet steps through the thicket. Stands a second with him.

"I'm sorry," he says, his voice clear and low. "It was my call, stoppin' at that barn. We shoulda pressed on last night. Found another setta wheels. Shoulda got the hell away from the Charger, at least."

The Charger had been out of gas. Stopping somewhere had been inevitable.

Jimmy had been suffering one of his migraines as they ditched the muscle car. He'd taken his pill, but he'd wanted to lie down for a bit to let it kick in. Just a few minutes, he'd said.

They'd been up for two days and driving most of that time. And the straw pile had turned out to be more comfortable than either of them figured it would be. Instead of a few minutes, they'd slept for over ten hours.

"It's not your fault," she says. "It's nobody's fault."

He takes her hand and squeezes it, and Scarlet goes on.

"We wouldn't be out here if it weren't for me. You know that."

"Don't talk like that. You never asked for what you got. And we're never going to let it happen again. That's all that matters."

Her eyes look watery, he thinks, but she nods.

"Anyway, we still have our freedom," he says. "For now."

She takes a long drink from a water bottle, and then they get moving again.

They've walked for a long time now. Left the farm behind hours ago. Most of the personal items they'd taken with them had been ditched along the way.

Jimmy still has a duffel bag of money and a change of clothes tucked under one shoulder. Probably less than $15,000 cash total, he thinks, but most of it is in small enough bills that it takes up a lot of space, surprisingly heavy to lug around in the Florida heat.

If he'd known ahead of time that they'd have to flee on foot through dense foliage, dragging the whole wad of cash along with them, well… maybe he'd have planned things a little differently. But it's too late for that now.

As it is, every time the bag gets caught up on some blackberry prickers and Jimmy has to stop to rip it free, he thinks about how much easier this would be if they could stow the money somewhere. Dig a hole out here in the middle of nothing and come back for it once things have calmed down.

But no… no. The money is everything. It's the whole damn point. He'd never risk leaving it.

And just inside the zippered flap on the side, he has the little .38 snub nose he's used on all of the stickup jobs. There is a second gun, almost identical to the first, shoved even lower in that same pocket. This pair forms their only protection left against all that stands in their way.

Everything else — everything — they'd dumped in a creek just wider than a sidewalk some miles back. Scarlet had been overheating, feeling dizzy, so they'd thrown it all out at Jimmy's insistence. They'd stood and watched some of it float downstream. Watched the heavier pieces sink straight to the bottom.

Maybe that'll fuck up the police dogs, Jimmy thinks as he remembers it. He assumes they're already on the scent. With all that stuff that smells like them spread up and down the stream, maybe the hounds will get confused. He doesn't really figure so, but he likes thinking it's possible.

They leave the clearing and press themselves back into that vaguely jungle-like growth around them. Here, spiky palm fronds jut out of the ground, and long tufts of hanging moss dangle from the tree branches like thick green beards.

The ground slopes downward underfoot, eventually going muddy where the grade bottoms out. Jimmy thinks they might be hiking into swampland, which makes cold sweat prickle on the back of his neck.

He'd heard, once, that if you were ever stranded in the Everglades, the sheer density of venomous snakes in the swamplands made it safer to stay in the deep water and take your chances with the alligators.

Thankfully, they aren't so far south as that. Still, he'd rather avoid the muck — and the snakes — if they can.

After a few hundred feet of soft slop, the ground banks gently upward in front of them, and the mud gives way to dry land once more. They pick up speed without the wet stuff sucking at their shoes.

Jimmy's stomach grumbles. He wishes they'd kept a bag of chips or something. Doritos. Snack cakes. Pop-Tarts. One of those little Hostess pies. Anything.

What little food they'd had was gone now, some left behind in the Charger, some still snugged in Scarlet's backpack, which he'd last seen floating along in that creek.

He tucks his elbow into the papery bulk within the duffel bag. Feels it compress into his side, the bag heaving out a little breath.

Fifteen thousand dollars. Not even that much.

All we have to start a new life far from here.

Not nearly enough, but...

He stops then. Looks over his shoulder. Listens for what feels like a long time.

He half-expects to hear the dogs tearing through the woods. Or maybe the chuff of a chopper circling overhead. Those will come sooner or later.

But there's nothing for now. Just that endless chirp of insects, their many voices threaded through this stretch of wilderness, something restless about the tiny creatures.

The bugs are only going to be here a brief time — just a day or two for a lot of 'em — and they mean to spend that time at full throat, full volume, screeching into the void.

Maybe that makes sense, Jimmy thinks. Maybe it makes more sense than how a lot of people live.

He pushes himself forward finally. Feels Scarlet hustling alongside.

Soon enough, this whole swath of wilderness will be

crawling with law enforcement. And if not that, the dark will fall.

He means to get the hell out of here before either of those can happen. Has to. Their lives probably depend on it.

He swipes the back of his hand at his brow. Feels sweat sluice down the side of his face. Then he realizes Scarlet is staring at him.

"You OK?" she says, her eyes crawling all over his face, something worried in them.

Can't let her know.

Gotta say something.

"I'm good. I was just thinking, I guess. Remember when we walked into town in the dark that one time?"

"I remember. You were out of cigarettes. All fidgety."

"It was only two years ago, but it feels like it was longer, you know? We walked like six miles along the side of the highway. No streetlights. Nothing. The cars would come past, headlights sweeping over everything. So bright. And scary. Like you knew they probably wouldn't see you until the last second. And you knew half the people in the county driving at night were drunk and all that.

"But then the cars would be gone, and the dark would come back, and that was even scarier. I remember it was like I could see the white line along the edge of the lane, but only if I didn't look right at it. Seemed more like I could feel it there. A purple glow or something. Just barely even there. That and the stars were about all I could see. And it was just such a crazy feeling, walking into nothing, only that tiny line to guide us at all.

"But I held your hand, and I knew we'd be OK.

"And we were. We got through it. And that's why I know we'll be OK this time, too. Like, I hope we don't get stuck out here in the dark, but if we do, we'll make it through like we always do, yeah?"

She nods. He takes her hand and squeezes it again.

But a few paces later he has to let go to weave through some oak branches. They fall quiet after that, and the daylight leaks out of the sky like it's draining into the horizon.

Jimmy scans the gaps in the thicket to the west again. That orange glow remains, but he can't see the sun anymore. Too low. Soon enough it'll be gone.

His throat feels dry. Sandpaper flaps trailing from the back of his mouth down into his belly.

He glances at the water bottle dangling from his fingers on a plastic loop, but he doesn't drink any. He needs to save it. If they might be stuck out here for a full night, he needs to save it.

The foliage thickens, and their pace slows, but they keep pushing. Soon the green around them starts to go gray as the light wanes.

It could be worse.

It could be way worse.

If Jimmy had to pick either of the bad options ahead of them, he'd take the dark over the cops. At least the dark would conceal them — not from the dogs or a chopper's spotlights, but it would have its benefits.

If the cops caught up to them, they'd need a lot of luck to get away.

Almost as soon as he thinks these things, the woods grow a few shades lighter around them. Not daylight. Not even close. But not quite as gloomy as it'd been.

He doesn't want to get his hopes up, but that doesn't matter about twenty feet later.

They spill out onto a dirt road just as the purple tones of dusk bloom in full, overtaking the daylight. Walking out into the open beyond the woods feels surreal. Goosebumps pull at the skin on the backs of Jimmy's arms and make his scalp prickle.

Holy shit, he thinks. The relief gushes lightness into his head, makes him feel like he might faint.

But he can't let that show. He has to stay strong. For her. Out loud he says:

"Told you we'd make it, didn't I?"

Scarlet smiles, but she doesn't say anything. He can tell that part of her is still far away from here. The trouble shows as the subtlest crinkle in her brow.

They walk a while on the dirt road, able to really move now. At first it seems like they've only found a strip of dirt cut into the woods. Nothing else. A road to nowhere.

But just as the dark begins to settle from purple to blackness, they find a little double-wide with an old pickup parked in the driveway.

The vehicle — a Dodge Ram from the 70s or 80s — is kinda rusty looking. But the old shit is easy to hotwire. If it runs, and it must, it'll be more than they could have hoped for.

Jimmy glances at Scarlet, then at the truck, and then back at her. She nods, catching his drift.

They close on it slowly, quietly. Step off the gritty road onto a lawn that should cover the sound of their footsteps some.

He glides up to the passenger side door, the one that keeps the truck between the double-wide and his body. He has to be at least partially shielded from view, and there is a chance that the lights inside are glaring up the windows enough to blot him out completely, but he can't trust that idea, can't count on it.

He stays still for a few breaths. Watches the trailer.

The lone glowing windowpane is coated with gauzy curtains, lacy things that look like yellow spiderwebs or something with the way the light shines through. Beyond that he can see images flickering on a TV. Looks like monster trucks.

Jimmy snakes his arm into the partially open window of the thing and unlocks it. He keeps watching the glowing window beyond, bracing himself for any movement there. Anything.

The evening has cooled slightly, finally, but the sweat still seeps out of his pores like crazy. Beads gathering along his hairline and on his top lip, rivulets dripping down the rippled contours of the muscles on his back.

Finally he wraps his fingers around the door handle. Thumbs the latch. Pulls.

His heart thumps now. Harder than before. Faster, too. An

angry muscle punching in his chest.

The pane of steel swings open. The dome light clicks on. Pale light the color of French vanilla ice cream fills the truck cabin. Soft and off-white.

Jimmy waits. Listens past his gushing pulse. Watches the curtains for any lurch or jump.

Nothing inside the trailer moves, save for the monster trucks leaping on television.

So far so good.

He slides into the cabin. Butt gliding over the length of the bench seat until he's snugged himself behind the steering wheel.

Scarlet waits outside the car. This is how they always do it. She is ready to flee right up until the last second. Just in case.

Jimmy fumbles his right hand under the ignition. Hooks three of his knuckles in a gap there like fishhooks.

He tears the plastic panel down. Then he fingers the wires to try to see what he is working with.

Even with the dome light, the murk in the cabin slows him down. It takes him almost a full minute to sort the six wires and determine which he needs.

The blade of his pocketknife slices the plastic skin of each wire. Then he peels back the ends of the two he needs.

Again, his eyes flick to those gauzy curtains. A lacework stained yellow by the incandescent bulbs beyond them. The TV screen flickers as giant trucks crush the hoods and roofs of indistinct sedans.

Jimmy keeps waiting for those curtains to twitch. For a dark part to form there as someone peeks out. But nothing moves.

He takes another breath. Feels that kick drum of his heart thudding in his chest, hard and steady.

He strikes the exposed copper of each wire against the other. Sparks leap and sizzle.

The truck's starter whines. The engine sputters a second and then catches, its rumble steadying.

Scarlet jumps into the passenger seat. Closes the door

gently.

Jimmy yanks the gearshift, and the truck lurches into motion.

He keeps it slow on the gravel. Keeps the lights off. Picks up speed as they hit the dirt road.

Jimmy watches those glowing lacy curtains in the rearview. Still waiting for motion there, something. But they rush down the rutted road, and the trailer and its windows shrink into nothing in that rectangular silver plane of the mirror.

Jimmy finally flips on the headlights. Watches the two beams lance out over the dirt track before them, a bunch of leafy foliage suddenly seeming to glow along the sides of the road.

They round a bend, and the house behind them disappears from view. They've gotten away. They've done it.

He reaches over into the growing gloom and squeezes Scarlet's hand again.

CHAPTER 17

Ellie's feet scuffed over the rough motel room carpet. Her eyes went from Courtney, who stood in front of the bathroom mirror applying her makeup for the evening, to the clock on the bedside table.

It was nearly time to meet John and Wes, which gave her a pang of panic.

She'd been wracking her brain for a good excuse to bow out of the whole "urban spelunking" thing ever since it had first come up. The most obvious was to simply say she wasn't feeling well, but then she would run the risk of Courtney wanting to stay behind, and Ellie hated the idea of her friend missing out because of her.

The truth was always an option, but Ellie couldn't bring herself to do that either. She tried to imagine what she'd even say.

Hey guys, so I did a little internet research into urban spelunking, and I discovered it's not only dangerous but also pretty illegal. There's a forum thread on a website called "DerelictUS" where all these urban explorers seem to brag about the number of arrests they've racked up over the years. Trespassing, breaking and entering, criminal mischief. To quote one posting, "If you're into urbex, and you haven't been caught yet, you've just gotten lucky. It's a matter of when, *not* if*."*

Yeah, the truth would be a good way to go if she wanted to look like the world's biggest chicken.

She couldn't stop picturing the Bud Light incident from middle school with Simone and Katie. Simone had swiped a can of Bud Light from her dad's fridge. Out in the woods, they'd dared each other to take a swig.

Ellie watched the two of them take turns sipping at the foam. Then they faced her.

"Here. Your turn."

The potential consequences flashed before her eyes. Kids got sent to juvie for this.

And worse: What if her parents found out?

Ellie took a step backward, like maybe putting distance between her and the can would help.

"Uh… I… don't think I should."

"Why?" Katie asked.

"I just…"

"Maybe she's a narc," Simone said.

"I wouldn't do that."

"That's exactly what a narc would say," Simone said.

"I won't tell anyone. I promise."

Katie pulled her lips into a pout and mocked her in a high-pitched voice.

"*I won't teww anyone! I pwomise!*"

"Look, she's gonna cry."

And now, all these years later, Ellie felt the sting of tears in her eyes again.

She shook her head, trying to clear the memory and the emotions that came with it.

Pull yourself together, she thought. *You're a grown adult.*

Old enough to not care if the others thought she was chicken, surely.

Surely.

That was it. Ellie needed some air. She grabbed her bag and rushed to the door.

"I'm going outside," she said, yanking the motel room door open and nearly bowling straight into John, who had one fist in the air, poised to knock.

John did a quick stutter step to the side and dodged out of the way, but Wes, who was standing behind him, head bowed over his phone, didn't see her coming. And she was moving too quickly to stop herself.

She plowed into him, her forehead colliding with his. The force of it knocked her teeth together.

"Whoa!" John said, steadying Ellie as she stumbled backward. "Where's the fire?"

"Shit. Sorry. I didn't..." Ellie stammered. "Shit."

She felt an absurd level of relief when Wes laughed it off.

"It's all good," he said, rubbing his forehead. "I've got a thick skull. No damage."

Courtney appeared in the doorway.

"Are we ready to go?"

And before Ellie could do anything to stop it, she found herself beside Wes in the cramped backseat of John's car, on the way to the Burdick Murder House.

The closer they got, the more certain she was that she would be arrested tonight.

Ellie tried to imagine calling her parents, telling them she was in jail and needed bail money. The thought made her stomach lurch. And what if her school found out? Would she get kicked out? All of those tuition dollars, down the drain. All of her hopes and dreams, gone in a flash.

I've got to think of a way to get out of this.

Wes leaned forward, telling John to take the next left.

They turned off the commercial strip and rolled through a neighborhood lined on both sides with gnarled live oak trees. On one side of the street was a park crisscrossed with brick walking paths. On the other, a mix of houses from various eras — restored Victorians, mid-century bungalows, cracker cottages with screened porches.

And then Wes pointed at a lot that was so overgrown, at first all Ellie could see was a fence boxing in a tangle of trees and shrubs.

But in the fading light, she caught a glimpse of a hulking structure beyond. The brick facade stretched five stories.

"That's it," Wes said. "The Burdick Murder House."

Ellie reeled at the notion that her time to get out of this was nearly up.

Hurry, idiot. Think.

But her mind was utterly blank.

CHAPTER 18

The truck engine growls out a throaty sound. Loud. Raspy. Struggling a bit like maybe it's growing tired.

The steering wheel throbs against Jimmy's hands. A tremor that crawls through his palms and fingers and shimmies into the meat of his forearms.

That same rumble thrums through the whole vehicle. Vibrates the floorboards. Rattles the rusty spots on the passenger door, somehow sounding like bedsprings.

Jimmy only half-hears. He tunes it out. Focuses.

Escape.

Escape.

He can't shake the fear. Not yet. It holds his body rigid in the driver's seat, makes him forget to blink for long stretches.

They fishtail off the dirt track and onto legit asphalt, tires screaming bloody murder. From there, Jimmy leads them out away from civilization, guiding the stolen pickup truck on a circuitous path through rural roads that all seem to lead deeper into nowhere.

The series of lefts and rights weaves them past orchards and soybean fields and more woods, ultimately putting them on a state route that snakes right alongside the Atlantic. They rocket north, obeying Jimmy's only instinct for the moment — *get away from Durango Beach.*

Scrubby growth occupies much of the coastline here, weeds and small trees about the girth of a cigar, patches of sand shining through the green in a way that looks mangy.

The last of the color drains from it all as they speed by, the darkness blooming in fast motion, like a time-lapse video of the day becoming night. All those leaves go from green to olive to dark gray over the course of a few minutes.

The adrenaline still clenches the muscles in Jimmy's face.

Little spasms that grind his molars together.

And even in this moment of intense fear, the land strikes him as a feminine thing. All those curves, maybe. The sand dunes. The hills. The way the beach gets slick right along the edge of the water.

He keeps watching the rearview. Waiting for a flicker of police lights. Or the headlights of the enraged owner of the truck somehow trailing them, rifle leaned out of the window, ready to kill.

But there's nothing there. No one. Just that strip of road getting swallowed up by the wild land, stretching back as far as he can see.

His eyelids flutter, and somewhere deep inside the vault of his skull, the neurotransmitters start to flip over into something else. Lightness. Tingling.

He almost feels like he was browning out for a second. Hands cold on the wheel. That roiling in his head.

And then Scarlet is there. Touching him. Leaning her face into his. Kissing.

When she speaks, her voice is right up close, cooing like a dove in his ear.

"You did it, baby. We did it."

Heat flushes his face. Fevered liquid in his cheeks.

All that fear lifts, a weight coming off of him, a dizzying lightness where the leaden feelings had been. The sense of freedom, of airiness, of the vast empty space all around him, around both of them, is almost overwhelming.

Like maybe this feeling is something else he can never tame, too breezy, too light, like he might just float away from here, sucked out of the driver's side window, drifting up into the heavens, suddenly out of control in a whole new way.

And the ice coursing through his veins somehow shifts from fear to excitement — that almost identical sensation in his limbs, in his core, somehow changing meanings in an instant.

Scarlet is always talking about that. How adrenaline can make that hard left turn from paralyzing in its negative force to exhilarating in its positive charge. Intense joy and crippling fear seem to walk the same pathways, an almost indiscernible line the only thing separating one experience from the other.

And he drives. And he watches the road. And some distant part of him ponders that notion, turns it over and over.

A car crash is terrifying.

A roller coaster is thrilling.

The physical experience is about the same.

Scarlet kisses his neck now. Lips gently touching and pulling away. Still murmuring praise against his skin in between.

"You did it. You did it."

Jimmy reaches past her. Unzips the duffel bag where it hugs against her right hip.

Keeping his eyes on the road, his fingers find the zippered hole. He plunges his hand into the bills there.

Tens. Twenties. Lots of singles and fives. The fifties and hundreds have been bundled in rubber bands, their density sinking them to the bottom. Most everything else lies loose inside the bag. Flaps of paper currency lapping at his hand like so many tongues.

He snakes his arm a little past wrist deep. Feels that cool money touching him, the funny material, not quite cloth and not quite paper.

And he breathes. Deep in. Slow out.

A current seems to surge out of the bag and into him. Electricity flowing out of the money and into his flesh.

Only when he touches this money does he trust it, does he believe it. Damn near fifteen thousand dollars. Not enough to live on for long, but enough to get away. Enough for that.

He grasps a handful of the bills. Lets them slip through his fingers. Faint papery sounds rasp where the edges brush the thick skin of his palm.

They've wrangled their future to the ground. Seized control of it.

Taken it.

For the first time in either of their lives, they rule their own fates. For the first time, they set the terms.

And the evidence of that, the way forward, the shape of things to come, lies within the canvas walls of this duffel bag. He can touch it, feel it, hold it in his grip, and put all his faith into it.

Now he kisses Scarlet back. Leans over to kiss that hard line of her jaw just under her ear.

"We can get outta here now," he says. "Zip along the gulf, and then cross into Mexico. Never to be seen again, at least 'round here."

She flinches. Pulls away from him. Hesitates.

Her voice sounds harder when she answers. Flatter.

"No. The plan was to get to twenty before we cross, so we'll get to twenty. Anyway, we should probably ditch the truck sooner than later. I think the guy saw us. In the trailer? I saw his silhouette stand up in front of the TV."

He pulls his hand out of the money and grips the wheel harder. Two hands choking it.

For a second, his back stiffens. Resisting her doubt, her commands.

He wants to surrender only to the idea that they are free, that he doesn't need to worry for this next little bit. Wants to feel safe for once. Wants her to feel it, too.

But just as quickly, the tension flees his muscles. She is right. She has always been the one keeping them one step ahead of the law. He isn't going to fight her on it now.

"Guy didn't seem the type to call the law, maybe," he says, the words coming out as he thinks them. "But you're right. We'll dump the truck in the next town. Maybe get something sportier, if we can. Faster. Then we'll put some distance between us and here. After that, we can lie low for a while. No need to rush. Rushin' is what leads to trouble."

She nods slowly. Then she rests her head on his shoulder and a big breath rolls out of her, somehow making her seem smaller after.

He can tell, glancing down at her, seeing the blank expression on her face, that the wave of post-escape excitement has already drained from her. Her mind is working, pulling her away from the here and now, making her calculate five or ten moves ahead the way she always does.

"We'll get through this like we get through everything," he says. "And they'll still be talking about us around here, long after we're gone. Running their mouths. The legend slowly expanding every time the story is told. That's how these things work.

"But we cut ourselves a path through the south. Took what we wanted. And we got ahead. Me and you? We got out of a bad situation, right, and we moved up a rung on the ladder in the process. For now and for always."

"That's what they don't allow."

"What?"

"Getting ahead. You can't just get ahead. In life. In society. Not like this."

He blinks at his own reflection in the rearview, tries to make sense of what she is saying.

After a second, Scarlet goes on.

"You know they spend more money tracking down bank robbers than what the robbers steal? On average, the massive police operations cost more than what the robbers took in the first place. So the public, the taxpayer, ultimately pays more than if the government had just covered the cost of the robbery.

"But the point is to keep control, to maintain that social order, to let the people know they can't just rob a bank and better their lot in life. Keeping that closed off is more important than the money involved.

"That's what they're really policing. The right to move yourself up a few rungs, the power and privilege that come with it. They'll do anything to guard that line, pay any price. It says a lot about who the police really serve and protect, ya know?"

He wonders how she knows these things, the statistics, the monetary impact of bank robberies, but the curiosity only lasts for a second. She knows a lot of things. More than him, that's for sure. Always reading. Always learning. Soaking up information, processing it. His brain has never seemed to work that way, not in school and not in life.

He looks at her in the green glow of the dashboard light, and for the millionth time he thinks about how he'd be nowhere without her. Locked up or on drugs. Maybe dead, though it's harder to be sure of something like that.

He needs her more than she needs him. It isn't a feeling so much as an absolute truth.

"You know I'd do anything for you, right?"

She smiles for the first time in a while, teeth glowing in that soft light from the speedometer.

"I know."

And a little thrill runs through him, erupting from his gut and bursting outward. Like fireworks inside, to see her happy.

"I'd do anything for you, too," she says, and then she starts kissing his neck again, moving upward. He can feel her eyelashes tickling his ear.

A siren screams somewhere behind them. A lone warble. Mournful and distant.

But alarming nonetheless.

CHAPTER 19

Ellie thought her prayers had been answered when John rolled right past the murder house without stopping. But then he wheeled around the block and into the parking lot of a Walmart Supercenter, explaining as he drove.

"Urban spelunking pro tip number one: always park a safe distance away from the exploration site. Parking right in front of the place would be a dead giveaway if there's any kind of security."

At the mention of security, Ellie's stomach curdled. Her hand tightened on the edge of her seat, and she felt like she might throw up.

"Of course, you have to balance that with parking close enough to be able to make a clean getaway if anyone *does* show up," John went on. "Thankfully, we've done our research and know the perfect place to stash the car."

He selected a space near the back corner of the building. Despite the evening hour, there were enough people shopping late that their car didn't seem out of place.

John pulled the key from the ignition, and everyone climbed out, except for Ellie.

She felt frozen in her seat. Unable to move.

This was it. Her last chance. And the funny thing was, she really *did* feel physically ill now. It wouldn't even be a lie if she said she was sick.

But then the laughter and mocking voices of Katie and Simone echoed in her ears.

Something thudded against the door inches from Ellie's face, and she jumped.

Courtney leaned down so their eyes were level and stared at Ellie through the pane of glass.

"You coming, ding dong?"

Ellie found herself nodding as she unlatched her seatbelt.

"Yeah," she said, climbing out of the car.

Wes was leaning into the open trunk when she joined the group. He pulled out a backpack and slung it over his shoulders. Once he closed the trunk, John pointed his key fob at the car and engaged the locks.

"Let's rock and roll."

He led the way around the back of the building. Past a row of dumpsters. Where the pavement ended, there was a guardrail and then a wall of greenery that seemed to shoot straight up.

John hopped onto the guardrail and gestured at the foliage barrier.

"Believe it or not, the back of the property is straight through here."

"We have to walk through all that?" Courtney asked.

John nodded and then headed straight into the thick of it. Right away, he was swallowed up by the undergrowth as though he'd entered a portal. Courtney followed with no hesitation, then Wes.

Ellie stood on the other side of the guardrail, shifting her weight from one foot to the other.

Too late to back out now, she thought.

So she sighed and stepped over the guardrail, one foot and then the other, and allowed herself to be devoured by the thicket. It felt like stepping into a dark room, her surroundings now rendered in shades of black, blacker, and blackest. She had to stop and get her phone out so she could turn the flashlight on.

The LED blinked on, and now Ellie could see about a six-foot radius around her. Vines and fronds and branches in every imaginable shade of green.

The others had already disappeared from sight, so she held still and listened for them, straining to hear over the buzzing, chirping background noise provided by the insects.

Finally, she heard Courtney's voice not far ahead.

"The place we drove past… it kind of looked like an apartment building to me."

Ellie hurried forward now, her eyes tracing the ground for anything that might trip her up. Within a few steps, she spotted Wes's form just ahead of her.

John's response filtered back from his position at the head of the pack.

"Right."

"But you called it a house."

"Burdick Murder Apartment Building doesn't have the same ring to it."

"And this Burdick guy… you said he was a serial killer?" Courtney asked.

"That's right."

The only sound for several seconds was the swish of the leaves and branches they brushed past. Ellie swatted a mosquito that landed on her arm.

"Well, come on," Courtney said. "What's his story?"

John chuckled.

"All in due time."

Courtney made an impatient sound.

"Don't worry, I'll go through all the gory details once we get there," John promised.

They trudged another twenty yards or so through the thick vegetation before they came to a sudden halt. Ellie wasn't sure why until she looked past the stretch of rusty chain-link fence and saw it.

Beyond the wire barricade, the Burdick Murder House rose up from the ground, lit by eerie silver moonlight.

CHAPTER 20

Unlike the panic of their earlier drive, the interior of Detective Taft's SUV held placid this time as the two detectives jetted back out into the boonies. They wove down country roads in the swamp, the air conditioner fighting to keep up with the heat and humidity still going strong even as the day faded.

Tonight's destination? The Citgo station where their victim, Justin Higgins, had worked. They'd arranged an interview with the owner of the franchise.

Stinson stared out the window at scrub flitting by. She'd been picturing Elmer and his dogs again, frozen in their final poses, when Taft started talking. He must have been thinking of the same.

"You ever watch any near-death experience videos on YouTube?"

Stinson's eyelids fluttered. It felt like waking up.

"No. I mean, not that I remember."

Taft nodded once. His hands fidgeted on the wheel.

"I like 'em. They're all different, but they all make it seem like none of what's happening here really matters. In a good way, I mean."

Stinson's eyelids did that blinkity hitch again.

"What does that mean?"

"Well… it's like everybody talks about going to some kind of peaceful place, I guess. They talk about beauty and a sense of togetherness, of existence somewhere that's not physical. They're all completely divorced from earthly things and concerns. Plunged into a happiness or satisfaction or something. And they're all kind of reassured by the experience.

"A lot of 'em, when they get brought back, they're kind of mad about it. Like they don't want to come back. I don't know. I guess that makes me feel better."

Stinson was quiet for a few seconds, thinking. She shrugged.

"I don't know," she said. "I kinda think that when you die, you die, and that's it."

The SUV thumped over a rough patch of road, and then the ride smoothed out again.

"There was this famous comedian," Taft said. "I guess this must have been on a podcast I was listening to a while back. He said that when he was young he got hit by a car, and then *bam*— he was in this peaceful place. Total tranquility and stillness and shit. And this voice came to him and said, like, 'Do you want to continue living as, uh…' Well, then it said his name, but I can't remember. But let's say it was me, it'd be like, 'Do you want to continue living as Brant Taft?' And I'd be like, 'Uh, hell yeah. Let's do this.'"

Taft chuckled to himself.

"What did he say?" Stinson asked.

"The comedian? He said yeah."

She was quiet for a couple seconds.

"Did he regret it?"

Taft's brow crinkled again.

"I think maybe he wondered if it was the right choice. I don't remember for sure. Why? Would you say no?"

"I don't know. Maybe. I mean, I'd be curious, I guess. If something like that happened. Curious about what might be next. Here, this is it."

She pointed.

Taft whipped his head around. The gas station was coming up on the left, looking kind of eerie with most of the lights off.

He jerked the wheel, pulled in at the last possible second, and snugged the Bronco into a parking spot. Stinson felt a strange sense of inertia at lurching and then stopping so quickly, like a rogue wave rolling through her gut.

They strode over the empty parking lot, gas pumps off to their right, broken glass gritting under their feet. The big Citgo sign — a kind of orange and white plastic bulb — held dark, but the LEDs overhead buzzed in a hum lower-pitched than that of the mosquitoes flitting everywhere.

The Citgo was closed, a fact made clear by the cardboard flap taped to the door with thick lettering Sharpied in black scrawl, poor grammar and all: *Were Closed.* Still, the owner of this particular franchise, Mike Morgan, was visible through the windows, messing with a toolbox on the main floor. He knew they were coming.

The trip here had been Stinson's call. While search teams and techs tore up the woods, hopefully apprehending Jimmy and Scarlet any moment now, she figured it best to try to hammer down the case against them. Hauling the perps in was one thing, building a narrative to convict them in court was another. She took pride in getting the story down in black and white on interview transcripts, giving the prosecutor more than enough material to work with. To her, that was the meat and potatoes of a detective's job, building that narrative.

Taft rapped his knuckles on the glass door, and a few seconds later, the owner's dark shape stepped out from behind the beer poster plastered over the window. With a flick of the wrist, he unlocked the door and let them in, a half-smile on his lips.

"Come on in. Still cleanin' up the mess, I'm afraid."

They stepped into the bright space, bags of chips and two-liters of Pepsi stacking the shelves around them. They followed the owner's lead off to the right, and Stinson studied the man.

Mike Morgan's deeply tan skin and full head of dark hair probably made him look younger from a distance, but the wrinkles visible up close showed him to be in his early fifties at least. Stinson thought he looked like the kind of guy who spent a lot of his free time on a boat, and it wasn't just the tan. There was something relaxed in his body language, a kind of freeness and confidence of movement she associated with boat people. The Hawaiian shirt unbuttoned to the sternum merely cemented the impression.

He moved back to the side window just off the cash register

and worked at taping another flap of cardboard over the broken pane. A dustpan full of glass shards sat at his feet as he worked.

"Now that the scene has been released, we're plannin' to open up tomorrow morning, but I won't be able to get a real window in here for a couple weeks. Gotta special order it. Guy's coming from all the way over in Tampa to install it. Just hope it doesn't rain anytime soon."

He *scritched* a length of duct tape off the roll, bit the edge to cut it off, then massaged it over the edge of the cardboard.

Stinson couldn't help but think of the glass bursting in the video. The wild look in Jimmy Maddox's body language. Shards raining down to the floor.

"We wanted to ask you a little about the victim," she said, her voice interrupting her own mind movie. "Justin Higgins worked here for… three years, was it?"

Morgan slapped another piece of duct tape onto the line where the cardboard touched the frame, only making eye contact for a second and then looking back to his work. The chipper tone left his voice for a moment.

"It's too bad about Justin. He was a good kid. Well, he wasn't a kid, but I still thought of him that way, I guess. But yeah. That sounds right. Yeah. Three years."

"What else can you tell us about Justin?"

Now Morgan stepped back. He fiddled with the roll of duct tape in his hands. Blinked a few times and looked up into the lights as he thought.

"Well… we weren't real close. I never saw him outside of work, and I only come in once or twice a week unless there's a problem, but… Justin was a funny guy. Made everyone laugh. Always had his nose in some book by or about a famous comedian. Usually old school. George Carlin, Garry Shandling, Steve Martin, stuff like that. He should have done something in that field — comedy. Easier said than done, I guess, but… From what Trish, another cashier, said, he'd sent out some movie scripts that got a lot of positive feedback when he was younger. But it's like then he got stuck in this dead-end job clerking at a gas station and couldn't break out of it."

He fell quiet, still blinking and looking up into the lights, and Stinson decided to let the silence linger, to let him think. Taft looked like he was about to speak, but she gave him a look, and he held off.

Morgan licked his lips. Gave the gentlest shake of his head.

"I feel guilty, you know. I know it's not my fault. Sometimes this kind of thing is in the cards, and there's maybe nothing anybody can do about it.

"But I feel like I should have known him better or something. Justin. Here he was, this interesting guy, working in my gas station for what wound up being the final three years of his life, and what do I really know about him? He liked Steve Martin. That's about it."

He shook his head again. Finally, he let his gaze fall from where it'd gotten stuck on the lights up above. His eyes met Stinson's, flicked to Taft's.

"Wish I could tell you something that might help or something. But I don't think I can, really."

His shoulders tilted to one side. Then he ticked his chin toward the back of the gas station.

"I put coffee on the Bunn. Something to keep me awake while I clean up. Y'all are welcome to some if you want."

Taft happily agreed, and Morgan walked him back to get a giant Styrofoam cup of coffee.

Taft drank it black. Got that bitter half-smile on his face that coffee always seemed to give him. They'd gotten to talking about Morgan's background — he was originally from Tennessee. Moved down to Florida in his late 20s. He'd just always loved the beach. Drawn to that place where the ocean hits the sand like the water had some magnetic force.

"I always said I'd get me a boat if I could. Growing up, starting probably — oh, let's say second grade — that was what I drew pictures of in art class. That and trucks with tank treads. Anyway, these days I'm out on the water daily. Living the dream, ya know?"

Taft was about to ask another question, but the radio at his hip started squawking.

"All units. All units. Suspects spotted. Jimmy Maddox and Scarlet Burlew were last seen near the intersection of Barrymore and Doty in a stolen 1981 Dodge Ram pickup, pale blue."

Taft's mustache and eyebrows twitched in unison.

"How the hell did they manage to get out of the woods unscathed? There had to be dozens of officers out there."

But Stinson barely heard his question.

"Barrymore and Doty," she said, repeating the road names. "That's close, isn't it?"

Both their heads turned. They gazed out the window into the parking lot where Taft's SUV sat alone.

Then they ran for it.

CHAPTER 21

The hairs on the back of Ellie's neck stood on end as she stared at the murder house. There was something menacing about it. A voice in her head said, *Don't go in there. This place is evil.*

But John had peeled back a panel of fencing where it had come loose from one of the support posts and was ushering them through. Wes and Courtney were already on the other side, and John had turned to face her.

"Go on," he said, gesturing that she should go next.

Her gaze went to the building again, to the ivy snaking around the foundation and up the brick exterior. The patches of green brought to mind a piece of moldy bread. Plywood covered the ground floor windows and doors, and there wasn't a single window on the upper floors that didn't have cracked or busted out panes.

It's just an abandoned building, she thought. *All abandoned buildings look creepy. A building can't be "evil." That's ridiculous.*

She crouched down and tried not to look at the No Trespassing sign posted on the fence as she wriggled through the gap.

Just blatantly ignoring the signs, she thought. *Totally cool with that.*

The graffiti marring the walls of the building told Ellie that people ignored the warnings often enough, which should have made her feel better. Clearly, trespassing happened frequently, which suggested security was lax if not altogether nonexistent. And yet she couldn't stop herself from imagining there were security cameras hidden all over the place, possibly recording them even now.

The grounds in back were just as overgrown as the front, with unkempt mulberry trees and castor bean shrubs interspersed in the waist-high grass and milkweed. It tickled against Ellie's legs as they moved in single file toward the building.

John led the way right up to the foundation of the place and stopped.

"We should do a shot here, since he buried some of the bodies in the yard," he said.

"Shut up," Courtney said. "You're just saying that to try to scare us."

John only chuckled.

Wes dropped his backpack and pulled out an expensive-looking camera.

While Wes fiddled with the camera, John got out his phone and skimmed through some notes he'd made, periodically murmuring some of the words and phrases aloud.

"August 1986, Lucille Montgomery, da-da-da… three bodies." He nodded to himself and then looked to Wes. "We ready?"

"Yep."

"Gimme a count, maestro."

Wes held up a hand and used his fingers to silently count down from three.

"Wait!" John said, sounding panicked. "Where's your hat?"

Wes dropped his hand.

"What?"

"The merch!" John plucked at the Spelunking Monkeys logo printed on the chest of his shirt. "You gotta wear your merch!"

"But I'm not even on camera."

"I knew it," John said, hands on hips. "You don't like the merch."

Wes tipped his head back until his face was pointed at the sky.

"I said it was fine!"

John turned to Ellie and Courtney.

"Did you hear that? It's 'fine.' Not 'cool.' Not 'hype.' Not 'lit.' *Fine.*"

Wes sighed and bent over his bag, rifling around until he found the branded baseball cap. He snugged it on his head.

"There. Happy?"

John's mouth still hung in a pout.

"John, the merch is dope as hell," Wes said. "The only reason I didn't have my hat on is because the bill gets in the way of the camera."

"Oh. I didn't think about that." John looked suddenly abashed. "You don't have to wear it then."

Wes flipped the hat backward.

"Nah, it's cool. I can wear it like this." He lifted the camera again. "Here we go."

Wes started the countdown again.

Ellie watched some sort of transformation happen to John as soon as the camera was on. He was already a lively guy, but he seemed to have an extra glow about him now.

"What's up, Lunkies? It's me, Johnny Boy, with my main man Wesley manning the camera, as yoozh." He clasped his hands together. "And we also have some special guests this time. Courtney and Ellie. Say hi, ladies."

Wes swung toward them. Courtney instantly smiled and waved, like she'd been prepared for this all along. Ellie just stared like a deer in headlights.

Wes swiveled back to John.

"We're on location here in Durango Beach, Florida, and oh boy have we got a treat for you. Our true crime fans in the audience might already have an inkling of where we are. That's right. We're comin' at ya live from the Burdick Murder House."

He turned and gestured at the building, holding the position almost like a statue.

He let the newscaster face drop.

"Cut. How was that?"

Wes lowered the camera.

"Perfect."

"Cool. So according to my research, the bodies were found near a bed of rose bushes around the foundation of the house. I'm thinking maybe over here?"

Wes nodded.

"OK, so what if you stand right at the corner, and I shoot with the fifteen-millimeter so that the building sort of looms over you?"

"That's fucking gold," John said, hurrying to the spot Wes had pointed to. "How's this?"

With a twisting motion, Wes took the original lens off his camera and glanced over at Ellie.

"Does one of you want to be my assistant for the night?"

Courtney shoved Ellie so that she stumbled a step and a half closer.

"Ellie will do it."

"OK, just hold onto this for now." He handed her the lens, pulling another from the bag and attaching it to the camera.

He crouched down on one knee, adjusting the focus.

"Let me take a few stills first," he said, and Ellie heard the sound of the camera's shutter.

With almost no direction from Wes, John changed his pose slightly every few seconds. Hands on hips. Hands in pockets. Looking at the camera. Looking over his shoulder. It was clear they'd done this before.

"That should do it for now," Wes said. "You ready?"

John nodded, and Wes started another silent count.

"In August of 1986, a resident of the building by the name of Lucille Montgomery was taking her morning stroll on the grounds when she noticed something amiss. A patch of disturbed earth right here along the foundation of the building, near the rose bushes she was so fond of. Upon closer inspection, Mrs. Montgomery made a grisly discovery. Protruding from the soil was a partially decayed human hand.

"She summoned the police, who immediately launched an investigation. They excavated the area around the rose bushes and uncovered not one, but three sets of human remains. All young men between the ages of seventeen and twenty-three. All found with plastic bags tied around their heads, suggesting they'd died by asphyxiation. And that was only the beginning."

John froze again for a few seconds before telling Wes to cut.

"You're, like… really good at this," Courtney said, echoing Ellie's thoughts almost exactly.

Because he really was good. John's natural charisma and energy translated to someone totally at ease in front of the camera. He oozed confidence.

John grinned and made an elaborate bow.

"Why thank you, milady. But the real magic happens on there," he said, gesturing at the camera. "Give 'em a little peek, Wes."

Wes angled the small display so they could see it and ran through some of the still shots he'd taken before.

"These are just the raw files, of course. I'm going to have to do some gamma correction, probably tinker with the white balance—"

"Relax, Francis Ford Coppola," John interrupted. "I'm sure what you have looks fine."

Seeing the photos, Ellie understood now what Wes had meant when he said the building would appear to loom over John.

"It's really creepy," Ellie said. "And I mean that as a compliment."

"Yeah, what the hell? I had no idea you guys were gonna be so profesh," Courtney added.

Wes gave a sheepish shrug. While he took a few more still photos of the exterior of the building, John turned to the girls and rubbed his hands together.

"Here comes the fun part."

CHAPTER 22

Taft's SUV chewed up the rural roads. Barreling forward. Headlights spearing out over the beach.

For a brief moment, Stinson could see the dark water there. The sea's churning surface a rippling black thing, unknowable. The twin beams of the headlights were made puny trying to stretch over the vastness, made useless against that kind of deep.

Then Taft ripped the steering wheel hard to the left, and the image panned out of the frame of the windshield. Erased from the glass.

A new road elongated before them. Black trees jutted on one side. Tall grass and scrubby beach growth on the other. Textures painted there in a soft focus, not quite real in Stinson's eyes.

Breathe.

The wind came by reflex. In through her nose. Out through her mouth.

Keep breathing.

She reminded herself out of habit more than anything conscious. A mantra that pulsed in her head in moments of stress.

Breathe and keep breathing.

Her heart flexed. Thumped against the meat around it. A frightened thing. It seemed to rise higher in her chest, the muscles there conspiring to try to funnel the hammering organ toward her neck, toward her throat. Like if it got the chance it would make the leap through her lips and get free. Make a run for it.

The radio burbled to life, interrupting.

"Car 19 has eyes on a pickup, westbound on Swamp Hollow Road. Just off Barrymore. Speeds of at least 75, 80. Appears to match the description of the stolen vehicle in the area. I think this is them."

The voice coming over the radio seemed calm, totally at odds with the tension in the SUV. Stinson and Taft looked at each other, then at the radio.

"Swamp Hollow and Barrymore," Taft said to himself. "That's less than a mile from here."

The dispatcher responded to the call. Her voice harder than his, cutting through the speakers.

"Car 19, if this is a chase, you should have your sirens on."

"Negative. Uh… Car 19 is pulled over on the shoulder here. They're coming right at me. I'm getting out to throw the spike strip now."

Spike strip, Stinson thought.

Holy shit.

This is really happening.

"All nearby cars standby," the dispatcher said. "All nearby cars standby. Chase procedure is in effect near the intersection of Swamp Hollow Road and Barrymore. Car 19, let me know when the spike strip is down."

New voices chimed in one by one.

"Car 7 copies. I'm on my way."

"Car 13 moving to block the intersection at Swamp Hollow and Talmadge."

"Car 7. Anybody nearby, grab some intersections. Let's cut 'em off."

"Car 11 inbound. I can block the corner at Swamp Hollow and Barrymore."

"Car 7. I believe there were choppers inbound for the search on Elmer Ferguson's property. Hell, let's get those redirected to Swamp Hollow if we can. Eyes in the sky."

Taft spoke into the mouthpiece on the radio, the weird double of his voice on the speakers sounding deeper than the real thing, sleepy and delayed a fraction of a second.

"This is Detective Taft. Detective Stinson and I are in the area in my personal vehicle. Should be on the scene within a minute or two. Let's shut 'em down."

The dispatcher's sharp voice cut in again, brighter than the rest.

"Car 19, please report when the spike strip is down."

The line held dead for a few seconds, and an icy feeling spread over the surface of Stinson's body all at once, pulling her skin taut.

Something was wrong.

Taft yelled in the driver's seat. A sharp sound that cut off quickly. Almost sounded like a small dog barking.

Stinson spun her gaze back to the road ahead. Scanned for the pickup. Her heart beat even harder than before.

Where?

Did he see them?

But the road lay barren ahead. A tube of empty space cut into the woods, a strip of craggy asphalt running through it.

No pickup truck. Nothing.

Taft made a little sucking sound. Pained. And then he whimpered, a soft moan that made the fine hairs on Stinson's arms prick up.

She double-checked the road. Nothing.

What the hell?

Finally, she glanced over at her partner. It took her a second to process what she was seeing, the disparate pieces of the tableau eluding her understanding, and then all at once she knew.

He'd spilled his drink as they'd rounded the last turn. Piping hot coffee all over his lap. The tall cup of black stuff Mike Morgan had poured for him at the Citgo.

Taft whimpered again. Made a hiccup sound somewhere deep in his throat.

Stinson took in the details one by one.

The Styrofoam cup lay on the floor between his feet. Capsized and empty.

His face beamed red. Jaw clenched and shaking. Bottom teeth exposed by parted lips.

And then his khakis — stained dark in a puddle shape. A cloud of steam still drifted up from his crotch.

They rounded another corner, centrifugal force pulling Stinson's shoulders to the left. Something about that little drift felt dreamlike, surreal. This whole night felt off and otherworldly. The harsh reality somehow held at arm's length.

The car straightened out on a new road. That pull let go.

Is this Swamp Hollow Road?

She'd missed the sign. Glancing over her shoulder showed her it was too late to check now. The dark had swallowed the sign some time ago.

The dispatcher shrilled over the speakers, renewing that queasy feeling in Stinson's gut.

"Car 19. Please respond. Are you there?"

CHAPTER 23

They followed John through the tangle of the aforementioned rose bushes, and even though the corpses had been discovered decades ago and were long gone by now, Ellie couldn't help but feel like she was treading on a grave.

Courtney must have felt the same, because she said, "Ew, why do we have to stand right where you said they found a bunch of dead bodies?"

John pointed to a narrow basement window that was level with the ground and perhaps eighteen inches tall.

"Because that's how we get in."

The window was covered with plywood, but when John stooped down and grasped the edge, he was able to lift it out of the way. Someone had already pried it off, apparently.

The wooden frame of the window was rotted and grimy, with peeling white paint. Fat stems of ivy twined around the opening, with protruding aerial roots that looked like pale worms. Beyond the empty panes, Ellie only saw inky blackness.

Courtney's eyes went wide, and she shook her head.

"No way."

"Come on, it's not as bad as it looks," John said.

"It *looks* like a psycho murdering clown lives in there."

"Don't be ridiculous. That clown moved out of here weeks ago. I'll go in first, OK?" John offered. "You'll see. It's fine."

He got onto his knees and went in feet first. He was there one second, and then the gaping hole of the window seemed to swallow him up.

The seconds ticked by. There was a scraping sound followed by silence. Just when Ellie started to worry something bad had happened, the light from John's phone flared to life. He beckoned from the other side of the opening.

"See?"

Courtney huffed out a breath.

"If I get murdered, I'm taking you down with me," she said, scooting closer to the window. "And there better not be rats in here."

Courtney shimmied through next, then Ellie, then Wes.

With everyone inside, Ellie took a moment to study her surroundings.

To their right sat a massive boiler. The surface was covered in rust, and various gauges and valves stuck out along the pipes.

On the left was a floor-to-ceiling cabinet that reminded Ellie of the lockers they'd had in her high school. Enameled metal in an industrial gray-green color, chipped at the corners where the steel had started to corrode.

Wes pulled a portable lighting rig from his bag and turned it on, and they got their first look at the expanse of the cavernous basement.

Junk littered the floor in random piles, some of it covered in so much dust it actually formed solid clumps. There were boxes of old records and books, warped and water damaged. A humongous boxy TV that looked like it was from about 1982. An assortment of furniture — broken dining room chairs and a wooden dining table with scorch marks on it.

Holes in the walls showed where pipes had been ripped out, probably scavenged for scrap metal.

"Ew, this place is definitely infested with rats," Courtney said.

John moved deeper into the space, skirting around a tangled nest of old window blinds. He stopped in front of a strange little door in the wall, perhaps three feet wide by three feet tall.

"What is that?" Courtney asked, sounding on the brink of hysteria.

"I think it's..." he said, grasping the knob.

Don't open it, Ellie thought, wanting to say it out loud but unable to find her voice.

John yanked the door open, and Ellie couldn't help but

hold her breath, imagining him being grabbed by some kind of ghoul or monster and dragged into the darkness beyond. But this was real life, not a horror movie, and nothing happened. Ellie breathed again.

"Yes! Bring the gear over here, Wes. I found the crawlspace."

John hunched down and took one step inside the tiny space.

"You're not actually going in there," Courtney said.

John shot her a demented smile before disappearing inside. A moment later, his slightly muffled voice filtered out through the open door.

"Oh yeah, this is solid gold. The floor in here is still actually dirt and everything!"

Courtney and Ellie stepped back while John and Wes set up the shot. Ellie noticed for the first time that the tripod had small wheels on the bottom, so Wes could wheel it around like a dolly. He gave John a count and then slid the camera through the door.

"After a thorough search of the grounds, the police moved inside the building," John began. "Tenants had complained about a smell coming from the basement all summer long, but the superintendent of the building, Arthur Burdicks, told everyone it was just some dead rats, which he'd poisoned after discovering an infestation. A brief search said otherwise. The smell was coming from something much bigger than a rat. Here, only shallowly buried in the dirt floor of the crawlspace, investigators found another three bodies, bringing the total victim count to six."

He frowned at the end.

"Did I say 'Arthur Burdicks,' with an 's'? I'm gonna do another take. Also, do you hear that dripping sound?"

They all went quiet and listened. Sure enough, Ellie heard a steady *drip, drip, drip* echoing from somewhere at the opposite end of the space.

"We should try to isolate that. Use it as some background

ambiance throughout."

Wes wheeled the camera back through the door, and they did it all over again. When John finished this time, he gave a little fist pump.

"Nailed it. OK, I'm coming out."

Wes stepped aside so John could squeeze through the small doorway.

"Cramped in there," John said, standing upright and stretching.

"They seriously found bodies in that crawlspace?" Courtney asked.

"Yeah."

"And you went in there?"

John shrugged.

"Man of the people. Gotta give the audience what they want."

Wes took some still shots of the crawlspace and then replaced the lens cap on his camera.

"Alright," he said, hoisting the tripod off the ground. "Let's head upstairs."

The door to the stairwell was metal with a pebbled glass window set in the center. The glass had been broken at some point, and Ellie could see several individual spiderwebbed points of impact.

Courtney's voice came out in a whine.

"Why does everything in this place have to be so creepy?"

John was at the front of their group, with Courtney clinging to his arm. The door screeched as they pushed through, and Courtney made a gagging sound.

"What is that smell?"

It hit Ellie as she crossed the threshold.

"Smells like… sewage."

The stairs thudded hollowly under their feet as they

climbed to the first floor.

"And that brings us to urban spelunking pro tip number two," John said. "Always breathe through your mouth."

Halfway up, John paused and clicked his tongue.

"Guess that explains the smell."

Courtney gasped.

"Is that—"

Ellie drew even with them, and then Wes. John had his light pointed down at the floor, illuminating a substantial pile of feces.

Courtney lurched backward.

"Ew! That is so disgusting!"

Each one of them made sure to give the excrement a wide berth as they continued upward.

Exiting the basement stairwell, they found themselves in a long corridor lined with doors. It made Ellie nervous to stare down the hallway, as if someone or some*thing* might pop out of any one of the doors at any moment.

"Hey, Wes. I bet you could get a sweet dolly zoom shot of this hallway."

"Definitely," Wes said, setting the tripod down and removing the lens cap.

He had Ellie aim the lights down the hall while he did his thing, slowly rolling the tripod backward. He finished, and John led the way to what had formerly been the main entrance of the building.

The arched front door led into a small foyer with built-in benches and a wooden staircase spiraling up like a nautilus shell. The parquet floor was water-stained and buckling, and it made cracking sounds as they walked over it that reminded Ellie of a hundred mouse traps snapping shut.

John led the way up the stairs, his voice echoing strangely around the stairwell.

"I figure we shoot the last of my segments up in Burdick's apartment first, and then we can explore the rest of this place. Get some B-roll in the other apartments and whatnot."

They climbed three flights up and entered another murky corridor lined with doors. John pointed a finger at one of the apartments.

"That's it," he said, jogging ahead of the group in excitement.

He pushed the door open and froze there on the threshold, his eyes stretching wide.

"Holy shit."

CHAPTER 24

Jimmy sits up straight, pulling away from Scarlet's touch. His eyes latch onto the rearview, stare into the darkness behind them like maybe he could see through it if he fixes his gaze intensely enough.

Nothing there. No spinning lights. Just shadows cut into the shape of trees. Empty space over the asphalt.

He listens then. Tries to figure out if the howling siren is getting closer or not.

He can't tell for sure. It isn't loud. The grinding truck engine swallows the moan off and on.

Something flashes in the mirror finally. Way back. Just a red shimmer in the air somewhere behind them — moving, sweeping lights — and then the police cruiser takes shape beneath it.

It isn't headed their way. Turning instead. All those lights brushing across an intersection, maybe headed toward the trailer where they'd hot-wired the truck.

Still, it is too damn close.

"Shit," Jimmy hisses, talking to himself. "Gotta get off the main road."

He takes a hard left at the next opening there. Tires squealing faintly. Potholes rocking them around, the asphalt pocked and rough like the surface of the moon.

Then they rocket on. Moving out into more nothing. More fields growing crops on both sides, though he can't identify the plants in the dark. Little bushy-looking silhouettes in neat rows.

Something about leaving the ocean behind feels wrong, Jimmy thinks. The sea. The beach. That is their good luck charm, maybe. Something that provides. Gives them energy. Gives them life. He can feel the force of it pulling away.

But the tension in the truck seems to recede. The police lights are long gone. The siren's cry has died out entirely. All their troubles are that much farther away, at least for this moment.

Jimmy finds Scarlet's hand with his. Squeezes it.

And he realizes that it is this — not the money — that he can trust whenever he touches it, that he can put his faith into.

And that it is only them inside the truck. Only them. The world outside, all of it, seems a threat to them, a burden, a sea of trash to push their way through. Nothing more. None of it quite seems real, not compared to them.

A couple miles flit by. The crops fade away, the rows of plants giving way to another stretch of woods.

Gnarly trees and branches flank both sides of the asphalt strip, huddling close. Dark limbs that only seem to become real when the headlights glint through them for a split second, black imprints in the light that disappear back into the shadows as soon as they pass.

And then he sees it.

The taillights on the side of the road. Two eyes glowing red.

"Is that… a cop car?"

Their headlights reach over the asphalt, brush up to the car's roof where the rack of lights sits.

And then there's a man there. A cop in a black uniform. Standing just in front of the cruiser.

His body coils, and then he flings one arm out before him. The motion makes it look like he's throwing either a bowling ball or a picnic blanket onto the road.

Instead, something extends from his outstretched arm. The spike strip elongates, reaches out over the highway.

Jimmy slams on the brakes. Jerks the wheel hard to the left. Veers.

Too late.

The spikes are down. Blocking their way.

He can only yank the wheel the other way. Turn toward the cop car. Try to cut just in front of it and miss the spikes by driving onto the shoulder there.

His foot crushes the accelerator. They build speed. Race for the gap.

A sound cracks like a gunshot as the left front tire is punctured.

The truck jolts. Rocks. Lowers on that side.

But they're still going. Still flying. Their momentum unperturbed.

And then the cop is there. A dark thing in front of them. A smeared shadow in the shape of a man.

They bash into him.

His details come into focus as the lights flash over him, and his body rolls up onto the hood.

Eyes wide. Lips parted. Arms rising.

He slaps face-first into the windshield like a bug. And then he's flung away.

Knocked by the force of their momentum. Catapulted. Ejected with great violence.

He soars.

Arcing.

Higher.

Shoulders slowly rotating in the air. Laying him out flat like Superman, belly down. Something almost graceful about the motion.

Sailing. Drifting.

The headlights catch him again. Surround him. Seem for just a second to hold him in midair like a tractor beam.

But the forward thrust continues. Momentum shoving him onward.

Arms and legs limp. Flailing like noodles.

He plunges lower at last. Gliding to the ground and then going choppy, going rough, as the asphalt grips him.

He hits the road and skids for a long way before he comes to a stop. Holds motionless.

The truck, too, jerks to a stop. No air inside. No breathing.

They sit there a long moment. Silent. Looking at the body.

Looking at the red darkness seeping out in slow motion, shiny where the headlights touch it.

The cop lies face down. Feet stretched over the white line. Most of his body draped over the shoulder. Loose gravel strewn about the section of asphalt where his face is planted.

Jimmy keeps waiting for the cop to move. For his chest to hitch in a breath. For his arms to scrabble to push him up.

But the body keeps still.

CHAPTER 25

They all stood just outside the door of Arthur Burdick's apartment, staring into the dim space.

Wes studied the walls inside, which were absolutely covered in graffiti. Much of it was sloppy scrawls. Penises and pentagrams and anarchy symbols. Phrases like, "Burdick is coming for you" and "You're next" and "Hail Satan 666" all layered over the striped wallpaper.

But the centerpiece on the wall directly across from the doorway was the intricately detailed face of a demon. Red skin, yellow eyes, black horns, and long, pointed white teeth. It was familiar to Wes, somehow. And also unnerving.

Unlike the careless scribbles in the rest of the room, whoever had painted the demon had real artistic skill. And that somehow made it more unsettling. Why would someone come here, in this abandoned ruin of a place, and take such care to paint this very sinister image?

"Did we just hit the jackpot or what?" John said, turning to grin at Wes.

And of course he was right. The fact that it was creepy and ominous was going to make for great footage.

John finally took a step inside the room, and Courtney grabbed his arm.

"Don't go in there!"

"Why?"

"I don't like it."

John chuckled.

"You're not scared of a little graffiti, are you?"

"It's not that. I feel something. A presence." She looked at Ellie. "You feel it, don't you?"

Ellie shook her head.

"Don't try to pull me into your woo-woo mumbo jumbo

nonsense."

"It's cool. You don't have to come inside if you don't want to," John said, sliding from Courtney's grasp and moving farther into the apartment.

Wes followed him in, past the splintered jamb where someone had once kicked the door in, and the two of them stood admiring the demon face on the wall.

It reminded him of something. But what?

And then it clicked.

Jason.

As an apprentice tattoo artist, Wes's brother always had a million art books from the library scattered around his apartment. And now Wes remembered one about Japanese yōkai.

He remembered that book specifically, because he'd found it when he and his mom cleaned out Jason's apartment, and his mom had remarked that she "had no idea he was interested in Japan." She made comments like that the entire time, seemingly half-mystified, half-annoyed.

And he wanted to say, *Yeah, that's because you didn't know him. You stopped paying attention to Jason when he was about ten years old. That's why you said in your "not-eulogy" at his "not-funeral" that he loved cars and basketball and played that fucking Ed Sheeran song from like 2011 and told everyone it was "one of his favorite songs." You haven't learned anything new about him in fifteen years.*

But he didn't say any of it, because as much as he found his mom to be quite lacking as a parent, she *was* grieving. What would have been the point, anyway? It wasn't like she could change any of it. What was done was done. Jason was gone, and she'd never really known him, and now she never would.

Dimly, he realized that John was talking.

"...use this as a background, obviously, but let's go check out the rest of the place."

Wes nodded in agreement.

The girls were still standing outside the door, but as he and

John headed deeper into the apartment, Ellie took a step inside.

Courtney squealed in a panic.

"You can't leave me, too!"

"We came all this way," Ellie said. "I want to see."

Courtney hesitated for a split second before scurrying through the door and latching onto Ellie's arm.

The floorboards creaked under their feet as they passed a bathroom with grungy yellow tile and peeling toile wallpaper. There was more graffiti here, including a figure with three butt cheeks painted across the shower stall.

"Triple butt," John said. "Classic."

Finally they reached what must have been Arthur Burdick's bedroom. Along with the same sort of slovenly spraypainted symbols and phrases they'd seen elsewhere in the house, there was a large message on the back wall that read, "COME SMELL MY KNIFE."

John rubbed his hands together.

"So we start in front of the graffiti wall, right? And then when I say, 'their final grim discovery,' we start moving down the hallway, ending up in here for the final shot."

"Got it," Wes said.

They headed back out to the front room. Wes got in position while John checked his notes one last time, and then they began.

"After the discovery of the additional bodies in the basement, the police did a systematic search of every apartment in the building. It was here, in the third-floor apartment of Arthur Burdick, the aforementioned super of the building, who'd excused the terrible smells coming from the basement by saying it was dead rats, where police made their final grim discovery."

John began walking backward down the hallway, and Wes traced his movements with the camera.

"In Burdick's bedroom, investigators found a seventh body. This one was the freshest of the bunch, just in the early stages of decomposition. The body was positioned sitting up in

Burdick's bed, dressed in Burdick's own pajamas, wearing a blonde wig, and covered in makeup to conceal the fact that the skin had started to turn an unnatural color."

John came to a stop in the center of the bedroom.

"Unfortunately, by the time the police had made the discovery in Burdick's apartment, thus implicating him as the killer, he had fled. A statewide manhunt ensued, and three days after discovering the bodies of Arthur Burdick's victims, they found the body of Arthur Burdick himself, in a nearby wilderness preserve. Burdick had died from a self-inflicted gunshot wound. A note in Burdick's pocket read, 'I know I should feel guilt for what I have done, but there is only an emptiness inside me. The same emptiness that began all of this in the first place. I am sorry for the families.'

"Five of the seven victims were eventually identified by police, and investigators were left to wonder if there may have been others. Unfortunately, the answer to that question, along with the names of the unidentified victims, died with Arthur Burdick."

Courtney and Ellie gave John a smattering of applause when he finished. He put his hands together in a mock-prayer position.

"Thank you. Thank you." He turned to Wes. "We should get some still shots of this place. Especially that mural in the living room."

Wes nodded and swapped lenses on his camera. He took a series in the bedroom, then moved down the hall, snapping a photo here and there.

In the living room, he used three different lenses to photograph the demon face from various angles. While he worked, his mind wandered to his brother again.

After the divorce, both parents had remarried and started new families, and it often felt to Wes like he and Jason had been left behind. Inconvenient reminders of past mistakes. They may have been present at various family functions, but he always felt a certain separateness.

And so the day his brother had disappeared, it felt to Wes like he'd lost the last true member of his family. The shared family history was his alone now.

"—alright?" John said and nudged Wes's shoulder.

Wes blinked.

"What?"

"I'm asking if you're alright."

"Yeah, I'm fine," Wes said, shrugging.

"You sure, bro? You were just kind of standing there in a daze. It was like you got hypnotized by that demon face on the wall."

Wes squirmed internally. He didn't want to explain that he'd been thinking about his brother. He already felt like an idiot for the way he'd dumped everything on Ellie at the beach earlier.

So he was glad when Courtney gasped and clapped a hand over her heart.

"Oh my God, I told you I felt a presence! What if Wes is possessed now?"

Ellie and Wes burst out laughing at the same time, and the tension was broken.

He slung his camera bag over his shoulder.

"Come on, let's check out the rest of this place."

The apartment next to Burdick's was devoid of any graffiti, though empty beer cans and bottles littered the ground, along with a smattering of cigarette butts and a crushed McDonald's fry box. Clearly a hangout spot, maybe for local kids.

The room had wood paneling and faded floral wallpaper in mustard, avocado, and brown.

"This place is like a time capsule," Ellie said, moving toward the coat closet next to the door and peering inside.

"I know, right?" Wes agreed, snapping a few pictures.

Courtney nudged one of the beer bottles with her toe.

"So after the murders, everyone who lived here just, like… left?" she asked.

John nodded.

"The town actually paid to move everyone out. I mean, who'd ever want to live here, right?"

"Why didn't they tear it down?" Ellie asked. "Like the building Dahmer lived in? Or John Wayne Gacy's house?"

"The town wanted to bulldoze it," John explained. "Offered to buy it from the owner. Or I should say *owners*. See, the guy who originally built the place back in the 30s died in the 1970s and left the building to his five children. Four of the five were on board to sell the place to the town, but there was one holdout who wanted more money. So the city walked. And no one else wanted it. It sounds like they kept trying to rent it out after that, but there were no takers. For obvious reasons. Eventually they just kind of left it to rot."

There was more floral wallpaper in the kitchen, this time in a pattern of pink and green. Jagged holes in the drywall showed where yet more pipes had been ripped out for scrap. Crumbs of plaster formed distinct trails on the floor, revealing the path of each new visitor as the white powder was tracked into the various rooms particle by particle.

"You notice they didn't touch the pipes in Burdick's apartment?" John asked.

Wes thought back. The walls had been vandalized in other ways, but they had been entirely intact.

"You wouldn't think someone desperate enough to steal pipes from an abandoned building would be the superstitious type," he said.

John chuckled and started to say something else, but then he stopped abruptly.

"Where'd the girls go?"

That was when the screaming started.

CHAPTER 26

Taft's vehicle breasted a hill. Stinson felt her stomach begin to float, an upward drift catching her innards at the top of the crest. The meat of her made weightless in the updraft.

Then they plunged down the slope, and gravity ripped all at once, a fist clenching at her gut and pulling her back down. She braced one hand on the dashboard and thought it looked like a starfish suctioned there.

The SUV sped into the pocket of light perpetually running out in front of it. The way it barreled down that road slit into the woods made Stinson think of a bobsled shooting down the track.

Trees flitted by. Dark flutters pulsing in both sides of her eyes.

But Stinson watched the dark wall just beyond the headlight's reach. It seemed to roll out in front of them, always there, somehow keeping its distance.

Bugs appeared there. Fresh clouds of them thrust into the light like flung grains of rice, swirling around and around each other. Mindless things. Chaotic.

And then the red and blue smears pierced the darkness in the distance.

Police lights.

Two cruisers huddled on the shoulder. Lights twirling.

Stinson noted the lights catching on a seam running out across the road. Glinting metal. A prickly thing.

So they'd gotten the spike strip down… but then where was the stolen pickup truck? Jimmy and Scarlet?

Taft rolled to a stop behind the parked black-and-whites. Stinson was about to ask where the hell everyone was when a uniformed officer darted out from the shadows at the side of the road.

He bent forward, and the spike strip glided toward him. Looked like a snake bellying over the asphalt. He was pulling it out of the road.

Damn. Had they missed Jimmy and Scarlet somehow?

As they exited Taft's vehicle, the uni hurried up to them. Stinson noticed then how big his eyes were. How ghostly white his complexion looked.

She knew him, but he was a rookie, and it was a beat before she could come up with his name.

Dan Ford. One of those gawky types that seemed to be all knobby elbows and bulging Adam's apple. An attempt at a mustache coated his top lip, hair the shade of a pecan, just longer than stubble.

"I wasn't sure what to do other than cover him with a blanket."

"Him?" Taft repeated.

And then Stinson remembered there were two cruisers parked here, not one. But only one officer…

She gazed out at where the headlights of the vehicles glinted off the expanse of asphalt. Empty and flat.

But no.

Not empty.

It huddled on the shoulder maybe a hundred feet from where they stood. One edge of it reached off the pavement and touched the edge of the woods.

Her eyes traced over and over the blanket-covered shape, the lump. A crumpled bulk against all the asphalt worn smooth.

Without a conscious thought, Stinson's legs had carried her over to the body, and now she stood over it, frowning. Taft and the uniform had followed.

The humped back made her think of a dead rat she'd seen at the edge of a parking lot once — bloated into something huge and grotesque. Legs akimbo like it'd been in flight before it landed in this spot.

"Who—"

She couldn't get the words out. Maybe because she couldn't decide on the appropriate tense. Who *is* it? Or who *was* it? The former seemed incorrect. The latter, too cruel.

"Wilton, ma'am. Barry Wilton. He's…" The Adam's apple bobbed severely. "He was dead by the time I got here."

Taft fell right into Detective Mode. He lifted one corner of the blanket, revealing the mangled body underneath. Took a good long look at the deceased and let the cover fall back in place.

He crossed his arms and turned to Officer Ford.

"Did you see what happened?"

"No, I only got here maybe a minute or two before you. Saw Wilton's car and wondered where the hell he was. Thought maybe I'd get to rib him about having to duck into the woods to take a leak in the middle of all the excitement. But then I saw him there in the road, and I…"

His voice hitched and cut out, and the night sounds of the crickets and frogs swelled around them.

Usually they arrived on a scene sometime after death. But this man had been alive only minutes ago. They'd heard his voice on the radio. It seemed wrong that they couldn't simply go back a little bit and redo things. Change the course of events.

Ford was talking again.

"…went out to the bar with Wilton just the other night to celebrate. His girlfriend is pregnant. Jennifer."

Taft groaned.

"Ah, Christ. That's fuckin' tragic."

Ford's hand drifted up to touch his forehead.

"I don't… am I gonna have to be the one to tell her? Because I found him and all?"

"The girlfriend?" Taft clarified. "Oh, geez. No, son. Don't you worry about that."

Ford's eyelids fluttered.

"I mean, it's not that I wouldn't do it, if I had to. I just… how do you tell someone something like that?"

Taft clapped a hand on his shoulder.

"That'll all be taken care of. You did what you could, alright?"

He nodded, his head seeming to pivot on that protruding Adam's apple.

"What about Jimmy and Scarlet, though? Maybe I should have gone after them, once I saw he was dead and all. But it just didn't feel right, leaving him here, alone..."

Stinson didn't realize she was still staring at the blanket until it moved.

Well no. It was a trick of the light, obviously. The flashers on the cruisers creating that weird strobe effect that made it impossible to—

Holy shit. It moved again.

It had been almost imperceptible, just a shifting of one of the wrinkled spots, but the blanket had definitely moved.

She dropped to her knees and ripped the fabric free.

"Stinson, what are you—"

From this angle, she could see part of Wilton's face, half-mashed into the asphalt. The muscles in his jaw twitched, and then his eyes opened. Nothing "almost imperceptible" this time.

Stinson's head snapped up, and her gaze met Taft's.

"He's still alive!"

CHAPTER 27

By the time John and Wes rushed into the bathroom, the girls had devolved into fits of hysterical laughter.

The slumped figure in the tub was nothing but an old store mannequin, missing its legs.

"Jesus," John said, heaving out a breath. "You guys scared the shit out of me."

"It's not our fault," Courtney said, still laughing.

Ellie pointed at the beat-up form.

"Yeah, blame whoever left their creepy mannequin here."

Wes suddenly waved his hands in the air, shushing them.

"Did you hear that?"

"Hear what?" John asked.

Courtney narrowed her eyes.

"Oh, come on. If you're trying to get us back for scaring you, we didn't do it on purp—"

She was interrupted by a muffled *thunk* sound.

"What was that?" she hissed.

"I think it came from out front," Wes whispered, leading them into the apartment across the hall.

He crept up to the window and peered outside. Two men in matching uniforms were climbing out of a white SUV parked next to the front door. The side of the SUV said "A-1 SECURITY."

"Shit," he whispered. "We gotta go."

They hustled to the stairs, four pairs of feet thundering down the steps. Ellie wished they could move quieter, but at the moment, speed took priority.

They were halfway down the basement stairway when they heard the rattle of a chain and then the hinges of the front door squealing open.

The four of them froze on the stairs, and Ellie was sure each one of them was holding their breath.

"...ever hear about Sawney Bean?" He didn't wait for a response, just plowed ahead talking a mile a minute. "He was the leader of this cannibalistic clan in Scotland in the 1500s. Supposedly they killed and ate over a thousand people."

"This was Sean Bean? Like Ned Stark?"

"No! Sawney. Short for Alexander, I guess. The clan was only like 45 people, total. That means they each ate like 22 people or something, if you average it out."

There were two guards, but it seemed one of them did most of the talking.

"Anyway, that legend was the inspiration, at least partially, for *The Hills Have Eyes*. That's Wes Craven's second movie, you know?"

The fact that the guy was yapping nonstop was actually helpful, as they could tell by the way his voice grew distant that they were moving away from the basement door.

"Wait. That's the one with — what's his face — Freddy Krueger?"

"No. No! Are you serious?"

"Of course not. I just like messing with you. So damn gullible."

There was some nudging and hand motions between Ellie and the others, and then the four of them began tiptoeing the rest of the way down to the basement.

Their feet scuffed softly over the concrete floor as they made a dash for the window. John laced his hands together and boosted Courtney out first.

Overhead, the floorboards whined and cracked under the boots of the two guards as they searched the first floor. The chatterbox was still at it, but his voice was too muffled now to make out the words.

Wes handed his gear through the window to Courtney, and then John laced his fingers together again and gestured that Ellie should go next.

"You go," she whispered.

He shrugged and turned, hoisting himself up to the window. He was part of the way through when the sound of splintering wood rang out.

The sill, apparently more rotted through than they'd realized, broke loose and tumbled to the basement floor with a deafening clatter. John fell back through with it, stumbling into Wes and Ellie.

Again, everyone froze.

"You hear that?"

The chatterbox's voice sounded directly above them, and the words were quite clear now.

"Yeah," the other guard said. "Sounded like a crackhead just knocked over a bunch of junk in the basement."

The footsteps overhead quickened now, heading for the stairs. John scrambled to his feet and heaved himself up again, but it was too late. By the time he cleared the window, the guards were almost to the bottom of the basement steps. There was no way Ellie and Wes would make it through in time.

Ellie turned to him, her eyes wide with panic.

The thing she'd feared all night was about to come true.

They were going to get caught.

CHAPTER 28

Jimmy and Scarlet ride a while on the flat tire. The rubber loop flaps against the wheel well, a loping rhythm. It sounds a bit like someone is beating a rug against the fender.

But inside, the truck holds silent. An atmosphere taut with shock. Dazed.

Jimmy blinks. Looks out at the night through glazed eyes.

He only kind of sees the road ahead. His eyes take in the image, peer straight into that tunnel of light the headlights push in front of them, the open road an expanse of reflecting asphalt, but his mind mostly filters it out.

Instead, his focus swings inward. Tumbles thoughts like a high-efficiency dryer.

They've killed a man. Run him down in a stolen pickup truck. Knocked him something like a hundred feet, body skittering over the macadam.

Jimmy blinks, finally, at the thought. Solemn for a moment.

But some instinct rails against what his brain has just told him. Objects.

It was life or death. Him or us.

I'll pick us every time.

He blinks again. Hard.

Except… it wasn't life or death. Not really.

We'd have gone to prison. Hell, we probably still will.

I chose freedom. For now, at least.

I chose it over a man's life. And now I have to live with that.

Scarlet speaks up from the passenger seat. Her voice seems still in a way that calms him.

"No sirens, right?"

He listens. Tunes his ears past the *thump-thump, thump-thump* of the flat tire glugging along.

Silence seems to stretch out in all directions outside the

truck. That's good.

He shakes his head.

"Flip on the radio," she says.

"The radio?"

Now she nods. Her eyes stay fastened to the rearview as she talks.

"Local news might have an update. I doubt we've lost 'em for long, but maybe the… scene back there will slow 'em down just enough to give us a chance."

Jimmy fingers the truck's stereo. Starts twisting the dial, scanning past obnoxious pop music and twangy country songs.

Scarlet keeps going.

"If we can make it to the next town before we have to ditch the truck… well, it'd help our odds a lot. Last thing I want to do is to have to run into the woods again. We got lucky last time. By now they'll probably have choppers ready to go. Dogs."

The ride grows bumpier beneath them second by second — the loping gait of the pickup getting wonkier and wonkier, like an animal whose limp is getting worse. But so far the truck is still moving along at a pretty good clip, at least.

A road sign pops up, its contents growing legible as they race toward it. Glowing white letters on a green background. All caps.

SWAMP HOLLOW

6 MILES

Jimmy's brain tries to do the math in a hurry.

Six miles at 60 miles per hour. Six minutes.

Longer if we have to slow down, but…

Maybe we'll make it. Maybe.

A voice drones on one of the radio stations at last. It clicks and woofs at first, distorted, but Jimmy dials in the tuning, and it comes clear mid-sentence.

"—ccording to police officials, the search for the responsible party is ongoing. This follows the earlier reports of the brutal murder of 66-year-old farmer Elmer Ferguson and his dogs this afternoon, so stay alert out there, folks. There are dangerous people in this world."

Jimmy feels his brow furrow. He snaps his head over to face Scarlet.

"What the fuck is he—"

But she shushes him right away. Index finger to her lips.

Her other hand shoots out. Clicks off the radio. Fresh silence swells in the truck.

And then the sirens moan somewhere behind them.

CHAPTER 29

Wes's fingers closed around Ellie's wrist and pulled her into the dark. She realized they were moving into the steel janitor's cabinet she'd noticed earlier in the night.

He slid into the taller side and drew her in with him, both of them elbowing into a mess of rotting mops and brooms. Wes swung the door closed just as they heard the basement door screech open.

There was barely enough room in the cabinet for the both of them. Ellie's arms were folded up and resting on Wes's chest while his were wrapped around her waist.

Through the louvered air vent at the top of the cabinet door, Ellie could see a few parallel slices of the basement. The beam of a flashlight swept over the floor. Not far behind, the first of the guards came into view.

"What's that stench?"

Ellie recognized this voice as the chattier of the two guards.

"Aww man! I stepped in something." He groaned. "Yeah. I think it's poop."

There was a wheezing sound then. The other guard was laughing.

"You didn't see that pile of shit in the middle of the stairs?"

"What the hell, man?" the chatterbox whined. "Why didn't you warn me?"

"Not to step in shit? Didn't think that was the kind of thing that had to be said."

"See, this is exactly what I was talking about earlier. You always treat me like I'm stupid."

The other guard snorted.

"Like stepping in a pile of shit makes you seem like a genius. Anyway, I'm pretty sure it was human if that makes you feel any better. Human feces."

"Why would that make me feel better?"

"I dunno. I just know that to a homeless guy, pretty much anything can become a toilet. It's kind of a freeing thought, you know?"

Ellie could hear the thump of Wes's heart through his chest. She tried not to think about how his body felt pressed against hers. But their faces were practically touching. Every time he exhaled, she felt the warmth of his breath caress the side of her neck.

She couldn't help but notice, too, that he smelled nice, though it wasn't a strong scent like cologne. Something more subtle, like the lingering fragrance of his laundry detergent or shampoo.

When it came right down to it, she didn't hate how it felt being this close to him.

And then — was she crazy or did Wes's lips just brush the side of her cheek?

A little lightning bolt of excitement ran through her, until she realized he was only trying to find her ear.

"Can you see anything?" he asked, his voice so low she would barely call it a whisper.

She nodded, then realized he couldn't see her in the darkness of the cabinet.

Ellie turned her head until she felt Wes's hair tickle the end of her nose and whispered back.

"I think they're over by the boiler."

They went quiet, listening. When the guards spoke again, it sounded like they'd moved to the far end of the basement.

"There's lotsa ways to be smart, you know. Like, when I watch *Jeopardy!* I know a lot of the answers. Just because I don't have some kind of poop detection radar system or ESP or something, that don't mean I'm a dummy," the chatterbox said.

There was a long pause.

"What the fuck are you talking about?"

"You brought up… I mean… I'm just sayin'… maybe I can't move things with my mind, but I know stuff."

That wheezing laugh came again.

"Wait. Do you think ESP and telekinesis are the same thing?"

"What? I— No." The chatterbox huffed out a frustrated breath. "Why do you have to be such a dick?"

Ellie stared out through the grate in the cabinet door and caught a glimpse of the two guards as they continued searching the basement. She leaned in to give Wes an update, and their foreheads bonked together. It sounded in Ellie's head like two coconuts banging into one another.

Ellie let out a quiet puff of laughter.

Wes gripped her waist tighter and shushed her, but she could tell by the way his chest was shaking that he was laughing too. And now that they'd gotten started, it was like they couldn't stop.

Ellie balled the front of Wes's shirt in her fist and buried her face in his shoulder, trying to stay quiet despite the tears rolling down her cheeks.

They were still convulsing with silent laughter when the footsteps of the guards came back over to their side of the basement.

"Looks like they're gone, whoever it was," the chatterbox said.

"Yeah. Probably came in through that window right there and slithered right back out when we showed up. Suppose we oughta tell the management company they need to have someone come board it up."

The hinges of the basement door let out their telltale squeal.

"Only a matter of time before someone pries it off again, though."

"Eh. Keeps us in a job, don't it?"

As the steps receded, the tension seemed to break, and they were finally able to stop laughing. Ellie was slightly out of breath, and her abs hurt from trying so hard to hold it in.

When the clatter of boots reached the top of the stairs, Ellie slid toward the cabinet door, but Wes held tight to her waist, stopping her.

"We should wait until we hear the car leave, just in case," he said.

Suddenly very aware of the feel of his hands on her, she felt a strange little pang in her chest and knew she was in trouble.

She swallowed, trying not to make a cartoonish gulping sound.

"OK."

They waited and listened. And all the while, Ellie argued with herself.

This isn't a thing. Can't be a thing. In a few days, it's back to the grind of law school. There won't be time for a boyfriend, certainly not a long-distance one at that. It will never work. Let it go.

But she couldn't deny how thrilling it felt to be this close to him. How much she wanted to move her head two inches and press her lips to his.

Her thoughts churned like an angry sea. Waves crashing together as she fought the feelings swelling inside.

And she must have fallen into somewhat of a daze, because suddenly Wes was shaking her gently.

"Hey. I think we're good."

"Right," she said and practically burst out of the cabinet.

The air in the basement seemed cooler and drier compared to the small, enclosed space of the storage locker, and something about that seemed to snap Ellie out of her ridiculous romantic fantasies. That and the lingering poop smell, maybe.

They approached the window and looked out. John and Courtney were nowhere to be seen, but she supposed they were staying out of sight until the coast was officially clear.

They took turns wriggling through the window, and then they began wading through the overgrown backyard toward the fence.

As the twisted wire came into view, Wes stopped abruptly and tapped her arm so that she halted too.

"Figured we should give them a minute," he said and

gestured to the shadowed place under the big creepy tree on the other side of the fence.

Ellie squinted. She spotted a figure under the tree but couldn't tell if she was looking at Courtney or John.

Then she realized it was Courtney *and* John, but their silhouettes were melded together in an embrace. Making out.

"Oh," she said, feeling strangely embarrassed. "Good idea."

She winced and rubbed at her elbow then, realizing it was throbbing.

"You OK?" he asked.

"I banged my elbow climbing out of the window. It's not a big deal. Just hurts a little."

"I know how we can fix that," Wes said.

"Oh?"

"Yeah. We just cut your foot off."

Ellie laughed a little, confused.

"Uh… what?"

Wes shrugged.

"Sorry. That's what my dad always said when I was a kid. 'Oh, your tummy hurts? We'll just amputate your foot, and then you won't even notice the stomachache anymore.'" He shook his head. "I never thought about what a weird thing it is to say until I said it myself. So that's cool."

At the sound of Courtney giggling, they both turned their heads toward the sound.

"Guess they finally came up for air," Wes said.

"Yeah. We should probably hurry before they start up again."

The grass swished and whispered around them as they made their way back to the fence. Wes went through first, then held the loose panel aside for her.

"Thanks," she said, and when she met his eyes, she thought again of how much she'd wanted to kiss him in the janitor's closet.

But she was right when she said it wouldn't work. Couldn't work.

Still, they'd shared a weird, tense, amusing moment together in that closet, and now he felt like an old friend.

She supposed she could live with that.

CHAPTER 30

The flat tire *thump-thumps* one last time, and then there is a lowering sensation in the cab of the truck. A sinking feeling, almost a kind of suction. It tilts the driver's side downward like the vehicle dips its shoulder on one side.

The tire is gone, Jimmy knows. The tattered loop of rubber has torn free of the rim, left itself behind them somewhere. The tread probably looks like an alligator's back humped on the side of the road.

He stares into the darkness in the black mirror. Looks for some sign of the tire there, maybe still flitting along like a tumbleweed.

But he sees only the gloom of the empty road stretching out behind them. Shapeless and motionless.

The warble of the sirens draws closer now. Louder.

Still no red lights twirling back there, though. At least that's something.

One thing going right.

The truck shakes. Rough vibrations thrum up through the body and rattle the bench seat beneath them. An uneven tremor. Something violent in it.

With the tire gone, the rim grinds against the road. Metal on asphalt. Makes an awful grating sound.

Brightness pulls Jimmy's eyes away from the mirror. He scans the area in front of them, only making sense of the orange flutters after a second.

Sparks. The rim kicks up sparks where it grates against the asphalt. Looks like a lighter's flint wheel spinning without end, orange glitter shooting out from that point.

The truck's speed has fallen steadily ever since the tire ripped free. They're only going about 25 miles per hour now, and even that feels iffy, the whole vehicle shaking like it's going into convulsions.

It occurs to Jimmy that they'll never make it into Swamp Hollow. Not like this. And if the cops were to come upon them now, they'd be powerless to get away. A low-speed chase has a way of wrapping up quickly.

When Jimmy speaks, his own voice sounds droll in his ears. Much calmer than he feels inside.

"'Spose I should pull over?"

Scarlet sighs and nods.

He doesn't hesitate. He yanks the wheel to the right, and they veer down into a shallow ditch and then climb the other side into a grass field.

"Try to get way back in the weeds," she says. "Our best hope is they don't find the truck for a while. Without that, maybe they won't know where to start searching."

They crush through the foliage, and Jimmy once again checks the mirrors. They have to be leaving a trail of beaten-down grass even if he can't see it in the ruddy glow of the taillights. Maybe in the dark it won't be so noticeable to a passing car. He hopes so.

He flips off the headlights, and they creep forward a few more feet, now moving among a sparse copse of trees. The shadows bloom thicker here, and the weeds are tall enough to touch the driver's side window. Grass seeds like heads of wheat tap the glass and patter at the hood and fenders.

Suddenly Scarlet is lurching forward. Hand fluttering at the dash.

She cranks the volume knob on the stereo. That voice on the radio sharpens into focus.

"—getting word, unofficially, about the critical injury of an unnamed police officer on Swamp Hollow Road during the course of a police chase. We're told Life Flight has been activated—"

The sense of relief that washes over Jimmy is so strong he almost feels like he is melting into the bench seat of the truck.

He's not dead.

I didn't kill him.

Thank fucking Christ.

His eyes slide sideways, and he can tell by the set of her jaw that a weight has been lifted from Scarlet's conscience as well.

They sit still for a few seconds. Just breathing.

Scarlet hisses then.

"Shit. Here they come."

She ducks. Something nonsensical about the movement.

Jimmy kills the engine by instinct, and the green glow of the dash lights cut to black around them. The shadows from outside suddenly flood into the cab.

Only after does he see the red glow smearing across the rearview. He cranks his head around to watch.

The police cruiser crests a hill and zooms their way, building speed. The car somehow looks muscular in the dark, a tapered thing, angular and moving aggressively. It rises with every dip, bobbing, somehow looking like it might lift off and take flight.

The headlights sweep over the ground. Their glowing edge drawing up on them. Plunging closer.

And Jimmy braces himself. Feels the muscles in his shoulders hunch just a little. Feels the tip of his tongue slither against the backs of his front teeth.

He can only picture the cruiser pivoting their way. Riding out into the field. The harsh glow of the headlights exposing them.

Without looking away from the cruiser, he paws at the zipper on the side pocket of the duffel bag. He can feel the snub-nosed gun just on the other side of the canvas, a bulk encased in coarse fabric.

The siren grows closer. Louder. A screaming thing now. Shrill.

He gets the gun free of the bag. Feels its grip snug against the web of his hand. Swings it into the open, the barrel pointing in the vague direction of the oncoming cop car.

An acrid taste appears on the back of his tongue. Acidic like pizza sauce gone sour.

The cruiser zips right by them, never slowing. It mounts and falls over another hill. Sinks behind the land. The spinning lights whip out of view all at once.

"Holy hell, that was close," Jimmy says, his voice suddenly sounding as tight as he does inside.

"That guy didn't see the truck — thank Christ — but someone will. We've gotta get going."

They climb out of the truck, Jimmy looping the straps of the duffel bag over his shoulder, all that money wedged into his armpit.

The distant sirens instantly seem louder as soon as his feet touch down. Closer. Spiky in his ears. Nerve-wracking. The warbling tones turn sharper now that he's outside with no windows blocking the sound, no truck engine grumbling out white noise.

At least it gives them a sense of where their pursuers are. Gives them something to run away from.

He follows Scarlet into the tall grass, growing momentarily nervous as her silhouette dulls in the shadowy stuff under the trees. It looks like she dissolves into the darkness there, turns liquid and dissipates. A few steps later, she solidifies again before him, though. He can see the sharp angle of her shoulders, those hard lines blacker than everything else around them.

He still has the gun out, the snub nose pointed down into the weeds. Again his stomach gurgles. Queasy as he looks down at the nickel body of the pistol glowing in a box of moonlight for a second.

Would the gun even do them any good in the dark like this? He doubts it.

Still, it's probably better to have it at the ready. Just in case.

Scarlet knifes through the brush, bushwhacking a trail, and Jimmy tails behind. Dense trees replace the weeds, and the ground under his feet turns softer and more open, the canopy above blocking out light and life. It's not until his foot sinks ankle-deep into a boggy hole that he realizes they're walking through a swamp.

Guess we should have seen that coming, Jimmy thought. *They probably don't call a town something like "Swamp Hollow" for no good reason.*

He wonders, not for the first time, how big the town might be.

Based on the name alone, he guesses small. But 3,000 people small or 300 people small, he doesn't know.

Maybe it doesn't matter. So long as there are cars to steal, it will do. And they won't linger there very long no matter what.

Something prickles on the back of his neck, and he smacks the mosquito away. Almost immediately, another takes its place, biting the back of his hand.

Gonna get eaten alive out here.

Scarlet picks up into something approaching a jog, zipping away from him. Jimmy can hear her feet squelching in the muck.

He struggles to keep pace. The straps of the duffel bag gnaw into his shoulder, and the canvas of the bag keeps bumping into his ribcage, the awkwardness slowing him. Every fifth step, his heel finds a soggy spot and sinks down into the slop.

Somewhere behind them, the sirens swell in volume again. Bearing down on them.

Jimmy peers over his shoulder just in time to see another set of twirling red lights go screeching by, the glow fractured by the meshwork of branches between him and the road. Flickering.

Like the last, this cruiser never slows. It disappears over the next hill. Swallowed by the sloping land, at least from their point of view.

So far, so good.

He lets out a big breath and keeps moving. Hustling to match Scarlet's pace.

They trudge deeper into the thicket, and the darkness only seems to deepen. The inky clouds of the separate shadows congeal into one great gloom, a collective thing, a black sea they can only try to get through.

Sometimes Jimmy isn't sure what he is seeing. He senses the trees around him more than sees them, feels the darkness of them, and he trusts the feeling and weaves around them, pressing deeper and deeper into the murk.

The sirens shrink into something tiny somewhere behind them. The sounds of the swamp slowly expand to fill the night.

Insects chirp. The wind whispers. Leaves rattle and whisk against each other.

And that black sea opens now. A vast emptiness all around. A nothingness that seems to stretch into forever.

Jimmy feels minuscule. Enveloped in darkness. Plunging into it.

He stares straight into the void, the black nothing he paradoxically thinks of as a thickness. Scans it for any sign of anything.

Nothing.

Nothing.

It seems impossible that the dark could ever end. If there were any light out there, he would see it, wouldn't he?

A pinprick would show somewhere before them, signifying the gleaming bulb some miles from here.

Or the fluttering orange of some distant lighter flame dancing in the breeze.

Or the snubbed red ember at the end of someone's cigarette.

Something.

But the darkness holds all in its grip. The whole universe as far as he can see.

They slog on. Constant sucking sounds accompany their footsteps now. A sheet of fresh mud underfoot, smooching at the soles of their shoes.

He shivers. Finds himself almost wishing he could hear the sirens again. Or see those red flashers ripping by. Anything but this.

The slurping footfalls stop in front of him, and his own feet likewise halt out of instinct.

He listens. Waits.

"There," Scarlet says, her voice low and husky.

Again Jimmy's eyes scour over the distance. He sees only black.

"Where?"

He feels her fingers slither down his arm. When she reaches his wrist, she yanks his hand up, directs it off to his right a little.

"There."

He squints that way. The black sea remains undisturbed. Still waters.

"I don't—"

But then he ducks his head, and he does see.

A wan light seeps through the branches. Not the pinprick he'd pictured before. More of a diffuse glow. Subtle. A faint grayness pouring through the woods, somehow reaching them. He doesn't think he'd have noticed without her literally reaching his arm into it.

She lurches forward. Faster now. Dragging him along by the wrist. Sloppy footsteps splish-splashing along.

They duck under a copse of cypress trees, and now Jimmy can really see the source of light.

The rectangular glow sits higher than them. Pale yellow. Still small enough that he can block it out by holding up his thumb.

A window.

A house.

CHAPTER 31

The night insects were trilling and chirruping in full force on their trek back to the car. Wes and Ellie had to almost shout over the cacophony as they regaled John and Courtney with the tale of how they'd stashed themselves inside the closet to evade the security guards.

"I think this calls for a celebration," John said, and everyone agreed.

They piled back into the car and were discussing which bar to head to when Courtney pointed at Ellie.

"What's all over your clothes?"

Ellie glanced down and noticed for the first time that she was covered in cobwebs, dust, and smears of some kind of oily grime.

"Ew. I think it must have come from the inside of that janitor's closet."

Wes rubbed at a dark smudge on his forearm.

"Yeah, it's all over me, too. Feels like… grease."

John put the car in gear.

"Here's what we'll do. I'll drop you guys off at the motel to get cleaned up, and in the meantime, Courtney and I will scout out a good bar. You can meet us there in Ellie's car."

And so, after showering and changing into fresh clothes, Ellie and Wes made the short drive to Bobby D's Tiki Hut. Courtney had texted her that the bar's parking lot was full, but she and John had found a spot in the public beach lot next door. Ellie did the same, claiming an empty space at the end of the row.

When she and Wes got out of the car, Ellie paused to look down the beach, noting the dark silhouette of a lifeguard station backlit by the moonlight reflecting on the water.

Looks like a postcard, she thought.

There was a decent crowd inside the grass-roofed bar, and it took several minutes before they spotted John and Courtney at a table in the corner. A few empty shot glasses already littered the table. Apparently, they'd wasted no time getting started.

Wes offered to buy the next round, and Ellie followed him to the bar to help carry the drinks.

While they waited, she glanced down the length of polished wood and spotted the fighting couple from the beach sitting at the bar. The ones who'd found the dead body.

It struck her, again, that the whole ruckus over the body discovery had only been this morning. To Ellie, it felt like days had passed between then and now. So much had happened.

Courtney didn't even let Ellie set her mojito on the table before snatching it up and sucking half of it down through the straw.

"Mmmm, so good!" she said when she paused to take a breath.

Then Courtney's smile faded, and she squirmed in her seat.

"You alright over there?" Ellie asked, taking a sip of her drink.

"Yeah, it's just that we walked through the sand to get over here, and I tripped and..." Courtney started to laugh.

She leaned across the table, quirking her finger at Ellie.

Ellie inclined her head, but apparently this wasn't enough. Courtney grasped her by the arm and pulled her so their heads met in the middle. Her breath was hot and smelled like booze.

Courtney moved her face closer to Ellie's ear. This gave Ellie the assumption that Courtney would whisper whatever she had to say.

"I think I got sand in my hoo-ha," she said, at full volume.

"OK. That's lovely," Ellie said, wincing while she disentangled herself from Courtney's grip.

"That's what I get for not wearing underwear!" Courtney giggled.

Ellie shook her head and turned her attention to the

conversation underway between John and Wes.

"—so stoked. The footage we got today is going to make a killer episode. It's just too bad we had to cut the exploration short. That place was huge."

"We could always go back," Wes said. "But it might not be worth it. That security detail showed up way faster than I expected."

It occurred to Ellie that for all her anxiety about the adventure earlier in the night, she'd never asked if John and Wes had gotten busted during one of their excursions.

"Have you guys ever been caught before?" Ellie asked.

A cocky grin spread over John's face, and he sat up a little straighter.

"Not us. The Spelunking Monkeys always get away clean."

"We've been lucky," Wes said, his tone more wary. "And we've had some extremely close calls."

Ellie swirled the ice cubes in her drink with the straw.

"Closer than tonight?"

Wes blew out a breath.

"I've *never* been that close to security," he said. "I could have practically reached out and touched those guys. Probably the closest call was the time we got chased by a guard dog."

"Yikes," Ellie said.

"Yeah. I refuse to go inside a place if I think there even *might* be a dog now."

"What about the time we explored that whole abandoned tuberculosis sanitarium, and then as we were leaving, we looked back, and there was a guy standing in one of the windows, staring at us. And we just knew he'd probably been following us and watching the whole time."

"Shut up," Courtney said. "If you guys had told us that story before, I never would have gone with you tonight!"

John squeezed her around the waist.

"Why do you think I'm only bringing it up now?" His eyes went to her empty glass. "Looks like we could use another round. I've got this one."

Courtney waited until John was out of earshot before she let out a tremendous burp.

"Mmm, minty," she said, smacking her lips.

Ellie scrunched her nose.

"Gross."

Courtney stuck out her tongue and then swung herself upright and leaned closer to Ellie. Her lip gloss left a sticky smear on Ellie's earlobe.

"Also, I think I got sand in my hoo-ha!"

Just as before, she didn't bother with whispering.

"So I hear. It was a big night for you."

When John returned with their drinks, he looked spooked.

"OK, *that* was fucking weird," he said, keeping his voice low.

"What is it?"

"You know that guy from earlier… Duke?" John scratched his chin. "He was at the bar."

"The creepy beach bum guy who wants to wear Courtney's skin?" Ellie asked.

"Yeah, that guy," John said. "He insisted on paying for our drinks, too. 'On account of us sharing a cold one with him earlier' is how he put it."

"That *is* weird. I mean, not the paying for the drinks so much as him being here," Ellie said.

"I know, right?"

Wes shrugged.

"Is it that weird, though? This is a pretty small town."

"I don't know," John said.

"You think he's stalking us or something?" Wes joked. "Don't be so paranoid."

"Hey, I'm just saying, the guy gave off a certain unhinged vibe."

Ellie felt a tingle of discomfort then, almost as if she were being watched. She peeked in the direction of the bar, expecting to find the man with the slicked-up pompadour staring at their table. But she scanned the bodies around the bar, and not only did she not spot Duke, she didn't notice anyone looking their way.

Now you really are being paranoid, she thought to herself.

She took one last look anyway, and this time her eyes landed on one of the TVs mounted on the wall of the place. The local evening news was running another story about Jimmy and Scarlet again. A slick graphic in the corner said "21st Century Bonnie & Clyde." The reporter was just wrapping up giving a description of the pair.

"Authorities say Scarlet Burlew, 22, may sometimes wear a wig to disguise her appearance."

It struck Ellie that she was pretty much the same age as Scarlet, which seemed so strange just now. Instead of being in school or hanging out with friends in a bar, this girl was on the run, wanted for a whole string of crimes.

She wondered what might put someone on this path. Imagined the sequence of events that would lead a girl — who probably wasn't all that different from herself — to being a fugitive from the law.

Ellie briefly lost herself on this train of thought until she was startled out of it by Courtney loudly singing along to the song playing on the jukebox a few yards from their table. She swayed side to side with her eyes closed, and then her eyelids snapped open. Ellie already knew just by the look on her face what she was about to say.

"Did I tell you that I think I got—

"Sand. In your hoo-ha," Ellie said with a nod. "Yes. You mentioned it. We're all aware. I think the whole bar is aware."

Courtney glanced around, as if realizing they were in public for the first time. But if she was embarrassed at all, she didn't show it. She threw back her head and laughed.

This was one of the things that Ellie admired most about her friend. Courtney was never embarrassed.

Ellie laughed with her, raising her glass.

"To your hoo-ha."

CHAPTER 32

Scarlet leads the way up the last slope, Jimmy following just a couple paces behind. They slow now. Climbing. Bodies tilted. Legs working.

The woods have thinned out around them, tall grass blanketing the hillside instead of trees. The blades brush at Jimmy's legs about knee-high, sometimes touching the hem of his shorts. It's that ridged kind of grass that seems to cling to everything in a way that reminds Jimmy of insect legs, almost a Velcro feel to it when it touches the skin.

Some tingle swirls in his belly now that they're so close to the house. He can't see the place just now — the hill is in the way — but he knows that they've reached another inflection point in their journey here.

Once they crest the top of this slope, the next chapter in their story will unfold, for good or ill. With good luck, they'll steal another car and jump out in front of the police again.

With bad luck…

The hill steepens underfoot. The grade pitching up toward the heavens.

And Jimmy looks up into the freshly open sky. No more canopy of interwoven leaves and branches above. No more blotting of the moonlight.

Now the stars poke tiny dots of brightness into the great abyss hung over them. And silvery starlight glints over the land itself, a soft glow like a night light.

They push harder now. Climbing in silence. Jimmy's thighs burn every time he digs in for another step, and his calves feel tight and dead, cylinders of clenched meat.

His feet slip every fourth step or so, the soil loose in places, as moist as chocolate cake. And the duffel bag full of money rocks against his side every time his balance wavers, a bulk knocking him in the flank to try to send him skittering back down the slope. But he keeps going, keeps going.

He can't really see the top of the hill. Letting his gaze flick up there leaves him with a vague impression of the line where the weeds cleave off into the night. Dark against dark.

He presses toward that spot nevertheless. Doesn't question it. Doesn't think about it. Just keeps moving.

It occurs to him that they've been at it all day. Got a measly few hours of sleep in that barn, and they've been on the run ever since.

The day became the night, and they'd kept running. Had the truck for what felt like ten minutes, though he supposed it was longer.

No respite. Nothing to eat except for half a bag of Ruffles or so, and that had been hours ago.

He takes out his water bottle at the thought. Drinks long and deep. At least they still have that.

Scarlet takes one more step, and her body rises off that tilted plane. She presses into a cleft in the weeds and disappears from view. A few steps later, Jimmy moves into the opening and makes the same transition.

The land flattens out at the top of the hill, and the weeds die back into a freshly mowed sod. The house swings into view, its two glowing windows staring at them like a pair of yellow eyes, the front door a dark mouth between the panes, somehow turned sideways.

It's a big old farmhouse with a wraparound porch. A pair of massive live oaks on either side of the driveway stretch their gnarled limbs in every direction.

Jimmy feels naked right away. Out in the open after so long under the cover of darkness and foliage.

He realizes there's a floodlight on the detached garage beyond the main house. The actual bulb is mostly blocked from their view by the peaked roof of the house, but the white light of the LED cuts a circle out of the darkness and spreads a pale glint over the grass.

They creep toward the house, and now for the first time Jimmy moves out in front. He keeps toward the shadows where he can. Sidling through the deeper blacks along a row of juniper trees, then moving close enough to the porch that the awning cuts a black swath for him to disappear into.

They circle the house like that, dashing through the well-lit areas and ducking to keep their silhouettes under the windows where necessary.

A TV casts flickering blue light onto the walls of what must be the living room. The glow swells and lurches, the walls brightening and darkening in unison.

None of the angles give them a view of who might be in there, however — the curtains are drawn over any windows that might offer a look.

Once they've walked the perimeter of the house without seeing anything else of interest, they proceed to the garage, which looks like it had originally been a carriage house. Jimmy avoids walking on the gravel driveway — something about footsteps on gravel has a telltale crunch that draws attention, in his experience.

But even if he can go around the rocks, he can't stay out of the light here. The LED bulb over the garage door floods this area with a white glow. Stepping into the light, Jimmy feels like he's wading into something, like there's a density to it.

He glides over the manicured grass. Sticks his nose right up to the window on one side of the converted garage. Cups his hand over the orbit of his eye socket to try to cut the glare from the LED bulb. Just next to him, Scarlet stands on her tiptoes and does the same.

Dark shapes winnow into focus on the other side of the glass. The bulkier stuff stays indistinct at first, but he can see tools hung on the far wall. Everything neat and orderly.

There's a tarp draped over something toward the back of the carriage house. A boat, Jimmy thinks. A small speedboat.

Then the closer curved shapes make sense all at once. A car. A sports car. He recognizes the body shape right away, and his heart beats faster.

A Ford Mustang. Not more than two or three years old.

"Awful new," Scarlet says.

"Well..." Jimmy says. "Whole lot faster than a beater pickup, anyway."

He knows what she means, though. Hotwiring won't be an option. Most newer ignitions have immobilizers that make it just about impossible, especially for someone in a hurry.

He steps back from the glass and checks the door out of habit. Locked tight. Of course.

He turns back to face the house, and his eyes latch onto one set of windows toward the back.

"You thinkin' kitchen?" Scarlet asks.

He nods slowly.

"Same here," she says after a second.

They creep that way with Jimmy out front again. He loops deeper into the yard to keep out of that glow casting down from the carriage house. Then he circles back toward the kitchen windows once he's beyond the brightest of it.

Sweat beads on his upper lip. He reaches up to swipe it away, feels the cold kiss of metal on his cheek. He'd forgotten about the gun clutched in his hand.

He keeps the weapon but passes the duffel to Scarlet for now.

Then he climbs three wooden steps to the back door, a paneled slab of cedar that offers no view. Bracing his hand on the wrought iron, he leans over the railing toward the window just off the stoop.

Again, he presses his nose right up to the glass. Gray light leaks into the kitchen from the living room at the other end of the house. A touch of the blue flickering from the TV seeps into the mouth of the doorway, though it doesn't quite enter the kitchen.

Still, he can see the black and white tile floors, sense the plane of the countertops along two of the walls. He gets the gist of the cupboards, appliances, and sink — all their shadowy bulks and clefts drawn in charcoal smears.

With the gun still nestled in his right hand, he fishes out his phone with his left. Thumbs on the flashlight.

The beam shoots through the window. Lights up a wooden hutch that houses a microwave and a bunch of country-fried knickknacks. Little cow-patterned things, mostly.

Jimmy sweeps the light along the counters. The glow flashes on the chrome of a toaster, the reflection bursting like a lens flare.

He brushes it past a coffee machine. Grinder. A bag of potato chips clipped shut at the top with one of those wide plastic things only grandparents ever seem to have.

He chews his bottom lip. Pivots his wrist. Keeps the light moving. Slowly, slowly.

The basket appears in the spotlight then. Right at the corner where the counter dead-ends.

Braids of wicker cupping… something. Even with the light gleaming on the outside of the basket, the inside remains in shadow.

Jimmy lifts his arm, angles the phone higher. The light stretches over the rim of the basket.

There.

The shadows shift, light and dark jumping in unison inside the basket. Then a tangle of flat pieces of metal emerges, each with jagged teeth cut into their sides. Jimmy's head goes light, tingly.

Keys.

The basket holds two key rings, each only holding five or so actual keys. But Jimmy recognizes the plastic rectangles also jutting from the loops. Bulky things like small bars of black soap.

Key fobs.

One or both will surely give them command over the Mustang. And one of the keys will let them into the garage, more than likely.

Jimmy thumbs off the light and steps back from the

window. Lets the smartphone slide back into his hip pocket. A cool breath rushes into him, fills his chest with sticky humidity. That excitement still froths in his head.

Now they know what they have to do. The next few steps lie before them. At their mercy.

They just have to get into the kitchen without alerting anyone inside.

Without thinking, Jimmy moves his free hand to the door handle. Then he sniffs a little laugh to himself.

"How much you wanna bet it's unlocked?" he asks in a whisper.

Scarlet smirks.

Out here in the boonies, people leave their doors unlocked all the time, don't they? Seems like a bunch of 'em bragged about it as much as they could, too. Like maybe if they said it enough times, they really would be safe. Like maybe the words would protect them, ward off people like Jimmy Maddox from their property.

But here I am, fucker. Here I am.

Pawing at your door.

Jimmy holds his breath.

He cranks his wrist, and the handle turns freely at his touch. No resistance.

He pushes. The cedar slab pivots on its hinges in what feels like slow motion. Quiet and smooth.

A slice of the black and white tile floor is unveiled at his feet. That soft light trickling in from the living room looks somehow purple now that he's up close. A glowing lilac shade tinting the white ceramic.

He takes one step into the room. Smells the faint scent of potpourri like a floral cinnamon roll in the air. Feels his upper body tense somehow at the aroma, like that Cinnabon stench marks his entry into foreign territory more than any other detail.

He loops his paw into the basket. Mucks around for a second. His tensed shoulder bounces the rest of his arm like a marionette, some tight rubber band feeling in the muscle.

There. His fingers find one serrated metal edge. Then another and another.

He clenches his fist, cinches both keyrings tightly in his hand. The cold metal quickly goes warm from his body heat.

Now his eyes slide back through the yawning doorway. He watches the TV's glow undulate on the wall there, the bruise-colored light splashing over the cow-patterned baubles. Nothing else moves.

His hand comes free of the basket. The one foot planted within the kitchen retreats across the threshold of the doorway, pulls him fully back outside.

He exhales. Slow and quiet. Feels that fizzy feeling in his skull intensify. Tiny bubbles bursting in the wrinkles of his brain.

Then he hands both key rings off to Scarlet. Takes another breath and holds it.

He swings the door closed. Slowly. Slowly.

Waits for a hinge to squawk like a dying gull.

Waits for footsteps to pound down the wooden planks of the hall.

Waits for the deep *click-clack* of a round being pushed into the chamber of a bolt-action rifle.

Nothing.

Nothing.

He snugs the door into the frame. Wedges it there without sound. He doesn't quite latch it, as the notion of the bolt clicking home scares him too much. Those metallic clicks could really carry.

He shoves his face up to the window beside the door again. Stares at that glowing rectangle of the hallway inside.

He finally peels his eyes away. Steps backward down one of the steps. Turns.

Holy shit.

The open space as he spins away from the house seems momentarily overwhelming. Disorienting. All that nothing stretching from here to eternity.

Too easy.

Like all of this was meant to be.

Now Scarlet pulls out in front, looking like a humpback from the duffel hoisted high on her shoulder. They shuffle back across the yard. Circle through the shadows toward the garage.

They pull up hard at the door. Scarlet lifts one set of keys and fumbles at the lock. Tries two. Three.

Little jangles spill into the night now. Metal jingling against metal, ice cubes in a tumbler.

Jimmy cranks his head around, looking back the way they've come. Again, he half-expects an old-timey farmer to come tearing around the corner of the house, a big lumbering oaf draped in flannel and overalls bursting out of the shadows and spilling into that circle of white LED light. Some deer hunting rifle almost looking twig-like wrapped in his kielbasa fingers.

But the yard holds still behind them. Not a blade of grass stirring in that patch of brightness. Crickets trill somewhere in the distance.

The next key plunges into the hole. Scarlet snaps her wrist to the side, and then the door is falling open, shoved into the shadowy interior of the carriage house. She tumbles in after it. Swallowed by the dark.

Jimmy goes to follow, steps into the doorway. A blur catches his eye. Something flailing in the shadows the other way.

Close. On him all at once. Not more than eight feet away and getting closer.

He doesn't have time to react. Can only take in the details.

Not a big lumbering oaf. A small man. Wiry. Lean and hard.

A face like well-oiled leather with a field of dark stubble sprouting over the narrow jaw and jutting chin.

The mouth cuts a hard line there. Flat and grim.

Little piggy eyes dot the middle of it all. Something harsh in them, too. Something cold.

It makes sense to Jimmy in a flash. The man has looped around the other side of the house. Probably exited through the front door and taken the dark way back here.

And then Jimmy's eyes shift lower. To the shotgun clutched in the man's hands. The double barrels gape at him like the nostrils of something big and mean.

And Jimmy remembers the gun in his own hand. Brings it up too late.

The man's body goes taut. Spine straightening. Arms tightening. Feet splaying to shoulder-width.

He swivels the shotgun a quarter of a turn. Levels it at Jimmy, center mass.

Then his forearms flex. His hands jerk.

He squeezes the trigger.

The shotgun snorts and bucks. The muzzle jets flame.

The boom splits the night. Only hatred in that roar.

The stock kicks back into the man's shoulder. Knocks him back half a step.

And the load of buckshot tears Jimmy Maddox in half.

CHAPTER 33

By the time Eddie Coombs walked into Bobby D's Tiki Hut, he was spoiling for a fight.

It had been a shitty day at work. Not that every day re-roofing houses in the Florida heat wasn't a shitty day, but today had been supremely shitty. All because that old bitch had called his boss to narc on him for kicking her dog.

He'd barely touched the stupid little mutt, and he'd only done it because the thing wouldn't shut the fuck up. Maybe that ancient crone should try her hand at doing a tear off in the heat and humidity with a dumbshit little dog screaming its head off the whole time. See how she liked it.

So sue him if he couldn't take one more minute of the high-pitched shrieking by the time lunch rolled around. He was only human. So he'd given the thing a nudge with his boot. It was one of those chihuahua mixes that looked like a fuckin' alien with the bugged-out eyes on the sides of its head. Stupid-looking and ugly as hell. Why'd people even have dogs like that? Thing was fuckin' useless in a fight.

If he ever got a dog, it'd be a pit bull. Now *that* was a dog. And he wouldn't have no useless pussy ass dog either. He'd have a mean sumbitch. He'd train it to fight so it was the baddest fuckin' dog in the county. Just like him. He'd like to see that stupid cuck boss of his try to get in his face then. Eddie'd have his dog rip the guy's balls clean off.

Unfortunately, Eddie didn't have the dog yet, so there'd been no ball-ripping to speak of when Jerry Plichta came down to the jobsite and chewed him out in front of his whole crew. Eddie had just had to stand there and take it.

Which looked bad, him being the senior man on the crew. Basically made him the one in charge, for all intents and purposes. So to have Plichta humiliate him like that in front of his guys? Total bullshit.

Just then, Chris and Jeff returned to the table with a pitcher and three glasses.

"I still don't see why I always have to pay for the first round," Chris was whining.

"Like I told you before," Eddie said. "Seniority."

"Yeah. Seniority," Jeff echoed.

"But that means I'll always have to buy the first round. That doesn't seem fair."

Eddie grabbed the pitcher and filled his glass.

"Not *always*, dipshit. In a month or two, someone new will join the crew. Then he'll have to buy the first round. You'll see."

Chris looked like he didn't quite believe this, but for once, Eddie wasn't bullshitting. There was a high turnover in the roofing business. None of the guys he worked with even two years ago were still on the job. Except for him.

And he liked it that way. Liked being the one who knew the most. Liked being the oldest one and therefore the wisest, by default. Liked being the de facto boss as long as their *real* boss wasn't around, which was almost always. Most of the guys he worked with were almost ten years younger than him. They looked up to him.

Chris here was a shining example. Eddie could tell Chris thought he was King Shit. Always laughed the hardest at Eddie's jokes. Volunteered to go pick up lunch for everybody. Was the first to agree to go out for a beer after work.

Eddie downed his glass in three gulps and let out an exaggerated *ahhhhh* noise.

"Nothing tastes better after a hot fuckin' day on a roof," he said and refilled his glass before Chris had even had a chance to pour one for himself.

"Fuckin' A right," Jeff agreed.

Chris nodded.

"Nothing better."

"Especially not after a day when that fat fuck Plichta comes around," Eddie said. "God, I hate that guy."

Jeff shook his head.

"Total dick."

Chris hurried to agree.

"Yeah, he sucks big time."

While Eddie waxed on about what a piece of shit their boss was, he simultaneously began scoping out the crowd in the bar. He'd love to take his aggression out on someone, and this place was ripe tonight. Stuffed to the gills with pussy ass college kids.

Eddie tried to envision how soft their lives probably were. Coming down here for some R&R after a grueling semester of sitting in a series of air-conditioned classrooms. Must be fuckin' nice.

He finished off the pitcher — Eddie had easily had half of it himself — and raised his eyebrows at Jeff.

"Your turn, Jeffrey."

Chris chuckled.

"Haha, *Jeffrey*."

Eddie rounded on him.

"You think that's funny, Christina?"

"What? No… if you're calling him Jeffrey, you have to call me Christopher. My full name."

"Is that right, Christina? I *have* to?"

"Well, no. I didn't mean…"

Eddie stared Chris down, feeling a malicious glee watching the younger man squirm. And also a touch of rage at what a coward he was. Eddie wanted to grab him by the shoulders and shake him so hard his head popped off. The image of Chris's head just flying off and blood squirting from the empty stump of his neck made Eddie laugh out loud.

Chris laughed too, probably thinking that Eddie's laughter was a sign that he'd only been messing with him. But for a second there, Eddie had been *this close* to punching him in the face.

Jeff returned with a fresh pitcher. Chris reached for it, and Eddie slapped his hand away.

"Ah, ah, ah, Christina. Gentlemen first."

"But your glass isn't even empty."

Chris's voice came out in a whine.

Eddie poured slowly, until the golden liquid reached the lip at the edge of his glass, his eyes on Chris the whole time.

Suddenly Jeff whispered under his breath.

"Shhhit." He glared down at his phone, his jaw clenched tight. "I gotta go."

"Already?" Eddie said.

"Yeah. I forgot that Jen's parents were coming for dinner tonight." He tucked his phone in his pocket and shook his head. "Jesus, she's gonna fucking kill me."

"Listen to this puss." Eddie mockingly repeated him. "'*She's gonna kill me!*' You're so fuckin' whipped."

Jeff got up.

"Whatever, man."

Eddie licked his lips.

"Hey, didn't you say she was into collecting handbags? Which one of her bags does she keep your balls in? Or does she carry them around with whichever one she's using for the day?"

Chris cackled as Eddie went on.

"When was the last time you actually *saw* your balls? Can you even remember? Does she let you have them back when you bone, or do you just, like, jizz a puff of dust?"

Jeff was in the middle of chugging the rest of his beer and held up his middle finger. Eddie had never really figured out how to get under Jeff's skin. He could razz him nonstop, and the guy never seemed to break a sweat. It was annoying.

Jeff finished off the glass and set it down with a *thunk*.

"See you guys at work."

"Unbelievable," Eddie said as Jeff walked away.

Chris grinned.

"So whipped."

"Eh, fuck 'im," Eddie said, holding his glass up. "We'll have more fun without him, am I right?"

Chris clinked his glass against Eddie's.

"Fuckin' A right."

CHAPTER 34

Jimmy flops into the open doorway of the garage. Sinks into the darkness with limbs gone slack. Chopped down.

He disappears into the gloom. Hits the floor with a thud. Dead weight slapping concrete.

Scarlet drops the duffel bag and stutter-steps back from the body. Silence roars inside her skull, like wind raging there without sound.

Then the words come.

Jimmy is dead.

Jimmy is dead.

She breathes in the dark. Hears the wheeze of it. Smells some pungent garage stink filling her nostrils. WD-40, maybe.

And then she dives toward the body. Presses herself into the darkness where he fell.

Her hands pat around the cool cement there. Smooth on her fingers. Calm against her fever.

Her touch finds Jimmy. A sheet of sticky heat covers a torso already going cold. His body perforated. His life leaking out.

Her hands climb him like two spiders. Belly to chest to throat.

She presses along the curve of the neck there. Finds the spot, finds the artery.

Her touch is light and still.

Waiting. Waiting.

Trying to listen over the thunder of her own blood, her own pulse, her own heart.

There.

His pulse touches her back.

A gentle thump taps at her fingertips. Heartbeat weak. A little erratic. Thready.

Movement shifts on the other side of the doorway. Draws

her eye.

The homeowner is there. Shotgun still raised. Beady eyes squinting to try to see into the dark inside the garage. He takes a careful step forward.

Scarlet lurches. Slams the door in his face.

His weight thuds against it. The knob rattles and turns.

And then she's leaning into the steel plank, too. Fighting him for command of the heavy door.

She thumps into it shoulder first. Whole body heaving. Feet sliding on the concrete floor.

The metal spirals cold into her shoulder, into her side. Her sweat-soaked skin and shirt absorbing the chill rapidly.

And all at once she steps back. Lets him shuffle forward. Lets the door glide a few inches into the space.

She can hear the soles of his boots. Choppy steps toeing up onto the threshold.

Then she lowers her shoulder and hurls herself into the door. Bashes it harder than before. Total abandon.

Better to break myself.

Better to die here and now than let him in here, than let him win.

The impact thrums through her whole body. The hurt a bad vibration rattling through the meat of her and whispering in her bones.

Pain.

The steel crumples her shoulder. Jolts her jaw and makes her bite her lip.

Pain.

But she can hear those boots again. Stumbling back. Wobbling.

She'd hoped to give him slack and get him off balance. Then knock him on his ass.

And it's worked. Maybe.

She pistons her legs again. Both hands suctioned to the steel. Pushing. Driving.

The door clacks home. Slams into the jamb. Hard enough

to jangle nails in jars and quiver the tools hanging on the wall.

And now her fingers work their way down the beveled steel. Scrabble over the cool metal like so many crab legs.

She finds the doorknob. Glossy against her moist skin. Locks it.

Then she stumbles back. Gapes at the dark outlines that separate the door from the wall. Not actual lines or contours so much as slight variations in the blackness.

Her heart thwacks. The cold seems to suddenly wrap around her, that dank garage air pressing itself against her soggy flesh.

The doorknob rattles. A violent shake. But the lock doesn't give.

He can't get in.

I have his keys.

She drifts a few steps backward. Heartened at the thought but only for a second.

Jimmy.

She kneels next to him. Can kind of see that sheet of red still pulsing over his torso. A stirring wetness in the dark there like a creek slithering through a forest at night.

Jimmy coughs then. His head turns. Scarlet can only tell by the glitter of his eyes blinking.

He's awake. Conscious.

His voice rasps out of him. Gritty and harsh.

"Did he… did he shoot me?"

Something about the nonsensical question sends a fresh chill over Scarlet's skin.

He's probably in shock.

But he's alive. He's still here.

He's going to make it.

He might.

She swallows before she answers. Deliberate with her words. Careful to keep her voice soft, soothing.

"You're going to be alright now. It's… You're going to be fine."

He coughs again. It sounds wet in his throat.

And for a second, Scarlet can't help but think about the little pellets spread all through him now. Flecks of lead lodged in the stringy muscle fibers. In his lungs. In his organs.

The man's shadow inks the window off to her left. A darkness wobbling over the glass.

The old man presses his face right up to the pane for a second. Cups a hand next to his brow. Steps back.

Then the flashlight from his phone lances into the room. A circle of light that dances over the concrete floor. Shaky movements. Sweeping up on her and Jimmy.

The light holds on them for a second. And then it rips out of the frame. Gone.

Fresh darkness floods the space. Blacker now, it seems.

Light and shadow twitch on the other side of the glass. Meaningless lurching and bobbing.

Then she sees the silhouette of the shotgun rising. That hard line drifting upward in his arms.

Scarlet loops her hands under Jimmy's armpits and drags him back from the pane. Scuffling steps pulling them deeper into the shadows. Jimmy's blood-soaked shirt and shorts hissing against the concrete.

The muzzle of the shotgun taps the glass. A small sound. Reminds her of something she'd hear in a dentist's office. One of those hooks touching the hard enamel of an incisor.

Scarlet braces herself. Waits for the boom. Waits for the rain of ripping pellets.

But nothing comes.

They huddle behind the fender of the Mustang. Out of sight for now.

There's more tapping at the window. Something smearing on the glass.

Scarlet pictures the man cupping his brow there again. Knowing he's lost them.

The light comes again. That phone flashlight spearing into the garage, its glow crawling over the floor.

The beam inches under the Mustang. Drifts back and forth over the concrete in slow motion. Glints on the dust motes they've kicked up.

But the light can't touch them. Not here, behind the wheel.

They don't move. Don't breathe.

And the light sweeps away. Swoops up over the car to touch the tools hanging from nails there. Slides toward the back of the garage.

The circle of light dances over a blue tarp covering a small boat. Moves faster now. Erratic.

It tries to stretch into the dark places along both sides of the craft. Angling for the deepest shadows.

But it can't quite reach.

And then the light is gone again. Out all at once.

Scarlet listens. Strains her ears to reach beyond this space.

Quiet.

Quiet.

Then the crunching comes. Heavy footsteps on gravel. Jogging. Trailing away.

He's running back to the house.

Maybe he doesn't know we have both sets of keys.

Or maybe there are backups. A garage door opener, maybe.

And if he has a phone on him, he could be calling the cops even now.

Shit.

Jimmy gasps for breath now. Wheezing. Scarlet realizes he's with it enough that he was keeping quiet before.

Her eyes have adjusted to the dark. She can make out a grayscale version of him now. The details fuzzy. A pixelated black and white picture in newsprint.

She shushes him. Coos near his ear.

"He's here now. Following us. You know that, right?"

"He just took off, I thought. Ran back to the house."

"Not the guy here. *Him.*"

He coughs, and then he's quiet for a few seconds.

"That other old man," he mutters, thinking out loud now.

"They said on the radio… Him and his dogs."

She nods.

"And we didn't do it. So who else?"

He's quiet again.

"How the hell did he find us?"

"Not like we're keeping a low profile."

Scarlet feels the muscles in her shoulders sag. Her neck goes slack. Her head droops.

"Maybe it's better this way. Getting arrested. Better than if he finds us."

Jimmy's voice comes clearer now. Intense.

"Take the money and go. Now."

Her whole body goes rigid at the suggestion.

"You have to come with me. I can—"

He shakes his head.

"It's all you now. Take the guns. Take the money. Take this guy's car, and get the hell away."

"I can't do this without you."

"You will."

"I'm just supposed to leave you here?"

Tears sting her eyes, and everything goes blurry around her.

"I'm bleeding out, babe. If I can make it until the cops get here, maybe I get to the hospital in time. Either way I'm done, you know? But you still have a chance. To have a life. To have freedom. To have all the things we always talked about. You got a chance. You gotta take it."

Breaths squeeze Scarlet's ribcage. An accordion going in and out. She doesn't say anything.

Jimmy licks his lips. Talks quieter now.

"All I care about is that you're happy. And safe. You know that? That's why we ran in the first place."

He coughs again. Harder this time. The hacking goes higher in pitch, ends in a throaty wretch like a vomiting dog.

He wipes the heel of his hand along his chin.

"When you open the garage door, this guy is gonna be out there. OK? He already shot once, so he's not going to hesitate.

Maybe it's better then, that I keep one of the guns. I'll cover you. Suppressing fire and shit. I can back him off, buy you time, but you gotta gun it out of here. And don't stop."

Ice crystallizes over the surface of Scarlet's scalp. Cold feelings. Dry and crackly.

This can't be real. It can't.

Jimmy keeps talking. Now he's the one trying for a soothing tone.

"Go straight for town. Yeah? Ditch this ride and get another one. Go to one of the tourist spots, maybe. The beach. Where everyone is partying and drunk. Lots of easy marks."

And now Scarlet is nodding along. It's all exactly what she would have suggested. Something about the strategy spoken out loud makes it seem to sprawl before her in three dimensions. It focuses her, calms her.

Life can seem so complicated, overwhelming, but it can always be broken down into a series of steps. This, and then this, and then this. The next action becomes all that's controllable, all that's real, and the simplicity of that comforts her somehow. It always has.

"OK," she says finally.

Jimmy half-smiles, crooked, something grim in it. Then his arm wags, and the gun lifts into view.

"Let's fuckin' go. I love you more than anything, babe."

Her voice comes out small in response. Pinched.

"Love you."

He grabs her hand one last time. She presses his knuckles to her lips.

Scarlet heaves the duffel bag over the center console and into the passenger seat of the Mustang and climbs in after it. The chill from the leather leaks through her sweat-sogged t-shirt. A cold hand cupping her back.

She pushes the button next to the wheel to start it. The plastic circle sinks and clicks at her touch.

The engine rumbles, and the dash lights flick on. A cobalt blue glow shoots out of the rounded speedometer and gas gauge.

Then she finds the garage door opener hooked to the visor. Fingers that.

The garage door jerks upward, and light spills into the garage slowly but surely as the thing wheels up the track. A curtain sliding out of the way. That harsh LED brightness encroaching.

The man is there about fifty feet back in the yard. Gaping. Then lifting the shotgun.

She wonders dimly if he'll have the guts to actually shoot his precious Mustang.

Jimmy rises up on one elbow. His other arm points the gun in the general direction of the man.

His arm quivers. Steadies. He squeezes the trigger.

The chunky little gun lifts and pops in his hand. A muzzle flash sparkling there. An orange flutter.

The man shuffles back all at once. Eyes wider than before. The shotgun tilts toward the ground as he does.

Scarlet shifts into drive. Jams her foot on the accelerator.

The Mustang lurches forward. Shoots out of the dark cave of the garage and into the artificial light.

Brightness. Exposed.

The car fishtails. Tires flinging gravel everywhere. Stones plinking against the wheel wells, against the undercarriage.

Scarlet wrestles with the steering wheel. Feels the back end of the car veering off to the side.

The man bobs up just off to her right. His bottom teeth exposed in a grimace. He starts to lift the shotgun.

More gunshots pop-pop-pop behind her. Smaller now. The muzzle flashes strobe in the mirrors, bright pockets of orange in the shadows within the carriage house.

She can't see Jimmy there. Only that snorting flame from his gun.

The man ducks and shuffles back again. Suppressed indeed.

And the treads of the tires seem to catch all at once. The wheels straighten out. All four working together now.

Scarlet hurtles down the gentle slope. Takes a hard left at the mouth of the driveway, throwing off more gravel. The car veers out onto the asphalt.

She flees into the night.

CHAPTER 35

Pete Murphy took a sip of his margarita, smacked his lips against the tartness of the lime juice, and leaned back in his chair with a contented sigh.

Coming over to Bobby D's Tiki Hut for a drink and some grub after a shift at the nursing home was his favorite way to unwind. And he needed it after today.

If he was being honest, he hated that damn place, even on a normal day. After a few hours in that sterile, hospital-like atmosphere, Pete always felt a little like a bug trapped in a jar.

But the pay was good, especially compared to most of the jobs here, so what could he do?

And he'd found the antidote. He popped into the Tiki Hut a few times a week and set himself right. He didn't mind that he was usually alone, though he knew a lot of people didn't care for dining out by themselves. He almost preferred it, because then he could just sit back and relax. Do a little people watching.

There was a good crowd for it tonight. Lots of tourists in for spring break. Mostly college kids, but also some families.

This was exactly what made the Tiki Hut his chosen hang out. Everyone here was always having a good time. They were lively. Engaged. Full of vigor. The complete opposite of the residents at the home, most of whom shuffled or scooted or wheeled around in a stupor.

Three guys came in and took a table nearby. Pete thought they were another group of spring breakers until he recognized one of them.

Eddie Coombs.

Pete had gone to school with Eddie's older brother, Gerald. Troublemakers, the both of them. Always getting suspended for fighting and smoking and whatnot. Actually, if he recalled correctly, Gerald Coombs had eventually been expelled for bringing a switchblade to school.

The whole family was like that. Something wrong in the genetics, Pete supposed. Or maybe it was being raised in an environment like that. Nature or nurture. Who could say? Probably a bit of both.

Pete dipped a fried shrimp in remoulade and popped it in his mouth. His eyes wandered away from Eddie Coombs.

One of the women a few tables over had clearly had a few. She was talking animatedly, with a lot of hand gestures, and projecting her voice just a little too loudly. She grasped her friend's wrist and leaned in to say something.

"I think I got sand in my hoo-ha!"

Pete chuckled to himself, finding it amusing despite the fact that he had no idea what the context for that statement might be.

He pulled a small notebook from his pocket that he carried around for moments exactly like this and jotted it down. Not everything he wrote in the book made it into his stories, but quite a few of them did.

Speaking of which, he might be able to finish the newest one this week.

Not that he was in any rush. He didn't really *do* anything with the stories, at this point. Almost no one even knew he wrote them.

He was honest with himself that it was fairly likely that nothing would come of the writing. And maybe that was OK. He'd keep doing it as long as it interested him. Figured you had to pass the time somehow. Some people ran marathons. He wrote his little stories.

He'd stopped telling people about the writing, because everyone acted like something had to come of it for it to be a valid hobby. Which was the funny thing about writing, compared to things like golfing and painting. His buddy Louis golfed every Sunday, and no one was ever asking him when he'd be in the Masters. Just like no one asked someone who paints in their spare time when their work will be featured at the Met. But when people found out Pete wrote short stories but didn't actually do anything with them, they looked at him like he was some kind of weirdo.

A voice startled him from his thoughts then.

"Can I get you another margarita?"

He glanced up at the waitress. Smiled.

"Yes, please."

His eyes followed her as she made her way to the bar, and that's when Pete spied Eddie Coombs shoving a college kid. Getting in his face. Classic Coombs bullshit.

Pete sighed and dusted panko crumbs from his fingers.

CHAPTER 36

Eddie and Chris drank and shot the shit for a while, until Eddie noticed the second pitcher was almost gone. He got out his wallet and made a show of peering into the billfold.

"Shit, I don't have any cash, and this place charges you like three percent if you use a credit card. Get this round, and I'll pay you back when I have the cash?"

Chris's face pinched together.

"You never paid me back for last time."

Eddie blinked. Playing dumb.

"What?"

"Last time. When we went out to O'Neal's. We got three pitchers, and you promised to pay for half, and you never did."

"Well shit, man. I musta forgot!"

Of course Eddie hadn't forgotten. It was one of the games he liked to play with people. How many more dimes and favors and good will could he squeeze from them? Just to see how far he could get.

Guys like Chris were just begging to be taken for a ride, and who was Eddie to argue with that?

"Tell you what… soon as we get back to my truck, I'll drive straight to an ATM and pay you back in full for the drinks here and at O'Neal's. How's that sound?"

Chris looked only half-convinced, but Eddie knew he wouldn't push back.

"OK. I guess."

Eddie clapped him on the shoulder. It was important to give them a little positive reinforcement every now and then. Like a dog.

"You're a good guy, Chris. The best."

The corners of Chris's mouth twitched upward.

It was too fuckin' easy.

Later tonight, when they got back to his truck, he'd pull the "drunk and belligerent" act, and even if Christina here really tried to push him on getting his money, he'd lose.

While Chris trotted off to the bar for another pitcher, Eddie eyed a group a few tables away. All girls. All dressed like whores.

He took a long look. If they were gonna flaunt it like that, why shouldn't he? Not that he'd touch any of 'em with his ten-foot pole, the stuck-up bitches, but he'd look.

He laughed to himself. *His ten-foot pole*. That was a good one.

"Look at these bitches," he said when Chris got back with the beer.

Chris turned and glanced at the group.

"Smokin' hot," he said, nodding enthusiastically.

"You think so?" Eddie sniffed. "Me, personally? I wouldn't touch 'em with my ten-foot pole."

He laughed again at his own joke, and Chris joined in.

Eddie filled his glass and continued his perusal of the bar. A mixed group huddled near the bar. Three guys, four girls. He did some quick math. Too many. If Jeff were still here, maybe.

He kept scanning. Zeroed in on a foursome. Two guys, two girls.

Eddie studied the girls first. The tall one was a looker, and her friend had nice tits. Still wouldn't fuck 'em, even if they were begging for it.

He moved onto the guys. One of 'em looked kinda big, but dumb. Probably a jock. Jocks always thought they were so fuckin' cool. So tough. But they only knew how to play by the rules. That put 'em at a real disadvantage when they got into it with someone like Eddie. Because Eddie didn't believe in rules. Especially not during a fight.

Next to the jock was a guy who looked like an art school fag. Real serious look to him, like he was always pondering something deep, but he was probably just thinkin' up new and imaginative ways to jerk off. Eddie'd give him something to ponder alright.

Yeah, this was the one.

Eddie focused on the guy for a good minute before he looked up, like he could feel Eddie's eyes on him. When he made eye contact with Eddie, he looked away and then back, like he thought Eddie would be looking elsewhere by now. That Eddie staring must have been a mistake. But it wasn't a mistake. This was a game Eddie had played many times before.

"You got a fuckin' problem?" he asked.

The guy blinked and looked away again.

Eddie snickered.

"What a pussy."

Chris twisted around to peer over his shoulder, like he'd missed something.

"What was that all about?"

"Just some faggot over there, staring at me."

For once, Chris didn't laugh. Instead, his face went all grave. He looked like someone had just told him his grandma had died.

"Hey man, that's… that's not cool." He swallowed. "One of my cousins is gay."

Eddie let his mouth fall open. Made an attempt to look contrite.

"Really?"

"Yeah."

"Well shit, man. I'm sorry…" He let the innocent act drop and smirked. "…sorry to hear you've got a groomer fag in the family, I mean."

Chris's cheeks had little patches of red on them now.

"Come on. He's not like that. He's a good guy."

Eddie hissed out a laugh.

"Calm down, Christina. You think I actually care if your cousin likes to blow other dudes in truck stop bathrooms?"

He didn't hear what Chris had to say next, because movement caught his eye, and he spotted the fruity art school priss heading for the bar.

Eddie watched like a bird of prey. Waiting for just the perfect moment. He had to time it just right.

When the time came, he cuffed Chris on the shoulder.

"They got horseshoes set up on the beach. Let's go play."

Eddie didn't wait for Chris's response. He slid off his stool and meandered across the bar, adjusting his stride by the millisecond so that at the exact moment the emo-haired pussy came around the corner of the bar with an armload of drinks, Eddie would be right in his path.

And it went just how Eddie wanted it to. He slammed into the prissy little fuck, and there was a small eruption of pale liquid from one of the glasses. A few drops landed on Eddie.

Eddie plucked at one of the wet spots on his shirt and gave the other guy a shove.

"Watch where you're going, cocksucker."

"What?" the guy said, obviously confused since Eddie was the one who had run into *him*. But Eddie had done this a hundred times.

Eddie closed the gap between them.

"I said, watch where you're fucking going."

"Eddie, man," Chris had a hand on his bicep and was trying to pull him back.

Eddie shook him off, his eyes still on his prey.

"You ruined my shirt. I'm gonna have to have this dry-cleaned, and you're gonna pay for it."

He tugged at his shirt again, which was one of his work shirts that had seen better days. Clearly not a garment that required dry-cleaning.

"Are you serious?" the little fucker asked.

"Yeah, I'm fucking serious." Eddie held out his hand. "Ten bucks oughta cover it."

"What's going on here?"

The jock had arrived. Perfect.

"What's going on is your clumsy friend dumped beer all over my shirt."

"Looked to me like you ran into him," the jock said.

Eddie sneered at him.

"Is that so?"

Chris was still pawing at him, trying to reason with him.

"Hey, Eddie, let it go, man. It's just a little beer. No big deal. Let's go play horseshoes, like you said. Come on."

Such a puss. Probably had never even been in a fight before. Well, Eddie would help him with that.

The art school wimp made a move to go around him. Eddie sidestepped and got in his face.

"Are you gonna give me the money, or what?"

"Fuck you," the wimp said, trying to get around him again.

Eddie reached out and knocked the drinks from the guy's hands, sending them flying up in the air. He watched the amber arc of beer spew from one of the bottles and land on a woman seated at the bar. She made a squawking sound that reminded Eddie of a dying chicken. Her husband's stool screeched as he jumped to his feet.

And then everything was happening at once. The wimp was saying, "What the hell?" And the chicken lady's husband was bellowing, "You spilled beer all over my wife!" And the jock was saying, "Not cool, man!"

It had begun. Eddie loved this part, where each millisecond bled into the next, so that when he thought back on it later, he had trouble separating the individual events.

He quickly analyzed the threat level of each man before him. The jock was the biggest, but the chicken lady's husband was the closest. Chicken cuck first, then.

Eddie gave him a dismissive look.

"Fuck off."

The man's face tensed as if he'd been slapped.

"What? What the fuck did you say to me?"

He got right in Eddie's face. It was perfect.

Let's do this, then.

Eddie hit him with a blinding right hook. There was a cracking sound as his knuckles connected with the man's jaw.

The chicken lady screamed as he went down.

Before anyone could process what had just happened, he gave the wimp a good push, which sent him stumbling backward into his friend. Eddie watched their faces, delighted at how shocked they looked. Like, *Oh, how could this be happening to me?*

The jock recovered the fastest and came straight at Eddie. He was ready.

Eddie cocked his fist and bounced on the balls of his feet like a prizefighter. He was smiling so wide he felt like the flesh at the corners of his mouth might tear.

He waited for the jock to get close, pivoting to keep a good angle.

Eddie was about to let loose when something clamped onto his wrist. Wrenched it to the side.

He spun around. Some fat fuck in scrubs had grabbed him from behind. Where had he even come from? And did he know these guys? He'd only seen four of them at the table — two guys and two girls. How did this guy figure into it?

Eddie decided it didn't matter. If this guy wanted a piece, too? So be it.

He tugged himself free from the guy's grip and readjusted his stance. Eddie stepped into the punch.

But the guy was way lighter on his feet than he looked. In one swift movement, he'd dodged Eddie's swing, slipped around behind him, grabbed him by the scruff of the neck, and hurled him down.

Before Eddie had even realized what was happening, he was face down with the guy's fingers still digging into the flesh at the back of his neck, pinning him to the floor with one hand.

This wasn't how it was supposed to go. Some meddling bystander wasn't supposed to know fucking ninja moves. It was fucking bullshit.

Eddie struggled.

"Get off me!"

He felt the fingers tighten.

"Are you going to behave?"

"Fuck you," Eddie said, spittle flying from his lips.

He squirmed some more, but the guy had him good.

"You're going to stay down there until you promise to behave."

A feeling of utter frustration welled in Eddie's chest. He realized he was on the brink of tears.

"This is bullshit. Get the fuck off me!"

"I ask again: Are you going to behave?" The man's words were slow and measured, like Eddie was a child or some kind of idiot.

Eddie nodded and hated himself for it. But what choice did he have? The oafy motherfucker clearly wasn't going to let up until he did.

"When I let go, you're going to get to your feet and leave."

Eddie sniffled, barely holding it back now. He nodded again.

"Say it."

When Eddie didn't speak, the oaf gave him a little shake.

"Say it."

"I'll fucking leave, OK?" Eddie's voice cracked, and he loathed what a little bitch he sounded like. "Now lemme go."

The fingers loosened and came away. Eddie scrambled to his feet and fled before he started to cry in earnest.

Jesus, he was pathetic.

He hadn't even had the guts to look the guy who'd bested him in the eye.

Fucking pathetic.

CHAPTER 37

Detective Stinson crunched over the gravel driveway with two paper cups in her hands. She drew up on the area where light pooled around the mouth of the garage door. Watched the swarm of insects trying to hurl themselves into the gleaming orb of the floodlight above.

Detective Taft and a pair of techs stood there, just shy of the structure. Heads bobbing. Hands gyrating.

The scene looked oddly sparse. Just a few techs and detectives walking the grounds. But it made sense, given the circumstances.

Almost all of the uniformed officers had moved on, giving chase to the stolen Mustang. The last of the flashers was already trailing away by the time Taft had ripped into the driveway. And then, almost as soon as they'd stepped from Taft's vehicle, the paramedics had whisked Jimmy Maddox away to the hospital.

Jimmy and Scarlet were here. Both of them. Right here. Just minutes ago.

She clenched her jaw. They'd barely missed them.

But no. No. We got one, she reminded herself.

Jimmy was in custody, albeit on the way to the hospital. Somehow that didn't seem real yet.

She swallowed. Told herself that truth again. Tried to force it to sink in.

We got him. We got Jimmy.

A bolt of triumph flared inside of her and waned almost as quickly. The satisfaction wouldn't stick. Something still felt off. Wrong. Like a tag sticking up from a t-shirt collar, grating at the back of her neck.

She pondered that for a few paces, her mind gnawing at the edges of the feeling. Maybe it was just the fact that one of them was still out there. That it wasn't over.

One down, one to go.

When she neared the garage, Stinson extended her left arm, the paper cup jutting toward her partner. He took the coffee and sipped.

"Starbucks," Taft said, his eyebrows jumping a couple times. "A frickin' latte, huh? Tonight must be some kind of special occasion. These babies cost about thirty bucks a pop or something like that, no? I can't even afford the down payment on a coffee like this."

"I don't know. One of the techs brought a couple drink carriers full and offered, so I grabbed."

Taft took a long sip and said, "Ahhh. Tastes better knowing it was free."

Stinson shrugged.

"Not for the tech."

"Well… tastes better knowing it was expensive then, maybe. I don't know. Good as hell is all I know." He took another drink. "Don't know if you heard the latest update on Officer Wilton, but word is he made it out of surgery. They got him in a medically induced coma for now, and he's far from out of the woods yet. But so far, so good. He has you to thank for that."

Stinson nodded once. Thanks was the last thing she was concerned with. She just hoped the guy pulled through. It was hard to believe all of that had happened something like an hour ago or more now. The chopper swooping overhead, loading up Officer Wilton, and jutting back into the sky.

Her eyes drifted past her partner to the tech beyond him.

A small-framed woman, older. Stinson recognized her, but it took a second for the name to pop to mind. Hernandez. Sue Hernandez. That was it.

CSI Hernandez faced the gaping garage door with her head angled down, eyes pricking into the ground a few feet in front of her, slow-blinking like an intelligent cat. Stinson followed her gaze.

The pool of blood looked black in the half-light. It sheened there, an inky island, shinier than all the matte concrete surrounding it.

That's his blood, she told herself. *Jimmy's blood.*

And she sat with that idea a few seconds. Let the weight of it settle.

"Dude lost a lot of blood," Taft said over her shoulder. "Wonder if he'll make it."

Now they both went still. Staring. That continent of Jimmy's hemoglobin holding their eyes steady.

Stinson felt that vague discomfort rise in her again, some creeping sense that something about all of this was wrong, that something in the numbers didn't quite add up. She tried to walk herself through it.

Jimmy and Scarlet come blowing into town. They stick up the Citgo in Peachtree. Come out of there with something like $635.

They end up taking the clerk from the scene. Maybe their intent is harmless. Maybe not. But he has a heart attack on 'em.

They panic. Dump the corpse outside a motel.

She sucked in a big breath and let it out slowly. The thoughts kept hurtling on.

That's all straightforward enough, I guess.

But sometime the next day, maybe early afternoon, Elmer Ferguson discovers he's had guests sleeping in his barn. Jimmy and Scarlet.

The couple flees into the woods, and the farmer gives chase. Releases the hounds.

And that's where the picture gets murky. That's where there's a piece missing.

Because somehow, someway, Ferguson and his dogs end up full of buckshot. It seems like…

Stinson's eyes slid over the empty spot where the Mustang should be. Then they drifted back to the puddle of blood.

It seems like…

"Someone else is involved," she muttered out loud.

Taft lifted his head.

"What?"

Stinson found herself slightly embarrassed to have voiced the half-digested thought, heat touching her cheeks.

"I don't know. Something about the Ferguson murder. The brutality of it. It doesn't fit with the rest of their crimes. I'm thinkin'… I don't know… what if there's someone else involved in all of this?"

"Uhhh, are you forgetting that they ran Officer Wilton down and put him in a coma?" Taft asked.

"Could have been accidental, losing control when they hit the spike strip." She saw the way Taft's eyebrows lifted. "Look, I'm not saying the two of them are saints, but—"

Footfalls chopped out throaty sounds in the gravel behind them before she could say more. Stinson turned back to see Sergeant Booth waddling up the driveway.

"Just got fresh word about Maddox and thought y'all would want to know," he said, eyes bright. "He's in critical condition at Presbyterian. They're getting fluids in him and all. Looks like he's gonna make it. Lucky fuck."

Stinson and Taft looked at each other and then back at Booth.

"Are we happy about that, or no?" Taft asked. "I can never quite tell."

"So long as he's breathing, he can help us fill in some of the details," Stinson said. "I still have a few questions, I guess."

Taft made a show of rolling his eyes.

"I mean… when do you not?"

Stinson ignored him and took a few paces toward the garage, pulling up just shy of the line where the gravel gave way to concrete. Her neck hurt. She kept pawing at it every minute or two, fingers kneading at the tight strands of muscle.

Taft fiddled with his radio somewhere behind her, and after a second she could hear the rapid-fire chatter of the ongoing chase. Voices hissing and spitting, the speaker crackling with the energy of it.

Stinson tuned it all out. Too tired. Let the unis run the

Mustang down.

"I guess they got a team down from Newaygo County now," Taft said. "Assisting on the hunt for Scarlet, I mean."

Stinson looked back at him just as he turned the radio down to a whisper.

"Yeah, I heard something about that," she said. "I kinda figured it was our cue to bow out. We did what we could as far as the chase, right? A couple of suits."

Taft half-shrugged and then nodded.

"Right. Let the pros do their thing. Now the raging manhunt will carry on without us. Hell, we're more useful piecing the story together anyway. On that front, I kinda figure our next move is paying ol' Jimmy Maddox a visit bright and early tomorrow morning. Figure there's a decent shot he'll be out of the ICU by then."

At the mere thought of sleep, Stinson felt some of the tension drain from her neck.

"So we're actually getting some sleep tonight after all, huh?"

Taft smiled.

"Yeah. Why not?"

They plodded back over to the driveway to where Taft's SUV was parked.

"Wanna get a bite to eat on the way back?" Taft asked. "I know a place that deep fries everything in hydrogenated grease, just the way you like it."

CHAPTER 38

Ellie and Courtney were in the bathroom when the fight started, emerging at the exact moment the redneck-looking guy threw the drinks Wes was holding in the air.

The next several seconds were a blur. There was a lot of shouting. The male half of the arguing couple from the beach was suddenly in the mix. And then just as quickly, he was crumpling to the floor.

Wes and John lurched backward at around the same time the female half of the arguing couple screamed her husband's name, though to Ellie, it sounded less like she was concerned and more like she was admonishing him for getting hit in the face.

And then a man in hospital scrubs had the redneck face down on the floor, and that was it. The fight was over almost as soon as it had begun.

The man in scrubs bent and said something to the redneck in a voice too low for her to hear. When the nurse finally released his grip, the redneck got to his feet and made a beeline for the door.

"That was your last strike, Eddie," the bartender hollered at his back. "I don't want to see you in here again."

The bartender shook his head, looking disgusted.

"Piece of trash." His eyes landed on the man in scrubs. "Thanks for taking him down, Pete. Consider tonight's bill taken care of."

"Actually…" another voice broke in. It was the guy who'd been punched in the face. "I'd like to pay for his meal, if I could."

Pete looked sheepish.

"That's really not necessary."

His voice was quieter than Ellie would have guessed.

"Of course it is," the husband said. "In fact, I'd like to buy all of these folks a round so we can toast to you."

Now Pete looked really embarrassed, but John jumped in and started making introductions, and soon they had all gathered around the bar for shots of Captain Morgan.

The husband and wife were Dan and Tanya, from Missoula, Montana.

John nudged Pete and leaned in conspiratorially.

"So where'd you learn moves like that? You do aikido or something?"

Pete was more relaxed now, post-rum. He chuckled and shook his head.

"Oh, nothing like that. I work in a nursing home on the med-psych unit. Lot of residents with Alzheimer's and dementia. And sometimes they have… outbursts, I guess you could call them. We have to be able to deescalate the situation in a way that keeps us and them safe."

"Well whatever it was, it was baller as hell."

"Yeah, you laid his ass out flat," Dan said. "Have to admit, though… I'm a little disappointed. I woulda loved a chance to clean his clock."

Tanya rolled her eyes.

"From the floor?"

"Hey, the guy sucker punched me," Dan said. "And even then, I was back on my feet in two seconds. Never let it be said that I can't take a punch."

Ellie glanced over at Courtney and gave her a look.

Here they go again.

Courtney smiled and reached out to place her hand on top of Tanya's wrist.

"I just want to say, I think it was pretty romantic the way your husband stood up for you."

Tanya blinked. Her eyes slid over to Dan, and she studied his face like she was seeing him for the first time.

"Yeah… you're right."

She nuzzled into her husband's neck.

Courtney caught Ellie's eye and winked.

"Hey wait," John said, pointing at Pete. "You said you work at a nursing home? The one just down the road here?"

"That's the one."

"You know they found a dead body over there this morning? Down in that ravine?"

Pete nodded.

"I actually spoke to one of the detectives. They thought our residents might have witnessed something."

"Did they?"

"Unfortunately, no."

Ellie noticed that Dan and Tanya were now making out. Dan was pawing the front of his wife's blouse. Ellie's nose wrinkled, and she looked away. She thought she might prefer it when they were fighting, if she was being honest.

Tanya's head suddenly snapped up, and Ellie was just drunk enough to worry that she might have spoken her thoughts out loud without realizing it. But Tanya grabbed her husband's face.

"Baby! It's our song!"

"Huh?"

"On the jukebox! It's playing our song." She got to her feet and pulled him with her. "Come on. We have to dance!"

Ellie watched Tanya elbow through the crowd to get closer to the jukebox, her husband in tow.

"I'm pretty sure this is the longest we've ever seen them go without bickering," she pointed out. "And I think it's all because of Courtney saying it was romantic when Dan got punched in the face. I don't know what kind of sorcery that was, but cheers to you."

Pete had lapsed into a silence that had lasted several minutes, but he suddenly sat up straighter and looked around.

"Hey! You guys want to see something cool?"

"What is it?" Courtney asked.

Pete grinned.

"It'll be better if it's a surprise."

"A man who knows how to cultivate a bit of mystery," John said, patting his shoulder. "Count us in."

CHAPTER 39

Scarlet plunges into the dark. Pedal pressed to the floorboard. The Mustang an angry beast at her command.

She looks through the windshield at a road all smeared with her tears. Everything reduced to a soft focus. Soggy and indistinct. Crystals pirouette where the light touches her wet eyelashes.

The idea that she's abandoned Jimmy hits her in waves. New agony crashing over her every few minutes, somehow worse than before.

His absence is made visceral in this moment. Something vital ripped out. A gaping hole left in its place.

An empty heart left in her chest. Still beating, but what for?

The duffel bag in the seat next to her only amplifies the feeling. Money. Money she doesn't even want. Money trying to replace something that really matters, the *only* thing that matters.

She wants to roll down the window and heave the black canvas bulk out. Let the duffel bag soar into the ditch.

Throw everything away.

Instead she lifts herself an inch or two out of the bucket seat. Strains to put all of her weight onto the accelerator. It jams into the floor, but she still presses harder, harder. Shakes with the effort.

The speedometer quivers. Pushes past 90. 100. 110. Finally it hovers just shy of 120.

The headlights bore a tunnel into the dark, and the Mustang hurtles through it. Impossible speed. Black branches blur past. The road signs never quite come into focus.

The whole world muddies around her as the speed peaks. A clouded thing, dark and without meaning.

The sense of forward momentum, of velocity, is

exhilarating. Seems to give purpose to the meaningless smudges of the world outside.

Me.

What I want.

That's what is real. It's all that's real.

The rest is nothing. An abstract painting. Oil-based blotches and whorls.

I pass through it. I stalk what I desire.

And when the time comes, I don't hesitate.

I leap for the throat.

She pictures Jimmy again lying on the concrete floor of the carriage house. His t-shirt pocked with pellet holes. His insides leaking out of him. That ashen complexion settling over his features.

And she sobs again. Harder than before. Whole body shaking.

He's still there now, probably. Lying on the cold concrete. Body heat draining rapidly. Sucked into the cement along with his blood.

The whimpers squeeze out of her. Involuntary. Quaking her chest. Squeaking and almost crunching in her throat, in her sinuses.

Heat. Fever.

A feeling like scalding fluid flushing her face, filling her cheeks. Bloated. Water-logged.

She can't stop now. Can't clamp it down. No control.

The awful sounds blubber out. And her red face twists up. Skin all bunched into snarls.

Powerless.

Nothing.

And the pain bursts in bright motes behind her eyes. Detonations of misery, grief, despair.

A crippling, lonely feeling. Sweat crawling down her back.

Nothing left.

Nothing.

The Mustang lurches all at once. Slides out from under her

command.

Skidding. Careening.

Now she jams the brake instead. Muscles it to the floor. Tires shrieking.

The car fights her. Slowing some but thrashing. Unbridled.

The back end of the car drifts forward. Pitches the vehicle into a sideways skid.

She blinks. Clears her eyes. Tries to make sense of that dark blur throbbing at the windows.

Empty space.

Nothing that makes sense.

A voice speaks in her head. Jimmy's voice.

"Gotta steer into the skid."

Steer into the skid.

Again, she stares into the pulsing blackness out the windows. All those rushing blots. None of it means anything to her.

Steer into it. What the fuck does that mean?

And then the car straightens out some, and she can see it.

A dark bulk. A tree trunk as fat as a sumo wrestler lunging for the front end.

She jerks the wheel. Into the skid or not, she doesn't know.

The Mustang spins. Bending. Coiling. Pressing her against the door.

The seatbelt slices a diagonal line into her chest, digs into her hip. Sharp as razor wire.

Pressure.

Light and dark flitting at the windows.

Confusion.

The darkness swirls around the car. A vortex opening, trying to suck her into the black nothing.

Her eyes flit and swivel. Try to make sense of anything in that spiral of black outside.

And all at once the squawk of the tires cuts out. That pressure releases her from the door.

The car jerks to a hard stop. Final.

The peace blooms in an instant. Just the hum of the idling engine. A soft sound.

Nothing moves. Nothing breathes.

The stillness aches in her. Crawling on her skin. The inertia somehow overwhelming.

She shudders. Shoulders convulsing. Tries to shake that awful motionlessness off her. Tries to make it stop.

The tingling roils to a peak on her neck, on her arms, every follicle pricking up, and then it starts to die back.

She sucks in a breath. Looks around. Surprised to see the world a solid thing around her, shapes and contours that make sense.

Rural Florida. Some country road cutting through mucky-looking woods.

The front end of the car straddles the shoulder. Aims the headlights off into the trees. She's somehow kept it on the road.

She breathes. Stares into the empty space, into the nothing between the trunks and branches. Concentrates only on her breath.

And slowly her gaze sinks lower, lower. It scans the shadows beneath the flat plane of the dash. Focuses on some knobs and buttons there. The digital face of the stereo gone dark.

She's been staring for several seconds when she realizes that what she's looking at is not a car stereo. It's too complicated for that.

A full dial pad like a phone occupies the right half of the unit. Multiple knobs flank the sides. The screen seems larger than any she's seen on a stereo.

She turns up the volume knob and a sharp pop emits over the speakers. Then the screen flips on and a few blue LEDs around the unit brighten all at once.

Rows of colorful text arrive on the screen. Red. Orange. Yellow. She reads the top.

"Durango County Sheriff's Department."

And then the police chatter blooms out of the speakers.

Deep cop voices that sound tiny with the volume so low. She turns it up.

A police scanner.

She wonders, for a second, if the Mustang's owner might be one of those volunteer types. Listening in on the scanner and trying to rush to crime scenes. But then she gets swept up in the tangle of voices.

"Car 6. The suspect fled south on Mangrove Road in a Blue 2022 Ford Mustang. I repeat. Blue 2022 Ford Mustang. Florida license plate OU945. Last seen heading south on Mangrove Road. Near the Everly intersection."

"Car 2. Roger that. I'm in pursuit."

"Car 9. Heading for Mangrove Road now."

"Car 12. Yep yep. I'm on my way there, too. Got the dog pack after her now. Let's run her down, boys."

They're coming for me. Right now.

And I'm just sitting here.

She listens for sirens blaring somewhere beyond the windows but hears nothing as yet. Maybe going 120 for a bit has given her a chance.

A new voice speaks on the radio, sharper than the rest.

"Dispatch to car 6. Can you confirm that the other suspect is in custody now?"

"Car 6. Affirmative. Our male suspect is resting up at Presbyterian Hospital now. He's gut shot, but he got through surgery and they think he'll live."

"Car 12. One down one to go. And hey, the docs think he'll make it, but you never know. Could be we'll get lucky."

But Scarlet isn't listening to the voices anymore. She's thinking.

She slowly releases her foot from the brake. Guides the car back onto the road and brings the speed back up, this time not letting it get over 90 mph.

She has a plan.

CHAPTER 40

The bar was so packed that Ellie and the rest had to follow Pete in single file as they made their way outside. On the way, they passed Dan and Tanya, who were practically dry humping on the dance floor now.

Pete led them through a back door that opened onto the beach. The surf crashed gently into the sand, muffling the faint jukebox sounds still coming from the bar behind them.

They proceeded down the shore, parallel with the water, past the parking lot and the lifeguard hut. Pete swung his head from side to side, sometimes turning around to watch behind them, as if he was looking for something.

With the moon shrouded behind a bank of clouds, it grew darker and darker the farther they got from the bar, and the music from the Tiki Hut dwindled until Ellie could barely make it out over the sound of the waves.

Eventually it was so dark that Ellie could only see where she was going based on the stark black silhouettes of the palm trees against the not-quite-black sky.

What cool thing were they possibly going to see out here in the pitch blackness?

The paranoid part of her brain wondered if Pete was luring them out here for some nefarious purpose. She'd heard enough stories about tourists being robbed. But that wouldn't make sense, would it? He was vastly outnumbered. And they knew his name, where he worked.

The farther they walked, though, the more Ellie began to doubt his intentions. This was weird, right? And what did they really know about this guy?

Her eyes had adjusted enough now that she could make out the faint outlines of her companions around her, and she closed in on Wes. She wanted to ask if he was getting weirded out, too. But then she realized Pete had stopped ahead of them.

They formed a loose huddle, and Pete lifted his hand, one finger aimed at the sky.

"There," he said.

Ellie looked up and sensed the others around her doing the same. She waited. Nothing happened.

She opened her mouth to say, "What exactly are we looking at?"

Then she saw it.

A bright slash of white streaking through the velvety blackness. A shooting star.

"Oh!" Courtney squealed. "I saw it!"

"It's the Lyrids meteor shower," Pete said. "Always peaks this time of year. The April Lyrids have the distinction of being the longest running meteor shower on record, with the first known observance in 687 BC."

"Damn," John said, with real awe in his voice.

They all stood there, their heads tilted back, whispering excitedly whenever they spotted the next glowing arc in the sky.

"There's another one!"

"That time there were two. Did you see?"

They'd been watching for several minutes when Ellie remembered you were supposed to make a wish when you saw a shooting star.

What should I wish for?

Wes was standing next to her, and his elbow brushed against her arm. She smirked to herself and shook her head.

Don't be stupid.

"Hey," Courtney said, spinning around. "Where'd he go?"

"Who?"

"Pete. He's not here."

Ellie cast her eyes about and realized Courtney was right. It was just the four of them standing there in a circle. Pete was gone.

She squinted into the hulking forms of the nearby palm trees but saw no one. It was like the guy had just disappeared.

"That's weird, right?" Courtney said. "Like to not even say goodbye? And how did we not hear him walk away?"

"Because maybe he *didn't* walk away," John said.

"What?"

"Because he was—" John lurched forward and grabbed Courtney. "—a ghost!"

"Cut it out."

Courtney swatted at him, though she was clearly amused.

"I don't know," Ellie said. "John has a point. We did go disturb a bunch of graves today."

"Shut up," Courtney said, turning annoyed. "You said you didn't believe in 'mumbo jumbo.'"

Wes tapped his chin thoughtfully.

"You know… I just realized we completely forgot to cast a circle of protection. Any spirits we encountered there could have just followed us right out."

"You guys are *not funny,* and also, I hate you," Courtney said, spinning on her heel and marching back toward the bar.

John jogged to catch up with her, scooping her up and tossing her over his shoulder. She shrieked with delight.

Ellie took a step toward them, intending to follow, when Wes stopped her with a hand on her elbow.

"It's a really nice night. Wanna take a walk down the beach?"

The salty ocean breeze sent Ellie's hair fluttering around her face.

"Just us?"

The moon had emerged from the clouds, and she could make out more of her surroundings now. She tried to study his face, to see what might be read there, but she could only really see the chiseled line of his jaw. Shadows cloaked the rest.

He shrugged.

"Why not?"

Ellie swallowed and glanced back at the ever-shrinking silhouettes of John and Courtney.

"OK, then. Let's take a walk."

CHAPTER 41

Ellie rolled her head from one side to the other as she and Wes paced toward the water. Keeping her face pointed up at the sky while they watched the meteors had left the muscles in her neck sore.

Her feet sank into the sand, ankle-deep sometimes, like the beach was trying to swallow her up. It made her gait a little wobbly.

She was, perhaps, a bit tipsier than she'd realized. She doubted any of them were sober enough to drive at this point.

It would be a quick Uber back to the motel, at least. Or they could probably even walk, if they wanted to.

Wispy clouds drifted past every minute or two, partially obscuring the moonlight. The fresh dark swelled the shadows up into something bigger, and then the moon and stars chased them away again.

Wes came to a stop a few feet shy of the water's edge, and Ellie stopped as well.

They stood. Quiet.

The water heaved itself up onto the shore. Slapping and rolling and sizzling. She could only vaguely sense the foamy surge, the wet movement of it almost unreal. But the sound was sharp, loud, real in her ears, the churning white noise drowning most everything else out.

She looked over at Wes. He stared out over the horizon where the black sea reached out for a blacker sky, reached out for eternity. There was a faint crinkle between his eyes, as if he were concentrating on something.

Ellie chewed her lip. Waited for him to turn his head. But his face remained pointed toward the water.

She swallowed. Loud. A nervous cartoon sound that embarrassed her beyond reason. Heat plumed in her cheeks.

"What?" Wes asked.

"Huh?"

"Did you say something?"

"No, I—" She stopped herself just shy of explaining that she'd swallowed too loud. "No."

"Oh."

They fell quiet again. Let the silence stretch out to fill the empty space.

Her heart sank.

When he'd first asked her to take a walk, she'd told herself not to assume. Not to get her hopes up. And yet…

She swiveled her head back toward the colorful lights decorating the bar in the distance and tried to will away her disappointment. No matter how things went with Wes, she somehow ended up feeling like a fool. Over and over again, and she was doing it to herself. Torturing herself.

God, what was she even doing out here?

The sound of the surf subtly changed pitch then. Louder. Deeper.

A wave slammed into Ellie's legs, the icy water gushing up and over her feet.

She let out a surprised yelp, heard Wes do the same. They both scrambled backward, fleeing for dry land, laughing as they did.

Ellie attempted a graceful leap over the last bit of the retreating wave. And then she pitched a little too far to one side, felt the ball of her foot punch the loose, wet sand at an awkward angle.

Her arms windmilled in the air, trying to right herself. But it was no use.

She was going down.

The night seemed to throb around her. The dark. The stars. Everything moving, bending, heaving.

Falling.

And then Wes's hands were on her waist. His arms circling her. Holding her. Lifting her back up.

They stayed still like that for a second. An accidental embrace pulling them chest-to-chest. She could feel Wes's heartbeat thrumming against her ribcage.

Ellie had a sudden flash of the janitor's closet again. The press of his body against hers. The smell of him. The way his breath had fluttered on her cheek.

To hell with it, she thought.

She kissed him.

CHAPTER 42

Ellie's brain did backflips and set off fireworks, celebrating her boldness.

I did it! I kissed him!

And then Wes pulled away. Blinked at her.

The look on his face was indecipherable, which instantly fed her self-doubt.

I've made a terrible mistake. I read things completely wrong. He's not into me at all.

Then she realized he was smiling.

"You beat me to it."

She shook her head, not understanding.

"What?"

"I've been trying to work up the nerve to do that all night. But you beat me to it."

"Oh," Ellie said, her face flushing with relief. "Well in that case, I triple-dog dare you to kiss me."

Wes let out a breathy laugh.

"Everyone knows you can't turn down a triple-dog dare."

He reached for her again, his grip tightening on her waist, pulling her closer as their lips met.

And this time, she resisted the urge to think too much in words and instead anchored herself in what she was feeling. Cataloging the sensations.

The softness of his lips against hers.

The taste of him. Like a boozy Bomb Pop.

The heat coming off his body where his torso pressed against hers.

Her hand slid over the flat plane of his chest. Rested on the coiled ball of his shoulder.

Wes moved his head lower to kiss her neck, his breath hot against her skin.

She opened her eyes, and the night thrummed around her again. Alive now in a new way. The moon and stars and sea all pumping in time with her heart.

The moonlight cast luminous bars through those wispy clouds. Slanted them over the beach.

And the stars poked through most of the darkness hung up above. A whole mess of glitter hovering up there. Blazing.

Ellie had forgotten what this felt like. Or had it not been like this before? The magnetic pull between her body and Wes's felt new.

She obeyed the instinct. Pressed herself to him. Felt the rock-hard length of him pressing against her groin. She grasped his hair and pulled his mouth back to hers, kissing him long and deep.

No, this was definitely new. She couldn't remember ever feeling this level of desire. She *wanted* him.

His hands crept from her waist and down to the hem of her shorts. He slid one hand up her thigh, and a pleasant shiver ran over her skin.

His fingers reached the cleft between Ellie's legs. She took a step back.

"Sorry," Wes said, his voice slightly hoarse. "Was that too far?"

She shook her head. It wasn't far enough. Her whole body was thrumming with desire. Pulsing.

But they were too exposed here. Too out in the open.

"Come on."

She took his hand and guided him away from the water.

Without that wan light shimmering off the top of the sea, the way grew darker with each choppy step. She gazed out across the beach, considered the tiny lights puncturing the darkness over the tiki bar.

Her car was there, parked right where the asphalt met the sand, but that was too close to other people. It wouldn't do. They needed privacy.

And then out of the darkness, the hard lines of the lifeguard hut took shape ahead, and Ellie smiled.

It was perfect.

"Here," she said, pulling Wes closer to the structure, then releasing his hand to climb up the small ladder to the platform above.

She scrambled onto the deck on all fours. She wondered if she should worry about splinters, but the boards felt worn smooth with age.

A second later, Wes clambered up beside her. They wasted no time.

Their lips found each other once more. Hungrier now. Wanting.

Heat surged outward from Ellie's core. Prickling in her cheeks.

He ran a thumb over her collarbone, and she sighed with pleasure. Breath feathery in her throat. Chest fluttering.

She felt no doubt now. Wanting Wes was the only thing she knew, the only thing that mattered.

His hat went first, then he leaned back and peeled his shirt off. Flung both over the side of the platform and out onto the sand. The arc of the t-shirt looked like a swooping gull.

Ellie giggled and followed suit. Shedding her own shirt and tossing it away.

Then Wes shrugged and started fumbling with his belt.

He gave her his phone to secure in her purse, and then shucked his shorts down over his knees and ankles. Those too went over the side.

Ellie wriggled out of the rest of her clothes, knocking her purse overboard in the process.

The bag flopped down into the sand with a soft thud.

"Oops," she said, and they both laughed.

They wouldn't be laughing if their phones were broken, but she supposed they'd worry about that later.

She peeked through a gap in the boards as she tossed her clothes over. Watched the dark flittering of the fabric as her shorts plummeted down to the earth.

She shivered. Naked. The cold breath of the ocean breeze whispering over moist flesh.

She'd never done anything like this before. Not with someone she'd just met.

But it felt right. It made sense. It made more sense than anything.

And it didn't need words to rationalize, justify, or explain.

Ellie blinked and stared into the sky. The roof blocked out one square of the heavens, but the stars gleamed everywhere else.

She reached for Wes in the dark. Ran her fingers over his stomach and onto his chest, riveted musculature silky against her fingers.

He pulled her close, and the feel of his bare skin against hers was electric.

And she lost herself in the sensations. Drawn into the pleasure.

His lips on her neck. His hands on her breasts.

That heat built in her again. Intensifying. Compounding.

It escalated quickly. Stages of foreplay flying past. She was ready and willing. She didn't want to wait any longer.

And then he stopped all at once. Rolled away from her and froze there.

"What is it?" she asked, worried she'd done something wrong.

When he spoke, it was a low rumble, almost under his breath.

"I think I heard something."

They held rigid.

Listening.

The wind blew in off the water, hissed and whistled over the top of the sand, moaned against the wood of the lifeguard tower.

Ellie's mind snapped to Duke, the beach bum with the Elvis hairdo. He'd asked whether Courtney had done any modeling, but maybe he'd settle for stalking and spying on her and Wes instead.

Or what about that Pete guy? Why had he brought them all the way out here and then disappeared like that?

But if there was anyone out there, Ellie couldn't hear them.

Without Wes's body heat reflecting back at her, the cold nipped at her naked skin. Sent goosebumps rippling over her flesh.

"Anything?" Ellie asked, keeping her voice small.

The quiet stretched out a few more seconds.

"I don't know," Wes said finally. "I thought I heard a—"

And then something thumped in the sand just beneath them. Something heavy.

"Shit," Wes said through gritted teeth. "I bet they're trying to steal our stuff. Hang on."

He pulled away from her. Moved into a strip of moonlight just along the wall of the hut. All the contours and divots of him rippled in the silvery glow.

Then he braced his hand on top of the railing that ran around the platform. Flung himself up and over. His erection bounced once, and then he disappeared over the side.

CHAPTER 43

Stinson jerked herself awake in the darkness. Shoulders quaking. Body folding itself into an upright position involuntarily.

A big breath scraped into her throat as she moved. Dry like flaps of fine grit sandpaper sliding around in her chest cavity.

Then her eyes snapped open. Swiveled like ping pong balls in her head. Scanning everything.

But the room that gaped back at her was familiar, even in the dark. The dormant ceiling fan. The telltale NordicTrack with garments draped over it like a coat rack.

It was only her bedroom.

She took a couple deep breaths. Smeared a hand over the left side of her face, fingers icy from the adrenaline rush. Then she let her head plop back down onto the pillow.

Her back felt clammy against the sheets. It took her a second to realize the bed was moist.

Night sweats.

She frowned at the thought.

That wasn't normal. A nightmare? Some kind of PTSD-like response? The job didn't get under Stinson's skin like it might for others. Even on nights when she'd worked grisly murder-suicides, she slept like a baby.

So what's different this time?

The alarm clock blazed 12:49 in blood red, digits hovering above the nightstand. So she hadn't been down long. Maybe an hour. That explained the gritty feeling like sand in her eyes.

She stared up at the dark ceiling, and her mind started working the puzzle of the afternoon's events once more, shifting the pieces against each other. Jimmy and Scarlet. The chase and the path of destruction left behind.

It *almost* all fit the obvious narrative — the crime spree

passing through town. But something had been off from early on, a puzzle piece that just wouldn't fit with the rest.

Elmer Ferguson and his dogs.

Stinson pictured the bodies — one human and three animals — laid out a few hundred yards from the barn where Jimmy and Scarlet had spent the night. A series of shotgun blasts had taken them down. Probably a pump-action to get that many shots off before the dogs had been able to react.

So where was the gun? No one had seen any sign of a shotgun on Jimmy or Scarlet before or after the incident. Not on any of the surveillance footage going all the way back up the coast and not during any part of the local chase.

Something still itched at the base of the detective's brain. A prickle needling her like a splinter.

She closed her eyes and let her mind go still. The space inside her reached out into the dark, shadowy tendrils stretching. Seeking.

Video clips flickered inside her skull. Remembered news footage projected there in bursts of light.

Jimmy pulling a gun on a gas station clerk.

Their vehicle du jour tearing out of another parking lot.

Smirking mugshots pinned to the corner of the screen.

Endless news anchors talking about them with glowing awe, all affecting a similar tone, trying to capture some sense of infamy, of grit, the whole modern-day Bonnie and Clyde thing.

But what if that isn't the full story. What if… what if it's not quite how it seems?

The idea was close now. Right there. Somehow just beyond her reach.

She resisted the urge to let frustration take her. Instead she kept her mind blank, kept her inner world placid.

After a few breaths, the stillness rose up again. And the space inside grew bigger once more. A sprawling vortex reaching out for the heavens, out into the endless deep.

What if Jimmy and Scarlet aren't just running for the thrill of it?

What if they're running from something? Or someone? Not just the police, either. Someone who is a threat. Someone more dangerous than the both of them. Someone who killed Elmer Ferguson and his dogs.

What if Jimmy and Scarlet are running for their lives?

She swallowed hard as the words settled over her.

Running for their lives.

Yes.

Yes.

That makes sense.

Stinson sat up in bed. She fumbled at the nightstand for her glass of water and drank, long and deep.

Pictures from the scene flashed in her head as the cool liquid glugged home. She tried to retrofit the idea of another person being involved, someone chasing Jimmy and Scarlet, into the images. If she could find some evidence to corroborate the theory. Anything.

She remembered the Charger tilted into the ditch with the driver's side door hanging open. The gravel driveway leading up to the barn. The beaten path out into the woods.

The techs would have logged footprints the best they could. The muddy spot where Ferguson went down? Maybe that would be something.

But that was all she could think of, as far as forensic possibilities. At least for now. Her shoulders sank a little at the realization.

She'd check on the prints tomorrow. She had her doubts there'd be anything to it.

She laid back down and started to drift toward sleep. A lightness coming over her.

And now her mind wandered further back. Earlier.

She imagined that high speed burn toward Ferguson's place. Trees flitting by. Sunlight fluttering through the branches. The dotted yellow line strobing in the middle of the road.

And then her mind made another leap, found the other

missing piece all at once.

And now she was throwing the blanket back. Scrambling to her feet. Hopping from foot to foot as she slid on a pair of pants.

A clean shirt swathed her face and snugged down over her torso, the fabric softener stench clinging to her nostrils. The holster went up and over next.

They'd seen it parked in the weeds not a mile out from Ferguson's farm, way back when all of this started. It hadn't seemed pertinent at the time, given what they knew.

But if there was someone else at the scene, someone following Jimmy and Scarlet, someone who might have killed Elmer Ferguson and his dogs… Well, they had to get out there somehow, didn't they?

As soon as her jacket was on, she swept through the house. The image still burned in her head as she grabbed her keys and moved for the door.

An almost muscular-looking thing tucked in the weeds, in the shadows. Perhaps the key to the whole case.

The white Camaro.

CHAPTER 44

Wes pawed at the sand with both hands like a cat in a litter box. He scrabbled forward on hands and knees. Patting everywhere, everywhere.

But his fingers found only the surface of the beach. Sand pocked with the divots of all those endless footsteps. Miniature dunes and valleys.

The panic blindsided him all at once. Turned the rivulets of sweat on his back into ice in an instant.

They're gone.

Our clothes.

My room key. My wallet. Her purse. Our phones.

All gone.

We're going to have to walk out of here naked.

Something clicked nearby, and his skin contracted. He froze. Listened.

Someone is there.

After a second, he pushed himself up onto his knees. Stayed like that, half-upright, straining to hear over the sound of the surf.

He felt alone in the open. Exposed. Especially in his nakedness.

He licked his lips. Squinted as though it might help him see in the dark.

A voice hissed out a whisper somewhere above him and a few feet to his right.

"Make sure to get my purse."

Electricity jolted through him. He shivered a second.

Ellie.

Just Ellie.

He nodded in the dark. Remembered a second later to answer out loud.

"Purse. I'm on it."

He kept digging around. Something frantic in his movements. Fingers clawing up involuntarily. Jaw clenching and unclenching in rapid bursts.

The sea of sand seemed a vast thing in the dark.

He stopped then. Took a breath.

He wheeled his head back. Used the vague outline of the crisscrossing beams of the tower to reorient himself. He'd veered farther away than he'd thought.

Seeing how far off course he was made him wonder if he was being an idiot. Had he actually heard anything? Or was his drunken mind conjuring something out of nothing?

He'd been *this close* to having honest-to-God "sex on the beach" with an amazing, smoking hot girl, and he'd gotten spooked and panicked.

Dumbass.

A quick U-turn pointed him back toward the foot of the tower, where the clothes should have landed. He swept his hands over the ground. Waxing on and off.

His hands found small, knobby things on top of the sand. Cool and glossy. He knew they were just shells and pebbles, but touching them made him think of a mouthful of teeth spit out here.

Finally, his hands brushed against fabric gone cool. Fingers hooking and catching in one of the pockets. His shorts.

He patted them up and down. Found the bulge representing his wallet.

Holy shit. Yes.

The elation flooded his skull. Tingled on his scalp. Made him feel about three times drunker in an instant.

He kept patting around, the fistful of shorts somewhat in his way now. Wagging back and forth like he was using them as a rag to try to clean the beach.

He stood. Slid the shorts on. Felt a bunch of sand dislodge from his knees as he did. All those grains like tiny shards of glass trying to grind his skin down to something smooth.

He got back down on his hands and knees and continued the search.

He found her top next. Thin material. Kind of silky. A minuscule amount of fabric compared to the heft of his shorts.

For just a second, he considered the notion that he might not find her shorts. Pictured her walking out of here with just a shirt on. Buttocks exposed as she stepped into the lights of the parking lot. Winnie the Pooh style.

He sniffed a laugh. Shoved the shirt down into his pocket. Kept looking.

His own t-shirt came next. A wad of knit fabric, still just a tad moist from his sweat.

He pulled it over his head. Weathered a clammy claustrophobic feeling as the wet material momentarily sheathed his face and blotted out the night.

It felt funny, tight on his shoulders, awkward around the neck. He hoped he hadn't put it on backwards, but he could sort that out later.

Her purse. He needed to find her purse. Both phones were in there.

In his drunken state, he didn't remember what it looked like. He imagined it as a clutch. Small and hard.

His hands fumbled back and forth, sweeping and raking at the sand, feeling only emptiness. Maybe he should ask her what it looked like, not that it'd help much in the dark.

The next clump of fabric he came upon felt grossly damp. His boxer briefs. Heavy with the Florida sog. He shoved them in the opposite cargo pocket and kept going.

Nothing.

Empty.

He slammed a fist into the sand.

He was going to be so screwed if he couldn't find his phone.

He gritted his teeth and turned around again. His fingers raked at the same section of beach a third time, sweeping back and forth, and his knuckles punched into the side of her purse. Knocked it over.

A big breath heaved out of him. The pressure valve in his head venting the frustration that had built up.

Then he managed to hook a hand through the strap on the side.

The outside of it felt glossy, and he couldn't remember what kind of material it was. Leather? Vinyl? Something else?

A quick rifling of the purse's innards revealed her keys and wallet to be intact. Both phones, too. Good.

He pulled his phone out. Then he tried to hook the strap over his shoulder, but it was too small and awkward to be able to continue the search. He huffed again.

He flicked the flashlight on his phone on. Swept it up to the edge of the lifeguard tower.

The circle of illumination shot up the wooden planks of the wall. Steadied there. It pained his eyes.

"Ellie?"

A beat passed before she answered. Then he could see, just barely, her face poking through the gap between the floor and the railing.

"Yeah?"

"Got your purse." The phone's light went shaky as he stepped up onto the second rung of the ladder and held the clutch out to her. "Here."

Her arm was a black snake slithering over the side of the platform. Its mouth clamped down on the strap. Tugged it free from his grasp.

"You got it?" he asked.

"Yeah."

"OK. I'm still looking for your shorts."

The search resumed. The light skimmed over the beach, bouncing slightly as it did a full 360-degree rotation. Nothing there. Nothing but sand and pebbles.

He squinted and circled again. Slower this time.

The beam lanced into the dark. Crept over the ground.

A hump in the sand caught his eye some fifteen or so feet away, and he walked for it. Closer inspection revealed that it was his Spelunking Monkeys hat. He'd almost forgotten about it. John would have been furious if he'd come back without it. He was so proud of the merch.

He reached his hand out for the brim, but just then the wind kicked up and carried the hat down the beach.

"Shit!"

He heard a thump back toward the lifeguard tower. Thought it must be Ellie coming down to help.

"I got it. Stay there, and I'll be right back."

He sprinted after the hat, trying to keep the bouncing flashlight on it. It cartwheeled down the beach like a tumbleweed, staying just out of his reach for some time.

Finally, it rolled to a stop. Wes let out a sigh and snatched it up, planting it securely on his head.

When he turned around, he couldn't believe how far he'd gotten from the lifeguard hut. He jogged back, once again picturing Ellie walking back into the light of civilization bare-assed, and shook his head. Would be kind of hilarious if he couldn't find her shorts. He could offer his boxers, but they were kind of gross. Maybe he could wear the boxers and give her his shorts, but he doubted his belt could even cinch tightly enough to keep them on her.

"Almost lost my hat," he explained as he drew up on the hut. "And you heard how crazy John is about *the merch*. He would have killed me."

When there was no response, he aimed his light up at the platform.

"Ellie?"

It struck him again how quiet it was. Too quiet.

He scrambled up the rungs of the ladder. The beam of light bobbing alongside.

At the top, he thrust the phone forward. Watched the shaft of light vanquish the shadows there. Found what he'd somehow already known he would.

The platform was empty.

CHAPTER 45

With her gaze fixed on the horizon, the dotted line in the middle of the road seemed to be rushing straight at Stinson's Accord. The glowing strips of yellow disappeared as she rushed past, like her car was eating them up.

She tore out into the sticks, hurtling back toward Elmer Ferguson's place. The car felt agile at her touch, fully awake even in the middle of the night. Excited for whatever came next.

That overgrown swamp sprawled in all directions once again, the pools of muck shimmering silver in the moonlight. Twisted things rose out of the bog, plant life cast only in silhouette. It looked like the kind of primordial landscape that would birth monstrous creatures, Stinson thought, grotesque beings rising out of the black gloop.

The road sign glittered green and white when the headlights caught the lettering. Highmore Road.

The detective jerked the wheel to move that way, and the sedan obeyed. She crept down the road, eyes trying to scan the dark places.

The road sloped upward beneath the tires, the grade gently lifting out of the wetlands, and trees thrust up from the ground where the swamp had been. First, it was a scattered mix of stunted trunks and saggy branches, everything gnarled like arthritic fingers. Soon enough, full-blown woods bloomed from the soil, with sprawling fields of low-lying crops interrupting more and more. Stinson didn't recognize any of it, not in the dark, but she knew she must be getting close.

Dark features filled both sides of the road. Tall weeds like spiky hair. Shadowy trees. Strange-looking fields of soybeans that looked almost fluffy in the low light.

Stinson tried to puzzle out something familiar. Eyes shifting to try to take all of it in.

All at once a floodlight beamed into a gap in the foliage, hard lines slicing a neat box out of the weeds, the LED glow slanting down on a ribbon of gravel passing through the opening. The clearing seemed jarring after all that tangled mess of foliage. A manmade thing that didn't belong here.

Stinson slowed her vehicle and examined what she could in the sliver of light. Squinting a second, she could make out the barn in the distance where the light was mounted, the farmhouse off to the right of that.

She knew it, of course. Elmer Ferguson's place. The awareness gave her a little shiver, knowing what had happened here just a few hours prior.

It looked different in the dark. Vacant and a little ghostly.

Anyway, reaching the house meant she'd gone too far. She swung into the driveway to turn around, heard the tires dig into the gravel, saw the bloom of the taillights tinting the road red in the rearview.

Now the sedan slithered back the way it'd come. Slowly. Carefully.

Stinson squared her shoulders toward the driver's side window and watched the dark world slide past in slow motion. Her pulse thumped in her ears, a hollow sound, slow and steady.

A couple minutes later, she found it, or thought she did. Hard to tell from inside the car.

She pulled over. Parked with the tires straddling the shoulder. She left the car running as she climbed out, the Accord's engine a faint hum against the endless chirping of bugs out here.

The humidity swirled around her. A heavy thing. Some remnant of the Florida heat still clinging to it.

Her boots clopped across the asphalt. She swung her flashlight toward the spot.

The weeds were still matted down there. A hollow carved into the green. This was the spot, all right.

But the Camaro was gone.

Gone.

Shit.

She stared into the empty spot a few seconds. Blinking. Some dejected feeling settling in her gut.

Probably not relevant to the case, anyway. At least, the odds would lean that way.

A car parked out in the boonies? Could be anything.

She told herself that a couple times as she trod back across the street, but she couldn't quite believe it.

She climbed back into her car. Felt the humidity sealed away from her as she closed the door.

She tossed the flashlight onto the passenger seat, rested her hands on top of the steering wheel, and took a couple of deep breaths.

She sat in the quiet like that for a while. Her eyes looked out toward the empty road where the headlights had sheared back the darkness, but she didn't really see it.

The stages of grief passed over her quickly enough.

She wasn't sure what she'd been expecting. That the owner of the Camaro, if he or she were even involved in the case, would still be sitting here? That he'd spontaneously confess to killing Ferguson and chasing Jimmy and Scarlet, if either of those things were true?

The dome light clicked out, plunging the interior of the Accord into gloom. She shook her head.

Her hand found the gearshift and pulled. The sedan lurched forward once more, slowly and steadily getting up toward the 55-mph speed limit.

The night seemed empty now. A cold dark nothingness surrounding the car. Empty space reaching out to form the heavens.

And that bright electricity spinning behind Stinson's eyes seemed to fade as rapidly as it'd come. She checked the clock on the dash. Not quite a quarter 'til two. At least she'd get back home in time to get a few hours of sleep.

A fresh stiffness kinked her neck. She stretched and rolled her head from shoulder to shoulder, felt the balled-up muscles flex and quiver.

And she almost missed it.

The headlights glinted off the side — a graze more than anything. The side of her beam caught an angle of glossy enamel and flashed for just a second in the corner of Stinson's eye.

A fraction of a second. But it was enough.

She slammed on the brakes. The Accord screeched and stopped dead on the empty road, those taillights puddling red behind it again, the ruddy glow dusting the mirrors.

She craned her neck all the way to the right. Looked out at the square of land framed by the edges of the passenger side window.

An outbuilding perched on a small hill there. A corrugated steel thing that stood some twenty-five feet high and looked like it might house up to five large tractors. It must be part of the next farm over from Ferguson's.

Exposed dirt lay in front of the roll-up garage door, mashed earth where the grass had been worn down to mangy patches by the traffic. Stinson could kind of make out the cleaner track lines curling toward the field where the tractor tires had gashed two neat rows.

But her eyes didn't follow the trail. They stayed close to the darkest shadows along the side of the building.

There, set at an angle with its nose just about touching the building, was the white Camaro.

CHAPTER 46

Ellie was dazed. In and out.

Her mind cleared in waves. Ripples. Concentric circles billowing outward on a pond's surface.

She found herself plunging into the dark along the beach. Her feet half-staggering, half-dragging through the sand.

One sweaty arm clutched around her ribcage, held her up. Guiding her along.

Not Wes. She knew it wasn't Wes. Someone smaller. Shorter.

And she was naked. Why was she naked?

Then she remembered being up on the lifeguard tower. She and Wes about to… and then he'd heard something.

He'd jumped down, been trying to find their clothes. And that was where things got fuzzy. She was pretty sure she'd fallen at some point. Hit her head.

Cold metal pressed into her back like a sharp knuckle. Even in her confusion, she knew what it was. Remembered the way it had glinted in the moonlight as it was shoved in her face, and the voice told her not to make a sound.

A gun.

The fear entered her bloodstream like an iced coffee. Tingling and prickling all through her.

The panic twittered and popped in her head. The voice inside suddenly urgent.

Do something.

Think.

Keeping her head still, she shifted her gaze all the way to the left. Tried to get a look at the one half-carrying her along out of the corner of her eye.

The silhouette there looked small. Thin and bony. Maybe an inch or two taller than her.

When the shadow spoke, it started making more sense.

"Faster," the girl whispered behind her.

And Ellie was awake now. Lifting her knees.

They walked on in that strange embrace. The gun had moved, now jammed into the side of her neck. And that arm looped around her likewise slid higher, hooked around her at collarbone level.

All four feet shuffled along beneath them, chopping in and out of the sand like the pointy spears of crab legs. Building speed.

They wove through a cluster of palm trees, aimed for the streetlights in the distance. Civilization slowly swelled before them, populating with detail.

Ellie hugged her arms to her chest. Naked and embarrassed even in the dark, embarrassed even with the cold steel of a snub-nosed handgun shoved into her neck. It didn't make sense, but it was so.

Her skin itched. Grainy and sweaty. Sand plastered everywhere. Somehow she knew that the crawling on her flesh would be worse when they stepped into the light, like the bulbs would sting and blister and flay her nude form.

Wes's voice echoed out over the sand, somewhere back there, sounding small.

"Ellie!"

She turned back automatically. The gun pressed harder into her flesh.

"Keep moving."

Wes's voice was tiny. Distant. If he yelled again, it was swallowed by the white noise roar of the wind and sea. That choppy blue churning. Always churning.

They kept to the shadows as they drew closer to the parking lot. Silhouettes flitted in the pale light there. A couple climbing into a sedan, one door and then the other popping closed.

Ellie inhaled, preparing to scream.

The girl with the gun whispered in her ear. Some grit to it.

"Make a noise, and it's all over."

The muzzle prodded harder at her neck for a second, and then it let up. Ellie nodded, wanted her to know she would comply.

She'll let me live if I listen.

Right?

A woman.

A woman with a gun is better than a man with a gun. Less cruel. More empathetic. More reasonable.

Maybe.

The slope of the beach leveled out and tall grass slithered against her calves. Cold and tickling.

Headlights flared over them. A car passed by on the curving road ahead.

And then Ellie saw the silhouette of the vehicle. A cruiser. A cop car with the telltale lightbar jutting out of the top.

Wes.

Wes called the police.

They're already here, already looking for me.

Ellie waited for her captor to react, to slow, to stop. But they trudged on like it was nothing. Barreling straight toward the parking lot and the road beyond.

Ellie held her breath. Sent out a mental message to whoever sat behind the wheel of the cruiser.

I'm here. Right here.

Please.

But the police car zoomed past without slowing. It rounded a bend that catapulted it out of sight. Heading somewhere down the beach.

Ellie felt her middle deflate, her shoulders sag. A big breath emptied her out.

And then reality struck her.

No one is coming to save me.

They plodded on for four more steps. The black road sucked down the volume of the cruiser's engine until it was gone completely.

Her captor's body quivered against her back then, made a

little choked sound. A single gasp chirped out of her and hung in the air. It almost sounded like she was crying.

What the hell?

What if she's insane? Totally unhinged.

The pinpricks of light dotting the black sky grew into larger spheres as they got closer and closer to the parking lot. The collective glow seemed to swell. Advance. Intensify. Beating back the shadows bit by bit.

Finally, they left the sand, stepped over a concrete wheel stop and onto the blacktop. The tar still held some of the heat from the day, and after so long on the sand, the firmness felt wrong against Ellie's feet.

They scurried along the edge of the lot now, mostly keeping cars between themselves and the bar. The gun had moved lower, shoved into the small of Ellie's back now.

Up close, the streetlights turned everything just a little gray. The cars reflected discs of the sickly yellow glow from the lamps, but everything else looked like the life had been sucked out of it. Ellie had never felt more naked in her life and longed to dive back into the shadows.

They stopped behind a big SUV, and the girl with the gun fished around in Ellie's purse with her free hand. Ellie took the chance to study her, able to see the facial features for the first time, albeit cast in gray.

Dark curly hair framed the girl's face. Young. Maybe 20 or 25. The jaw was sharp and chin strong under a half-snarled lip. The planes of the cheeks angled and divoted. Big eyes stared down into the black hole of the purse, and it was those that somehow registered for Ellie.

Holy fuck.

The hair is different. Dyed. But it's her.

Scarlet.

Scarlet Burlew.

Scarlet's fist emerged from the purse, the key ring dangling from it. She held it by one key so the others all jangled and drooped like something wilted.

"Which one?" she said.

Ellie stared at the keys, not understanding.

"What?"

"Which car?"

Ellie turned to scan the rest of the lot. Pointed to her Corolla a few rows up from them.

They swooped for it.

CHAPTER 47

The night stained the Camaro's enamel an inky shade, and it had been moved perhaps a mile farther down from the Ferguson place compared to where she'd first spotted it. But Stinson knew it was the same one she'd seen earlier. The slight bump of the fenders, the generous width of the grill. She knew.

She stared at the vehicle for the span of several heartbeats. Eyes fastened to it. Jaw slack though her lips weren't parted.

She didn't think it was a brand-new model — maybe something like three or four years old — but it was modern enough to look out of place here in the middle of nowhere. And parked along an outbuilding like this? No way. Out in these parts it was almost exclusively older model pickup trucks. Rusted relics that had seen multiple George Bush presidencies.

An inner monologue spurred her from her stillness.

This is the car. And it doesn't belong here.

She licked her lips. Tasted salt.

Her hands cranked the wheel, and her foot let up on the brake, though her conscious mind barely registered these motions. Her focus had seized onto the muscle car and wouldn't let go.

Her vehicle eased forward. Crunched up the gentle slope of the gravel driveway, crushing clumps of grass on the way.

To Stinson it felt like a zoom shot in a movie. That image of the Camaro swelled and tightened.

Her car pressed into the open just before the outbuilding, and suddenly she felt exposed. Naked. Vulnerable.

Her shoulders hunched. She flicked off the headlights. Sat in the dark a few seconds. Then she killed the engine so the taillights would die, too.

The darkness became complete. Black nothing encased the car.

She sat, waiting for her eyes to adjust.

It took two full seconds for the building to reappear before the windshield, its lines grayer now and fuzzy.

The metal under the hood of her car plinked a few more times and then fell quiet. The stillness of the scene seemed pregnant, loaded, ready, somehow, to burst into action.

But all held motionless outside. Even the breeze that had riffled through the leaves had receded.

Stinson's heart punched in her chest. She swallowed, and it sounded loud inside the car. Juicy.

Looking around, she noted the expanse of low, bushy crops beyond the steel siding of the building — probably soybeans. Then she scanned the copse of woods lining the edges of the field. Nothing moved in any of these places.

She was alone. She knew that. But she couldn't shake the feeling that she shouldn't be here, like she was a snooping kid or something. Like she'd get in trouble for this.

I'm a homicide detective, and I've got probable cause to check out this vehicle, she reminded herself, though it didn't soften the anxiety all that much. She fixed her posture like that might screw her confidence back up, shoulder blades squeezing together, chest expanding.

Then she looked out the driver's side window. She wished, for some reason, that she could see the ground just there, but without her headlights brightening the way, the murk had thickened enough to make that impossible.

Full dark. Now that she was face-to-face with the blackness, she didn't want to go out in it, but she knew she would.

She dug a flashlight from the glovebox and set her phone in the inside pocket of her jacket for easy access. She'd get a quick snap of the license plate and come back to the car to run it.

The dark seemed to resettle over the scene. The night overtaking whatever flare of exposure she'd felt a moment before.

She stepped out into that cavernous humidity again. The mugginess pressed around her body, sheathed her in dankness, something revolting in it, and the fine hairs pricked up on the back of her neck.

But the night felt open around her. Like getting out of the cabin of the car had taken some lid off, exposed her to the endless sky above. In a way, she guessed it had.

The beam of her light swung in front of her. Sliced a tunnel of brightness into the gloom. Then it bobbed along with her gait as she started forward.

Her heart rate picked up into a gallop as she strode up on the car. Her pulse glugged in unison in her neck and in her ears.

As she closed in on the Camaro, she shined her light into the windows. Sweeping it over the front seat and then the back. The heel of her free hand drifted down to the butt of her Glock and unsnapped the holster as she did.

What she could see of the car's interior looked clean. Nothing notable.

Her breath felt feathery in her throat. Fluttering over her lips, over her teeth. She realized that she was breathing through her mouth to keep quiet and felt foolish again.

There's no one out here.

Nobody but me.

She closed her mouth and shuffled forward a few more steps. Felt the soles of her shoes crush and grit at the dirt underfoot.

The angle of the shadows changed as she got closer. The dark shortening, the light expanding.

Soon she was standing right over the Camaro, looking down on the innards laid bare. The light brushed over the entirety of the front seat once again and then the back.

Empty.

The interior was spotless. Not even so much as loose change or a ketchup packet in the cup holders. She found herself disappointed by the tidiness. It wasn't like she'd expected to find some kind of smoking gun — literally or figuratively. But she still had no clue about the vehicle's owner.

No feel at all for who this person might be.

Her breath came easier though, and her hand slid away from the Glock. She placed her palm flat on the hood. Still warm.

Then she rounded the back of the vehicle, brought her light down to the license plate. Time to get what she came for.

The blue and red letters told her right away it wasn't a Florida plate. A little cartoon of an airplane and the text *First in Flight* occupied the top of the rectangle. What looked like cattails jutted up from the bottom.

She swallowed hard, and her eyelashes flickered over her field of vision like moth wings.

A North Carolina plate.

That's where Jimmy and Scarlet are from.

OK. Maybe this is *something.*

Adrenaline rushed through her, that same ecstasy she always felt when one of her hunches led to something. Sometimes she thought it was the rush that kept her getting out of bed in the morning, the moment when the puzzle pieces snapped together.

Her scalp tingled, and her phone suddenly felt broad and awkward in fingers going numb. She just needed to snap a quick pic, and then she would run the plate number.

She bit the end of the flashlight like a fat cigar to free up both hands. Then she swiped and jabbed at the screen to flip it into camera mode.

The phone seemed a little sluggish. Hanging on a blank screen. She waited.

A bead of sweat wept down her temple. She swallowed with her mouth open around the flashlight. The clenching in her throat reminded her of lying back in the dentist's chair.

She stared into that black screen, and her head buzzed with the desire to run this plate, to see who the hell this person was, to make that next leap down the track the evidence was leading her on.

Finally, the phone screen winked to life. She aimed at the

plate, let the blurred image on the screen tighten into focus.

She tapped the screen. The camera flashed.

There.

Got it.

She sniffed a little laugh to herself. Stared into the glowing version of the Camaro plate on her screen.

And then footsteps crunched in the darkness beyond where Stinson stood.

They were moving toward her.

CHAPTER 48

Wes gaped at the empty boards before him. The lifeguard hut lay vacant. Ellie was gone.

He jumped down from the ladder. Turned to sweep his flashlight out over the beach.

The beam crawled over all those cupped spots in the sand. It moved from left to right, a clockwise motion of glow slowly rotating around him.

But it didn't quite make it all the way.

His phone blipped and died, and Wes was thrust into the dark.

Alone.

He huffed in a funny breath. It felt like the darkness was cinching around him, the nothingness drawing tight like yanking the drawstrings on a hoodie.

He frantically thumbed the power button on his phone a dozen times, but it was no use. His phone battery was dead.

He made himself stop and think.

OK, she probably had to pee or something, right?

He spent the next minute scrambling around the perimeter of the tower and the nearby trees, whispering Ellie's name into the shadows, hoping to find her every time he turned a corner.

But he found nothing.

"What the fuck," he whispered to himself, remembering that this was the second person to mysteriously vanish into the darkness tonight.

For some reason, the thought of Pete and the shooting stars also reminded him of seeing Duke and his Elvis hairdo at the Tiki Hut, and how Ellie had thought it was creepy.

You think he's stalking us or something? Wes had said.

Jesus. What if he had been?

Don't be ridiculous, he thought. *There's got to be a logical explanation. Like maybe she went back to the bar, for some reason.*

He fumbled with his phone, realizing he could simply call her.

Then he remembered that his phone was dead.

Damn it.

He went to tuck the phone in his pocket. Found a wad of silky material there.

It was a second before he recognized it as Ellie's shirt.

And he'd never even found her shorts. Which meant that wherever Ellie was right now, she was nude.

Try as he might, he couldn't come up with a logical explanation for *that.* No way did she walk off stark naked of her own volition.

He thought of his brother then. Walking into those woods never to return. All those questions left unanswered.

No. This can't be happening. Not again.

He called out, his voice raspy.

"Ellie!"

He turned the other way. Cupped his hand around the side of his mouth.

"Ellie?"

The only response was the *swish-swash* of the water climbing the beach.

The panic was arriving now, welcome or not. He tried to force himself to stay steady. To scan the dark in all directions for any sign of movement.

He slowly swiveled. Looked for any stirring in the shadows. Tried to listen over the thumping of his heart. For footsteps. Or anything.

Nothing.

Nothing.

Nothing.

He ran for the parking lot in the distance, for the palm trees decked out in colored Christmas lights. *The tiki bar.*

The sand pulled at his ankles. Made him feel like he was

barely moving. A conveyor belt spinning the wrong way.

As soon as the bar sharpened into view, he started shouting for help. But he remembered how loud it had been inside with the music and the crowd and knew it was unlikely anyone could hear him.

He tore past the first two rows of cars, grabbing the first person he saw, just shy of the front door. A meathead-looking frat guy with a backwards red hat and a goatee.

"Call 9-1-1!"

The guy stared at him with glazed, drunken eyes.

"Wut?"

Wes pressed his face closer.

"Call. 9-1-1."

The guy squinted his fratty eyes, still seeming confused, and Wes had the sudden feeling that he was in one of those nightmares where no one could hear or understand him.

Then the frat guy blinked and went slightly cross-eyed, and Wes realized he was wasted.

He abandoned the drunkard. Pushed through the doorway and knifed through the crowd until he reached the bar. He flagged down the bartender, his voice coming out loud and wavery, and this time several people heard his plea.

No less than four people whipped out their phones, the glowing screens lighting their chins from below.

Then a girl with a surface piercing in the middle of her cheek was passing her phone to him. He didn't understand why until he heard the 9-1-1 operator on the other end asking him to explain the nature of his emergency.

Emergency.

The word sounded strange in his ears. Overly dramatic somehow. He recognized some urge to cling to denial. To continue plumbing the depths for a rational explanation.

But no. There was only one explanation.

Ellie had been kidnapped.

And then the words spilled out of him in a rush he couldn't keep up with.

He had a difficult time relaying what had happened to the operator. The order of things kept getting jumbled in his head, and he sputtered out details that were hardly pertinent, like the way his hat had almost blown away in the wind or how he had never managed to find Ellie's shorts.

In the end, it didn't seem to matter. The operator told him the police would be there shortly and to please stay where he was.

He handed the phone back to the girl with the piercing and stood frozen for several seconds, unsure of what to do now. Just stand and wait? It seemed crazy.

Then he remembered John and Courtney. He had to tell them.

He turned away from the bar, scanning. Courtney had been talking about wanting to dance earlier, he recalled. He waded through the crowd over to the small area near the jukebox that had been cleared for this purpose, but John and Courtney weren't there.

He reversed course, returning to the table they'd been at earlier in the night. Another dead end.

Wes grasped the sides of his head.

What if they'd left? Gone back to the motel, assuming Wes would ride back with Ellie.

His stomach felt like it was wadding itself up, a wet beach towel clenching in his gut.

And then he spotted them in a small crowd just outside on the back deck. A bank of ashtrays stood nearby, their stone mouths full of sand and cigarette butts. He churned his way through the packed bar, determined to do a better job explaining the situation than he had with the 9-1-1 operator.

Instead, he blurted out, "Ellie's gone," the moment he reached them.

"Gone? You mean, she left?"

Wes shook his head.

"No. No, someone took her. We were on the beach… and then we… she…"

Again, words failed him. He felt the ball of fabric and held it up. Ellie's shirt.

He watched the change in their facial expressions as it sunk in.

"Holy shit," John said.

"Well who was it?" Courtney asked. "Did you see?"

"I didn't see anything. It was like I turned my back for one second, and…"

"Did you try to call her?" Courtney was already getting out her phone.

"My phone is dead."

Courtney scrolled through her contacts and dialed Ellie's phone. It rang and rang with no answer.

"OK, what about her car?" Courtney said. "Is it still here?"

Wes hadn't even thought to check. They jogged out into the parking lot, Wes leading the way.

"We parked down at the end, right near the edge of the beach." He slowed and then stopped in his tracks, pointing. "Right there."

The spot where Ellie's car had been sat empty like a missing tooth.

CHAPTER 49

The man stepped out of the gloom and into the half-light, still moving toward the Camaro. Stinson could see the cut of his shoulders first — broad and corded with muscle, clad in a white t-shirt that looked the shade of a plum in the dark. She pegged him to be maybe 28.

She jammed her phone into the inside pocket of her jacket and drew her Glock. Only after the weapon was trained on the man did she remove the flashlight from her mouth.

"Durango Beach PD. Stop right there," she said, her voice coming out hard and loud. Harsh in the quiet.

She swung the flashlight beam onto him. His hands had been up even before she'd spoken, she realized. He took one final step into the spotlight and stopped, and she could see the big smile on his face, the twinkle in his squinting eyes. She shifted the light down onto his chest.

"Don't suppose you know the owner of this here Camaro?" he asked, his southern accent thick.

Stinson blinked. She quickly reassessed the situation. The smile. The raised hands. Him asking about the Camaro. There was something relaxed in his body language, too. Nothing tight in the neck or shoulders. No fear in his eyes.

She let out a breath and felt her own tension wane just a little.

"What's your name?"

"John Turner."

"You got ID that says so?"

"Yes, ma'am."

He took a step forward, but Stinson cut him off.

"Stop. Not yet. You'll walk over here when I tell you to."

He stopped again. Lifted his hands higher.

Stinson adjusted her grip on the Glock.

"Are you the owner of this property?" she asked.

He was still grinning away. Eyes swaddled in rims of darkness like he'd put on eyeshadow.

"Not mine, no. It's my uncle's place. Amos Turner. I just work here. Pretty sure we've got ourselves a trespasser."

She drew up on him as he spoke. With the flashlight in her teeth again, she patted him down with her free hand. He wasn't armed.

"That'd be the owner of the Camaro?"

She backed off again as she asked.

"Yes, ma'am. I was just— Can I put my hands down?"

Stinson nodded once. His hands fell to his sides, and she lowered her Glock, pointing it at the ground but keeping it out and ready.

"Thanks. But um… yes, ma'am. The intruder and the owner of the Chevy are one and the same. Or so I suspect. We picked up a creeper on the security cams, and that's when I noticed the car parked out here."

Stinson hadn't noted any cameras as she walked up on the car, an observation that raised her suspicion level again. Still, it'd make sense to keep an eye on an outbuilding that was presumably loaded with tractors and other high-dollar equipment.

"And what do you think this *creeper* is up to?"

He shrugged those thick shoulders.

"Dunno. I just come out now to check it out. We've had buildings vandalized over the years, though it's usually just kids with spray paint. But last summer we had a fire set on one of Uncle's properties a couple counties over. Chicken farm. Killed a bunch of birds. Now here, it's mostly equipment. And hell, I don't know if anyone would try to run off with a 40,000-pound combine or something, but… it'd make for quite the police chase."

His face had gone serious while he spoke. Now that grin brightened again.

"Anyhow, since you're an officer of the law and all, you

wanna help me take a look?"

Stinson nodded again.

"One thing first."

She walked close again and patted him down a second time. Had him empty his pockets. No weapons on his person. Just a wallet and a can of Skoal.

"I take it the car is empty?" Turner asked, pointing back that way.

"Yeah. Clean, too."

Turner hooked his thumb over his shoulder, pointing at the thicker copse of growth behind him.

"I figured as much. Last saw him creeping through the woods toward the old pump house. Figured I'd take a look at the car before I waded into the prickers. Wiry looking sumbitch, too. Arms long enough to drag his knuckles on the ground when he walks around, you know. What's the word? Gawky."

Stinson started walking the way he'd pointed, and Turner fell in beside her. They wove around a couple bushes, and then the thicket cinched closed before them. A wall of green.

"He was right in there. Might wanna ditch the light," he said. "He sees us coming, he'll take off, you know?"

Stinson gazed down at the flashlight in her hand. In the dark, it kind of looked like the hilt of a sword with a blade of light beaming out of it. She chewed her lip a second and then clicked it off.

The dark closed in on all sides. A blooming void that wanted only to swallow her up.

She forced herself to breathe. Big breaths. Steady.

After a few seconds, her night vision started to come back in stages. The moonlight glinted through the leaves, and the tree trunks took on shape and then texture. The images sharpened little by little.

When Turner spoke again, his voice came out in a whisper with some rasp to it.

"Want me to take point?"

"Go for it."

He started into the foliage, that V-shaped torso knifing into the weeds. Lunging steps lifted his knees up high and set them down with care. He was surprisingly light on his feet considering his bulk.

Stinson followed. In a way, she was relieved to have him out in front. Easier to keep an eye on him that way. He wasn't armed, but some part of her still didn't like the idea of having him at her back.

They glided deeper into the patch of woods. Noise erupted under Stinson's feet now and then, leaves grinding, twigs snapping. She was able to blunt the sounds some by keeping her feet and ankles soft, flexing into each step, but she couldn't stay as quiet as Turner out here. Not even close. She supposed that came with knowing the land.

Despite the fact that he couldn't be over thirty, he had an oddly old-fashioned way of speaking. Some of the turns of phrase reminded her of her Grandpa Stinson.

He stopped all at once. His back went upright and locked there. Then he raised his right fist, elbow lifting into a 90-degree angle from his shoulder, all of this just faintly discernible in the dark.

It was a familiar signal, one the local SWAT team used to indicate "freeze." She wondered if he had law enforcement experience. Maybe military.

Turner's fist turned to two fingers pointing into the bushes ahead. He repeated the motion a couple times.

Stinson scanned the foliage that way. She could only make out the blobs of the bushes there. Thick prickly things, the texture of the needles looking spiky along the edges.

She turned back toward Turner and shook her head, not sure if he'd be able to read the gesture in the dark.

He took a baby step her way and leaned in. Up close he smelled vaguely like tobacco and leather. Some other masculine note that Stinson couldn't place. He was practically breathing into her ear now.

"In them brambles. You see?"

He pointed again, two fingers jutting into the scrub, and she followed the trajectory of them. Stared into the gloom.

But no. Stinson didn't see.

Wait. Maybe there was something there.

A vague shape. Darker than the rest.

She took a short step forward. Squinting hard.

She'd hoped the shape would congeal into something specific — square shoulders tapering to hips, arms and legs jutting out of a torso, a skull, a face, anything — but it didn't.

It was about the size of a person squatted down, though, she thought. Roughly the right shape for that. Maybe.

Then again, it wasn't moving. At all. No twitch of the ribcage showing signs of breath. No quiver of the muscles trying to keep still.

She fingered her flashlight. Itched to click it on, to thrust that glowing beam on them now, whoever they might be.

But that would send them running, and she could so easily lose sight in the brush, in the dark. She chewed the inside of her cheek.

Better to get closer first. Better to flank them.

Yes.

Yes.

If Turner moved off to the left and she hooked in from the right side, they'd stand a better chance of cutting the person off if they bolted. Like hunting rabbits, Stinson thought. It was all about taking the right angle.

She smiled to herself. Felt a single silent laugh puff from her nostrils.

Then she turned to whisper the plan to Turner, expecting to find him still hovering over her left shoulder. But the space was empty.

The big lug wasn't there.

Stinson wheeled around just in time to see the blur lurching for her. His fist corkscrewed. A wild hook that caught her high on the side of the head.

CHAPTER 50

Static burst inside Stinson's skull. Stars exploding over the fresh darkness inside.

She staggered. Felt her consciousness blinking in and out. The woods around her flickering out of existence and returning. Reality itself gone touchy.

She twisted as though to get away. Hips and shoulders rotating. Too late.

She fell. Dead weight plummeting into the dead leaves below. Gravity a rough thing just now.

She bellyflopped down. The ground slapped her core. Jolted through all of her. Paralyzed her lungs.

And her consciousness sucked like a drain at the bottom of a hole. She turned to look up, barely mustering the movement. The dark surrounded one tunnel of brightness — the pinpoint of awareness left to her.

And he loomed over her. Big and mean. An angular thing chiseled out of granite.

He lifted his foot. The waffle tread of his boot visible for a second in the moonlight. Poised to stomp, to squash her like a bug.

She squirmed. Scrabbling and wriggling on her belly. Sliding herself forward a foot or two. Trying to get her gun arm out from under her bulk.

Useless. Powerless.

Her free arm flailed forward. Fingers clawing at the earth, gouging grooves into the black soil. Reaching again, finding something solid now.

A rock. A flat boulder jutting several inches from the ground. Too big to lift.

But her fingers found purchase in its craggy body. She gripped a crack. Pulled herself. Kicked with both legs.

That wormed her forward a couple feet all at once. Her head and shoulders shifted up and over the big rock. It propped her top half off the ground.

Her gun arm came free at last. Unpinned. She lifted it.

And then his foot crunched down on the back of her head. Smashed her face into the stone.

Her nose cracked and flattened. Her teeth shattered against the inside of her lip. Strange shards tumbling in her mouth like Chiclets.

And the dark exploded inside. Blotted out those motes of brightness all at once. The dimmer switch cranked all the way down.

Nothing.

Nothing.

But she bobbed back to the surface right away. Like diving off the high dive. Sinking into the deep. Popping back up. Lifted into the light, into the hurt.

His boot smashed down again and again. Slamming her head. Cracking her neck. Mashing her face into a pulp against the coarse exterior of the boulder.

Battering.

Pounding.

Wet slapping like a mud puddle.

Bolts of pain flaring steadily. New hurts joining the chorus.

Heat and confusion lurched and spit in her skull. She somehow clung to one sliver of consciousness. Felt it all. Lived it all.

Needed to fight. Somehow.

She blinked hard. Saw red and black smearing her vision.

Her life leaking. Draining.

She tried again to lift the Glock, but her shoulder wouldn't budge. She blinked once more and swiveled her eyes over to that dark weapon at the end of her arm.

An inert bulk. Matte black against her sheening skin. She couldn't even wiggle the fingers clutched around the grip.

She felt only pins and needles where the hand should be,

where the limb should be. A sucking emptiness where all feeling should be from the neck down.

The darkness swirled inside. Boiling and agitated. Jagged red flashing again and again where his boot battered into the back of her skull.

And the wind kicked up. A humid breath swishing over the land, churning up leaves. A big gust snuffling over her cheeks, over her forehead, over everything, pluming clouds of dust like smoke. Something angry in it, something thrashing with life.

And that crimson strobe inside got bigger and bigger until it blotted all other visions out. Imprinted that pulse over her retinas, over her being.

Red and black.

Light and dark.

Just that and the wind on her face. Nothing else. Nothing.

And then even that cut out.

CHAPTER 51

A calypso jingle shrilled somewhere off to Taft's left. A MIDI synth trying to sound like a steel drum melody. Guitars skanking out tinny upstrokes on the offbeat.

He rolled to the bedside table, feeling blindly for his phone in the pitch black of his bedroom. His fingers fumbled over the surface, bumping into a lamp and a bottle of water before finally landing on the phone.

Blinding light thrust from the screen and speared his pupils as he turned it toward his face. He squinted and swiped at the greenish blob there. Brought the phone to his ear.

"Taft."

The chief's voice sounded painfully chipper in his ear.

"Sorry to wake you, detective, but we just had an abduction on Durango Beach. One of these college kids down for spring break."

"OK," Taft said, closing his eyes and massaging the lids with his free hand. "You know Stinson and I are working this whole Jimmy and Scarlet thing, though. The Ferguson murder and all that. Malsook and Bosa are up for the next case, I think."

"Yeah, that's the thing," the chief went on. "We think maybe this is related to the Bonnie and, er— Jimmy and Scarlet business. The stolen Mustang was found not two blocks from the abduction site, and it's looking like whoever kidnapped the girl also made off with her vehicle."

Something snapped and popped between the chief's syllables. Chewing sounds. Taft found himself focusing on the percussive rhythm more than the words.

"Are you chewing gum?"

"What?"

"Nothing." He forced himself to focus. "So, uh, Scarlet

dumped the Mustang, stole a fresh car, and took a hostage?"

The chief blew out a breath. The phone speaker fluttered.

"That's the current theory. It would fit their established M.O., seeing as how they took that big fella from the Citgo. Of course, I figure you'll have a better feel for it, having worked the case all day and gotten yourself elbow-deep in the particulars."

Resigned to the fact that he was, after all, not going to get any sleep tonight, Taft turned on the bedside lamp and swung his legs over the side of the bed.

"Have you talked to Stinson yet?"

"Nope, I was going to roust her next."

"I can do it," Taft offered, thinking of how she'd been ribbing him about hitting the pastries too hard that morning. "I owe her a pleasant wake-up call."

Taft confirmed the location of the abduction — just across from Bobby D's Tiki Hut — and told the chief he'd be there in fifteen. Then he fired off a quick text to Stinson, opting for the ironic, "You up?"

He padded out to the kitchen on bare feet and got the Mr. Coffee pumping. Then he jumped in the shower for three minutes, the water not quite reaching lukewarm before he got out. Maybe that was better, though. The icy water had roused him fully awake in a heartbeat, his skin tightening and his knees wobbling at the frigid touch.

Taft tried to imagine having the amount of energy required to keep a crime spree like this up. Scarlet and Jimmy had been at it for a long time now. Didn't they ever get tired?

He toweled himself off to the throaty drone of the bathroom vent. Slicked his hair back. Dressed in a hurry.

Then he filled a travel mug with as much coffee, sugar, and cream as it would hold, sipping at it so he could get the lid on without the top spilling over. Two swallows later and the caffeine already roared in his veins, prickled in his eyes at a high amperage. He thought of a Ray Bradbury title by way of Walt Whitman, *I Sing the Body Electric.*

He tapped Stinson's name on his contact list as he walked out to his SUV, and the phone gurgled in his ear. She hadn't responded to his text, could even still be asleep.

That wouldn't do. He couldn't deprive her of this wonderful late-night opportunity to serve and protect the public.

CHAPTER 52

His body flexes. Abdominals arching and hips coiling.

His right leg draws up like a piston. And all of him unwinds as his boot slams down into the back of the cop's skull.

He crushes her face into the rock.

He stomps and stomps. All of his force discharged, all of his weight expelled. The storm of his being loosed through the sole of his boot.

Long after she's gone, he keeps going.

The rage burns clean. Feels right. He can feel it cooking, cleansing. A molten fluid bubbling in the heat inside his head, boiling behind the mask of his face.

Bolts of pain shoot up through his heel, through the ball of his foot. Radiating like a steady flame in his calf muscle, sparking new hurt in his thigh.

At some point the words come to him. A whisper inside.

Curb stomp.

He stops and breathes then. Stumbles a couple steps back.

Bends at the waist. Hands on his knees. Great torso heaving and trembling.

Sweat drizzles down from his brow. Drips into the fronds of a fern.

The plant glints in the moonlight where the moisture touches it. Looks like it's dripping diamonds.

He closes his eyes and breathes. Sucks big breaths into the hollow of his torso. Wind spiraling into him.

His lungs blaze, two wildfires in his chest. It feels like his breath will never catch up, that his heart will only beat faster and faster until its red walls blow out like a tire.

But the breaths come easier in time. The flame inside dies back to cinders.

He opens his eyes and looks down at the broken form of the

detective.

Her body lies still. Frozen in that awkward final pose, half-draped over a boulder.

The glossy layer of blood smearing the rock is already going tacky, gummy along the edges. The puddle draws his eyes to the rumpled back of her head, and his eyebrows drift up.

Holy shit.

The way her face flats itself against the rock looks cartoonish. Surreal.

So grotesque, so seemingly impossible. A bad special effect in a cheap horror movie. Some polyfoam faux gore rendered here in flesh and bone.

A little laugh hisses out at the thought. Spit sizzling between his teeth in a hi-hat rhythm. Sixteenth notes.

Jesus H.

He sucks his teeth and shakes his head again.

Wrong place at the wrong time, little lady.

It's true. If she'd stopped here ten minutes earlier or later, she'd have missed him.

He'd driven back by the earlier crime scene looking for any sign of Scarlet and found none. A mile or two down the road, he'd decided maybe it'd be best to ditch the murder weapon. He was out of ammo for it, anyway.

He'd pulled into the next driveway, walked out into the scrub, and buried the shotgun beneath a few inches of topsoil and dead leaves.

Just as he'd stood, the little sedan pulled in. He could tell as soon as she got out of the car that it was law enforcement. Her body language practically screamed it — handling the gun, sweeping the flashlight.

And now?

Well, now here she is. A bloody mess.

The fickle turn of fortune makes his skin crawl. Life and death riding on a simple case of bad timing.

Ah well. I never did like lady cops anyhow. Always got a fuckin' attitude about 'em.

Uppity. All hot to prove that they're tough shit.

It occurs to him that something about her position on the rock calls to mind an altar. Makes the scene look ritualistic.

A sacrifice… but to what?

He breathes. Those twin flames in his chest have died back.

The air feels pure in his throat. Clean.

And part of him remembers a rogue gust of wind coming over them just as he'd started stomping on her.

It'd been dryer and hotter than the air felt now. Intense, too. High velocity, yes, but there'd been something more to it.

A charge in the air. A wave or frequency or something. Electricity.

He shakes the memory of the feeling off. Steps closer to the corpse.

He hovers his foot over her a second. Hesitates.

It seems funny to slow play this now. He's just stomped the life out of her, and now he's reluctant to touch her?

But she'd been alive before, hadn't she? A dead body is something different. Something sacred. Everyone knows that.

He slides his boot closer in slow motion. Hooks the steel toe under her shoulder. Jerks his leg upward and gives the corpse a flip.

The body rolls off the rock. Hips twisting. Limp arms flailing.

The dead weight plops and shudders for a beat before it settles on the flat ground.

And then it's still again. One hard turn and done. Something jarring in the burst of movement.

At last the broken face comes clear.

He sucks in a shaky gasp at the sight. Steps back from the gore and shakes his head.

The bladed bone of her brow shines white through the mess of pulp. Her cheekbones likewise form bleached patches against the red.

She somehow looks unrecognizable as a human being now. Animal, yes. Human, not quite.

He mops the back of his hand over his lips. Gapes into that face.

No matter how long he looks, his eyes can't make sense of it.

Part skull. Part scarlet slush that used to mean something. Something alien in the forms, in the planes.

It's wrong. Obscene. A grievance against nature.

That word comes to him again: *Impossible.* The profane image on display here cannot be real.

And yet here it lies before him. Not just real but his own handiwork.

He has performed the impossible. He smiles at the thought.

He's made this. Destroyed what she was and recast her into something new.

Maybe that makes sense. Maybe a miracle can be an act of destruction.

Creation has no monopoly on these things. Just look around at the world.

He takes that step back toward her. Tentative again, though he doesn't know why. Some reverence washing over him now.

The altar. The ritual.

Maybe there's something to all of that. Something he can feel even if he doesn't understand it on a conscious level.

Something primordial.

He kneels then and digs through her pockets. Takes her phone, her flashlight.

He plucks the badge from inside her jacket. Sits back to play with it a little. Flips the leather flap open and closed. He takes that, too.

Finally, he takes her gun from her slack fingers and tucks it into his waistband at the small of his back.

Who knows? It could come in handy.

CHAPTER 53

Dark. Emptiness.

Stinson drifts in the nothingness. Made weightless.

The long dark stretches out from her in all directions.

Cavernous.

Vast.

She sees nothing. Hears nothing.

Senses, somehow, that she's not alone. That this is a shared space. A gathering.

She floats in it. Awash in the tranquility. Lighter than air.

And she feels only peace here. A release from old worries. An untethering from where she's been, who she's been.

She tries to remember.

How did she get here?

What was just happening to her?

It's there, the memory. She can feel it like an itch inside her thoughts. The knowledge hovering, somehow, just beyond her reach.

Broken bits of that final moment flicker inside. More feelings than any kind of concrete scene.

She tries to force the shards of recollection to the surface.

But the images are gray and smeared. Meaningless smudges. Fragmented beyond all recognition.

The pieces won't cohere into a narrative. They won't make sense.

All she can conjure clearly is a memory of the wind. The feel of it.

That breeze heaving over her. Hot breath touching the exposed places.

Something striking about it. Something strange.

It didn't belong, the wind. Not where she was.

And she knows it must mean something. Something

important.

A harbinger or omen of some kind. A symbol bearing some spiritual meaning. Transmitted from some hallowed place.

She tries to follow it. Tries to trail it back from wherever it came.

But she can't. She can't.

So she lets it go. Surrenders to the mystery of it. Drifts again in this nowhere place. Weightless.

And she feels the others there and knows that they feel her too. Knows that all is known here, that all is understood. Shared by so many that it soothes her in some way.

And bright light floods this place all at once. A beam shot into the nothingness. Pale blue.

And it's clear, somehow, that the void is endless. Stretching into eternity, into the infinite. The light touching only a fraction of the whole.

Another plane. A universe of empty space that she finds herself a part of.

And that wind comes back. Flips on full blast like an air-conditioning vent. The rush of that endless exhale streaming over her, through her.

Moaning and sizzling as it passes. Whistling through the vacancy of her like a breath between teeth.

The energy trembles inside her. A surging current. Somehow part of her and not at the same time.

And a voice speaks now into the gleam, into the wind, into the void. Breathy and everywhere. Echoing funny. Like a choir of whispers overlapping each other.

"Do you want to continue living as Avery Stinson?"

CHAPTER 54

Wes had expected *a* cop car. Maybe two. Instead, a whole squad had descended upon the parking lot outside the club, and that was when he'd realized there was something more going on here.

"This is… a lot of police, right?" he'd asked as the cavalcade came screaming into view.

"Yeah," Courtney agreed.

They stood near the front end of John's car and watched the teeming law enforcement sprawl out over the beach. Trees of lights went up in the distance, lighting the way out to the lifeguard tower.

John scratched the side of his face, looking dumbfounded.

"At least as many cop cars as we saw this morning, dealing with the whole dead body scenario."

And even then, Wes hadn't put it together. It was John who finally made the connection.

"Oh shit. Do you think this has something to do with the Bonnie and Clyde thing? Jimmy and Scarlet?"

Wes felt like an idiot. He'd thought it might be creepy Duke out on the beach in the dark, and the two bona fide criminals terrorizing the area hadn't even crossed his mind. But what would they want with Ellie?

He thought about how the last guy they'd taken had ended up dead and felt suddenly sick to his stomach. Then he reminded himself that it had supposedly been natural causes. They hadn't killed the man. Hadn't really hurt anyone, as far as he knew.

Before long, a detective named Taft walked over and introduced himself. He asked Wes to show him exactly where he'd last seen Ellie.

They tromped down the beach to the lifeguard hut, and

Wes gestured at the small platform.

"We were up there. I heard a noise, thought maybe someone was trying to steal our stuff or something, so I jumped down here. By the time I'd gathered up our things, she was gone."

Naturally, Detective Taft wanted more details. What exactly were they doing at the lifeguard tower at this hour? What had Ellie been wearing when she disappeared?

It would have been embarrassing enough to recount these details to the detective at all, but with John and Courtney standing by witnessing the whole thing? Wes wanted to walk straight into the ocean without looking back.

Even more embarrassing was realizing how little he knew about Ellie. Detective Taft wanted her birth date, her home address, contact information for her next of kin, and Wes knew none of it. Thank Christ Courtney was there.

Taft handed Wes a sheet with six mugshot photos on it.

"Now I know you said you didn't see who took Ms. Levine, but take a gander at this, and tell me if anyone looks familiar. Maybe you saw 'em hanging around sometime earlier tonight?"

Wes scanned the photos. The second face on the lineup confirmed their earlier suspicions.

"That's Scarlet Burlew." Wes glanced up from the paper. "You think Jimmy and Scarlet took Ellie?"

The detective winced.

"Guess you've seen them on the news, then." He took the photo lineup back. "Look, it's way too early in the investigation to say anything definitive. Let's just say this is one of many potential theories. But the fact that the vic— that Ellie's car was taken… Anyway, did you see her tonight or not?"

Wes held his gaze a second before he answered.

"No."

Taft blinked.

"OK," the detective said after a second. "Well, I'll be in touch if I have more questions."

And just like that, they were dismissed. Taft plodded back

down the beach. Wes couldn't help but feel disappointed. He wasn't sure what more he'd expected, but the whole thing still felt unresolved.

Did you think the detectives would waltz in and pull Ellie out of a black hat, like a magician with a rabbit? You, of all people, should know that's now how it works.

He supposed he should feel grateful for the response they'd gotten. He remembered the way they'd gotten the brush off when they first reported his brother missing. How it had taken days before the police took them seriously and actually started looking for Jason in earnest.

Then again, he knew now that the massive police response was probably less about Ellie and more about Scarlet. Still, it had to be a good thing, having all these cops on the hunt.

He watched one group of cruisers rush out of the lot, while another mess of law enforcement personnel fanned out over the beach, combing the sand with flashlights. Looking for footprints, maybe. Or fibers? Would that make sense? He didn't know much about crime scene investigations. He bet Ellie would know, with all her true crime knowledge.

Standing in the parking lot and watching the operation, it occurred to Wes that, once again, he didn't know what to do with himself. Up until this moment, he'd had a purpose. Every second since Ellie had gone missing had a clear goal. *Get to the bar. Call 9-1-1. Talk to the police.*

And now that he'd done all that, he had no idea what to do. Was he supposed to go back to the motel? Try to sleep?

He crossed his arms over his chest. Felt the chill wind roll in off the ocean.

"Looks like something's happening," John said, nodding toward a cluster of uniformed men. "Check it out."

Wes trained his eyes on the commotion. Had they found something? A piece of evidence? Some kind of clue?

Their group moved closer to the line of police tape that had been strung in a perimeter around the lifeguard hut, but the men in the huddle didn't appear to be looking at anything in particular. They were just talking.

Then one of the flashlights suddenly broke off from the rest, running at full tilt in the direction of the bar. It was Taft. He climbed into his SUV and sped off, tires squealing as he careened out of the lot.

"What do you think that's all about?" John asked. "You think they found something already?"

Wes just shook his head. He had no idea what was going on.

CHAPTER 55

Taft wheeled onto Highmore Road, getting a weird sense of déjà vu as the strip of blacktop straightened out underneath him. The woods and soybeans looked eerie in the dark, shadowy and unfamiliar even if he'd driven past the scene just yesterday.

Or today, depending on how you look at it, he thought. *Jesus.*

But if his last trip out into the boonies had held the morbid promise of Elmer Ferguson and his dogs lying dead at the end of the drive, this one held something worse.

Stinson.

He swallowed in an acrid throat. Didn't let himself think the full thought.

Couldn't believe it. Wouldn't believe it until he saw it for himself.

He dug his travel mug out of the cup holder and took two big slugs of coffee. The scalding stuff he'd made an hour or two ago had cooled to something approaching lukewarm, and the acidic notes seemed sour on his tongue now.

Swirling lights caught his eye just ahead. Red and blue flutters between the tree branches.

He parked. Snugged the SUV along the shoulder of the road. And then his heart sank a little when he saw Stinson's sedan in the driveway. The techs were working it. Photographing the car.

Again, that denial rose in him, a beast raring up on its hind legs.

He'd rushed here from the beach as soon as word came down, some shock numbing him immediately as the words spilled out of the radio speaker. Feeling fled his hands and feet first, then the iciness crept up his limbs.

It couldn't be true. Couldn't be.

But then…

He'd been trying to call her ever since the kidnapping report came in. Sent a few texts. Now he thumbed through those unanswered messages.

You up?

Wakey wakey, Detective Stinson.

Dude?

Finally, he climbed out of the vehicle and made his way along the slope of the ditch until he reached the driveway. He walked right past the techs processing the car.

Then he sidled along the building and approached the clearing where more techs swarmed, white suits stark against the greenery. Cameras flashing. Hushed voices falling quieter still as they saw him coming.

His eyes snapped to the bulk lying at their feet, and a dry breath scraped into him.

Stinson was still there.

A broken thing. Face crushed.

And Taft couldn't breathe. Couldn't move.

A red smear. Features rubbed out.

So small. Bony and frail.

Taft choked once. Some involuntary sound grating deep in his throat.

And then he was fine somehow. He looked, he saw, he understood, but he didn't feel it.

Another wave of that anesthesia coursed through him instead. A morgue drawer chill of fresh dullness surging in his veins.

The techs all stopped and looked at him. Maybe they wanted to say something. Maybe they wanted him to say something.

But no one spoke. The silence vibrated in the air between them.

Taft locked eyes with one of the techs, and he nodded. Then he turned back toward the road.

He stomped that way, amazed at how the feelings, the grief, they couldn't get through. Couldn't touch him.

I must be in shock. That's all.

The feelings will come later. Maybe when I'm alone.

He stopped a few feet shy of Stinson's car. Tried to gather his thoughts, focus on the job he was here to do.

A deep breath snuffled in through his nostrils. The woods smelled like moldering newspaper.

Or maybe I've had this job too fucking long, stared death in the face too many times, and I can't feel anything anymore. Detached even when my partner dies. Fuck.

His head tingled now. Fizzy and numb. Legs going dead underneath him.

He grunted and started forward again. Wobbled a little and then righted himself.

He needed to keep moving. Walk it off.

Another twelve steps left him at the mouth of the beaten driveway, feet planted on those balding patches in the grass. And he took a few more deep breaths, and he felt the strength come back to his legs, felt the ground become solid under him. That lightheaded feeling receded as the oxygen flooded his bloodstream.

Maybe it's better to feel nothing, he thought. *Maybe it's the only way to do this job.*

He scanned the faces of the uniformed officers dotting the scene. When he spotted Sergeant Booth, he waved him over.

Booth jogged closer, something about his sloped shoulders reminding Taft of a penguin just now. The sergeant's eyes kept connecting with Taft's and flitting away, lips twitching underneath a sandy mustache as thick as a Cuban cigar.

He doesn't know what to say, either.

But it didn't matter now. Some mix of procedure and instinct took over, a kind of muscle memory coaxing a list of orders out of Taft's mouth. Booth would go to work executing them.

"The guy must have driven out here, so we'll check the

traffic cams in a five-mile radius. From two hours before T.O.D. to now. Hopefully there won't be a lot to sift through. If we find the car, we find the killer."

He tried not to think about his use of "T.O.D." instead of "time of death." Avoiding the word.

Taft turned and looked down the darkened road a second before he went on, eyes working the horizon line where the asphalt stretched out of view.

"And if any of the properties on this road have security cameras, I want the footage."

"Yes, sir," Booth said, that twitch in his lip receding. "I'm on it."

Booth relayed the message into the radio in his mitt.

And Taft felt better as soon as he'd taken control of the scene. Standard procedure would walk him through the rest of it. This part was normal. This part made sense.

"Anything else you want me on, sir?" Booth said. He looked like a dog begging his master to have him do another trick.

Taft squinted as he thought about it.

"I overheard the CSIs saying they'd already documented the tire prints here in the driveway. So I don't know. I think the traffic cams are our best bet. Maybe we'll get lucky on a civilian camera, too. Kinda doubtful out here in the boonies, but it always seems to work in the—"

And mid-sentence Taft choked and burst into tears.

Wet touched his cheeks. Heat flooded his face. The moans gargled in his throat, like he could tell part of him was trying to squeeze them off.

Booth gasped and cupped a hand under his nose as though to protect his 'stache.

Taft stared away from the other cop. Tears blurring his vision of the soybeans across the way.

Booth patted a hand on the detective's shoulder.

"Uh… you OK, Detective Taft?"

Taft took two steps out onto the road, and the asphalt seemed to tilt under his feet like the deck of a listing ship. He staggered another step and stopped.

And he breathed again, and that newspaper smell spiraled into his throat and sinus cavity. He could taste it on his tongue, the earthy note of the dead leaves.

Death.

Decay.

The crying stopped within thirty seconds or so. He turned back to see Sergeant Booth, eyes bugging out of his head. The guy grasped for words, stammering a little.

"Are we assuming this was… I mean, do we think Jimmy and Scarlet did this?"

Taft shook his head. He thought back to something Stinson herself had said.

Someone else involved.

"No," Taft said, his voice going thoughtful. "Jimmy would have already been gut shot in the hospital by the time this happened. And Scarlet? She's too small. Probably weighs about 115 soaking wet. No way she could do… that kind of damage. Besides, we think she was elsewhere when it happened."

He stared into the middle distance. Eyes spearing empty space again.

"There's someone else involved."

CHAPTER 56

Ellie's car rolled through town, slow and steady. The quiet inside seemed heavy, strained.

Scarlet looked small behind the wheel. A delicate form with fine features that glowed momentarily whenever the streetlights swept by overhead. Angelic.

There was something sad written into the lines of her face, the set of her lips, but Ellie saw some ferocity there, too. Determination molded into the arch of the brow. Something rigid forged in the musculature of her jaw.

Ellie hunched in the backseat. She still felt weird when the bars of light slanted into the windows to touch her nude body. Exposed. The planks of her flesh gritty and matte where the sand still clung to most of her. All those tiny grains scritching everywhere on the surface of her.

She looked out the nearest window. Suburban lawns rolling past. Spanish-style homes flecked with periodic bungalows. White picket fences divvying up the lots. Everything cast in charcoal daubs and swirls.

Freedom lay just on the other side of this pane of glass, but she couldn't touch it. The child safety locks would keep her penned in the backseat. Scarlet had seen to that right away.

Ellie kicked around at the thick shadows along the floor with one foot. Tried to feel for a bag or anything she or Courtney might have left in the car, maybe something that had gotten tucked under the front seat and forgotten.

But her toes found empty space. There was nothing there.

This is what I get for keeping my car spotless.

Everything she and Courtney had brought to Florida was locked safely in their motel room. Untouchable. It didn't leave her anything to work with, either to aid her escape or just to cover herself.

Check that. Everything was locked away save for her purse and phone, which Scarlet must have tucked away in her own duffel bag, the bulky thing currently riding shotgun.

A whine erupted, shrill and sudden. It made the hair on the back of Ellie's neck prick up. Her head rattled a little on her shoulders.

Sirens. They moaned in the distance. It sounded like a lot of them.

The swirling red and blue lights appeared not so long after that. Rising over a hill one after another. Colorful slices wedged into the darkness over the road in the distance, glowing smudges swirling around and around.

All at once, Scarlet wheeled into a small parking lot alongside an apartment complex. Snugged the car right up behind an Escalade.

She killed the lights and then the engine. The shadows bloomed around them like they meant to help conceal the car.

The line of cruisers, at least three, jerked straight for them. Rushed down the gentle hill.

Their headlights slowly spread over everything. Glinting off the asphalt and making every blade of grass glow on the lawns down this way. A flood of illumination.

But before Ellie could get her hopes up, the line of cars zipped past. Sirens fading.

Headed for the beach, probably. Looking for her.

Flying away from here as fast as they could go.

The quiet settled over the inside of the car again. Swelled to fill the empty space.

"You don't have any clothes in the car?" Scarlet asked.

Her eyes looked big in the rearview mirror.

Ellie shook her head.

The girl in the driver's seat clicked on the dome light and leaned over the center console. Went to work rifling through the duffel bag.

The shadows mostly hid what lay beneath those zippered flaps, but Ellie thought she saw strips of what had to be cash.

Lots of cash.

"Here," Scarlet said.

She thrust a hand between the seats. White fabric bunched at the end of her arm.

Ellie took the offering. She slid on the t-shirt a second later. It felt cool cocooning over her.

It was a man's shirt. Vintage. Like something someone might have won by knocking down bottles at a state fair circa 1986. A cartoonish font on the front said, "HOT DAMN! Here I am."

Another handful of fabric punched between the seats, khaki-colored this time. Ellie took it.

Like the shirt, the shorts were way too big for her. All wrinkled like they'd been wadded at the bottom of the bag for weeks. Still, it was better than being naked.

"Got a belt here, too," Scarlet said after a second.

Ellie laced the thing around her middle and cinched it tight. It gathered the shorts funny along the waist, the fabric rumpling like the mouth of a garbage bag drawn taut, but she was pretty sure they'd stay up.

"Thanks," she said after a second.

Scarlet nodded.

Ellie observed the girl up close now as they faced each other. She could see the wetness around Scarlet's eyes still.

So she was *crying before.*

Something fragile exuded from Scarlet up close. Vulnerability rolling off her like infrared rays shimmering over hot asphalt. The smirk from all the pictures on TV was gone. Delicate features had taken its place — the sad eyes, the slightest downturn of the mouth.

The pertinent question occurred to Ellie then, the thought arriving from nowhere all at once:

Where is Jimmy?

Could he be...

It would explain the tears. Would explain why she's alone, too.

The dome light clicked off and plunged Scarlet's face into shadow again. And now the sharper qualities slammed back into focus. The blade of the jaw, the square of the chin, something angular in the brow like some fierce bird of prey.

Scarlet started the car. The engine coughed and rumbled. Then the headlights snapped on, and they eased out of the parking spot, the wheel sliding against Scarlet's fingers, against her palms.

The town held still around them. No traffic. No movement.

Ellie settled back in her seat, and the upholstery felt cold against her sweaty back. She realized she'd already sweat through the fresh t-shirt, that she was going to spend the rest of the night soggy and uncomfortable.

A second later, movement in the rearview drew her eyes back to the mirror. Scarlet was looking at her. Their eyes met in the glass.

The driver took a breath before she spoke.

"Listen. This isn't going to make sense. Not at first," Scarlet said. "But I need you to do something for me."

CHAPTER 57

The air-conditioning vent breathed on Wes. He sat in the passenger seat of John's car, the windshield aimed at the beach where the search still moseyed along.

When Detective Taft had first sped off, Wes's optimistic side wondered if maybe they'd found Ellie. Now, watching the handful of officers left combing the beach, he thought not. Or maybe he knew it wasn't so.

In the backseat, Courtney yawned.

"You getting tired?" John asked.

"I mean… yeah. But there's no way I'm leaving."

"No way. Of course not," John agreed. "But I could go see if there's anywhere to get coffee around here."

As John wandered off in search of caffeine, Wes was glad Courtney had stayed behind. He felt a strange separateness from everyone right now — probably the guilt of being there when Ellie was taken and not being able to stop it. The presence of someone else nearby gave him at least some comfort. He may be pretty much useless, but he wasn't alone, at least.

John returned a few minutes later, his fingers hooked through the handles of a plastic shopping bag. He opened it and showed off a collection of energy drinks and canned nitro cold brews.

Wes wasn't thirsty in the slightest, but he figured the caffeine would do him good. He selected one of the coffee drinks and popped the tab.

John cleared his throat and began speaking in a hushed tone.

"So there were a couple of cops inside the gas station, and I overheard them talking. Remember Detective Stinson, from this morning?"

"Yeah. Why?"

"She died."

Wes almost choked on the cold brew.

"What?" he sputtered. "Like just now?"

John nodded.

"And the way they were talking… it sounded like it was bad. Like a bad death. Violent, you know?"

They were quiet for a few seconds. Courtney looked like she might throw up.

"Do they think Jimmy and Scarlet did it?"

John was mid-sip and shook his head without pausing.

"That's another bit of scuttlebutt I heard. Jimmy? He got shot. He's in the hospital now."

John's brow lowered, making his eyes look sunken for a second.

"But I guess Scarlet is still on the loose. I don't think she could have been the one to kill Stinson, though. From the sounds of it… well… I think she got beaten to death, the detective. Just seems more likely it'd be a man to do that, I guess."

Wes felt lightheaded. He could barely process all that John was saying. Something about another police officer getting run over as part of the police chase earlier in the night.

Jesus, this was bad.

His eyes went to the police and investigators that seemed to be twiddling their thumbs at this point.

"Why the fuck are they just standing around?" he said to no one in particular. "Why aren't they out on the streets, searching for Ellie?"

And as the first glimmer of dawn started to rise over the edge of the sea, Wes was struck by an urge to act. If the cops were going to be this goddamn slow, then fuck 'em. Because there was no way he was losing someone else this way. No fucking way.

Gray light leaked over the horizon. It pooled on top of the water, a puddle of light spreading toward the shore.

Wes turned and looked out over what he could see of downtown Durango Beach, roads snaking between the palm trees and buildings.

Ellie was out there somewhere. And he was going to find her.

CHAPTER 58

Ellie smoothed out the two twenty-dollar bills. Gaped at them like something in Andrew Jackson's face might make this night make sense.

The quiet expanded again. Filled the inside of the car like some high-pressure gas.

Ellie looked up at the Walgreens in the middle distance. A stucco box with glowing glass panels cut into it, the windows too painfully bright to stare at for long. The predawn gray was no match.

Scarlet slammed both of her hands on the steering wheel. The slap echoed off the windshield. She yelled hard enough that her voice broke up into a rasp.

"Just fucking go."

Ellie flinched.

Scarlet sighed, and her expression softened. The girl looked down at nothing as she went on.

"Look, I can't go in there. My mugshot is all over TV, you know? None of this is what it seems."

Ellie stared at Scarlet for another two seconds. Saw that incredible sadness emanating from her eyes. A hurt that seemed to roll off of her. Contagious.

"Just go, and we'll talk about it after," Scarlet said, her eyes fastening on Ellie's again. "I'll explain it then. I'll explain it all."

Ellie nodded. Then she shoved the forty bucks in her right hip pocket and climbed out of the car.

With the air-conditioning gone, the heat surrounded her immediately. The humidity pressed its damp body against hers.

The mugginess felt different at night. Heavier.

She adjusted her shoulders as though to shrug it off. Felt her sweaty t-shirt peel away from her shoulder blades. It made her shudder a little.

Finally, she turned to look at the way forward.

They'd parked at the back of the Walgreens lot, several rows away from the smattering of cars here at this hour. Ellie gawked a second at the glowing glass front of the store. It looked hollow from this far back. Empty space flooded with light.

Then she took a breath and started the ninety-foot march over the blacktop sea.

Her instinct was to hurry. Speed-walk. Get this over with. But she willed her legs to stay slow and steady.

Wind whistled around the stucco corner of the store and snuffled against the undercarriages of the parked cars. It ruffled the wide legs of her shorts, billowed in her baggy t-shirt.

As she got about halfway across the lot, the automatic doors swished open in the distance. A figure swept through the opening.

A man with a plastic bag dangling from one hand and his glowing phone in the other. Late 30s or so. Pointy features. Black hair swept back in a side part that seemed fussy.

He looked nice, she thought. Something soft in his eyes. He looked like someone who might help her.

She stutter-stepped once but kept going, heading right for the store. She didn't want Scarlet to see anything in her body language.

But she watched the man. Her brain on fire.

She could say something. *Call 9-1-1.* It'd be so fast maybe Scarlet wouldn't know.

She licked her lips. Felt the words right there on the tip of her tongue.

The guy swiped at his phone with his thumb. Kept staring into the abyss of the web browser there.

If he looks up, I'll say it. I will. I'll say it.

She could feel the itch of Scarlet's eyes on her back. A line of electric current drawn between her and the Corolla back there. She kept going.

The phone guy walked past. Gone. A couple seconds later,

his car door thumped somewhere behind her. He'd never even looked at her.

In a flash, Ellie wondered if Wes had called the police. Had they already notified her parents she was missing? How pissed off would they be when they found out she'd snuck away for spring break? She couldn't dwell on the thought long. The building was coming up on her.

She strode up onto the sidewalk fringing the building. That brightness leaked everywhere through the doors, through the windows.

And a weird reflection of her jiggled on the glass as she got to the door. Her proportions looked all wrong with the baggy clothes hanging off her. Stick arms and legs jutting out of all that fabric.

The automatic door whooshed out of her way. Erased that reflection all at once.

She stepped over the line into the glow. Squinted at first as her eyes adjusted.

And her heart hammered in her chest. A crooked knock, that little bit harder on every other beat.

thump-THUMP.

thump-THUMP.

She scanned left and right as she moved through the RFID scanners and fully into the store. Her eyes snapped to the three people she could see from here.

The guy behind the counter, to her left, flipped through a magazine. A star tattoo blotted one side of his neck. When he turned a page, she noted more black ink tracing down both arms and coating the backs of his hands all the way up over his knuckles. His jaw churned at a piece of pale purple gum she believed to be cotton candy-flavored, based on the scent in here. He didn't look up at her.

A customer — a middle-aged man with a deep tan and a camo hat — knelt on the floor and reached elbow-deep into a drink cooler. He fished around for a while before pulling out a tall boy of Lo-Carb Monster, the blue *M* practically glowing against the black of the can.

Way in the back of the store, she could see a pharmacist in a white coat, her figure encased in glass, walking the rows of medicine.

No one was paying attention to her. No one had even glanced at her. Still, she felt exposed in the open floorspace just inside the door. No cover here save for two spinner racks of mass market paperbacks. Stephen King elbowed up against Tom Clancy.

She pressed toward the aisles of inventory beyond, obeying some instinct to hide among them — a moth flying for the glowing bulb even if it didn't know why. And she felt better as soon as the wall of Pepsi products and potato chips sealed her off from the others present here.

The signs over the aisles guided her to the proper area. Still, she walked down the row of cosmetics twice before she found what she was looking for — hair dye.

She squatted. Stared at the rows of boxes. But she couldn't think. Couldn't quite make the cutesy color names make much sense to her reeling mind.

Champagne Blonde.

Cool Amethyst.

Iced Golden Brown.

Espresso.

Cherry Crush.

Christ. They sound more like beverages than hair colors.

She huffed in a breath to steady herself.

Reminded herself that the sooner she gave Scarlet what she wanted, the sooner this would be over.

Then she grabbed two boxes at random and headed for the beverage coolers. Grabbed a tall can of AriZona tea, pale green just like Scarlet had asked for. Next came the front counter.

She could feel her lip twitching as she put the boxes down next to the cashier's open magazine. She had the money all ready to go, too, the cloth-like dollar bills already snugged into her hand inside her pocket.

Still, the guy barely looked up at her. Eyes adhered to the magazine, he rang up the items, the scanner blipping thrice.

"That all?" he said finally.

She practically threw the twenties. The two bills skidded over the counter, half-crumpled again.

The cashier gazed down at them, and then he looked at her. He didn't quite smile, but his lips quirked up just faintly at the corners. Up close she could see he had a tear drop tattooed under his right eye.

"Well, alright," he said. "I guess that's all."

He bagged the stuff. Gave her the change.

She couldn't contain herself now. She ripped the bag away and speedwalked out of the air-conditioned space, just shy of jogging. Somehow that heat felt like a mercy when it enveloped her.

And she could just hear his voice call out behind her before the automatic doors swished closed.

"Hey. You have a real good night, Turbo."

CHAPTER 59

Wes leaned back on the hood of John's car, watching the sky brighten bit by bit. John and Courtney had immediately agreed to help Wes search for Ellie, but none of them had any idea where they should start. So they'd returned to the motel to regroup and come up with a plan. It also gave them an opportunity to shower and change clothes, and Wes had managed to charge his phone, too.

Wes squeezed his eyes shut, wracking his brain to come up with some way forward — a next step if not a full-blown plan. He flashed back to the lifeguard hut. How Ellie was there one minute and gone the next. How dark it had been. How fast she seemed to disappear.

John came out of their room in fresh clothes, his hair still wet. He glanced back at the neighboring motel room door.

"Courtney's not ready yet?" John asked.

Wes shook his head.

One of the doors several rooms down swung open, and Dan and Tanya spilled out. While Dan turned back to lock the door, Tanya embraced him and began kissing his neck. Apparently oblivious to the fact that Wes and John were only a few yards away, the couple fell back against the door in another of their prolonged PDA sessions.

John and Wes exchanged a glance.

Awkward.

They suffered in silence for a good two minutes until Tanya actually started moaning.

John cleared his throat purposefully, and the two lovebirds startled and broke apart. Dan looked a bit sheepish until he recognized John and Wes, and then he brightened.

"Oh, hey guys," he said. "Beautiful morning, isn't it?"

He and Tanya approached, hand in hand. Considering they

fought so much, the good spirits seemed odd, and it became clear that they had no idea about the disaster that had unfolded with Ellie last night.

"I guess you didn't hear what happened?" John asked.

Dan smirked.

"Did that scrawny redneck piece of trash come back?"

"No. It's Ellie," John glanced at Wes. "She went missing. Got, like, kidnapped right off the beach."

Dan's jaw went slack.

"What? By who?"

John shrugged.

"No one knows. And then that detective — the one who was asking questions here yesterday morning after you guys found the body — she got killed."

Tanya gasped and looked at her husband, stunned.

"Detective Stinson is dead?"

"Jesus," Dan said. "Are the two things related, you think?"

"Not sure how, but it seems that way." John sighed. "The whole thing is crazy. We're about to head out to try looking for Ellie, but it's like… where do you even start, you know?"

Dan pursed his lips thoughtfully.

"Could follow the detective. The big fella, uh… Taft. Stinson was his partner, so if there's anything to follow up on, clues or whatever… well, I figure he'd lead you right to it."

Wes and John locked eyes.

"That's a good idea, actually."

John leaped to his feet.

"You lock up our room, and I'll go grab Courtney."

Wes rushed to the door, fumbling with the keys for a moment. They had a plan now, and he felt jittery with this new sense of purpose. When he returned to the car, the couple was still there, having some sort of whispered debate that Wes only heard the tail end of.

"I thought you were taking me out to breakfast!" Tanya hissed.

Dan turned away from his wife as John and Courtney came

bustling outside.

"So hey, if you have room for us, we'd love to tag along. You know, lend a helping hand."

John eyed the backseat of the car.

"I mean, it's gonna be a tight fit in that backseat. But it's up to you."

"We'll be fine," Dan said, waving him off. "Won't we, baby?"

Tanya only glared at him, but Wes was barely paying the couple any attention by then.

Things were finally moving now.

CHAPTER 60

A line of gray bleached away the night just along the horizon, a pool of illumination staining the place where the road touched the sky. Ellie stared at the distant glow, somehow uneasy at the prospect of real daylight spilling over all of this, laying it bare, making it more real.

The Corolla ripped up the freeway, rocketing vaguely north. They rode in the left lane. A bunch of slow-ass SUVs and semis flickered by on their right like they were standing still.

Scarlet hunched over the wheel. Her body taut. Her eyes dead. Her mouth a grim flat line.

For now, they'd fallen quiet. Tense.

Ellie sat in the passenger seat, thinking back. Replayed the ride internally as she watched that glimmer of dawn swell in the distance.

First, Scarlet had needed to throw off the cops. Police were out looking for this make and model by now, but Scarlet had switched the license plates in a McDonald's parking lot off one of the exits some miles back. She'd unscrewed a Georgia plate from a metallic blue Hummer the size of a small tank. Left their tainted plate in its place. That should at least buy them a little time, Scarlet had said.

Then, as they hurtled north, Scarlet had explained things, at least somewhat. She'd kept her eyes on the road as she talked, something shiny in them as they caught the dash lights. The details had come out in a rush.

Jimmy had been gut shot on a farm outside of Swamp Hollow. According to the police scanner, he'd gone into emergency surgery at Presbyterian hospital and would likely be there recovering for days, if not weeks.

And then there was the other bit. The part she'd left cryptic.

The part that made her voice waver some as she told it.

This whole crime spree had never been about joy or thrills or anything like that, she'd said. Jimmy and Scarlet were on the run from someone. Someone dangerous. Someone who would stop at nothing to find them, to get them.

Scarlet had grown quiet at that point, and the ride had stayed that way ever since. The sound of Scarlet's breath became the only sound coming from either of them, something almost animal in the way it puffed through her nostrils.

Ellie listened to the drone of the tires humming against the road. Her thoughts spiraled out into empty space.

If Jimmy and Scarlet were the victims, it changed things, didn't it?

Running from someone, in fear for their lives, Scarlet had said.

But then Ellie had been dragged along against her will, plucked out of the night, her car stolen. That made her their victim — or Scarlet's victim, at least.

Scarlet hadn't even had the gun out of the duffel bag since they left the beach, and Ellie had done everything Scarlet told her to do. She hadn't seriously considered trying to run, not at any point.

What does that say about me? Ellie wondered.

The driver's words interrupted the thought.

"Why were you scared, do you think?"

Scarlet turned her head, and their eyes met. Ellie didn't understand.

"What?"

"At the store. You froze, you know. You were terrified to go in and buy some hair dye."

"Oh. I don't know. I don't get taken hostage at gunpoint that often. I guess I *don't* like it."

Scarlet sniffed, and it took Ellie a second to realize it was a laugh.

"I mean… I get that. But I didn't have a gun on you at that point. Just seemed like there was something more to it.

Reminded me of this dog I had way back. If I had something in my hand and held it up in the air, he'd flinch. He'd never been hit, not once, but he had this innate fear. You kinda looked like that."

Scarlet grabbed the can of tea from the cup holder and took a sip before she went on.

"Would you say that you're a fearful type of person? In general, I mean."

"Well, yeah. Definitely."

Scarlet nodded, and the conversation lulled. Strips of tar *thump-thumped* under the tires every few seconds. The highway's heartbeat thrumming through the car.

"Thanks. For buying the hair dye, I mean. And I— Look, if you help me out just a little bit more, I can try to pay you back somehow. I'm not… you know I've never planned to hurt you or anything like that. You were always going to be free to go, just…"

Scarlet seemed to search for the words. That tar pulsed six more times before she finished her thought.

"It'll be over soon. That's all."

Ellie nodded after a second. She didn't know what to say.

Should she tell her captor, *You're welcome*? *No problem*?

She turned to look out the window. Plant life blurred past in a homogeneous smear, colorless in the pre-dawn light.

The quiet settled. It seemed less tense than before. More comfortable. Maybe Scarlet's rambling thoughts had done some good.

"I used to be like you," Scarlet said, breaking up the quiet again. "Scared, I mean. This was back when I was younger, of course. I was just… sort of a meek person. Timid. A victim more than anything."

Ellie gaped at Scarlet and tried to picture it. Scarlet, a wimp? She couldn't quite imagine it.

"This whole outlaw thing got forced on me, really," Scarlet said. "Life or death shit. But I don't regret it."

Scarlet cranked her head toward the backseat to check the

blind spot and then switched into the right lane momentarily to get around a moseying Saab, the enamel mostly sun-bleached off the thing. Then she went on.

"See, life is for living. That's the thing. The universe was here billions of years before we got here. It'll be here billions more after we're gone. You only get this little bit of time. A sliver. You have to take chances, embrace some amount of risk, to live it to the fullest. Put yourself out there. Stick your neck out for whatever you believe, whatever you want. Calculate the odds.

"To make it have any meaning at all, you know you've got to make a stand somewhere. Once I figured that out…"

She trailed off for a few seconds. The tires hummed.

"It's like I read this article once. It was about these studies — neurological, I guess. Basically, to the human body, fear and excitement are the same thing. Adrenaline rush, increased heartbeat, dilated pupils — the physical responses are identical. Whether you're going down a roller coaster or going into a gunfight, your body goes through the same protocol. So what distinguishes the two is mental, it's what the stimulus means to you, how you interpret it, whether or not you feel safe. The difference between fear and excitement is perspective. Nothing more and nothing less. Does that make sense?"

Ellie held still for a second before she remembered to nod.

"So whenever I was scared after that, I started just telling myself, 'You're not scared. You're excited. That's all.' It kind of became this ongoing mantra in a way. I'd start reaching for more colorful words. 'You're thrilled. You're pumped. You're amped. You're elated.' Stuff like that. But eventually I kinda sanded it down to one word. Fun. 'This is fun.' 'We're having fun now.'"

Scarlet fell quiet then, maneuvering through another clogged spot in the traffic. Ellie let the monologue sink in, replaying snippets as she looked out the window at the first flare of real sunlight creeping over the edge of the world.

"Did it work?" she asked.

"What? The mantra?" Scarlet smiled. "Oh yeah. It's subtle at first, maybe. You start standing up for yourself. You start fighting back in small ways. But the next thing you know, you're holding up a liquor store and having a fucking blast doing it. You point a gun at some guy's face and inside you're asking yourself, 'Are we having fun yet?' Some burst of giddiness flowing through you.

"You get addicted to it, I think. The rush of it. And the… velocity of it.

"It's like everything speeds up, turns just this tiny bit overwhelming, all of reality winnowing down to the fine point of right now. The moment gets big, but you walk through it, and it feels good. So good. After that, video games and shit like that… they don't do it anymore, you know. You need the real thing.

"People like us, we start out shying away from contact. Wincing. Flinching, you know. But if you work at it, eventually, you're going into it headfirst. Into life, I mean. Leading with your face."

Scarlet looked over her shoulder again, eyes finding something in the backseat.

"Can you dig in the side pocket of the duffel bag?" she asked. "There's a pack of cigarettes in there. And a lighter."

Ellie undid her seatbelt and climbed halfway into the back, one knee resting on the console. Her head and shoulders hovered over the dark bulk of the bag.

Then she unzipped the pocket and wriggled her fingers into the breach. Coarse fabric pulled taut against both sides of her hand. It took some work to reach down into the hole.

But the first object she felt was neither the cigarettes nor the lighter.

The gun felt cool against her skin in that way only metal can. She recoiled for a second, drew her hand most of the way out of the pocket.

"You find 'em?" Scarlet asked, and Ellie's shoulders jerked.

"Um… Not yet. Must be way down there."

She took in a deep breath. Let it out slow. Then she eased her hand into the fabric mouth once more.

I could take the gun. Right now.

She licked her lips. Her fingers crawled deeper and deeper.

I could make her drop me off. Could get out of this situation. Have her go on her way without me.

Her hand slithered down to the gun again, and she wrapped her fingers around the grip. Felt the heft of it, the power of it, nestle into her palm.

But then she let the gun go and reached beyond it. There were a few other odds and ends inside. A pair of scissors. A compact metal doohickey she thought might be some kind of multi-tool.

Finally her fingers brushed the small box all the way in the bottom corner. She had to work at the cigarettes to finagle them up and out. Thankfully the lighter was stuffed inside the mostly empty pack.

She trusts me. She must.

She only wants to get Jimmy back.

I've never really done anything that matters before… but I think I can help her with that.

She handed the cigarettes over, and Scarlet lit one.

"Thanks." She took a hit, put the window down about half an inch to let the smoke out. "They're Jimmy's. The cigarettes. I actually quit a few months ago. But I guess now…"

Scarlet didn't finish the thought, and she didn't have to. Ellie knew what she meant.

The crack in the window made a steady suction sound like one of those dental tools the hygienist hooks into a patient's lip. The air outside felt fairly cool for now, that trickle of it whipping around in the car.

They raced into a new day, fleeing the small beach town, leaving Wes and the others behind. Even Jimmy was back there in the hospital somewhere. All of it in the past, in the rearview.

Ellie peered through the windshield at the horizon once more. The sun looked like a half-melted thing rising out of the ground — a molten orange disc off to their right for now.

Staring down the road, Ellie realized that she didn't know what the future held. But maybe that was OK.

This is fun, she told herself.

We're having fun. That's all.

CHAPTER 61

It wasn't until they were all inside John's car — with Courtney squeezed in back with Dan and Tanya — that the group realized they needed to locate Detective Taft before they could actually do any following.

"We saw him leave the scene at the beach, but that was hours ago now," John said.

"When in doubt, start with the simplest solution," Dan said. "Let's go down to the cop shop and see if he's there."

"Like, just walk in and ask for him?" Wes asked.

"No!" Dan chuckled. "I know what his vehicle looks like. Seen him roll up in it when we found the body yesterday."

John drove across town to the police station and eased into the main parking lot.

"We're lookin' for a dark blue Ford Bronco. One of the newer models," Dan said.

All eyes were trained out the windows, searching among the rows of cars in tense silence.

Courtney sat forward and pointed to a corner of the lot shaded by a line of magnolia trees.

"There!"

Sure enough, Wes spotted the navy blue Bronco tucked between two pickup trucks.

"Good eye," John said. "So… now what?"

Wes shrugged.

"I guess we wait for him to come out."

John wheeled out of the lot and found a parking spot on the street with a clear shot of the Bronco. From there, they watched and waited. And waited some more.

As the minutes wore on, Wes fidgeted in his seat, worried this whole thing would be a waste of time.

He reminded himself that even though he was sitting still,

he was being proactive. This was the plan they'd come up with.

But it felt counterintuitive, especially after witnessing all the activity when his brother had gone missing. The search parties on the ground. The rescue helicopters in the air. Days of combing the woods from dawn to dusk. By comparison, this effort felt… lackluster.

John put on some kind of industrial music with clicky-sounding drums, though he kept it at a mercifully low volume.

"I actually considered a career in MMA at one time," Dan said, continuing a conversation Wes hadn't heard the start of. "Kinda wish I'd had a chance to try out some of my old moves."

"MMA?" Tanya repeated.

"Yeah. You know, mixed martial arts?"

"I know what it stands for," she said, her tone dismissive. "But since when did you ever do any MMA? I've never seen you do so much as a push-up."

Dan sniffed.

"It was before we met."

Tanya let out a bitter laugh.

"Uh-huh."

Wes didn't understand couples who did this. Did they think other people thought the caustic banter was endearing? Because it was not.

He glanced over at John, who raised his eyebrows, and then made a show of patting his stomach.

"Dang, did you guys hear that? My tummy is a-rumblin'. I need to eat something. Who else is up for some grub? There's a diner right over there."

Wes wasn't hungry himself, couldn't imagine eating anything, but he was glad for the interruption.

Dan volunteered to take down everyone's order, since he "needed to use the facilities," to which Tanya snorted and muttered, "shocker."

Wes couldn't help but feel somewhat relieved when the two of them were out of the car. He was starting to wish they hadn't come along, even though Dan was the one who'd suggested following Taft in the first place. They reminded him too much of his parents and of all the family vacations they'd ruined with their incessant bickering.

He tried for a while to remember one family outing that hadn't been derailed by some fight over something trivial and stupid. He failed. He was certain there wasn't one.

Wes's eyes strayed from the smoked glass of the entrance to the digital clock on the car dash. They'd been sitting out here for at least forty minutes now, and it was impossible to say how much longer Taft would be inside. They might be waiting out here all damn day.

Dan and Tanya returned with two paper bags filled with food, handing out the various items everyone had ordered.

"Got coffee for everyone," Dan said. "Hope that's OK."

Wes had been certain he wasn't hungry, but now that he had the bagel he'd ordered in hand, he found himself eating ravenously and washing it down with scalding diner coffee that somehow tasted way better than anything he made at home.

When they'd finished eating, Wes gathered everyone's trash into one of the bags and got out to toss it in a nearby garbage bin. He glared over at the police station as he stalked back to the car. What was Taft doing in there, anyway? Shouldn't he be out somewhere, looking for Ellie? Instead he was probably stuffing his face with donuts.

Even more reason to take things into their own hands.

When he climbed back into the car, John gave him a wide-eyed look he couldn't discern at first. It was only once he settled into his seat that he started hearing snippets of a whispered argument between Dan and Tanya over the music.

"—unacceptable, and frankly? An embarrassment. We've been here for almost a week, and you've only taken me out *three times*! Some vacation."

Dan murmured something Wes couldn't make out.

"No. Takeout does *not* count," Tanya said. "You promised me *brunch*. That means a *sit-down* meal at a *nice* restaurant *with* mimosas, not greasy diner food out of a paper sack while we play *Scooby-Doo*. And what about the sunset cruise you said we were going on? The one that was going to be so romantic. This vacation is a joke."

Wes cringed. The awkward atmosphere in the car wasn't just thickening, he thought. It was congealing into a gelatinous mass of bad vibes.

Courtney suddenly sat forward, raising her voice over Tanya to be heard.

"Everybody shut up!" She gestured at the police station. "Look!"

The front door stood open, swinging wildly on its hinges, and Taft was moving so fast he was already halfway down the sidewalk.

The detective hopped into his SUV, backed out of his parking space, and sped out of the lot.

Wes's heart started thudding. He looked over at John.

He gave a wordless nod before putting the car in gear and following.

CHAPTER 62

Wes tugged the beanie lower on his head as he stepped up to the entrance of the drug store. The automatic door whooshed aside, and there was an electronic *beep-boop* to alert the employees that someone had entered.

Through the gap in the side of his sunglasses, Wes spied Detective Taft at one of the registers, talking to the clerk there. He breezed past the two of them, walking all the way down an aisle lined with make-up and nail polish. Then he swung around an end cap display filled with Easter candy and crept up the next aisle until the detective came into view again.

Wes stopped and adjusted his glasses. Pretended to study the rack of magazines in front of him.

He hoped the sunglasses and hat were enough to make him unrecognizable to Detective Taft. There'd been some argument in the car about who would follow the detective inside.

John had shrugged.

"I think it should be me. I'm not trying to brag, but I'm pretty stealthy."

"She's *my* best friend," Courtney argued.

"Now hold on a minute," Dan said. "This whole thing was my idea. Following the detective and what not. I should be in on this."

"Well you're not going without me," Tanya whined.

"Why don't we all go?" Dan suggested.

"Dude, that would be so incredibly obvious," John said. "It makes me question your ability to stay under the radar, honestly."

Wes had ignored them all, pulling on the hat and sunglasses and checking his reflection in the mirror before opening his door.

"I'm going. Alone." Wes's tone brooked no argument. "I'm

the one who let her get taken. This is on me."

Now inside, Wes selected a magazine at random and focused surreptitiously on the conversation happening at the front counter.

"I need you to take a look at a photo for me," Taft said. "Can you confirm this is the woman you saw this morning?"

Taft scrolled through some pictures on his phone, probably the photo of Ellie that Courtney had given Taft this morning as well as whatever the police had dug up on her social media.

The clerk squinted at the phone. His eyelids kept crinkling in little spasms, some kind of tic that scrunched up the teardrop tattoo under his left eye. After a few seconds, he nodded.

"I recognized the one photo on TV, and then these others. Yeah. That's definitely her. She was wearing, like, real baggy clothes, though."

"Now if you could take a look at another photo," Taft said, swiping at his phone screen.

"That's that Scarlet chick from the news!" He stood up straighter and his eyes went wide. "She has something to do with the missing girl?"

"I just need to know if you saw her."

"Well, as far as here in the store, I only saw the first girl."

"Can I get a copy of the receipt for the purchase she made?" Taft asked.

"Sure. Just a second," the clerk tapped at the keyboard connected to the register. "I can tell you exactly what she bought, though. Clairol Natural Instincts and a can of AriZona iced tea. The green tea one."

Taft jotted this down.

"A box of hair dye and iced tea? That's it?"

"It was multiple boxes of hair dye — two — but yeah. Nothing else."

"Did she say anything?"

"Uh… she seemed uptight. Quiet. I just remember she kinda threw her money at me. Two twenties all wadded up. I think that's the only reason I remembered her at all. I kinda thought she was a tweaker or somethin'." He pointed a finger at one of the security camera domes overhead. "I pulled up the security footage, if you want to see it."

Wes took a step closer as the clerk angled his computer screen so Taft could more easily see it.

There was Ellie, on the screen. His stomach fluttered at the sight of her. She'd been here. Right here. Five or ten feet from where he stood. It was reassuring and frustrating at the same time.

As Ellie's form flitted over the screen, Wes scooted back down the aisle a bit. He replaced the magazine he'd been holding and picked up a new one while he continued eavesdropping.

Taft was telling the clerk he'd need copies of the footage, and the clerk was explaining that he didn't have access to the raw files.

"We'll need a manager for that."

He grabbed a phone, punched in a code on the dial pad, and then his voice was suddenly blaring from the speaks overhead.

"Kim, you're needed at register 1. Kim to register 1."

The clerk replaced the phone on the cradle.

"It'll be just a minute," he said.

With barely a pause, his eyes whipped over to where Wes was standing.

"You need to buy something or leave, bud. This ain't a library."

Wes was so startled, he actually jumped and dropped the magazine, which he now saw was one of those trashy gossip rags. He stared down at a picture of one of those reality TV celebrities in a bikini with a giant headline in bright yellow text: *THUNDER THIGHS?*

He scrambled to retrieve the magazine, which kept slipping from his grasp. Finally, he snatched it up and placed it back on the shelf. When he turned, he found Taft staring at him.

Shit.

Wes spun around and hurried back down the aisle. He glanced once over his shoulder. Found that Taft didn't seem to be following him.

The automatic doors whooshed again, and he was outside. Home free.

He took two steps and felt a hand on his shoulder.

Taft whipped him around.

"Thought that was you." He gave him a hard look. "You following me?"

Wes gulped.

"No. I mean… maybe. Yeah."

He wasn't sure why he'd admitted it, but it wasn't like what they were doing was illegal.

Taft took a breath and then sighed.

"Look, I get it. You want to find your friend." A sad look passed over the detective's features. "But we're on it. There's nothing you can do for now, OK? Just step aside, and let me do my job."

Wes didn't say anything.

"If it makes you feel any better, I don't think Ellie is in mortal danger."

"You can't be serious," Wes said, staring at the detective. "She was *abducted*. How is she *not* in mortal danger?"

Taft folded his arms across his broad chest.

"I know everyone likes to play amateur sleuth these days, what with all the true crime crap on TV and the internet. But this case is more complicated than it seems on the surface. There are a lot of details the public isn't privy—"

But Taft was interrupted by a squawk over the radio clipped to his belt.

"Detective Taft? We just got a call from the highway patrol. The vehicle listed in this morning's APB has been located at Shelbyville Public Beach."

Shelbyville, Wes thought. *That's not far from here. Twenty or thirty miles, maybe.*

He remembered driving past it when he and John first came down the coast.

Wes and Taft took off at the same moment, sprinting for their cars.

The detective aimed a finger at him without breaking his stride.

"Don't you go getting any ideas, son. Just step back, and let the professionals handle this."

But Wes was already sliding into the passenger seat and punching the destination into the GPS on John's phone.

CHAPTER 63

They zoomed north on the highway. Wes watched Taft's vehicle disappear over a rise up ahead as people made way for the flashing emergency lights.

"I don't get it," Courtney said. "They found her car. Are you sure they didn't find Ellie too?"

Wes swallowed.

"I don't know. The dispatcher only mentioned the car."

The bagel he'd eaten earlier churned in his stomach as he considered the implications.

Detective Taft had said that Ellie wasn't in mortal danger. But what about the body from that morning? What about Detective Stinson?

Unbidden, an image popped into Wes's mind — the trunk of Ellie's Corolla slowly opening to reveal her body tucked inside.

No.

He shook his head a little as if he could clear the intrusive thought away the same way he might erase an Etch A Sketch.

Ellie is fine, he told himself. *Detective Taft said so.*

They spotted the scene before they'd even reached the Shelbyville exit. The public beach was just off the highway, and the knot of police vehicles clustered in the parking lot would have been impossible to miss. All those flashing lights surrounding Ellie's car.

Again, the image of Ellie in the trunk flashed in his mind.

Stop being ridiculous, he thought to himself.

John pulled into a gas station across the street from the scene, choosing a spot where they could observe from a distance, keeping well outside the police tape. But Wes was done sitting on the sidelines.

As soon as the car came to a stop, he jumped out.

He waited for a break in the traffic before stalking across the street. When he reached the beach, he found he wasn't alone. A group of civilians huddled up against the sawhorse there. Rubberneckers in bikinis and board shorts.

Wes found the whole thing distasteful. This wasn't entertainment.

He forgot his irritation when he turned and caught sight of the car for the first time. The trunk was open.

His heart seemed to stop for a second before taking off at a gallop like a spooked horse.

He couldn't actually see the inside of the trunk from where he was. Could just see the lid hovering in the air.

He froze as a tech stepped up to the gaping cavity and aimed a camera inside.

Oh God, Wes thought. *What is she taking pictures of?*

The camera flashed once, twice, three times. And then, with a gloved hand, the tech reached up and closed the trunk.

Wes's body went so limp with relief, he almost fell over.

John, Courtney, Dan, and Tanya joined him a few minutes later, along with more random people from the beach. The crowd grew to several dozen at one point, but as it became clear that nothing overtly exciting was happening, the group waned until nearly all of the gawkers had wandered off in boredom. It was simply a car parked haphazardly, to their eyes.

Wes was simultaneously glad and irked. On the one hand, he was pleased their nosiness hadn't been rewarded. On the other, he felt they should be forced to stay until they knew more. They had no idea what happened to Ellie yet. How could they just leave?

The temperature rose as the sun grew higher in the sky, and with no shade, the breeze off the water only offered so much relief. A bead of sweat ran down Wes's forehead. He wiped it away, not moving his eyes from the scene.

Somewhere behind him, Tanya was whining about the heat in a hushed tone, but he tuned her out. He'd just spied Taft chatting with some of the other police on the scene. Yet again, the detective didn't seem to be *doing* anything. He was only standing there, yacking.

At some point, a bottle of Gatorade was thrust in front of his face. Orange fluid lurching for the mouth hole.

"You should drink some of this," Courtney said.

Wes took a few gulps and handed it back. He wondered dimly who had gotten drinks and when, knew it would be considered polite to ask and say thank you, but he couldn't bring himself to pretend to care just now. He wanted to know what was going on with the scene. Ellie's car was here, so then where was Ellie?

Finally, after what felt like hours, Taft walked over to where they were standing.

"They're gone. Probably heading north, if they got back on the highway here. According to witnesses, the car was here for quite a while before highway patrol found it, so they could be a hundred miles from here by now."

"They?" Wes repeated, not sure he was understanding. "You're saying Scarlet still has Ellie?"

Taft nodded and looked out over the vast sea.

"I'm afraid so."

CHAPTER 64

Scarlet leaned over so far that she just about laid down in the driver's seat of the Hyundai. Then she felt along the contoured plastic under the steering wheel.

Her fingernail found a seam, and she dug at the cleft. Pulled. The plastic bowed, the gap curling like a grimacing mouth. Scarlet hooked two fingers into the chasm.

With one sudden motion, she ripped the plastic panel free. Let it drop to the floor.

The cavity gaped where the cover had been. A shadowy opening exposing one square of the car's innards.

And then, as though somehow delayed for a full second, a mess of wires and cables spilled out of the gap like a tipped plate of angel hair pasta. Bundles of fine threads tumbling forth in a multitude of colors.

Ellie watched all of this from the passenger seat, half-scanning the alley outside for any pedestrians as she did. Her eyes kept flitting back and forth.

Now Scarlet pulled a stainless steel multi-tool out of her pocket. Unfolded the pliers.

She prodded around with the needle-nose of the tool, sifting through the rainbow of cords with the fingers of her opposite hand.

"You got it?" Ellie said, her voice low.

A beat passed before Scarlet answered.

"Shit, I don't know. Jimmy usually does this part."

Ellie didn't like the sound of that. Didn't like sitting here in some random person's car. They were pinned down here in an alley, unable to really flee, at least for the moment.

She swiveled her head one way and then the other, eyes sweeping over the full expanse.

Cars surged by on the streets beyond their position. The

alley itself remained empty.

Still, she missed the familiar confines of her own car. And part of her worried about how that would play out.

They'd ditched it as part of Scarlet's plan. Left it somewhere conspicuous. The open loop made her uncomfortable, and she thought about her parents again. If they found out about *any* of this…

Can't worry about that now.

She let her gaze drift back to where Scarlet was wrist-deep in the rat's nest of wires. Her face contorted, and she shifted in her seat, as if straining for something out of reach.

She'd said Jimmy usually did this part, which implied that Scarlet had done it herself at least once. Didn't it? Except, what if *usually* meant *always*? What if Scarlet didn't know what she was doing at all?

Ellie clamped her lips together to stop herself from asking. It wasn't like pestering Scarlet about it was going to help.

Something rippled there in the corner of Ellie's eye. The motion drew her attention back to the mouth of the alley.

A man. Maybe mid-30s. White blonde hair slicked back. Broad shoulders. Black t-shirt and aviator sunglasses. He curled into the alley, torso pretty much squared at the Hyundai. Something jaunty in his step.

Ellie hunched down in the seat. Her voice sounded husky and strange when it came out.

"Someone is coming."

Scarlet kept working, wrenching at something under the steering wheel.

"Just play it cool."

Ellie caught her own reflection in the rearview just as she licked her lips. She looked like a nervous poodle.

Yeah. Sure. I'll just play it cool.

"OK. But, like, if this is his car, won't he… uh… freak out?"

"It's probably not his."

Now Scarlet bent forward, her face practically touching the ignition keyhole. The process seemed to be going in slow motion.

The man was about halfway down the alley. He hadn't changed trajectory at all.

"OK," Ellie said, the syllables coming out slowly. "But, just so you know, the guy is walking straight for us."

Scarlet let out a long breath. Her glare flicked up from the wires, but she wasn't looking at the encroaching man. Her eyes swiveled higher than that. Then her voice came out in a deadpan.

"Ah. Of course."

She flipped down the visor, and the keys tumbled into her lap.

Then she was jamming one home. Cranking the ignition.

The starter groaned, and the engine caught. The car jolted once as it started like a wet dog shaking the moisture away.

Outside, the man gave a start. His whole body rocking back half a step.

Scarlet's hand floated between the seats and grappled the gearshift.

Ellie's head kept snapping back and forth between the shifter and the pedestrian. Chin bobbling up and down.

He was moving again. Coming for them. Faster than before, maybe?

Scarlet put it in drive, and they lurched out of the parking spot, already building speed.

Ellie turned in her seat and looked back at the man as they left him in the alley.

"Huh," she said.

"What?"

"He just kept walking. Guess it really wasn't his car."

CHAPTER 65

Ellie clomped out of the lobby and into the parking lot, shaking the motel key in her hand. She held it high so Scarlet would be able to see it from her vantage point in the car. The sun scalded the back of her neck.

A bad smell wafted here, something salty and somehow reminiscent of French onion soup gone sour. But the odor fit the decor, Ellie supposed. Concrete blocks formed the motel walls, peeling white paint covering most of the facade. Red doors stood out from the dirty white. Gaping wounds in the brickwork.

The landscaping looked wilted and dead. Brown pine needles sculpted into bony shapes that must have been bushes once.

She walked seven doors down the sidewalk to the door of their room, number nine. Scarlet trailed along in the Elantra and parked outside the door. Then they hustled inside.

The interior lived up to the standard the cracked paint had set. Mud brown carpet shagged over the floors. Wood paneling shot up the walls.

A brown-on-brown look. Nice.

The orange bedspread gave a pumpkin spice feel to the affair, kind of pulled all the brown shades under the autumn umbrella. It really tied the room together, in Ellie's opinion.

She held out a cupped hand of change toward Scarlet and then gave her a small stack of bills to go with it.

"I got the room for an hour, like you said."

Scarlet nodded.

"As long as we hustle, that's all we'll need."

Scarlet pocketed the cash and led the march into the dark doorway of the bathroom. She flipped on the light switch and most of the bulbs above the vanity came on, buzzing like a nest of mosquito zappers.

Green linoleum stretched faux mosaic tiles over the floor. Black mildew laced the inside of a clear shower curtain going cloudy.

Scarlet held up the plastic bag from the pharmacy, the loops hooked over her left forearm. Ellie watched her double mimic her in the mirror.

"You're up first, so let's decide on colors," Scarlet said. "You want Mushroom Blonde or Sunset Peach?"

Ellie squinted like she was trying to look through the white plastic wall of the bag.

"Those can't be the real color names."

Scarlet fished them out of the bag. Held them up. They were the real color names.

"If I were you? I'd go bold and opt for the peach. But it's your call."

Ellie watched herself grimace in the mirror. Her throat flexed as she swallowed.

"I mean… Shouldn't I, like, bleach my hair first?"

"There's bleach already in it," Scarlet said. "Haven't you ever dyed your hair before?"

Ellie shook her head.

"Never?"

"My parents wouldn't let me."

She instantly wished she hadn't said it and winced when Scarlet chuckled.

"Well, what the hell? Why even ask for their permission?"

"It's not that… I'd never ask to do it in the first place, because I know how disappointed they'd be."

Scarlet made a *psht* sound.

"Girl, you can't let other people live your life. They already got theirs. They don't get yours, too."

The statement hit Ellie in the gut like a closed fist. She stared down at the boxes of hair dye, waiting until she regained the ability to speak.

After a few seconds, she flicked a finger against one of the packages.

"Guess I'll go for the Sunset Peach, then."

Then she was leaning over the side of the bathtub, warm water running over her head, soaking her hair, Scarlet's fingers splaying through the strands and rubbing in shampoo.

After her hair was clean, she toweled down, and they got to work with the dye.

She sat on the floor, another ratty towel protecting her rump from the green linoleum. Her head leaned back, neck resting on the edge of the tub.

Scarlet squirted the almost-magenta goo just along the roots, starting at the hairline and working her way back, massaging the dye in with a plastic-gloved hand that crinkled all along the way.

Ellie could really only see the bottle getting close and then the smudge of dye on those plastic fingers. It made a sucking noise like a ketchup bottle at a diner every time Scarlet finished a squeeze.

It felt strange, being so close to this criminal she'd seen on TV. Sharing this strange moment.

It seemed like she should dislike Scarlet or at least be angry at her, but she only felt empathy and a strange frustration that this was the path she'd chosen for herself. Maybe it was Stockholm syndrome. She didn't know.

She watched the girl up close, saw the intense focus in her eyes as she worked. Something electric animated this one. She seemed more alive than anyone Ellie had ever known. So why had she done the things she'd done? Scarlet struck her as the type of person who could do anything she set her mind to.

She felt overcome by a strange urge to defend her parents, suddenly. Worried that she'd given Scarlet the wrong impression.

"I don't mean to make them sound like bad people," she blurted into the silence.

Scarlet blinked.

"Who?"

"My parents."

"Oh," Scarlet said. "Sure."

Was she smirking?

"Because they're not," Ellie insisted.

"If you say so."

The smirk was still there.

After a beat, Ellie asked, "Well, what are *your* parents like?"

And then Scarlet got this look in her eye, and Ellie instantly regretted that she'd asked.

"Sorry," Ellie said. "I didn't mean to pry."

She'd gotten too complacent. Started thinking of Scarlet as, well… maybe not a *friend*, but as someone she could just have a regular old conversation with.

The quiet in the room only seemed to intensify the buzz shivering out of those light bulbs up above the mirror.

She was afraid to look at the other girl now, afraid that she'd offended her with her nosiness. But when she finally worked up the nerve to glance at the other girl's face, Scarlet didn't appear angry at all. Just lost in thought.

She recalled something Courtney was always telling her.

You worry too much.

Ellie inhaled and tried to let those worries fall away. Every pore and follicle growing sensitive, every detail sharpening into brilliant focus. Nothing left but the present moment.

And it suddenly felt right to Ellie somehow. This time. This place. This moment. This course of action.

She'd done the exact opposite of what her parents wanted for once. Gone out on her own. Gotten mixed up in something bigger than herself.

And it was scary. But maybe that was OK.

Maybe life should be scary sometimes.

She helped Scarlet apply the other box of dye, smeared the beige goo over the dark curls. Watched the black strands shift lighter and lighter over the course of the next twenty minutes.

"I'm gonna wash mine out first," Scarlet said, after pulling a small lock of hair loose and studying it in the mirror. "I've dyed my hair so many times this past month, I'm worried it'll fry it if I leave this on any longer."

Scarlet wrenched on the faucet. The water gushed and slapped the porcelain, and she wriggled her fingers in the stream to get the temp right.

She hummed softly as she ducked her head under the deluge.

Next it was Ellie's turn, and she once more put her head under the water. Felt the warmth stream over her skull. Felt the fluid momentarily clog her ears so the sounds inside seemed louder than those outside. She opened her eyes and looked at the brightness through that surging lens of the water.

A baptism, she thought. *A new beginning.*

She pulled her head out of the flow. Leaned over the empty tub and watched the rivulets drizzle down.

And she breathed. And her heart beat. And she was alive.

After a few seconds, she found a dry portion of towel and swiped it at her forehead and ears. Mopped the drips away.

A little snick sounded behind her. Metal gliding against metal. Familiar.

Scarlet gave the barber's shears another couple squeezes. "Just a little off the top, right?"

CHAPTER 66

Scarlet begins to talk as she drapes a towel around Ellie's shoulders and combs her hair into sections.

"You asked what my parents were like?"

"You don't have to tell me." Ellie shakes her head a little. "It's none of my business."

"No. I think it is," Scarlet says. "I told you I'd tell you the whole story, and there's still one bit I left kinda vague. My parents would be as good a place to start as any."

The scissors snick and a clump of salmon-colored hair drifts to the floor.

"I'll put it like this: I barely ever knew my dad, and that's not because he wasn't around. He was. But my mom was his second marriage — he had a wife and kids that he basically left for her."

Scarlet chews her lip, tries to think of how to best explain it. She's thought about it a lot, but putting it into words is something else.

"I think he thought he was escaping something by leaving them. Then my mom got pregnant, and it was like he was starting the whole cycle over again.

"But instead of leaving us like he did his first family, he just checked out instead. Don't think I ever exchanged more than two sentences at a time with that man, and it was usually along the lines of, 'Scarlet, go fetch me a beer from the fridge.' And I'd say, 'OK.' And then I'd hand him the beer and kinda stand there, hoping for… oh, I don't know what. And eventually he'd see I was still standing there, and he'd tell me, 'Now go watch TV or something.'

"And my mom, well… let's just say she didn't really want me around either. They weren't like some parents, not overtly abusive or anything. But they treated me like a bother. Like I was always in the way. I remember being six, and my mom showing me how to make Kraft macaroni. And at the end, she said, 'There. Now you can do it yourself.' And that was it. She pretty much didn't cook for me after that."

She shrugs.

"So it didn't take much for him to win me over. Shane, I mean. He just acted interested in me. Asked me what music I listened to and what movies I liked. But I'm gettin' ahead of myself."

She sighs. Goes on.

"We moved to Charlotte right after I turned sixteen. I made friends with a girl in my biology class. Gina. And Gina's older brother would buy Adderall from Shane, so that was how we ended up meeting.

"I was over at her house, and we were hanging out in the garage where Gina's brother had his drum kit set up. There were some old couches out there and Christmas lights, and sometimes they'd have parties there. Anyway, Shane showed up, looking for Gina's brother, only he had run to the store for Gina's mom and wasn't there.

"So we ended up talking with Shane a little while he waited for her brother to get back. I hardly thought anything of it at the time. But I guess he got her brother to get my phone number for him, and pretty soon we were talking all the time."

Scarlet steps around in front of Ellie and drags the comb through the front of her hair.

"He told me he was only nineteen at first, but I found out later that was a lie. He was 23. I can't say if it would have made a difference to me, though. There was something flattering about an older guy taking such an interest in me, you know? And at that age, you kinda think you're all grown up, even though you're still just a kid."

Scarlet isn't sure how much of this Ellie will truly get. From the sound of it, this one has lived a pretty sheltered life up until now. But she sees the girl nodding, smiling a little. Maybe she does understand.

"Eventually my mom found out about him, and wouldn't you know, that finally got her attention. Suddenly she was super interested in knowing what I was up to. Tried telling me I couldn't see him anymore, that he was too old, but I couldn't take her seriously. It was like, after all these years of not giving two shits, now you're gonna act like you care what I do, like you care about what happens to me?"

Scarlet falls quiet for a few seconds. Snippets of all the old memories flitting in her head.

"Anyway, right around the time I graduated high school, things got pretty bad at home with my mom. We were fighting all the time. So when Shane suggested I move in with him, I was all over the idea.

"I figured I'd get a job, split rent with him, but he insisted I stay at home. Said taking care of the place would be my job. And it seemed fun at first. Exciting. Felt like I was a real grown up. Living with a man. Just the two of us. No parents there to act like I didn't exist one minute and be all up in my business the next.

"He worked full time as a tow truck driver, doing repos, and the house was this run-down old place out in the boonies. So I was alone all day by myself. Didn't even have any neighbors to talk to. I didn't have a car. Didn't have any money of my own.

"And if I did happen to have any kind of plans — I went out a time or two with friends I knew from school — he wanted me to account for every second I was out of the house. He was jealous of everyone I talked to, even girls."

Scarlet stops cutting then. More memories coming in flashes.

"He didn't seem to want me to have friends or any kind of life outside of that house. I think he wanted it so I was reliant on him for everything. Because then… I'd be trapped."

She swallows, and it almost feels like there's something stuck back there. Poised to choke her.

"And I was."

She snaps out of the momentary daze and starts working the comb through Ellie's hair again. Snipping here and there with the scissors.

"Over time, he got more and more particular about things around the house. How I cooked. How I cleaned. If any little thing wasn't how he liked it, he'd get mad. Real mad.

"And you better believe that he expected sex whenever he got the urge. Whether I was in the mood or not was simply never a consideration."

Scarlet sucks in a long breath. She doesn't like to think about this. Likes talking about it even less. She'd escaped it all, and remembering it somehow draws her back to that time, awakens all the ancient feelings.

But she'd promised. Promised to tell Ellie the whole story.

She lets the breath out, and the words spill out with it.

"The first time he hit me was because I burnt some cornbread."

She avoids looking at Ellie's face when she says it. Worries what she might see written there.

"I started telling myself I'm going to leave. But I didn't know where to go. I didn't have friends, you know? And home didn't feel like a place I was welcome anymore.

"And then he apologizes, and it seems sincere. And you kinda just let it slide. Not thinking about it somehow becomes easier, the path of least resistance. I think a lot of things in life are like that."

She closes her eyes and shakes her head.

"So I stayed. And he changed. For a while. Maybe a month or two went by before something else set him off. I forgot to put the laundry in the dryer, or he 'didn't like the tone of my voice.' The cycle played out over and over.

"I'd been living in that house with him almost a year and a half when Shane got a DUI. Boom — automatic license suspension for one year. Kiss the towing job goodbye.

"So that's when he decided it was my turn to work. That's how he said it, too. Not, 'Hey, baby, I messed up and now you're going to have to get a job so we can keep paying the bills.' No, he acted like all along he'd been doing me a big favor, and he was tired of pulling all the weight."

She puts her hands on her hips then. The open scissors jut from her clenched fist.

"He sat around all day, gettin' drunk and high. Fiddling with his stupid car when the mood struck. And still expected me to come home after work and make dinner and clean up all the crap he'd left around all day and be ready to suck his dick on command."

She takes a step back then. Studies Ellie. Make a few small snips here and there. Then she nods.

"OK, turn around and take a look. Not too bad, right?"

Ellie spins so she can see herself in the mirror. Gapes at her reflection.

"I don't even look like me."

Scarlet grins.

"That's the idea." She lifts the shears. "My turn."

She turns her head from one side to the other in the mirror and starts chopping in a much more haphazard fashion compared to the care she'd taken with Ellie's hair. Talking about Shane, about the person she used to be, makes her want to punish herself a little. Penance for putting up with it for so long.

"So what was it like? Getting your first job?" Ellie asks.

"At first I was terrified. It felt like an eternity since I'd been around other people or socialized with anyone other than him. That does something to you. That isolation. That level of dependence. It gets under your skin. Makes going out on your own sort of overwhelming.

"I had no job experience to speak of, so the best I could get was bagging groceries at the Food Lion. And suddenly I had a boss and coworkers, and for eight hours a day, I was out of that house. Away from him. I don't think most people equate a dead-end job like that with freedom, but for me? It felt like salvation.

"I didn't have any plans at first. Didn't think of it as a way out, exactly. Just a reprieve. That's how much he messed me up, you know? He had me thinking I *couldn't* get away."

She pauses with the scissors next to her face.

"But then I met Jimmy. He worked at the supermarket too, and he'd do the goofiest shit for a laugh. We got to talking sometimes, and he would just listen. I hadn't had that for so long."

She brings the blades of the scissors together with a *snick*.

"I'd been at the Food Lion for a few months when I watched Shane almost beat a man to death. He was still dealing drugs here and there, and this guy tried to pay with some real crappy counterfeit bills. Shane lost it. Just threw the guy down and started kicking his teeth in.

"It felt like I was in a nightmare. Like it couldn't be real. This guy's face all bloody and mangled, not ten feet from where I was sitting.

"I don't know what Shane was thinking. I mean, I guess he wasn't thinking anything, because we were right outside a crowded bar when it happened. There were witnesses. Lots of 'em. And one of them called the cops. The guy ended up surviving but just barely. He was real messed up.

"Shane was in jail then. Awaiting trial. They said he was facing up to 40 years, and I was finally free."

Another snip takes a chunk of Scarlet's hair. The tuft floats down into the sink.

"I remember the house felt so empty. So quiet. It wasn't peaceful, though. More eerie. Like some negative energy was still there. Something restless.

"I got closer with Jimmy, and eventually we moved in together. *That* was peaceful finally. Happy finally.

"More than a year went by like that. It seemed like the worst was over, ya know? But then Shane got out. He hadn't gotten 40 years after all. Just 5. And good behavior knocked it down to 18 months plus the time served awaiting trial."

Scarlet lets out a sigh before she continues.

"That's when the stalking started. He slashed Jimmy's tires a bunch of times. Broke into our place and laid out some of my clothes on the bed. Clothes that he'd bought me. I went to the cops, but there was no evidence. Nothing to prove it was him doing it."

Scarlet stares into nothingness. Thinking.

"There was an escalation to it. Eventually there was a note. A blank envelope left in the mailbox. Letters cut out of magazines. 'Do you want to die?' When we got that, I figured that was our big cue."

Her eyes swivel to meet Ellie's in the mirror before she finishes the thought.

"Life has a way of pushing you into a corner, I think. When the moment comes, you change or you die. That's the way the universe works. Like evolution, you know?

"We had to leave. Had to do something drastic. Had to get so far away he could never find us. Or at least try."

She blinks in the mirror, and then her gaze steadies.

"So… here we are."

CHAPTER 67

John's car hurtled down the highway, tracing back the way it had come. The sun rose higher in the sky, and Wes found the glare leaking over everything somehow maddening.

No one spoke on the ride back to the motel. Even Tanya had stopped griping at Dan, seeming to have finally sensed that now was not the time.

Taft's words echoed in Wes's mind.

...they're gone. Could be a hundred miles from here by now.

Wes remembered his pathetic attempts to bargain with the detective before his friends had dragged him away.

"Can't you, like, trace Ellie's credit cards or something? Track her phone?"

Taft had sighed.

"We're doing that, and keeping an eye on all of her accounts, but... I'm sorry. Right now, we're at somewhat of a dead end."

Wes understood what Taft was saying, but he couldn't accept it. Surely they could do *something* more than they were already doing.

It was only when he saw the familiar "Welcome to Durango Beach" sign with the illustration of the crisscrossed palm trees that Wes snapped out of his funk.

This was a shitty situation all around, and the cops seemed pretty hopeless, but sitting around feeling sorry for himself wasn't going to help find Ellie. He knew that. If he couldn't rely on the cops, then clearly it fell back on him.

And yeah, their first attempt had been a bust. But that just meant it was time to come up with Plan B.

He sat up straighter in his seat, feeling a little less disheartened already.

First, he'd need to rally the troops. He wasn't the only one to feel the blow of finding Ellie's abandoned car like that. But it was going to be on him to keep everyone motivated.

Dan had been the one to suggest following the detective before, Wes remembered. And even though it hadn't been quite the breakthrough he'd been hoping for, they *had* gotten more information. Maybe Dan would have another idea.

Wes turned in his seat to address him but found that everyone in the backseat was fast asleep. Courtney's cheek was mashed against the window on one side, Dan's on the other. Tanya's head lolled on her husband's shoulder.

Blinking rapidly, Wes swiveled to face forward again.

John peered over at him from the driver's seat.

"You OK?"

"Everyone's asleep," Wes said.

John checked the rearview mirror and then smiled.

"Guess they were tired."

Wes nodded, trying not to judge. It seemed… wrong. How could anyone sleep at a time like this?

All three slept soundly until John brought the vehicle to a stop in the motel parking lot and turned off the ignition.

Everyone climbed out and then stood around somewhat awkwardly, as if each person was waiting for someone else to say something.

Wes figured now was as good a time as any to broach the subject of continuing their search efforts, but before he could say anything, Tanya spoke up.

"Well, we really hope you guys find your friend," she said, grabbing Dan by the elbow and taking a few steps away from the group.

"Oh…" Wes said. "You guys are leaving?"

Dan and Tanya exchanged a look. He thought maybe Dan would put his foot down again, like he'd done earlier this morning. But he gave a sheepish shrug instead.

"I mean, we gave it our best shot," he said. "And you heard what the detective said. They could be anywhere by now. I figure it's probably best to let the professionals handle it from here."

He yawned and stretched theatrically.

"Also? I'm, like, totally beat. And there's this boat ride we've been wanting to go on, so we really need to get some rest if we're gonna do that."

Wes didn't know what to say. They were going to just… continue on with their vacation like nothing had happened?

Before he could think of a response, the couple had disappeared inside their room.

He closed his eyes and let the anger swell. Observed it like an outsider. It seemed to fade after that.

What had he expected? They didn't really know Ellie.

The world goes on. With or without us. It was, somehow, the way of things.

Still, he couldn't help but feel like this was a setback, losing some of the party. They'd felt like a team before. Strength in numbers or something.

Courtney rubbed her eyes and sighed.

"I think Dan and Tanya have the right idea about getting some sleep."

Wes's head whipped around.

"You want to sleep?"

"I mean…" Her eyes slid over to John. "For a few hours, at least. Yeah."

Wes's eyelids fluttered open and shut several times.

"But Ellie is still out there."

"Wes, man…"

John clapped a hand on his shoulder, and Wes fought an irrational urge to slap it away.

"We're not giving up," John continued. "But we gotta get some sleep at some point. We can't keep running on empty. That's not good for anyone. Work smarter, not harder, right?"

That anger inside shot up like a bolt of flame. Steadied. Wes stared at them for a few seconds before finally nodding.

"Yeah. OK." He sniffed. "I guess you're right."

"We'll get some shut eye. Refuel," John went on. "Then

we'll be ready to rock again in a few hours. Yeah?"

Wes nodded again.

Courtney chewed her lip and glanced in the direction of her room.

"Would it be OK if I slept in your room? It just seems like it's going to be weird if I'm in my room all by myself."

"Of course, babe," John said. "We've got plenty of space."

Wes followed them inside. John emptied his pockets onto the table next to the door. Wallet, keys, phone. Then he stooped in front of the cooler and handed out bottled waters.

"Gotta stay hydrated." He swished a hand around in the ice that was now almost entirely water. "We should remember to grab some more ice when we go out later, too."

Wes wanted to scream.

Fuck everything that isn't us looking for Ellie right now.

Instead, he just nodded. Again.

There was some do-si-do-ing as everyone took a turn in the bathroom. Courtney went first, then John. When it was Wes's turn, he splashed some cold water on his face and then stared in the mirror as the rivulets ran down and gathered in droplets along his jawline. His eyes looked dark, pitted.

Let it pass. Let it go.

Let them fall asleep.

When he came out of the bathroom, the blinds had been pulled shut. In the dimness, he could just make out the twin lumps of John and Courtney snuggled together on John's bed. Wes flopped down on his mattress, not bothering to get under the covers. He gazed up at the ceiling, studying the popcorn texture and imagining it was the surface of the moon.

It was only a few minutes before he heard faint snoring from the other bed. He peeked over. He could make out more details in the gloom now that his eyes had been given time to adjust.

They were both facing his way with John in the big spoon position. All four eyes closed. Both faces slack. Placid.

Wes checked the digital clock and noted the time. He

decided on ten minutes.

Waiting was excruciating. His heartbeat accelerating like it could speed up the clock. But he wanted to wait until they were in a deeper sleep.

When the ten minutes was up, he slid out of bed and crept over to the table next to the door. There was a pad of paper with the motel logo next to the phone, and he stopped to scribble a quick note.

Couldn't sleep.

Hope it's OK that I took the car.

I'll be back in the afternoon, maybe.

Then he scooped up the key fob, careful not to let the keys jangle.

The door was tricky. As soon as he opened it, a blazing slice of sunlight invaded the velvety darkness of the motel room. Wes took his time, allowing the crack to grow only a millimeter at a time, so that the room grew brighter incrementally. He watched the two sleeping forms on the bed for any signs of waking.

When he gauged the door wide enough for him to squeeze through, he slithered outside and gently pulled the door shut with the softest of clicks. He felt a little thrill at having successfully escaped without waking the other two. It was the same giddiness bordering on nausea that he used to feel in high school when he snuck out of his parents' house in the wee hours.

The wind rolled in off the distant beach and riffled his hair as he jogged over to the car. He unlocked it, slid behind the wheel, and tugged the door closed.

All at once the sound of the sea cut out. It felt strange to be alone in such quiet, and that queasy-yet-excited feeling squirmed in his gut again like an eel.

He started the car and backed out of the parking spot, news radio burbling out of the speakers.

Where the parking lot opened onto the street, he stopped, trying to decide which way to go.

He made eye contact with his reflection in the rearview mirror. That narrow slice of his face staring back at him.

Now what, genius? it seemed to ask.

The radio suddenly spat out a familiar name, and he reached to turn the volume up.

"Detective Stinson is the first officer killed in the line of duty in Durango County since 1986."

The audio cut to what sounded like a snippet from a press conference, the chief of police talking.

"As the commanding officer of Detective Stinson, I can't help but feel that all the residents of Durango County have been made poorer. Robbed of a brilliant detective, a loyal friend, a dedicated mother. Stripped of one of our own and one of our best."

Details about how to donate to a memorial fund for the family followed before the report went on. Bits of the crimes were recapped, the murder out at the farm. The hit and run and stolen vehicle outside Swamp Hollow.

The disembodied voice coming from the speakers started talking about the weather, and Wes realized that was it. The report was over, and they hadn't even mentioned Ellie or anything about her disappearance.

He strangled the steering wheel, wondering why the fuck she didn't rank. Because she hadn't been killed?

He found himself steering the car out of the parking lot and turning left, not realizing that he had a destination in mind until he was actively merging into traffic.

He'd check out the crime scenes.

He probably wouldn't find anything the cops had missed. He knew that. Wes was *not* a detective. When it came right down to it, he had no idea what he was doing. Still, it was all he could think to do.

Because waiting around wasn't an option, even though that seemed like what everyone else wanted to do, from the police to John and Courtney, and even the media.

Whatever he tried had to be better than nothing, right?

Anything was better than nothing.

CHAPTER 68

Ellie eyed herself in the car mirror, not quite recognizing the person she saw there. The Sunset Peach dye gave her hair an almost pink hue. And the new haircut placed a row of choppy bangs just above her eyebrows.

She turned her head back and forth. Watched as the cuts in that face in the mirror shifted with each new position.

Crazy. Crazy how adding that harsh line above her brow seemed to change the angles of her face. It sharpened her jaw and cheekbones. Somehow brought out the subtle hollows of her cheeks.

The dye came through better than she would have guessed for something she randomly grabbed without even looking. The pale hair, too, seemed to morph her complexion into something milkier than before. The shock of bright color brought out some porcelain quality in her face that hadn't been there previously.

She could still see herself there, if she really looked. The lines around the eyes seemed to give it away.

But when she put on the chunky pair of sunglasses Scarlet had given her, the familiarity dropped away. She became someone new. There was something thrilling about it.

Finally, she let her gaze drift away from the mirror. Glanced down at the scrubs she was wearing.

The matte purple fabric bunched around her middle and encased her legs below. A little baggy, maybe.

Stupid-looking white shoes they'd bought at Walmart thrust out of the legs of the pants like chunky horse hooves. Bulky. They looked orthopedic or something. But they also seemed legit, Ellie thought. Just like something you'd see a hospital worker wearing.

Nurse Ellie.

That was the character she would be playing today. Any minute now.

She stared out the window. Endless rows of parked cars seemed to fill the land around them. An ocean of them, the sun glinting off the windshields, kicking up shards of harsh light in random patterns.

Then Ellie changed the angle of the rearview mirror. Slanted it so she could see a slice of the backseat.

And she watched for a second. Quiet.

Scarlet seemed a small thing, once again the up-close reality at odds with the image Ellie had gotten from TV. This strange creature adjusted her position in the backseat, looking frail with the gown draped over her. Intelligent eyes looking everywhere, taking everything in.

Gauze mummy-wrapped the top of the girl's head, everything from the brow up swaddled in white, a ketchup smear already soaking through the bandage material.

"You ready?" Scarlet said, leveling her gaze at Ellie in the mirror.

Ellie bobbed her head once, grabbing the keys from where Scarlet had tossed them on top of the dashboard. They hopped out onto a baking-hot parking lot.

Staying hunched, Scarlet pulled a wheelchair out of the backseat and unfolded it in the narrow row running between the cars. Then she sat down in the seat, making her bare feet dance in the footrests.

"Damn. Pavement's hot as hell."

Then she set about testing out different postures.

She hunched first. Shoulders stooped. Chin dipping down toward her chest.

Then she lay back in an overly relaxed pose. She pulled a white blanket over her lap. Nestled her head at a crooked angle. It looked like she'd fallen asleep that way, possibly fresh out of surgery and still medicated.

"This look OK?" she said, mouth half-slack.

"Looks great."

"OK. Let's go."

Ellie stepped in behind the wheelchair and started pushing Scarlet toward the towering hospital in the distance.

CHAPTER 69

"FARM STAND! FRESH ORGANIC PRODUCE! 1 MILE!"

This was the pronouncement painted on the side of a 1940s Chevy truck with rusting yellow paint. And sure enough, 0.9 miles down the road according to the trip odometer, Wes caught sight of a small wooden structure covered with a mural featuring anthropomorphic fruits and vegetables and a hand-lettered sign.

"FERGUSON'S FARM FRESH PRODUCE."

He slowed the car and pulled into a gravel area near the small building. A length of crime scene tape blocked the entrance of the driveway that Wes assumed led up to the house.

He climbed out and just stood for a moment. Hesitant to cross the threshold. But there was no one here to stop him, and he'd come all this way…

Finally, he ducked under the tape and walked up the drive. The crunching sound of his feet on the gravel seemed impossibly loud in the stillness.

A barn came into view and then a house. He paused.

It dawned on him that he had no idea what he was hoping to find. What exactly had he imagined doing once he got out here? Did he think he was going to bust out a magnifying glass and start looking for clues?

He pushed the negativity down. Got that strange feeling of separation between his awareness and feelings — a gap there he hadn't noticed before.

A well-worn path through the grass led off into the woods. Beyond the line of trees, Wes spied another slash of yellow police tape.

At the edge of the woods, he stood still a second and took it all in. Then he got moving again.

The chirping and buzzing of crickets swelled as he stepped

under the canopy, approaching the place where he assumed the farmer and his dogs were killed.

The corpses were gone, of course. But Wes noticed matted places in the leaves and brush where they had lain. Dark stains in the plant matter that he knew must be dried blood. And was it his imagination, or was there a faint coppery smell in the air?

He stared at the splotches for what felt like a long time. Shallow breaths rolling in and out of him.

He'd known exactly what had happened here before he'd come, and yet he wasn't prepared. Because suddenly, all the optimistic stuff everyone had been saying about Ellie — himself included — seemed like bullshit.

Someone died here.

How can everyone keep pretending she's going to be OK when someone died here?

He took a stumbling step forward, feeling lightheaded. He put out a hand and rested it on a nearby tree.

Panicking isn't going to help anything.

Just calm the fuck down.

He held in his next breath and let it out slowly. And again.

In time, his heart slowed, and he was able to shake off most of the dread. But the frustration he'd felt all morning lingered.

Whatever he'd hoped to discover, all he'd found here were bad feelings.

He spun away from the scene and began the march through the woods back to the house and the gravel drive. He was nearly to the tree line when he heard a branch snap somewhere behind him.

Wes froze and slowly turned to see who was there.

CHAPTER 70

Ellie pushed the wheelchair through the front doors of the hospital. Broad sheets of glass sliding out of the way automatically. She felt a lump in her throat as they crossed that line into the bright interior.

The chair juddered over a rubber floor mat. Then they hit the tile, and the ride smoothed out. The entryway bulbed out into a lobby which then elongated into a hallway beyond.

All of this floorspace bustled with life, teemed with movement. Hushed voices hissed over each other and reverberated throughout the area.

Just inside the door, they passed a waiting room clogged with people. A screen on one wall playing some house hunting show. Magazines splayed over a coffee table.

Then they wheeled past a gently rounded counter with a nurse behind it. She thumbed a phone with one hand while her shoulder held a landline to her opposite ear. Multitasking.

People. Too many people.

Ellie willed herself not to look at them. Tried not to care whether they were looking at her. She wished she could put the sunglasses back on.

Scarlet moaned and sort of rotated her head around like she could barely hold it up. She rolled her eyes up in her head every thirty seconds or so.

The people passing by looked at them out of the side of their eyes, but mostly they seemed to stare at the bloody gauze. Scarlet had said it was better to be conspicuous, to get everyone looking. If you could control that, get their guard down by drawing attention on purpose, you were better off. If people sensed you were trying to hide, they started looking closer.

Maybe she had been right about that, but Ellie still felt anxious.

When her nerves spiked, she stared at the strip of hair at the back of Scarlet's head.

A one-inch stripe of hair stuck out of the bottom of the gauze wrap. Scarlet had hacked her hair down to almost nothing with the shears, and what was left had been tinted Mushroom Blonde by the dye — a shade which somehow reminded Ellie of dirty dishwater.

They kept going. Kept moving.

Even with her eyes locked on Scarlet, the frantic energy of the hospital seemed to soak into Ellie's pores like a nicotine patch. The jitters seeped into her bloodstream, the beat of them building in her chest, in her neck, in her ears. With every inhale, it felt like something heavy was squatting on her chest.

She aimed the chair for the place where the lobby narrowed into a hall. Somehow she felt like that would feel better. Smaller confines. Less activity. Less spectators. Just a tube of drywall carrying them deeper into the structure.

Three gurneys pushed past on the opposite side of the walkway. Two empty. One holding a dazed-looking patient, an old woman slow-blinking up at the ceiling.

Then they crossed that line into the corridor. The walls choked off the high ceiling, hemmed in the vast space. Long fluorescent bulbs refracted off smooth tile floors here, harsh reflections made jagged around the edges.

Feet still squeaked everywhere and echoed funny in the long passageway. But the atmosphere shifted as Ellie had expected.

This was colder than the lobby, for one thing. The air conditioner oozed chilled air on them, and goosebumps plumped on the backs of her arms.

Signs jutted from the walls at every intersection, blue panels with white letters, hung up high like signage on the freeway. Ellie followed the pointed arrow left, heading for the ICU.

Then she flashed back to their prep conversation.

"The place is like ten floors, several hundred rooms. How the hell will we find him?"

"The intensive care unit is on the first floor. His room will be the one with the cop posted outside the door."

Ellie had digested that. It made sense, but she had a question.

"What if they've moved him?"

"Moved him?"

"Yeah, what if he's not in the ICU anymore?"

Scarlet's lips pursed.

"Then we'll figure out where he is. An elevator ride never killed anyone."

Ellie still had her doubts about that. At some point an elevator cable had probably snapped, the ensuing fall and crash killing the occupants. But she decided it would be pedantic to quibble about it.

Another waiting area sat empty to their right. Guy Fieri filled the TV screen, delivering a pork butt scrapple monologue to no one.

"Here," Scarlet said. "This is perfect."

Ellie knew what she meant. She left the chair in the aisle and walked over to the little Nespresso machine in the corner of the waiting area.

Her fingers trembled as she loaded a pod into the thing, and then the machine went to work. Hissing and groaning at first, then spitting coffee into a paper cup.

When the last drips had dropped out of the nozzle, she snapped a plastic lid on top and they went back to traversing the hall. The cup radiated heat against her fingers, and she could feel the coffee sloshing around inside, lurching up the waxy walls.

A pair of steel doors blocked the hallway ahead. A stern-looking sign marked "AUTHORIZED PERSONNEL ONLY" in severe red letters, all caps, wanted to bar their way.

"This is it," Scarlet said, just above a whisper.

Being careful not to slosh coffee, Ellie depressed the metal bar and shoved the door open. She half-expected security guards to leap on them or at least for some alarm to whoop once.

Nothing happened.

There was no one there. The empty hallway seemed eerie, though she could sense movement not so far ahead.

She held the door open with her foot and rolled Scarlet over the threshold. The wheelchair thudded over a steel sill along the floor.

They shoved on like that, and the door clicked shut behind them. About twenty feet beyond the barrier, the hallway broadened once more into a boiling mess of activity.

Nurses bobbed and weaved behind a counter, some of them toting clipboards, others loading trays and carts with something, possibly medication for their upcoming rounds. Everyone darted everywhere. Scrub legs swishing. Busy bees.

Two robed patients trekked through the area, choppy steps carrying them much slower than their nursing counterparts. Their IV bags wheeled alongside each of them on steel frames like coat racks. A nurse trotted beside one of them, holding the hospital robe closed in the back. The other walked solo, ass cheeks exposed.

Ellie's heart thumped harder as she pushed past the fresh crowd. Scarlet started doing that head twirl again. This time Ellie thought the motion looked like an asteroid locked in an uneven orbit. Wobbling as it spiraled.

They entered another hall, leaving the bulk of the foot traffic behind near the nurse's station. Some forty feet later, they approached an intersection.

The options made Ellie queasy. Her eyes snapped to the various hallways, one after another, three mouths gaping at her. They could keep going straight, or they could go either right or left. She had no gut feeling, no internal radar blipping.

"Which way?" she whispered, lowering her face toward the back of Scarlet's head.

The girl in the wheelchair held still for a second. Then she slid her shoulders over the back of the chair and let her head loll hard to the left.

Ellie took the hint and banked that way. They swerved around a mop and bucket cordoned off by a couple "Wet Floor" signs and padded to the left. Then the chair's course straightened out again.

Farther down the hall, a form took shape in the distance. Ellie could see that Scarlet's instinct had been right.

Sure enough, a cop sat on a chair outside of one room. He was reading the sports page. Eyebrows creased in focus. So far, he hadn't looked up at them.

Ellie slowed the chair. Surveyed the scene.

A meaty jaw seemed to dominate the cop's face, the cinder block chin somehow disproportionate to his pointy nose and light brow. You might think he was a professor of literature if you only saw the top half of his face, Ellie thought, but he was all beer-swilling, MMA-watching caveman from the mouth down.

"You ready?" Scarlet said almost under her breath.

Ellie swallowed hard, feeling queasy.

"Yeah. Let's do it."

CHAPTER 71

Ellie wheeled the chair toward the cop reading the sports page. He glanced up at them for a second and then went back to scouring the box scores.

Her pulse thrummed in her ears. The hand holding the paper cup suddenly felt numb even with the hot coffee trying its best to melt her fingers.

When she stopped just a few feet shy of him, he lowered the newspaper and peered over the top at them. Eyes squinting just a little. Mouth flat.

Ellie started churning out the phony charm. Her voice came out in a southern accent unintentionally.

"Hi! I saw that you were sittin' here all day, so I thought maybe you could use a cup of coffee."

He stared at Ellie. Then he stared at the cup of coffee in her hand. He tipped his thick chin toward Scarlet.

"What the hell happened to her?"

Ellie didn't miss a beat.

"Tubing accident. White water rapids threw her face-first into a rock, ya know? Anyway, here's your coffee."

His lip curled. For a second Ellie thought he was going to refuse — and then what the fuck would they do?

"Um… Hope you like Franch vuhnella."

Scarlet grunted, and Ellie realized that the girl had almost laughed at her pronunciation. The fake southern accent seemed to be getting thicker of its own accord.

She hovered the cup of coffee toward the cop. A forearm drift pushing it into his space.

He lowered the paper and stuck out a hand. Knuckles opening in slow motion like one of those claws in a crane game machine.

And then, just as his fingers brushed the sides of the cup,

she pretended to get her feet caught up in the wheelchair. She stumbled forward and flung the cup down onto him.

The loose lid toppled away.

Hot coffee leapt for him. Slapped down on the lap of his pants. Disappeared into him somehow. The fabric going dark.

Steam coiled up right away. The bottom of the sports page saturated and soggy.

And then he was up. Hissing through clenched teeth. Hopping from foot to foot.

"Hot. Hot. Hot."

"I'm so sorry. Oh my gosh. Let me help you. Here, there are paper towels in the restroom."

She grabbed him. One hand on his shoulder, the other on his forearm. She started guiding him down the hall.

He grunted. Pulled away from her. Shook his head.

"You wait here. Watch the room. I'll go. Just holler for me if anyone tries to get into that room."

"Sure. Of course."

He waddled down the hall. Gave the restroom door a forearm shiver and squeezed through the gap. The door swung shut behind him.

The girls looked both ways.

The hall was empty. Quiet.

And then Scarlet was up and scuttling into the room.

CHAPTER 72

Scarlet tiptoes through the doorway into the hospital room. She keeps herself low and quiet, a scuttling rat entering a new space.

She freezes just three steps inside the door. A little breath sucks between her teeth.

Jimmy is there. Laid out on the hospital bed. Asleep.

He looks almost dead. Ashen in pallor. Smaller and withered somehow. Like some doctor or nurse had wrung him out and hung him here to dry.

Her breath catches in her throat again, and then her heart thumps funny. Hollow, somehow.

Her eyes trace his arm down to where the handcuffs hook his right wrist to the stainless steel post of the bed. Two sets of cuffs looped together, presumably to give his arm some wiggle room. Something about that image spurs her forward again, brings the situation back into focus.

She crosses the room. Scans the blipping machines just next to Jimmy.

The IV pump hums in pulses. The heart monitor draws a jagged golden line over and over on the black screen, slow and steady.

She weaves around the bed and ducks low just next to the cuffs. Puts her nose right up to the chrome to get a good long look, eyes following the metal loop around, examining the serrated metal teeth as they disappear into the clasp.

Standard police crap. Good. Not a problem.

She rocks forward, leaving her squatted position to rest her weight on her knees. The tile instantly transmits its chill into her joints, and the refrigerated sensation starts crawling up into her thighs.

Then she digs her right hand under the back of the gauze

wrapped around her skull. Her freshly dyed hair feels crinkly and strange to her fingertips, like a lawn going crispy in a drought. She finds the crooked thing tangled in her hair. Detaches and removes it.

With the bobby pin out in the open, she bends the two sides apart from each other.

She turns her attention back to the cuffs. All of her focus zooms in on the little keyhole of the cuff hooked to the bed post.

And some aggressive feeling flares up inside of her. A bolt of heat rising from her gut, blazing in her skull.

She pokes the pin into the hole. Prods beneath the chrome shell of the thing. Starts working it around, feeling along the edges.

A thudding sound stops her. Her eyes flick to the open doorway, that rectangular slice of the hallway visible beyond it.

The restroom door clacks shut in the distance.

Then movement in the hall. Footsteps.

Someone coming, probably the cop.

He'll look in the room in a second, make sure everything's OK.

Scarlet retracts the pin and puts her head down. Uses the bed to screen herself from view.

She holds her breath. Listens.

The footsteps beat closer and closer.

Jimmy's breath lurches then. Stutters. That little steam hiss venting from his nostrils.

Scarlet glances up just in time to see his eyelids flutter.

Oh no.

If he starts talking...

She puts her index finger over her lips. Locks onto him. Wills him to keep quiet.

He peels his eyelids open. Blinks three times in rapid succession. Dazed for a fraction of a second.

His eyes open wide when he sees her.

And his lips part to speak.

CHAPTER 73

Ellie swirled paper towels from the ladies' room over the floor. The brown paper soaked up the coffee going lukewarm. Then she walked down the hall to the trash can to throw the soggy things away.

On the next round she worked slowly. Stalling. The paper towel sopped into something heavy and slowly disintegrated in her fingers as she swiped it over and over the tile.

Finally, with a fresh sheet of paper towel at hand, she froze. Held still with the brown paper pressed to the floor as though frozen mid-swipe.

She waited. Breathed. Counted in her head.

Better to just wait.

Better to leave part of the coffee puddle here, leave it intact, give myself a reason to stay a little longer.

Finally, just as her internal count reached 49, she heard the *click* and *whoomp* of the men's room door. Heavy footsteps clattered out into the hall.

She resumed wiping, though she kept it slow. Poking at the puddle more than mopping it.

The footfalls drew right up on her. She watched the approaching officer out of the corner of her eye.

He peeked into the hospital room and then sat down on his chair. He patted the folded newspaper like he was about to open it. But then he just squinted at Ellie.

His voice came out with some gravel to it.

"What happened to the other gal?"

Ellie smiled.

"Hm?"

"Your patient. The gal with the, uh…" He gestured at his head with a winding motion, pantomiming the gauze. "The gal who had the jet ski accident."

Is he testing me?

"Oh, it was actually a tubing accident. One of the other nurses took her off my hands while I stayed to clean this up."

He glared at her a few more seconds. The muscles in his jaw bulged a few times. Then his squint released, and he gave a reluctant nod.

He unfolded the newspaper. Right back to those box scores.

Ellie let her eyes drift over to the open doorway for a second. She should probably keep him engaged. If Scarlet could hear the two of them talking, that babble of voices out in the hall, she'd know she was in the clear to keep working.

She sat back from the coffee puddle, brought herself into a semi-upright position.

"I'm sorry," she said. "In all the, you know, commotion, I didn't catch your name."

"Lawrence. Er… Jim Lawrence," he said. He folded the top half of the newspaper down and stuck out his hand in the opening.

She shook it. All smiles.

"Nice to meet you. You know, I don't throw coffee on everyone I meet. Just feel like I should say that."

He half-smiled at that. It looked like he was about to speak, but Ellie kept chattering, cutting him off.

"Anyway, how is it? This guard duty, I mean. Is it boring having to sit here, or do you like the low-key thing?"

He dipped his head to the side for a second.

"If I'm being honest, it's a little boring, but I've done worse. You ask me, the poor souls stuck out working with the farmer and his dogs? That's the nightmare job. No thanks."

"I hear that," she said.

This time he was the one to cut her off.

"And you are?" he asked.

"Hm?"

His smile faded.

"What's your name?"

"Ohhh. Right. I, um…"

She felt her eyes drift down the hall. Mind blank.

Say something.

"Um…"

Idiot. Say something.

"I'm Scarlet."

Fuck.

Panic shuddered through Ellie's core. She felt her shoulders sag.

He squinted again.

"Scarlet," he repeated, his voice soft. "Like the, what's her face, the criminal gal on TV?"

Ellie shook her head. Hard.

"No."

His jaw flexed and held. Rigid muscles jutting under his ears. His cheeks looked all the more hollow.

"No?" he said, then paused for effect. "So your name *isn't* Scarlet like the girl on TV?"

She kept shaking her head for another two seconds and then stopped.

"Well… yeah. Yeah. It is. But I'm not… you know… her."

His lip quirked up on one side. He looked like he might be a little disgusted with her.

"Uh-huh," he said. "Well, you got a last name?"

"Smith."

"Scarlet Smith," he said. "OK. Nice to meet you, Scarlet Smith."

He shook his head and went back to the newspaper. He turned the page, and the paper fluttered and scraped.

Heart still thudding, Ellie took another paper towel swipe at the floor. Then she walked down some thirty feet or so to throw the soggy thing away. Her eyes stayed trained on the cop as she walked back.

He read the paper. Dead eyes blinking at the page. His former disinterest in her had returned.

OK.

He thinks I'm an idiot. That's all.

I mean, that's good, I think.

Better than the alternative.

Then something squeaked in the distance. Ellie shifted her gaze to the mouth of the hall.

A figure rounded the corner. A nurse. A nurse pushing a medical cart. A nurse with her eyes on the door to Jimmy's room.

Ellie started coughing as loud as she could.

CHAPTER 74

"You a cop?"

These were the first words to come from the man who stepped from the shadows of the forest at the Ferguson farm.

"What? No," Wes said, feeling oddly defensive. "Are you?"

He asked automatically, though it was clear this man was no cop. The dismissive tone with which he'd asked the original question was the first clue, and the way he was dressed was the second. A dirty white t-shirt snugged around his beefy torso, and a trucker hat snugged low on his brow, shadowing his eyes.

The man smirked, standing with his legs just more than shoulder-width apart. His stance reminded Wes of a movie superhero. Or maybe a supervillain.

"Hell no, I ain't no cop," he said, spitting into the dead leaves at his feet. "And if you aren't either, then how about you tell me who you are, and what you're doing here."

"I… my friend…"

A rambling explanation seemed to spill out of Wes then. It was a sloppy, disjointed account of Ellie's abduction and the aftermath, and he wasn't even sure he was making sense, but the man's reaction reassured him that he must be, because he nodded and raised his eyebrows and said things like 'no shit?' in all the right places.

"Damn," the man said, wiping the ball of his thumb under his lip. "That's quite an ordeal you been through."

Wes bobbed his head slowly and stared at the ground, feeling as if the retelling had taken something out of him.

The man took a few steps forward, his hand extended.

"Well, I'm Putnam. Shane Putnam. Don't think I said that before."

Wes took the offered hand and introduced himself in turn.

"I live on the next property over." Putnam gestured over his shoulder. "Seen your car parked down by the road and figured I better come see who was poking around Ferguson's land. Them damn reporters are bloodthirsty, let me tell you. They been after you for an interview yet?"

Wes blinked.

"Um… no. I mean, it just happened last night, and I spent all morning driving around, so…"

"Well, it's a matter of time. I can promise you that." Putnam shook his head. "Back when I was a youngster — still in high school even — a local girl went missing. Neighbor of mine, matter of fact. Wendy Morehouse was her name."

He paused, looking suddenly wistful, then laughed.

"Shoot. I haven't thought of Wendy in quite some time. Brings back all sorts of memories." He sighed. "Anyhow, she lived right down the street from me, and there used to be this little store all the kids in the area walked to when we wanted a soda or some candy. One evening — it was summer break as I recollect — Wendy went out for a Coke and never came back. Her parents called the police, and the whole town came together to try to find her, organizing search parties and whatnot. I volunteered myself, actually. Still remember stalking through the woods, poking the underbrush with a stick, looking for clues. Any sign of her that might tell us what happened."

He trailed off, lost in the memories, it seemed.

Wes crossed his arms.

"So did they find her?"

Putnam snapped out of it, his head swiveling to face Wes again. He smiled, which gave Wes hope that the story had a happy ending.

"Well… can't say they did, unfortunately. It was like she vanished into thin air, you know?" He snapped his fingers. "There one second and gone the next. Not a single clue left behind."

Wes felt a chill run through him. The story was too familiar. Like his brother. And now Ellie.

Shane straightened and cleared his throat.

"Of course, things with your friend will turn out different, I'm sure."

Try as he might, Wes didn't feel convinced. Everyone kept telling him it would all work out, that Ellie was probably fine, but the longer this went on, the harder it felt to keep believing that.

"Why should it turn out any different?" Wes asked. "Bad shit happens to good people every day."

"Well, all I can say is that in Wendy's case, there may have been more to the story. Rumors around town that she wasn't missing at all, for example. That what really happened is that she'd run away. I don't think her home life was all roses and sunshine, if I'm honest. Her parents were real strict, religious types. Kept her on a tight leash. And you can only keep a girl caged up for so long before she's gonna want to rebel. I reckon she run off with a boyfriend, and that's why no one ever found hide nor hair of her."

Wes thought that if that were true, someone would surely have heard *something* of the girl after so many years had passed, but he didn't see much point in pressing it. And maybe it made the guy feel better to tell himself this girl he used to know was still out there somewhere.

"But listen to me carrying on," Putnam said. "Only reason I even brought up Wendy was because the whole thing caused such a ruckus. Between the police and the folks from the news media, our neighborhood was a 24-hour circus for some time after she went missing. All sorts of Nosy Nancies come pokin' around, wanting interviews with anyone that knew Wendy. They didn't care if you knew her well or even at all, just that you said you did. Figured I'd warn you, is all. Anyhow, I'll quit ramblin' so as you can get back to your search. Best of luck to you, now."

"Thanks," Wes said, giving an awkward wave as he turned to go.

"Say…" Putnam called out to his back. "You wouldn't want

some help, would you? I know my way around town pretty well. And I have a police scanner."

That piqued Wes's interest.

"You do?"

CHAPTER 75

Scarlet works the tip of the bobby pin around the rim of the keyhole again. All of her focus seems to zoom into that small space — the universe shrinking down to a rounded cavity about a tenth of an inch tall.

She dips the pin. Shoves and scrapes. Quiet sounds erupt from the work, noises that remind Scarlet of a dentist gently prodding that little hook into someone's teeth.

"Yeah… I figured you'd come," Jimmy whispers, smirking.

The scratch in his voice breaks Scarlet's concentration. She shushes him silently.

"Knew you'd be back. Not like you could stay away. And what's with the mummy wrap?"

A breath vents through her nostrils. She jiggles the bobby pin in her hand.

"I need to concentrate, so shut it."

Jimmy tilts his head.

"Oh, of course. I'm sorry, your highness. Pardon my interruption."

He sounds hurt, but when she glances up at him, he's grinning like a jackal. She watches him for a couple seconds, that smile unwavering, and then she goes back to working on the lock.

She sticks the exposed tip of the pin halfway into the top of the hole and bends it into a roughly 45-degree angle. She pulls the pin free and checks the bend. It looks good.

Then she jams it in deeper, so that the entirety of the exposed part of the pin disappears into the hole, and she bends it the opposite way. When she pulls it out, the pin now has a kink at the end that seems to match the one in Scarlet's memory. In a way, it looks like a key already.

"Coulda just unscrewed the arm of the bed," Jimmy

whispers, shaking Scarlet out of the zone again. "No fancy stuff. Just takes a screwdriver."

She whips her head up and glares at him.

"What?" he says. "I'm just sayin'."

Just as she starts working, he whispers again.

"How the hell did you learn to do this, anyway?"

She sighs.

"I watched a video on the internet. Some crazy Russian guy. He said it's really easy."

"That's funny. Man, the internet is nuts. You know? You ever see that video of the boulder falling off a mountain in Kazakhstan or something and smashing the SUV? Fuckin' bonkers."

She glares at him again.

"Are you high?"

He laughs at that, a noisy enough thing to snap Scarlet's eyes to the doorway for a second.

The babble out there between Ellie and the guard continues. It sounds like Ellie is having a good time of it, at least.

After a second, Scarlet realizes that Jimmy had thought she was joking.

"Seriously. Are you on pain meds or something?"

His grin falters some at that. Eyes staring straight ahead.

"I don't know. I mean, I guess I probably am. Heh." He chuckles to himself. "Yep. You get shot in the gut, they prolly dope you up pretty good. Guess that's why I've been in such a good mood. I thought it was just my positive mental attitude or somethin'."

Ellie starts coughing in the hallway, and Scarlet feels her eyes go wide. Jimmy stares at her.

"What is it?"

"Someone's coming."

Scarlet ducks, pressing her face into the side of the mattress and curling herself into a tight ball. A second later one of Jimmy's blankets flaps off the side of the bed and drapes over her. The shadow around her swells, and the fabric muffles the sounds.

Still, she can hear the wheels of the cart grating and squeaking into the space.

"You're up," a woman's voice says. "Good."

Scarlet swallows. Wishes that she could melt into the mattress.

"Yeah," Jimmy says. "Thirsty, too. You got any water in that cart or what?"

The nurse mumbles something Scarlet can't understand. The wheels of the cart pull up short and stop squeaking.

Scarlet waits. Listens. She doesn't dare breathe now.

Then suddenly the footsteps are closer. Right on top of her.

Something thumps on the tray hovering over Jimmy's bed. Then he makes an exaggerated *Ahhh* sound.

"Thank ya," he says.

The nurse mumbles something else. A bunch of wah-wah sounds pouring out of her like Charlie Brown's teacher.

Then Scarlet feels the blanket lift off her. It glides up a few inches, that fabric sliding over her, stopping just shy of revealing her.

"You want this on or off?" the nurse asks.

"Leave it," Jimmy says, tugging the blanket out of her hands. "It's there if I want it."

The nurse huffs.

"Fine. I'll be back in a bit."

Her shoes squeak around the bed and away. Then she pushes the cart on down the hall, that shrieking wheel growing smaller and smaller.

CHAPTER 76

Scarlet's heart still knocks against her ribcage as she paws the blanket free from her face. The fabric crumples to the floor, forming a semicircle around her knees.

The room's brightness assails her eyes now. The sunlight spills in through the windows, glowing boxes angling across the room.

She breathes that air-conditioned air, feels the chill swoop into her lungs.

The brush with the nurse seems to have sobered Jimmy some. He still smiles at her, but it seems less demented than before. She can see some new clarity in his eyes.

When he speaks, his voice comes out dry and small.

"Give me the blanket."

She scoops it up and pushes it up onto the bed. His cuffs jangle against the metal arm of the bed for a second as he takes and unballs the fabric.

"You work. I'll keep watch. If anyone starts in, I'll hide you under this again."

She nods and scoots back to the place where the cuff connects to the bed post. Lets her vision, her concentration, zoom into that cleft once more.

Her hands shake a bit as she maneuvers the bobby pin between her fingers. Too much adrenaline. But there's nothing she can do about it now.

She works the pin in the keyhole. This time she wrenches hard, winding all the way to the left.

A click emits from deep inside the steel housing. A soft sound. Something letting go.

A breath vents through Scarlet's nostrils. She swishes a hand at her brow as though swiping hair out of her face out of habit. Finds only the gauze there now.

She knows the sound signifies the double lock pin sliding out of the way. Good. Halfway done.

She removes the pin from the hole. Changes the angle of the bent little sawtooth on the end of it. Then she jams it in again, wedges it under the nub inside the keyhole and pries straight upward.

The leverage forces the metal inside. She can feel the spring fighting her, but not very hard.

The ratchet teeth of the lock lift out of the way. Surrendering.

She hooks a finger into the metal loop and pulls. The strand eases out of the lock housing, smooth and soundless.

Then the open cuff falls free from the bed rail. Tumbles down into the soft blankets there and holds still.

Scarlet gapes at it for a second.

Holy shit.

I did it.

"Nice," Jimmy hisses.

Scarlet pushes herself to her feet. Knees wobbly from the head rush.

Then she thrusts her hand out to Jimmy.

"Shouldn't we…"

He holds up his wrist with two pairs of handcuffs dangling from it.

Scarlet shakes her head.

"We can pick the other later. Let's get out of here first."

Jimmy takes her hand. He grunts as she pulls him out of bed. His snarled lip and nose tell her what kind of pain he's feeling as his abdomen flexes, no matter what kind of medication he's on.

He stands still for a second. Torso hunched.

"Are you OK?" she asks.

Shallow breaths sizzle between his teeth. After a second, he nods.

Scarlet still holds his arm, ready to pull him along if need be. They move for the window, the world a vibrant thing just on the other side of the glass, all that empty space stretching out into eternity.

But they only make it a few paces before Jimmy pulls up short.

The cords hooking him to the machines jerk him back a half-step like a dog reaching the end of its chain. He grimaces again. Then he wraps his fist around the IV tube snaking into his wrist.

"Wait," Scarlet says. "Don't."

Jimmy's bicep ripples and jumps, but he stops himself just shy of pulling the tube free. Then he glances up at her. The pain shines bright and hot in his eyes, and his chin quivers like he's about to cry.

"Soon as we unhook those, the machines will start squawking," Scarlet says. "The nurses will be here within seconds. Not to mention Officer McFuckface sitting out in the hall. Let me do this first."

She strides to the window. Starts yanking on the metal handle there. It's old and sticky, but she can feel it starting to give.

"McFuckface," Jimmy whispers somewhere behind her. "Could be, like, a breakfast sandwich at McDonald's or something. Or French toast strips. McFucksticks, maybe."

Scarlet ignores him and keeps going. She examines the window as she works. It reminds her of what they'd had at her middle school when she was a kid. The panel of the window that will open, once she gets it, is only maybe a foot tall and swings outward, pivoting from the top. Not much of a gap. They'll have to lay themselves flat and slither through.

The handle thwacks as something inside gives, and then it swivels out of the way all at once. Defeated.

Scarlet sucks in a deep breath and keeps going. Testing the window, it feels pretty stiff as well.

She puts both hands on the glass and shoves as hard as she can. Bending at the knee, dipping her hips, pushing off with both feet, arms shaking.

The glass barrier puts up more of a fight than the handle did. It shivers a little but doesn't really budge.

Scarlet keeps pushing. Her fingers squeaking against the glazing.

And her jaw clenches. And her cheeks flush. And the muscles in her arms lurch and strain and shimmy.

The window pops as it leaves the frame. Cracks once like a small caliber gunshot.

Panic thrums through Scarlet's body. But she doesn't dare stop now. She pushes harder.

And then the sash thrusts out into the open.

Scarlet loses her footing, loses her balance. Her vision wheels out over the opening.

She stares down at a flourish of landscaping detail some four or five feet down. Can feel herself sinking into the breach.

Hot wind sniffs and snorts at the opening. The outside world licking at the edges of the window frame, trying to take her.

But she braces a hand on the top sash and rights herself. Snaps her shoulders up. Turns back to Jimmy.

"Nice," he says again.

She hustles over to him, and together they rip the IV tube out and remove another mess of wires that attach to small white pads stickied onto his chest.

The machines screech and whoop. Tattling on them in a shrill voice.

But by then they're already out the window.

Ellie pushed the empty wheelchair back toward the front of the building. Moseying. Keeping her gait slow, her progress steady. One of the front wheels pulled to the left just a little, like a wonky shopping cart, but she didn't mind that now.

She was done here.

Finished.

Free.

Giddiness burst inside her head. Popping champagne bottles. The brightness of endorphins gushing into her brain. It made her scalp tingle.

She'd helped Scarlet get Jimmy back, and now she was done. She had gone above and beyond what she and Scarlet had discussed. Had distracted the cop while the two of them got out. She'd managed, even, to catch just a glimpse of Jimmy's sky-blue hospital gown as it fluttered out the window and disappeared behind the wall.

Probably just missed seeing his butt crack, she realized. *What a loss.*

Her lips quivered at that, a laugh almost escaping. Better to suppress it, though. Keep a straight face until she got out of the building.

What's that British saying?

Keep a stiff upper lip.

She pushed the wheelchair around a corner and put a straight line between her and the exit. Ecstatic on the inside. Placid on the outside.

She didn't need to push the chair, she knew. Could ditch it in any of these empty stretches of hallway or shove it into one of the restrooms. But it felt better, somehow, to have something to do with her hands. A prop.

Another stretch of hallway passed, those squares of tiling scrolling underfoot. Soon, the front doors took shape in the distance.

Sunlight streamed through the glass. A box of brightness marking out the threshold in glowing highlight.

She could just leave now. Be done with this. Go back and find her friends.

That's what Scarlet had said. "Help me get Jimmy out, and you're free to go."

She'd even offered money for the help — 1500 dollars, which seemed an oddly specific amount. Ellie had refused it.

But now she was here. Facing that glowing exit to the

building. Drawing another step closer to it with every second, every heartbeat.

And somehow, up close, the prospect of walking away felt a little wrong. Like she was leaving a task half-finished. Incomplete.

She'd done something here. Taken some step in life. Something that couldn't be taken back.

She'd taken a stand for something. Believed in something. Acted on it.

Yes. That was it.

She'd *acted* on something. Gone for it. She'd never really done that before, at least not that she could remember.

She plunged down the last strip of hallway and shoved into the lobby as she digested the thought. The wheelchair pulled to the left again, and she corrected course.

Or maybe I was abducted and ended up identifying with my captor a little too much? Been manipulated by her.

Stockholm syndrome.

Could be that.

The room bustled around her — nurses and patients flitting around like moths — but Ellie's thoughts found a still place internally. A calm. A quiet inside that blocked the outside world.

She pondered the *why* of what she'd just experienced. Tumbled the narratives like a clothes dryer, tried to solve for the meaning.

Had she really asserted herself, or had Scarlet used her?

On a gut level, neither explanation felt quite right. One had to be truer than the other, though. Right?

Scarlet had done what she had to do to get Jimmy and survive. That was all.

She'd grabbed Ellie to get a car, and then she'd enlisted her for further help. Maybe that help was forced at first, but Ellie'd had plenty of chances to get out.

The wheelchair pierced that glowing box where the sun streamed through the glass. And the light enveloped Ellie. Lit her up. She juddered over the floor mat, pressed through the door.

And she wondered where Jimmy and Scarlet were. Probably long gone by now. She remembered the hospital room as she'd last seen it — the bed empty, the window open, Jimmy's gown fluttering out of view beyond the glass.

Outside, she pushed the wheelchair off to the side of the front doors. Left it in a bed of mulch there.

And then she stepped away from the building and into the bright sunlight.

CHAPTER 77

Scarlet plops down into a bed of cedar mulch that runs along the edge of the building. Hands and knees sinking into the pile. Her weight seems to catch up a second later, driving the heels of her hands into the wood chips like pylons.

Then she scrabbles out of the way, reddish bits of wood flinging everywhere.

And now Jimmy's body worms through the gap of the open window. Spilling into the breach.

He seems to fall a long time. Sinking in slow motion. Hospital gown billowing, inflating, whipping against itself like a small flag.

He grunts when he hits down. Scarlet can see the jolt of the impact thrum pain through him. He curls into himself, chest and belly going concave.

"You good?" she asks.

He glances up at her. Teeth locked in a grimace that looks like a sad smile just now. After a second, he nods.

She gets to her feet and takes Jimmy by the hand. Helps him up.

Then she turns and gazes out at the sea of cars off to their right. The parking lot stretches out and out and out. Little shimmies of heat distortion ripple the air above the asphalt and some of the hoods and windshields, the air itself a bending, tortured thing.

They rush toward the lot. Building speed. Scarlet scans the rows of vehicles, trying to orient herself. She doesn't have any feel for where the car might be. But she can worry about that as they get closer.

People mill about here and there among the cars. They look like ants from this far out.

And an ambulance wails in the distance. Rushing closer.

The warble seeming to change speed as it moves.

Strange thoughts occur to Scarlet as they jog across the hospital lawn, the words inside oddly calm, drifting up from some deep, detached part of her mind.

It's weird, somehow, how life keeps going. Proceeding as usual. They are in the midst of pulling off some daring escape from police custody, picking locks and jumping out windows, fighting for their freedom, for their lives, but to the rest of the world it's just another day. Any other day.

With or without us. It all keeps going and going.

They round a corner, and the front entrance reveals itself. They'll need to weave around a decorative hedge to get to the parking lot. Not a problem in and of itself.

But this will bring them close to the foot traffic surging in and out of the building.

People.

Her eyes jump over to Jimmy.

The handcuffs still dangle off his right side. A Christmas ornament twirling and swaying along with his gait. Shiny.

Just seeing the loose metal makes Scarlet wince.

But they can disappear in the jumble of cars in the lot. Weave out among all those hunks of steel. Keep low. Shielded.

They just have to get there, and everything will be OK.

She runs faster as they near the hedge. Jimmy grunts again as she yanks on his arm, gets him up to a sprint.

And she watches the front of the building off to her right. Wants to see if anyone notices them, notices Jimmy.

An older couple pads toward the front doors, hand in hand. The glass swooshes out of the way, and they walk inside.

Two seconds later, the doors whisk shut behind them. Sealing the building off.

And the exterior of the hospital holds still then, save for Jimmy and Scarlet. An almost eerie quality to the motionless scene like a vacant amusement park.

Empty sidewalk cells draw pale lines over the deep green of the front lawn. All the benches lay barren.

Scarlet's vision zooms in on the stone ashtrays just outside the front doors. Round columns with deep ridges etched into the sides. Colorful rocks embedded in the cement. Beds of sand set on top of each. Cigarette butts jutting out at every angle.

A single line of smoke curls out of one of those ashtrays. The image pulls Scarlet's skin taut. Makes her breath catch in her throat. It's the only proof that anyone has been here, she thinks.

Deserted.

Desolate.

They've hit a lull that seems striking and strange in this moment. Like maybe the whole world could be empty now.

Scarlet veers around the edge of the laurel bushes. Traverses a fat square of sidewalk. Steps down off the curb.

Hot asphalt touches the soles of her bare feet. Sun-baked. Like a cast-iron pan pressing its warmth into her flesh. She barely notices.

Fifteen feet. In fifteen feet, they'll be across the lane and walking among the fleet of cars. In fifteen feet, they'll be free.

Jimmy stumbles stepping off the curb. His hand yanks hers. Wrenches her arm lower.

And their stride wobbles. Slows.

Scarlet's feet clap against the pavement. Clomping and sending shocks up the lengths of her legs. Jolting her ankles, her knees.

She fights for balance. Wrestles against gravity. Drives herself upright.

And then they are there. Slipping between a pair of parked cars.

Scarlet hunches low and snakes deeper into the lot. Jimmy follows.

CHAPTER 78

Detective Taft hunkered over a laptop in a dark room. Alone.

The screen flared to life as it booted. The rectangle of white light was stark against the darkness around it.

One of the uniformed officers who'd set him up down here had flipped the lights off on their way out, and now the big detective was too tired to get up and turn them back on.

The darkness reminded him of being a school kid, how the teachers always turned off all the lights when they'd watch a movie in class. This was the AV room, which made it appropriate, he supposed.

He cupped a sleeve of McDonald's French fries in one hand, pulling and shoveling with the other. The fries tasted salty on his lips.

He was happy to have something to try to help settle his stomach. He wasn't looking forward to this next task. Oh, it needed to be done, and he was anxious to get on with bringing Stinson's killer to justice, but something about watching the footage, knowing that one of these cars held the killer — a killer who was still out there now — unsettled him.

Maybe it was seeing up close what had been done to his partner. The level of brutality.

The traffic cam footage from the night of Stinson's murder had all been pulled and loaded for him. Now he just had to get to work watching it.

From what he'd been told, there were thirteen total clips featuring five distinct cars — not counting Stinson's. Not a busy night at all, but out in the boonies in the wee hours, such was the norm.

The video files were listed in chronological order, so the ones closest to the time of Stinson's death would come last. Still, they were all within an hour of the murder, so Taft would look at every one.

He clicked the first file name, and the screen went black as the media player popped up. A second later the image there whirred to life.

Headlights flared in the camera lens for just a second, and then a beat-up Ford pickup rolled through the intersection, past the traffic cam. It was white, maybe late 90s or early aughts.

Taft rewound the clip a few seconds. Paused it just after the lens flare.

First, he ran the tag. Punching in the six digits and hitting submit.

Three dots pulsed on the screen for a few seconds. Then the results came, a block of text populating the screen all at once, white lettering on a black background.

The truck was registered to one Clifford Marshall, 67 years old. His address wasn't far from the Ferguson farm. Probably another farmer himself, and unlikely to be involved in the murder. Just an old man headed home.

Once he had the vehicle registration, he switched to a different browser tab and logged all of the information in an online form that would be added to the case file. Not quite as backwards as having to fill out a paper form, which had been standard procedure in the department until just four years prior. The system was dated and slow as hell, not much more advanced than an old GeoCities site, but it beat writing everything by hand.

The next clip featured the white truck again as it passed through the next intersection. No help.

The following four videos featured a Buick Skylark registered to one Barbara Johnson, a resident of Swamp Hollow and 81 years old. The woman seemed lost and possibly drunk, turning around twice, waiting too long at the traffic lights, the Buick weaving in all four clips.

Could just be really old, Taft thought. *Drunk with age. They should have a breathalyzer for that.*

Sorry, lady. You blew an 81. I'm afraid that's too old to drive.

Anyway, I'm going to go out on a limb and say she's not our murderer.

Taft sniffed a laugh to himself and tossed a fry nub into his mouth. Then he loaded the next video.

The next two cars offered up the first legitimate suspects.

Three videos showed a two-tone Toyota MR2 driven by 23-year-old Cyrus "C.J." Rodgers, a resident of Miami. Even beyond the paint job, the car looked to have had custom work done — a spoiler and some rims adequately pimping it, in Taft's opinion, to make it wildly out of place out in soybean and orange country.

And Rodgers had a criminal record. No felonies. Nothing violent. Three arrests for possession of a controlled substance, Xanax apparently being the drug of choice in this case. A couple more charges for minor-in-possession of alcohol dating back to his high school days.

What Mr. Rodgers was doing in *this* neighborhood in the middle of the night was anyone's guess. It was curious enough for Taft to jot down a few notes.

Could be something. Could be nothing. We'll see.

Two clips showed a 2012 Mitsubishi Mirage, a hatchback with a grayish enamel finish that the manufacturer labeled "Starlight Silver." The little car rolled through the intersection with a badly crumpled front right fender and dents and dings pocking the rest of it. One of the back tires visibly wobbled in the second clip.

Guy drives this thing like he has contempt for it.

The Mitsubishi came back registered to one Calvin Kerns, 34 years old and a resident of one of the roughest parts of northwest Jacksonville — Royal Terrace. Like the neighborhood he lived in, Kerns had a history of violence.

Over the last sixteen years, he'd been charged with assault and battery some twelve separate times. A carjacking charge put him in jail for a few months, and an armed robbery charge that might have locked him up on a long-term basis got dropped.

So what was he doing out in the sticks? Taft didn't know, but he'd sure as shit be finding out.

He jotted more notes. Pen scratching out quiet sounds against the paper.

Then he moved to load the final few videos, knowing that they would feature the last car. The mouse click seemed quiet in the empty room, and he suddenly felt more alone.

Black nothing inked the laptop screen. Then the video flicked to life.

And there it was. A white Camaro plunging through the intersection. Taft got a chill as soon as he saw it.

The car flitted across the screen, right to left. Disappeared out of the frame. He watched the video twice.

He didn't have a good angle on the plate, so he loaded the next clip.

The screen shot to black again. The laptop breathed gently, exhaling in the quiet space.

Taft brought a fry nub to his mouth. He wasn't hungry anymore, but nerves somehow kept his hands and mouth busy.

The video flared on the screen. This time the Camaro came straight on, jounced a little over the worn asphalt.

Taft let it play through. On the second pass, he waited for a clear view of the plate and jabbed the pause button.

There.

He stared at the plate. His mouth stopped moving mid-chew.

North Carolina.

Holy shit.

That's where Jimmy and Scarlet are from.

An icy tingle prickled all the way down his back.

He switched to the other browser tab and ran the plate. Dug into the sleeve for another fry.

Waited.

Waited.

The dots bounced on the screen over and over. Taft stared into them, entranced.

When the computer spat out the information, he almost choked on a fry.

CHAPTER 79

Scarlet works a diagonal path through the maze of cars. She can feel Jimmy a couple paces behind her, can hear him wincing now and again when his gut hurts, sharp breaths hissing between his teeth.

The cars form constricting walls of glass and metal penning them in, and it feels strange to walk such a narrow path now after crossing that wide-open space to get here.

Her focus extends past the vehicles at close quarters. She scans the periphery. Tries to spot some landmark, something familiar.

But nothing sticks out. The never-ending rows of sedans and SUVs… they all look the same. The periodic light poles thrusting up overhead could have been identical quintuplets. Like so many things in life, the parking lot becomes an endless repeat.

Some magnetic force seems to pull her to the back left quadrant of the lot, and she obeys. She turns sideways, sidles between an F-150 and a Blazer.

She imagines what the two of them might look like from afar — her with the gauze encasing her head, the ketchup splotch showing through the bandages, shiny and red. Jimmy hunching, bobbing up and down as he lopes along. Both of their hospital robes pluming and jouncing.

Escaped mental patients. That's what they must look like. Especially if anyone can see the improvised jewelry dangling from Jimmy's wrist. Police-issue Smith & Wesson handcuffs, double-lock.

The aisle opens wide before Scarlet. She rushes into the void.

And something registers somewhere in her brain. Something familiar here. She's not sure what it is.

Her head cocks to 10 o'clock. The Hyundai sits just there, maybe fifty feet ahead of them on the next aisle over.

Something sharpens in her mind. All of reality sifting to that pinpoint — the Elantra sitting, waiting. Waiting to take them away.

She picks up speed. Lengthens her stride.

And she feels the grain and rough texture of the dirty asphalt underfoot, the heat of it trying impress itself into her heels and toes. Searing the imprint there.

She glances back to find Jimmy. He's fallen a few paces behind. Face red. Grimacing worse than before.

His right hand grips a wad of his hospital gown, arm rigid at his side. It adds an uneven hitch to his gait.

Scarlet realizes he's using the gown to conceal the handcuffs.

Smart.

Three rows before their destination, she darts left. Follows the ribbon of blacktop that slices between a couple of small pickup trucks.

Almost there.

Almost there.

But then she finds herself stopping short. Ducking behind the flank of an orange Jeep.

A big boat of a car — a Lincoln, maybe — idles in the next aisle, directly in front of the Hyundai. Parking them in.

She peeks over the Jeep's fender. Peers through the glass of the vehicle blocking their escape.

The driver stares down at the device in his open hand, chin tucked to his chest.

Fucker's just sitting there, playing with his phone.

Scarlet swallows. Tries to think.

Jimmy creeps up beside her, keeping low. He gets down on his knees, sucking wind. One forearm cradles his belly.

And he gazes at her. Something wild in his eyes.

"What is it?" he asks, voice soft.

"That car is blocking us in."

Jimmy breathes.

"Could ask them to move."

Scarlet tilts her head.

"And if he recognizes us?"

Jimmy's face holds placid.

"So we wait for him to move."

"The cops will be here any minute. We need to get gone."

"Well, shit. It's one or the other. Ask or wait. Lemme take a look."

Jimmy lifts his head over the hood of the Jeep. Squints at the car in the middle distance. He sucks in a breath.

"I know that guy."

He ducks back down. Blinks a few times.

"Know him how? From where?"

"He tried talking to me after I woke up from surgery. Name's Bosa."

He swallows, and some lump rises and falls in his throat. His eyes swivel back to hers.

"He's a detective."

CHAPTER 80

The phone felt cold against Taft's ear, against the side of his face.

"Subject wanted for questioning. The name is Shane Putnam. That's P-U-T-N-A-M."

But the detective felt distant from the talking. Separate. Still alone in that AV room, alone in the dark.

His voice vibrated in his neck and spilled from his lips, words pouring out of him and into the receiver. His body kept going, functioning, communicating, working the case, doing his job. But Taft's consciousness had pulled away from the here and now, crawled deeper inside himself. A snail retracting into its shell.

Chief Bannon said something back, but all Taft could feel was that separation between him and the rest of existence.

"I told you how Stinson had a hunch there was someone else involved with the Jimmy and Scarlet thing? Well, I think this is the guy," he said, his voice much slower than his thoughts. "The one who killed her and Elmer Ferguson."

He was making a leap here, he was aware of that. Due process and all that crap. But he'd known the instant he'd seen those cold eyes in the DMV photo that Putnam was their guy.

"He drives a 2021 Chevy Camaro. White. North Carolina plate."

He read off the tag and swiped his free hand down his face like maybe he could wipe the alienated feeling away. His fingers passed over his field of vision, brushed over his mouth, but nothing changed.

The chief's voice gurgled in Taft's ear now, but the words seemed to be going through him. Flowing. Surging. Sinking and vanishing like water draining into the dirt.

Still, some part of him tracked what the man was saying.

Some part of him was still real.

"Amen to that," he found himself saying. "Spread the word, far and wide. Let's nail this dirtbag."

The chief asked him to hold on the line while he passed on the APB info to dispatch, and Taft did, though he didn't know why.

He staggered into the darkest corner of the AV room, stepping out of the glare blazing out of the laptop screen.

The dark closed around him. Swallowed him.

And all of this was happening to him. He wasn't doing it. Wasn't controlling it. Was he?

It was all just happening.

CHAPTER 81

Shane Putnam's white Camaro sat at the mouth of Elmer Ferguson's driveway, just next to where Wes had parked.

"Come on, you can ride with me," Putnam said, giving a little wave. "I can drop you back here when we're done."

Wes hesitated, his eyes on John's car. He felt a strong urge to not abandon it.

"I don't know... You think it's OK to just leave the car sitting here?"

Putnam grinned.

"Why? What do you think's gonna happen to it?" He scratched his chin. "Course, I forget you city folks have cause to be concerned about car theft and the like."

"It's not that—" Wes started to say.

"I mean, if you're that scared, I guess we could drive separately." Putnam shrugged. "Just seems a waste is all."

Wes's previous urge to not leave the car was replaced by an urge to prove he wasn't some scaredy-cat city boy. And Putnam did have a point. There was probably no harm in leaving the car parked on a country road for an hour or two.

"No, I'm sure it's fine."

Wes pocketed the keys and walked over to the passenger side of the Camaro.

Putnam started the car, then paused to light a cigarette. He swung the car around and pointed them back toward town.

Wes's eyes slid over the interior, searching.

"Didn't you say you had a scanner?"

Putnam tucked the cigarette between his lips.

"Oh shit, yeah. Almost forgot."

Putnam reached under his seat and came back with a small walkie-talkie-looking device with a digital screen. He thumbed a switch on the top. The device beeped, and the volume swelled as he turned the knob.

"—report from a citizen in Swamp Hollow." The dispatcher's voice was almost monotone. "There's a stalled vehicle blocking northbound traffic at the intersection of Twelve Oaks and Creekside Road."

"We're lucky," Putnam said. "Some jurisdictions have started encrypting their transmissions. Means you can't listen no matter how much you might want to. But most of these small-town places? Shoot." He shook his head. "Heck, I've heard tell there are still places that haven't even switched to digital yet! Can you imagine? Still using the old analog system like our granddaddies?"

"Crazy," Wes said. "So where are we going, anyway?"

"Well, I heard some chatter on the scanner earlier, right when I saw your car, about a possible sighting of the bandit girl at a motel out in the sticks toward the north end of Durango County. What's her name again? Charlotte or something…"

"Scarlet Burlew," Wes said, not sure how anyone could forget.

"Scarlet!" Putnam's eyes flashed as he repeated the name. "That's it. Yeah, there was a potential sighting a little while back."

Already Wes was seeing how useful this scanner might end up being. It was a lucky thing that he'd run into Putnam, and the man had turned out to be so eager to help.

"So wait," he asked. "She's still here? In Durango County?"

He couldn't help but think of the detective insisting that Scarlet and Ellie were long gone.

"Sounds that way, at least not so long ago. Eyewitness account, apparently."

"Was it Scarlet alone? Was anyone with her?"

"Dunno. I figure we go take a look and find out for ourselves."

They fell quiet for a while. The wind swished against the Camaro.

"You here for spring break?"

"Yeah."

"Figured so. Real popular place this time of year." He bobbed his head a little as he spoke. "You stayin' at one of them fancy resorts?"

"Oh God no. Couldn't come close to affording that." Wes watched the greenery out the window whiz by in a blur. "We're staying at the luxurious Sea Spray Motel."

Putnam chuckled.

"So this Ellie, the one you're lookin' for… how long have you two been romantically involved?" Putnam asked.

Wes blinked rapidly.

"What? I never said— what makes you think that?"

Putnam wheezed out another laugh.

"Shoot, I could tell just by the way you talk about her," Putnam said, gesturing with his cigarette. "I don't want to say it's *obvious*, but if the shoe fits…"

Wes's cheeks felt warm, and he smiled sheepishly.

"Well, the truth is, we just met. She's staying in the next room over, and we sort of ended up hanging out and… yeah."

"Ah!" Now he sounded triumphant. "A whirlwind vacation romance. I should have known. Now let me guess… you probably been tellin' yourself all the while that it's just a little fling, but she got under your skin, didn't she?"

"I guess so, yeah," Wes said, still blushing.

Putnam elbowed him.

"Yessiree Bob! I thought so! I can always tell."

They'd just reached the outer edges of Durango Beach proper when there was a sudden burst of activity on the scanner.

"Twenty-four-twenty, uh… we have a, uh… a bit of a situation over here."

The voice was male and sounded somewhat panicked.

"Jesus wept, Lawrence," a gruff, more authoritative voice responded. "How many times do I have to tell you to use the damn codes?"

"Uh oh, sounds like we have a little bit of po-lice drama

going on," Putnam said, turning the volume knob on the scanner higher.

"Ah jeez. OK," the one they'd called Lawrence said. "Uh… there's a… ten… um… ten-thirty-two?"

Someone chuckled over the radio.

"Aren't you stationed inside the hospital, two-four-two-zero?"

"Uh… yes, sir?"

"A ten-thirty-two is requesting an intox operator. Did you pull a patient over for reckless driving of a wheelchair?"

There was laughter and then more ribbing from his fellow officers. When they calmed down, Lawrence tried again.

"Alright, alright. We have a ten… forty-two?"

"For fuck's sake, Lawrence. Just tell us what happened."

"OK. Well… the, er… the ten-fifteen from earlier? He, uh… seems to have… absconded?"

"Did he say ten-fifteen?" Putnam perked up. "I think that's a prisoner in custody."

"Two-four-two-zero, are you saying what I think you're saying?" the gruff voice asked.

"I don't know! I'm saying the ten-fifteen… the guy! Jimmy Maddox… he's gone! And I need, like… assistance over here."

Putnam jerked the Camaro into a U-turn.

CHAPTER 82

Ellie strode down the long strip of concrete leading out toward the parking lot. Glancing over her shoulder, the hospital already looked smaller behind her, its bulk shrinking little by little.

Even through her sunglasses, the daylight gleamed everywhere, palm fronds gently bouncing in the wind on both sides of the path. There was something exhilarating about it all just now, the freedom of it, the lightness of it.

After so long in the air-conditioned tomb of the hospital, the heat outside actually felt kind of nice. She knew the feeling would pass, that the humidity would get heavier and heavier, that the soggy feeling would encase her entire body in feverish moisture.

But for now the warmth felt good, the open expanse of air stretching out all around her, the sunlight slanting down from the heavens to touch her skin. It reminded her, in some way, of a childhood impression she'd always had — what a lizard sunning itself on a rock might feel. Safe and warm.

At the end of the sidewalk, she stepped down onto the asphalt of the parking lot. The soles of the cheap Walmart shoes felt tacky against the hot cement. She moved through the throng of vehicles now.

But she looked past the crush of cars crammed into the lot. Fixed her gaze on what lay beyond them.

Her eyes danced on the traffic moving in the distance. All those cars whooshing past, stopping and starting at the intersection.

There. That way lay a return to her normal life, to the regular world, and all the streets led to it. Her friends. Her motel room. None of it was so far off now.

Maybe she could get a cab or something once she got out to

the street. Or maybe she'd just walk. It might be two or three miles to the motel, but what would that take? Maybe forty minutes or so?

She imagined getting back to the room. Shedding the scrubs. Climbing into a scalding shower. Steam pluming everywhere. This whole excursion would be cleansed from her skin, purged with hot water and a few squirts of Courtney's body wash.

As if on cue, her scrubs crinkled faintly, a soft sound pulsing with each step, the smooth fabric rubbing against her knees, swishing between her thighs. She looked down at the pants.

That feeling grew stronger, somehow, at the sight. She couldn't wait to get out of these clothes, get out of this parking lot. Be done with all of this. She couldn't wait to get back to Wes.

The image of him flashed in her head. The way his mouth pulled into a smirk when he made a joke. Or the way his hair was always falling in his eyes.

She wondered what he was doing now. Looking for her, maybe?

It suddenly occurred to her how worried he'd probably been when she disappeared, especially given what had happened with his brother. She hoped he hadn't been too distressed.

A hatchback with a busted muffler rumbled down the aisle of the parking lot. Violent sounds shuddering out of the thing, revving up into a higher pitch as it plunged her way.

Ellie hugged all the way to the left side of the row to let it pass. Trekked alongside the line of bumpers there.

She glanced up at the sky again. Clouds stark white against the blue. The sunlight seemed to be going orange as the day progressed. The once-lemony light taking on a darker, more saturated tint.

And then movement drew her eye back to the lot.

A figure wearing scrubs bobbed up from between the cars.

A man. Hair all matted down in the back. Shoulders hunched funny.

He stared over the hood of a Jeep for a few seconds, and then he ducked back down amidst the cars.

Some part of Ellie's mind leapt like a fish — enthralled, excited — before the meaning of what she'd seen reached her conscious mind.

Not scrubs. A gown.

Jimmy.

Jimmy was still here. Hiding in the parking lot.

But why?

Ellie kept walking. Staring that way. The meaning came to her as she moved.

They're stuck.

She found the stolen Hyundai, some few rows up and to the left. Then her eyes shifted to the Lincoln blocking them in. Its idling engine was barely audible from here, a low hum reverberating over the top of the asphalt.

A memory came of the machines in Jimmy's room shrieking as soon as the two of them had fled. Ellie hadn't waited around to see the aftermath, lest she get caught up in it. That was what Scarlet had told her to do.

She twisted her head, peered over her shoulder on one side and then the other. Checked behind her out of the corner of her eye.

A woman with red hair pushed a stroller toward the front doors. Closer, a slow string of people filtered into the lot, spreading outward into the cars.

The cavalry wasn't here yet, but they would be. Any second now, this place would be swarming with cops.

She turned back toward the Hyundai. Cut left between the cars.

Jimmy and Scarlet huddled in the next row over. Scarlet's head wheeled around when she heard the footsteps.

Ellie gave her a little nod, tried to make it barely perceptible should anyone be looking this way.

Then she stepped out into the aisle and strode for the Lincoln.

The man inside wore a suit and swiped at his phone in little bursts. He didn't look up as she approached.

She rapped her knuckles on the glass, and he jumped like a marionette, elbows lifting funny. She noted the gun holstered to his hip right away.

A cop?

In a suit?

Must be a detective.

And if he's just sitting here, he must not know that Jimmy's escaped yet.

He jabbed the button on the door, and the window whirred as it lowered. Air-conditioned coolness wafted out of the opening.

Ellie laid on the southern accent even thicker than before.

"Sorry to trouble ya, but can I ask you to move your car? Just a few feet up would do it."

He frowned. Lips pursed. For a beat, Ellie worried he recognized her. Then his eyes drifted down to take in her scrubs, and it looked like his complexion went a touch red. Ellie had to stop herself from laughing.

People really do see what they want to see.

"See, I've only got thirty minutes for lunch, and getting to the Taco Bell and back can be iffy, when there's traffics. Lookin' to get me a Crunchwrap, I guess. They discontinued the 7-layer burrito sometime back for some dumb reason nobody apparently knows. So yeah. Crunchwrap."

His gaze went flat as she yammered, something glazing over in his eyes as he watched her lips move. When she finished, he took a second to respond, and in the silence, she could hear tinny voices emanating from the police radio mounted under the dash.

"Twenty-four-twenty, uh… we have a, uh… a bit of a situation over here."

"Jesus wept, Lawrence. How many times do I have to tell

you to use the damn codes?"

The detective reached over and turned the volume down. The burble of voices became unintelligible.

"Uh… sure," the detective said. "I'll get out of your way. Sorry. Enjoy your, uh, Crunchy Wrap."

The Lincoln seemed to hiccup as he shifted into gear. He eased forward, that window whirring up.

Ellie stalled then, fidgeting as though getting something out of her pocket, slow to make her way toward the Elantra. She had a dim memory of hitting the lock button on the keys before handing them over to Scarlet.

Scarlet had the keys. She studied the Lincoln from the corner of her eye.

If he waits and watches, he might wonder why I'm not getting in the car.

The big car slowed again, taillights flaring red at the corner of Ellie's vision. The brake pads squeaked faintly as he stopped.

She glanced back. Saw the cop's head angled toward the rearview mirror, neck all lengthened and tight. Watching.

Shit.

She turned the slight corner to get to the driver's side door. Heart thumping pretty good.

What do I do?

But then there was an electronic beep, and the car doors unlocked with a mechanical *thunk*. Her eyes slid over, and she spotted Scarlet and Jimmy squatted at the end of the row, grinning.

Ellie's fingers sank into the recess around the handle. She pulled.

The door made a sticky sound as she pried it out of the frame, and then it swung free. She hesitated a second and then slid into the driver's seat.

The Lincoln still loitered just a few cars down. Maybe he was going to wait until she actually left. Maybe he'd gone back to dicking around on his phone, not even paying attention to her.

She didn't want to look too closely. Even with the sunglasses shielding her eyes, it felt like she'd be jinxing something to angle her head that way.

The back door inched open. Ellie watched in the mirror as Scarlet and then Jimmy slithered through the crack and crawled over the backseat, keeping so low that their chests skimmed over the upholstery. It reminded Ellie, somehow, of a video she'd seen on the internet of a three-toed sloth dragging itself across a road.

"You good?" Ellie said, pretending to adjust her makeup in the mirror.

"Yeah. Thanks, Ellie," Scarlet said. "Let's get out of here."

Ellie jabbed the button to start the car, and they were off.

CHAPTER 83

Ellie gripped the wheel, foot lightly pressing the accelerator. The car responded to her touch, hastening into the stream of traffic, then slowing down to match the pace of the herd.

"That's good," Scarlet said from the backseat. "Keep it slow and steady. For now, anyway."

Ellie nodded, took a quick glance over her shoulder as she did.

Jimmy and Scarlet held hands in the back, sitting close, still wearing their hospital gowns. They looked like one of those movies about cancer kids falling in love, Ellie thought.

They knifed through a neighborhood of old Victorian homes. Mansard roofs here and wraparound porches there. Big green yards separated the houses from the road.

Ellie felt a tremor in the tendons of her wrists and relaxed her grip on the steering wheel. She reminded herself to breathe. Felt the wind suctioning through her nostrils.

Her body seemed to be going through the motions of panic, but the fear hadn't touched her mind yet, at least not fully. She wasn't sure what to make of that.

Jimmy spoke up then.

"Can't believe the cops ain't floodin' the hospital parking lot yet. Wonder what the hell—"

Scarlet shushed him, interrupting with a hiss and then holding up an index finger.

"Listen."

The inside of the car fell quiet. The tires thumped over a craggy spot in the street.

And then Ellie heard it.

The sirens wailed in the distance. Mournful voices all tangled together.

They seemed small. Far away.

But they were fading in. Swelling in volume. Definitely getting closer.

At last, a trickle of fear seeped into Ellie's bloodstream like ice water. She watched the horizon, waiting for the cruisers to appear there.

Scarlet's voice still sounded calm.

"Pull into this driveway up here on the right. All the way in, and then kill the engine."

Ellie forced her gaze away from the street. Found the driveway.

She guided the car up the concrete ramp. Eased them down the length of the drive.

The plot of grass rolled along outside the window, and a house painted the shade of the ocean seemed to grow as they drew up on it. Ellie watched the windows but saw no movement.

Hopefully these people aren't home.

The driveway curved gently at the end. The front end of the Hyundai snugged up just shy of a garage door, and then Ellie tapped the button to shut off the engine.

The quiet shuddered through the car. Fresh and strange.

And the sirens seemed all the louder outside. At least three of them. Screaming bloody murder.

They all ducked low then, heads below the dash level.

Ellie watched a narrow rectangle of the street behind them in the side mirror. Eyes flicking over the glass even as nothing moved there.

They waited. Listened.

The sirens built in volume, soaring toward a crescendo. It felt like the end of a dramatic symphony piece. The tension surged. The end was near. Any second now.

Ellie watched the reflection. A Volvo cruised past.

The sirens kept getting louder. Beyond what seemed possible. Shrieking like a boiling kettle. Piercing.

And finally the mirror flared with light and movement. Six cop cars raced past, headed for the hospital, red and blue lights smearing from one end of the glass to the other.

Despite her fear, Ellie felt a strange relief at seeing them. The waiting was over. Her chest loosened, and a big breath came in.

And just as quickly as they'd appeared, the cops were gone. Past. The sirens seemed to change pitch, going flat and elongated as they rushed away, like some of the urgency had already seeped out of them.

No one moved for another thirty seconds. They held silent as the sirens shrank back down to bird voices.

Scarlet was the one who finally broke the quiet.

"I think it's clear. Let's go."

CHAPTER 84

"How far is the hospital from here?" Wes asked.

Putnam sped up until he was riding the bumper of a silver Subaru.

"Five or ten minutes, maybe more if we keep getting stuck behind these molasses motherfuckers."

When there was a break in oncoming traffic, he gunned it and passed the silver car. Wes gripped the sides of his seat. Putnam's aggressive driving style made him nervous as hell, but on the other hand, he was kind of impressed that he was going this hard when he didn't even know Ellie.

As they drove, more updates filtered in over the scanner.

"We have a citizen witness on the line, a nurse who saw two Caucasian females entering the building," a female dispatcher was saying. "She believes one of the females might have been Scarlet Burlew."

Wes's heart rate, already slightly elevated by the way Shane was swerving in and out of traffic, ratcheted up another notch.

"Did you hear that?" he said. "Two females, and one of them was Scarlet? The other one has to be Ellie!"

A grin spread over Putnam's lips. Something about it looked demonic to Wes.

"Oh, I heard alright."

The scanner blipped again, and another dispatcher broke in.

"County dispatch to north-end county units, prepare to copy ATL. Be on the lookout for suspect in last night's officer-involved homicide outside of Durango Beach."

Wes sucked in a breath. Last night's officer-involved homicide? They had to be talking about the murder of Detective Stinson.

"North Carolina license plate 1-7-2 Ocean Yellow David."

The dispatcher's voice was strikingly calm, almost flat, considering she was talking about the suspect in a murder. "Again, ten-twenty-eight is 1-7-2 Ocean Yellow David. 2021 white Chevy Camaro."

It felt like time slowed down as Wes processed what he'd just heard. Had she said a *white Chevy Camaro*?

"Suspect's name is Bertram Shane Putnam, and he is assumed to be in possession of multiple firearms. If located, detain and advise, using extreme caution."

The words hung there in the air, and Wes felt the blood drain from his face.

The chatter on the radio kept going. The basics were repeated, but the turn of phrase "armed and dangerous" caught Wes's ear this time.

He couldn't bring himself to turn his head, could only work up the courage to glance at Putnam from the corner of his eye. The driver stayed focused on the road, looking so calm it was almost like he hadn't heard the scanner broadcast the APB for him. Was that even possible?

Adjusting his position, Wes crossed his arms over his lap with the left arm on top. With his right hand tucked under his left elbow, he inched his fingers up to his pocket. Slowly tugged at his phone.

With the phone in hand, he peeked over at Putnam again. His face was placid. Maybe he was so fixated on driving, he really *hadn't* heard.

Wes swallowed, his throat so dry it felt like it was coated in sand. He brought up the dial pad.

9.

He sneaked another look at Shane.

1.

Almost there.

1.

And then Putnam's hand clamped down on his wrist.

"Now, now, now, Wes..."

He ripped the phone from Wes's grip in one clean motion

and tossed it out his open window.

"You won't be needing that."

He turned to Wes, his mouth stretching into that evil smile again.

"Look," Wes said, his voice shaking. "I don't want to make any trouble for you. So just let me out, and I won't say anything to anyone. OK?"

"Hmm…" Putnam made a show of pursing his lips and rocking his head side to side, like he was considering it. Then he clicked his tongue. "Nah. I think you should stay. Me and you should see this thing through to the end."

Wes didn't like how ominous that sounded. His eyes went to the scenery whizzing past.

He had to get out of here. Had to bail out. The thought of jumping from a moving vehicle turned his insides to ice, but he had no other choice. He'd close his eyes and count to three.

One…

Two…

Just as his fingers brushed against the door latch, Putnam floored it. Wes lost his hold on the handle as his body was thrown back against his seat.

"You wouldn't be gettin' any wild ideas, now would you?" Putnam asked, chuckling a little.

Wes stared at the speedometer.

65.

70.

75.

Wes pictured himself scraping over the asphalt, rolling like a tumbleweed. There was no way he could jump out now.

Putnam jerked the wheel, and the Camaro swerved over the yellow line. They passed an SUV on a blind curve and only narrowly missed colliding with a truck coming their way.

And still he didn't slow down. The pitch of the engine's whine rose higher and higher as they hit 80, then 85.

Wes's hands were claws, clinging to his seatbelt like that might add an extra layer of protection.

He's going to kill us, he thought. *I'm going to die.*

When the needle hit 100 miles per hour, Putnam lifted his head and howled like a wolf.

CHAPTER 85

Ellie guided the Hyundai back onto the street. Eased back into the flow of traffic.

"The highway ramp is straight ahead," Scarlet said from the backseat. "Maybe 5 or 10 miles."

Ellie bobbed her head. Tried to let her gaze creep all that way ahead, past all the fast-food places and gas stations and grocery stores.

They waited a few beats at a red light and got going again. It felt like they could disappear among all the other vehicles. Melt into the throng.

Then the sirens shrilled behind the Hyundai. Screaming in falsetto.

"Aw, fuck," Jimmy said, facing out the back. "Here they come."

Ellie grimaced. Held the wheel in that death grip again. Bolts of pain shot out of hands and wrists gone taut.

Her eyes flicked to the rearview mirror. Red and blue lights twinkled there, swirling motes of brightness creeping ever closer.

No way out now.

The cruisers looked like aggressive things. Muscular shapes reflected in the glass. Angular. A swarm of wasps speeding toward them.

And now that pain evaporated from Ellie's joints, hands going icy on the wheel instead. Numb.

Fear trembled in her core. Knotted the muscles in her gut. Something gurgling there. Frothing like the scum on top of a polluted river.

She knew, somehow, that she'd made some mistake in letting the terror inside, that a line had been crossed, that her ability to stave it off was gone now. Passed.

"I can't do this," she whispered, tongue touching her top lip as soon as the words were out.

"What?" Scarlet said from the backseat.

Ellie whispered again.

"I can't. I can't do this."

Scarlet sighed. Her tone hardened.

"No one can hear you. Speak up."

Ellie focused. Forced herself to project her voice, though she couldn't keep the waver out of it.

"I can't do this."

"Well, you have to."

"I can't. OK? I can't. This is not me. I'm not like you. I'm not brave or whatever."

Her hands clenched and twisted at the steering wheel as she talked. The Hyundai zoomed straight down the middle lane, ripping past a bunch of cars.

Scarlet worked to control her voice, her jaw tight, but Ellie could hear the rage just beneath the surface.

"Ellie. You can't just nope out of things when life gets hard. You can't just crawl under a rock like a pill bug or something and hide until the responsibility goes away. The real world doesn't work that way. Just drive. We need you. We're depending on you."

Ellie threw up her arms. Then gripped the wheel again.

She yelled.

"No! This is too much. I'm scared. And I don't know what I'm doing. And I can't."

She braced herself for the venom that would surely come from the backseat, the anger that Scarlet would unleash.

But the backseat held quiet.

Ellie watched the police lights twirling in the rearview again. The flashers were getting closer.

Then she turned her head to peek into the backseat.

Both Jimmy and Scarlet had turned to stare out the rear windshield. Something looked off about their body language — shoulders tight, arms rigid.

"He found us," Scarlet said, her voice soft.

Ellie turned back to the windshield. She checked the mirror again, tried to get a glimpse of what Scarlet was looking at, but she couldn't.

"What?" she asked, finally.

"That Camaro back there. It's *him*."

CHAPTER 86

Taft's SUV fell in with the cruisers tearing through town. He jockeyed for position among the swarm, working his way up a spot or two from the back of the pack.

Up ahead, the Hyundai leapt to life. It wove into the middle lane — the turn lane — and rocketed onward, building speed, leaving the normal traffic behind.

And some tingling snake squirmed in Taft's gut as he, too, glided out into the center lane and jammed the gas pedal to the floor. He chewed his top lip. Swerved around some stopped cars at an intersection.

And words came unbidden to his thoughts, spoken in a gravelly register inside his skull:

Joining the chase.

The pitch of the Bronco's engine heightened, its usual soft hum breaking up into a rasp, a growl. He hurtled past much of the chase mob, a mess of cruisers bogged down in the two lanes to his right for the moment.

A tangle of voices throbbed on the radio. Chaos. Taft couldn't make sense of the words. Not now.

The Hyundai seemed to swell in the windshield. Growing. Occupying more and more of the glass as he drew up on it.

When he got to within five or so cars from the front of the pack, Taft could make out the three heads within the vehicle. It looked like Jimmy and Scarlet sat in the backseat. A third person — an unknown female, from the looks of it — drove the getaway vehicle.

So who the hell is that?

Another accomplice?

A hostage being forced to help? Ellie Levine?

The hair didn't look right, but he didn't mull it for long. They could sort it out upon apprehending the scumbags.

They swooped down a hill, all the cars bobbing over a dip in the road. After that, the chase seemed to settle some, at least in Taft's gut.

The pace grew familiar, comfortable. The adrenaline slowed from gushing to a steady drip.

The cruisers closest to the Hyundai tried to flank it. Rolling up toward one side or the other.

If they could swipe their front end into the side of the rear bumper just so, they could get the Hyundai to spin out, Taft knew.

But the sedan seemed to get feisty every time one of the cruisers got close. Speeding up. Darting back and forth. Not letting either of them get an angle.

Whoever was driving — hostage or accomplice — she knew what she was doing.

Hell. I don't know. Maybe Scarlet is driving, he thought. *Could be a hostage in the backseat there.*

The approaching cruisers fell back as the road began to curve, not wanting to risk anything with oncoming traffic that'd be blind to them. The Hyundai pressed the advantage and widened its lead for the moment.

Taft let his gaze drift around for a second. He found himself looking at the other cars speeding along.

Most of the vehicles giving chase were cruisers, obviously, but he saw Detective Bosa's Lincoln in the mix. A white sports car just a couple lengths from the front of the pack stuck out. He didn't recognize that one.

From this angle, with part of the muscle car screened from view by other vehicles in the chase mob, he couldn't tell if it was a Dodge Charger or maybe a Mustang. Could be a Challenger.

And then he thought, *Could even be a Camaro,* and almost threw up.

His eyes snapped to the license plate. North Carolina.

Jesus fuck.

This is the guy. The one chasing Jimmy and Scarlet down the coast. The one who killed Stinson.

Taft's butt lifted a few inches out of the seat, and his foot pressed the accelerator pedal down all the way.

CHAPTER 87

Wes angled his shoulders toward the passenger side window. He stared at the green and concrete beyond. Freedom blurred past, just there, on the other side of the glass.

The city smeared along. Houses with the occasional strip mall or a payday loan place interrupting the residential sprawl.

It felt strange to watch it all go by, powerless to leave the Camaro. A hollowness bloomed in his gut.

But he recognized the neighborhood, at least. The Burdick Murder House wasn't far from here. Just past the next light, or maybe two, if he was remembering right. Something about the familiarity reassured him.

He turned his head enough to see the driver. Watched him out of the corner of his eye.

Putnam sat tall in his seat. Shoulders back. Chest out.

His fingers writhed and flexed against the steering wheel. It almost looked like he was massaging it.

The man mumbled under his breath as he drove. Hard syllables Wes couldn't make out. Then he laughed a little.

Wes felt his jaw muscles bunch. Two knots flexing under his ears.

"How are you going to get out of this?" he said, his voice coming out hard.

Putnam's eyebrows scrunched.

"Huh?"

"The police are everywhere," he said, pointing a thumb over his shoulder.

Putnam shook his head. Shrugged.

"It don't matter. If I get locked up, I get locked up."

He breathed loud, in through his nostrils, out through his mouth.

"All that matters is killin' that little bitch. Jimmy, too, if I can. I'd trade my life for that. No question. Hell, I think I already have."

He shook his head again.

"That's what your kind'll never understand. You just drift along in life. Rudderless. Don't have any real passion for anything. Just kind of gravitate toward comfort and convenience like they're the only values that mean anything to you."

He turned and looked at Wes. Stared at him.

And Wes could feel Putnam's eyes crawling on him, piercing him, judging him.

"Sometimes, when you love someone, it don't even fully make sense. Like Scarlet and me. If I can't have her…"

Wes found his shoulders rotating away from the window as Putnam talked. Drawn in.

"See, on all them movies, they make love seem like it can only be this thing of light. A weightless, soaring thing. Uplifting."

His eyes flicked back to the road as he talked, jabbed the space in the distance.

"But that's not always true. Not at all. Scarlet and me? The love I feel for her is a violent thing. A darkness that pulses in my skull and trembles in my chest and twists in my fuckin' guts and makes me want to fucking explode. It's like a black tide lurching and hissing and spitting inside of me."

Wes took in the details of the scene as Putnam went on. Found himself measuring the angle of the killer's arms leading up to the steering wheel. The placement of the gearshift, the parking brake lever. The lights on the dash, and the stereo.

"And the idea that she wants someone else instead of me? It makes me want to kill. Makes me want to destroy. Nothing else matters."

He was quiet for a second. Thinking.

When he spoke again, his voice went soft, light.

"I love her darkly, you know."

They held quiet for another three seconds. The wind tore at

the windshield, made a rippling sound. A bevy of sirens wailed somewhere just behind them.

And then Wes lurched, unlatching his seatbelt.

He ripped the parking brake lever up with one hand. Threw himself at the steering wheel in the same motion.

His chest slammed into the hard plastic ring. Ribcage quaking. Upper body draped over it.

He flailed. Found the wheel with his hands a beat later.

Then he cranked it as hard as he could to the right. Threw all his weight that way.

The Camaro shimmied for a second. Tires screeching like wounded birds.

And then it felt like reality itself careened hard to the right.

Tilting. Listing.

A sinking feeling.

Wes crashed backward. Off balance. One knee planted between the seats.

Somehow he held onto the wheel. Fought Putnam for control.

The car jumped the curb. Banged down. Metal thumping. Bottoming out. Shocks bouncing.

They zipped up onto a dirt parking lot, fishtailing, losing control.

And they hit something. Knocked it flat. The fence, Wes thought.

Clouds of dust kicked up all around them. Brown smoke blotting out most of the view. Gravel pinging against the undercarriage and wheel wells.

The brake pads hissed like steam engines. Angry. Somehow unable to stop the car.

Wes watched as the Burdick Murder House grew to fill the windshield completely.

CHAPTER 88

Detective Taft sat forward in his seat. Telescoped his neck. Jutted his chin out over the dashboard like this might give him some greater vantage point to see who was inside the Camaro in the lane to his right.

Tinted windows muted his view, but he thought there might be two heads hovering behind the glass, occupying the front seats.

The Camaro swerved hard to the right without warning. Tires shrieking.

It hurtled over the curb. Rocked up and down. Shredded the thin strip of grass along the verge, gouging muddy ruts in it.

Then it tore out over the dirt and gravel lot, heading for an abandoned building there. Flattened the fence. Careening. Fishtailing. A wild thing unbridled.

Taft felt that his mouth was hanging open and closed it. He narrowed his eyes.

No. Not just any abandoned building. The spooky old Burdick house.

The Camaro jerked and lurched, zigzagging over the lot. Conflicted about where to go.

The tires threw up gravel with every hard turn. Spitting rocks like slush.

Dust kicked up everywhere, a cloud hanging behind the muscle car, billowing outward in slow motion.

And weeds whipped at the undercarriage as it delved deeper into the unkempt lot, the throttled plants shaking around even after the Camaro had passed.

All five floors of the building loomed over the car. Made the vehicle look smaller and smaller as it drew closer.

Even with the haphazard trail, the car ultimately zipped straight for the structure. A heatseeking missile arcing for its target. Impact became inevitable.

Taft gritted his teeth. Braced his hands hard against the wheel. Clenched his gut.

The sports car slammed into the brick. Taft could hear the crack even through his closed windows. Thick like a snapping femur.

The front end crushed into the building, splintering like balsa, and then the vehicle's forward thrust stopped dead. The back end of the car hopped up and then down a beat after that.

Holy shit.

The Camaro held motionless then. Deathly still. Eerie.

And then black smoke fluttered out of the crinkled hood. A rising wall of murk leaking out of the wounded thing all at once. Dark tendrils coiling around and around.

Taft's eyes drifted from the Camaro to the Hyundai way out in front of the chase. He swallowed. Then he looked back at the smashed muscle car.

And some part of his subconscious mind did the calculus. Worked the angles. Divined the meaning.

He had to choose which to pursue, and he quickly did.

He got on the radio as he slowed and pulled into the lot outside of the abandoned building.

"Putnam's white Camaro just smashed into the Burdick house. Detective Taft in pursuit."

His mouth suddenly felt dry. Tongue all tacky like a leech trying to cling to his hard palate. He added one more sentence to his radio message.

"This is the guy who killed Stinson."

CHAPTER 89

Wes braced his hands against the dashboard. Watched the brickwork swell to fill the windshield.

And everything seemed to flip into slow motion.

The Camaro smacked into the brick with a boom like a shotgun blast. The front end crumpled and burst.

Wes could feel the section of brick wall buckling, the force of it thrumming through the Camaro, vibrating into his hands.

And then the props of his arms ripped out from under him. He flew into the dash.

White.

The world went white. Pluming. Filling his vision. Punching him in the face. Enveloping him.

Gravity held him down. Ground him into the white. All that forward momentum seemed like it would pin him there forever.

But the force let up as quickly as it came. Let up all at once.

Wes lifted his head. Saw the details of the pale balloon thing surrounding him. The airbag.

He looked around at a car interior now shaded by the brick looming over it.

He felt the last vestige of the crash still venting through the Camaro's body, one final jerk like an aftershock.

Then it crunched down in the gravel. Something gritty in the settling. Shocks all rough like blown-out knees.

And at last the car was still. Motionless.

Wes blinked. Listened.

Something hissed and then smoke plumed out from under the hood. Opaque black.

Wes pushed himself back from the airbag, from the dashboard. Arms feeling dead from fighting gravity. Muscles numb and rubbery.

He tried to breathe and found his throat tight, his face hot.

And then the smoke was jetting through the vents. The acrid smell suddenly everywhere. Black clouds jetting into the cabin.

Something scrabbled next to him.

Putnam was out and gone before Wes could react.

He juked around the car door, darting toward the building. He climbed over the smashed hood of the Camaro and then turned sideways to disappear into the cleft spot in the bricks.

Wes fought through the sagging airbag and flopped over onto the passenger door. Reached a hand into the smoke to find the door handle.

He pulled. Shoved. Wedged the door out into the daylight.

And then he clambered into the clear air. Staggering on numb legs. All his limbs vibrating.

He shuffled a few steps away from the smoking car. Feet crunching on grainy sand flecked with gravel.

He glanced back over his shoulder at the smoking car. Somehow, he didn't think it would blow, but he kind of knew he wasn't thinking clearly. Adrenaline and shock filled his head with strange emptiness.

All he knew was that he wanted to get away from the smoke, away from that awful burnt polyester smell. He wanted to get it out of his head.

He stumbled on. Stared at the ground.

Breathed heavy. Mouth open.

Clean wind entered him, that humid Florida feeling lacquering his throat, laminating his lungs.

But for now he didn't mind. Anything but the smoke.

Once he was a good fifty or so feet from the burning car, he leaned forward and put his hands on his knees. Stared out at the road where heat distortion whirled atop the asphalt.

Everything seemed distant now. His consciousness had sucked way up in his skull like a tortoise shell, and the rest of the world was far, far away. He stared down a tunnel at it all.

And then he saw the SUV whipping into the lot.

The Bronco cruised right up to Wes and then slammed on the brakes, skidding over the dirt and gravel to stop about a foot shy of him.

The detective, Taft, hopped out, and he stormed right up to Wes. Gun out. Something aggressive in his movements. Angry.

Then his eyelids scrunched up. Some look of recognition settled his features. He pointed the gun at the ground.

Taft glanced at the building and then back at Wes.

"He still in the car?"

Wes's head started swinging side to side before he could get the words out.

"No. He ran inside."

Taft turned and strode off.

Wes took a few more breaths. He felt lightheaded then, fresh weakness spiraling into his skull. He needed to find a place to sit down.

He pushed himself forward. Staggering once more. Feet skimming over the dirt.

He wanted to get over to that strip of grass along the road. But he didn't make it.

The blackness lurched up and wrestled Wes down to his knees. He could feel the gravel, warm against his legs, heat waves rising up from it.

He fought for balance. His head rotated funny, tilting in a loping circle like it meant to orbit his body.

Finally he tipped forward. Falling. Falling for the dirt.

The last thing he saw was the line of police cruisers streaming into the lot.

CHAPTER 90

The low light inside the abandoned building seems to cast a gray bloom over the guts of the structure. Sepia tones leach the color out of everything, and the shadows gather into charcoal fog in the corners, blacker than the rest.

Putnam creeps through the gloom and surveys the scene. He needs to think.

He finds the first floor of the apartment building dominated by ripped-out chunks of drywall — an open floor plan by way of someone tearing out all the copper pipes. Exposed studs seem the only thing between him and the exterior walls in some places. It feels skeletal, like he's looking through the ribcage of the structure.

He strides through some of the broken places. Ducks to pass through the holes in the walls.

Gray rooms brush past. Bedrooms and bathrooms hard to distinguish given the state of decay and plunder.

A pond smell wafts throughout the space. Water has definitely gotten in through the years, gallons and gallons.

One more gray room passes, and one more rough door punched into the drywall ushers him into the next space.

Some kind of lobby widens out before him then. A bigger space. Open.

Metal mailboxes line one wall. Corroded with green growth like an old penny. It seems to Putnam like the bandits would have pillaged that for scrap, too. Maybe they couldn't pry it out of the brick.

He steps forward, moves deeper into the lobby, and the ceiling opens to a giant staircase winding up the center of the larger chamber. He stands in the center and looks up at the banister and steps coiling up and up.

Five floors of empty space gape back at him from the

middle of that spiraling handrail flecked with newels and balusters. Something about the soaring emptiness ripples goose bumps over the backs of his arms.

And now he has an idea.

Putnam lurches for the mouth of the broad staircase, jogs up rotten steps. Thin carpet the color of algae lines the middle part of the risers and treads, leaving dark stained wood exposed along the edges. The wood shifts under his weight, moaning high-pitched sounds in some places and crackling in others.

He gains speed as he traverses the first two floors. Takes the steps two at a time. Then he pauses and peeks over the banister.

No one down there. Yet.

He keeps moving. Striding two steps over a landing and launching himself up the next flight of stairs.

His foot punches through a soggy spot in one of the treads. A mouth of rotten wood grips his shoe.

He goes down. Catches himself, bracing both hands on one of the risers. A breath woofs out of him.

Then he yanks. Kicks. The wood hooked around his shoe won't let go.

Finally he bends down and fishhooks one finger into the opening. Pries along the lip of jagged wood. Eases the edge of the rubber sole free from the hole.

And then he's moving again. Bounding up the stairs.

It occurs to some part of his mind that this is the classic movie mistake. The person on the run inexplicably heads upstairs. Backing themselves into a corner.

But this is different.

On the third floor, he leaves the staircase. Creeps a few steps down the hall.

He kicks open one of the apartment doors, peers through the open doorway and looks out the broken window beyond that.

He scans what he can, but the neighboring building blots out most of the view.

Better to go all the way up, if I can.

He runs back for the stairs. Mounts that upward slope again. Legs churning. Feet pounding.

On the next landing, he peeks over the banister again. Still nothing below. Just the blackened squares of the floor congealing into one murky surface that almost looks like a bog.

Maybe I'll get lucky. Maybe the cops want Jimmy and Scarlet more than they want me.

Those two have been on TV and shit.

Everybody wants a piece of that kind of celebrity. Everybody.

But he'd heard the APB on him. "Wanted in connection to an officer-involved homicide." So they know he's the one who rock-stomped the detective. Not great.

When it comes to cop killin', a pig never forgets.

He sniffs a laugh to himself as he climbs the next set of stairs. Still taking them two at a time.

At last he reaches the top floor.

He stops again and goes quiet, leans up against the handrail. Listens.

And he tries to slow his breathing, tries to hear past the thunder of his heart in his chest.

Finally he peeks over the rail. Lets his gaze zoom in on that boggy black surface below.

Still nothing. But something tells him to wait a few more seconds, so he does.

At last, footsteps sound below. Quiet at first but getting louder, closer.

He pulls his head back from the breach and listens again.

The heavy footfalls crunch over bits of broken glass. Hesitate. And then they start climbing the steps.

CHAPTER 91

It felt like an anvil was perched on Ellie's chest. The panic had grown heavy somehow — a leaden thing constricting her breath, squeezing her ribcage. Iron trying to punch a hole straight through her.

She drove. Wrestled the car for control. Faster, faster.

Red and yellow fast-food signs flitted by. Traffic still bunched at red lights, pooled at stop signs. Ellie maneuvered through the vehicles, knowing only that she needed to get out away from people, away from town.

Maybe there was no point. Maybe the police would run them down no matter what. But it felt like if she could just get them out of the city, they might have some chance of escape. Something.

Her eyes kept bouncing from the windshield to the side mirror to the rearview and then back to the road. Fidgety orbs swiveling in their sockets.

And the panic found voice in her head now and again. The fear itself congealing into language, words burbling to the surface.

You can't.

But she gripped the wheel tighter whenever the fright surfaced. And a second voice stirred to combat the first.

I can. I am. I'm doing it right now.

Police lights still twirled in the rearview. And Ellie found her palms going damp, slick against the wheel. Some sickly feeling yawing in her gut like she'd eaten too many blueberries.

I'm already doing it, and I'm fine.

She focused on her breathing. Deep breaths in through her nostrils. Slow breaths out through her mouth.

Waves. Waves of wind rolling through her. Ingested and expelled.

The breathing, and her focus on it, seemed to beat back the panic a bit. She could let the fear roll away with the outbound waves. Release it.

While Ellie drove, Scarlet chattered in the backseat. Some stream of updates pouring forth that Ellie couldn't really track. Now, as her mind cleared, she found she could understand the words spilling out.

Scarlet gasped.

"Holy fuck."

"What?"

"A bunch of police just veered off back there. Like most of 'em."

Jimmy spun in his seat until he was faced out the back. His voice came out high, confused.

"What the hell?"

They fell quiet for several seconds. Ellie didn't know what to make of it.

She glanced back over her shoulder to see both of them staring out the rear windshield, sitting on their knees, hands hooked over the headrests, something childish in the poses. And behind them, only three cars now.

"Well? What's going on?" Ellie asked.

Scarlet took a beat to respond.

"I don't know. Just keep driving."

Ellie forced herself to watch the road, but her thoughts kept straying to the backseat, to the rear windshield, wondering what might be playing out beyond that curved pane of glass. Checking the mirror revealed nothing significant.

Jimmy's voice came out lower now, some hint of awe in it.

"Hey… I don't see…"

"Yeah," Scarlet said. "Me neither."

Ellie licked her lips. Posed another question.

"What?"

Again, the response was slow to come.

"The Camaro is gone."

CHAPTER 92

Detective Taft surged into the building. Swept his gun before him. The left side of his face twitched in time with his heartbeat. Fast.

He slowed as he crossed the first room, let his eyes adjust to the gloom in here. Then he remembered the flashlight in his pocket. A mini Maglite Stinson had given him for Christmas last year. Or had it been two years ago? It bothered him that he couldn't remember.

He flicked it on and scanned the room.

A broken-down dresser slumped in one corner. Some kind of grain or beads flecked the floor, tiny black bits crunching under his feet. Cobwebs festooned corners and draped the pitted places in the drywall, stringy fibers providing permanent Halloween decorations here.

He stepped through one of the gaps where a wall used to be. Lumber going gray rubbed at the sleeve of his suit jacket as he passed into the next room.

Again, his gun brushed across the expanse in front of him, pivoting like a lawn sprinkler. He didn't remember drawing the weapon, but it was there. Out and in his hand. Ready.

He waded through ankle-deep trash in this room. Pushed the beam of his flashlight over the top of it.

Food wrappers. Wadded-up bags, both paper and plastic. Cans. Bottles. Junk mail torn to flaps.

Standing here, he could look right through the building in all directions, staring through the studs of the structure like he had x-ray vision.

He slowly turned around. Looked. Listened.

He shot his light in each direction. North. South. East. West.

Murky rooms stretched outward from here, mostly

indistinguishable from each other. He caught glimpses of trashed couches and busted La-Z-Boys. Moldering mattresses floating on a sea of trash.

It smelled like a pond here, he thought. Wet. Something stale about it.

Finally, he lowered his light again. He didn't feel the killer's presence. Not on this floor.

He pressed onward. Shuffled through another doorway and another breach in the drywall.

And then he found himself in the lobby of the building. A giant staircase dominated the space, something about it drawing him closer. He stepped one foot onto the first tread.

But he swallowed then. Stopped himself. He wanted to check the other doorways here first. Suss out his options.

An office sat just off from the mailboxes. It had been destroyed long ago. A wooden desk sitting at an angle where one leg had been cracked out from under it. Papers strewn about.

A utility closet occupied the doorway beyond that. An old mop slanted in one corner. A cracked plastic bucket just beyond that. It still reeked like Pine-Sol in the small chamber, even if he saw no bottles left.

The last door lay beneath the staircase. He padded over to it.

He threw the door open. Lanced his light into the darkness. Pressed his gun into it, too.

Empty space filled his field of vision. Black nothing that shocked him somehow. His brain processed it in fragments.

Stairs.

Leading down.

The basement.

The concrete floor at the bottom of the steps seemed to pitch away from him. Lurching along with the movement of his light. Something vertiginous about the movement.

His breathing went ragged for a second, but it steadied almost as quickly. The floor below held still once he got control of his flashlight.

Just a basement.

That's all.

He stepped back from the basement doorway. Listened to the knock of his heart shudder through his ribcage, reverberate in his skull.

So would this asshole go upstairs or down?

His gut told him nothing. He paced back through the lobby as he thought.

And he let his gaze climb the big staircase going up and up.

There.

Something caught his eye about halfway up. A wounded spot on one of the risers. It looked fresh.

Up it is, then.

He started jogging up the steps. Body pitching forward to fight the upward slope. Some part of him wondered if he was making a mistake.

But some parts of life could only be lived face-first, he thought. It sounded like something Stinson would say.

And he wished she was here now. Wished it more than anything.

He swallowed, his throat suddenly feeling gritty. That twitch in his cheek just kept going. Spasming. Felt like a jellyfish flexing in the flesh of his face.

He reached the top of the first flight of steps. Coiled around the landing to start up the second.

And then a bevy of car engines roared outside, a mess of tires crunching over gravel, racing right up on the building. Cruisers, Taft knew. The cavalry was coming.

Good.

We've got this asshole cornered now.

CHAPTER 93

Where the handrail dead-ends at the top of the stairs, Putnam finds a shadowy spot encased in drywall on three sides. He steps into the darkness there.

Then he gets down on hands and knees. Pokes his head between two of the balusters.

And he peers at that coil of handrail leading down and down. The posts look like the spokes of a bike tire, connecting the stairs to the rail.

Even with the mess of cops spilling into the lobby below, one set of footsteps lopes up the steps. Thundering over the wood. Way out ahead of all the rest.

He tries to see between the bars, to see who's leading this charge. His eyes trace back and forth, but he sees no one.

Whoever it is, he thinks they still have a couple flights to go, at least.

He focuses on the sound again. More feet pound the lower floors now, but he blocks those out. Concentrates on the closest.

Heavy footsteps. A big guy, maybe.

But fast, too. Someone athletic.

Maybe if I get the jump on the lead guy…

Maybe something like that would change the game.

Give him a little push into the rickety old rail, perhaps.

He feels his face pulling. Realizes he's smiling.

Something flits between the bars two floors down. A dark strobe effect playing at the light between the balusters.

Putnam gets a glimpse. Recognizes the person he sees.

The fat detective. He'd seen him working the beach scene, watched from the parking lot without anyone having a clue.

And Putnam pictures himself lying in wait. Hurling himself just as the big lug hits the top of the steps.

The movie bucks and lurches in his mind.

The big detective flopping into the handrail. The lumber splintering. Cracking.

The body flying out into the abyss. Plunging five floors to the parquet below.

And he wonders if the big body would punch right through the wood. Dump the detective into the basement below.

Probably would.

But then he watches the silhouette flickering on the other side of the bars again. When the detective reaches the landing on the fourth floor, Putnam can see the dark bulk at the end of his pumping arm.

A gun.

That erases any thought of shoving the wide load over the edge. Putnam swallows and tastes something acidic at the back of his tongue.

He eases back from the balusters, but not before the detective leans out over the rail just one floor below.

"Up here," he yells to the floors below.

And it seems like even more uniformed officers spill into the lobby then. Flashlight beams swinging everywhere. They all rush for the steps, filing onto the staircase one after another, the wood creaking in protest.

Putnam backpedals into the hallway, his view of all those flashlights brushing up the walls getting cut off as he backs away.

Fuck. Gotta get out of here.

He runs for one of the rooms.

CHAPTER 94

Taft swung his flashlight beam into one of the fifth-floor apartments. The glowing circle crawled over the floor, climbed up the wall, darted to one side and then the other.

Then the detective crept into the darkened space. His feet squished on shag carpet that felt like it might be soggy even now — he wasn't sure. He walked toward the tunnel of glow spilling out of his flashlight without quite reaching it. The glowing patch on the wall swelled as he crossed the room, an ever-expanding circle.

The pond scum smell seemed to have intensified on the upper floors. That made sense, Taft thought. The closer he got to the leaky roof, the more water damage he'd encounter.

He's here. Somewhere.

Maybe not this room.

But the son of a bitch has to be here somewhere.

He plodded forward. Mouth clenched.

The gun trembled at the end of his arm. The muzzle thrusting into the darkness.

And his heart hammered. And his chest quaked.

It felt like sweat was oozing out of him in a steady stream, salty juice slicking him from head to toe, the moisture tickling funny on the backs of his knees. Still, he pressed onward.

After three steps into the room, the shapes around him started to make sense in the periphery of his vision. The kitchenette. The broken plastic deck chair lying on its side in the corner.

Slowly, he brought the flashlight up. Clenched it between his teeth to free his hand.

Then he darted forward. Grabbed a handful of the fabric hugging against the wall and pulled downward.

The curtain rod ripped clean off the wall with two snaps.

The drape flapped down along with it, a billowing parachute of dark green fabric sinking in slow motion.

And bright light shot through the window where the curtains had been. Piercing.

Taft squinted his eyes to slits. Brought that free hand up to shield his brow. Adjusted the tooth grip on the flashlight.

He staggered back a couple steps. Then he forced his eyes to open, swept the gun around the studio apartment.

Two steps shifted him to the door on the left-hand side of the room. He kicked it open. Exposed a bathroom darkened like a tomb.

He charged into the small space. Stomped on the wadded-up shower curtain in the corner to make sure no one was squatting under it.

There was nothing here. No one.

Shit.

A breath huffed out of him. Involuntary.

He plucked the flashlight out of his mouth. Flicked it off. Tucked it in his pocket.

Then he turned back to get a better look at the main space. Needed to walk the room to be sure. See it in the daylight.

Mold crawled up one of the far corners of the room. Black and green staining the walls, creeping over the edges of the kitchen cupboards.

The carpet had a hole melted into the middle of it. A blackened crater that went all the way down to the wood underneath.

He opened the fridge and every cabinet door. Found an old magazine sprawled under the kitchen sink. Eric Bana on the cover. Nothing else.

Only once he'd cleared the room did he realize the pond scent was different here. It smelled like a wet animal. Some doggy bath stench wafting everywhere.

And the carpet wasn't wet — at least not at the moment. It was just such a deep 80s pile that it felt loamy and plush under foot.

Out in the hall, the voices rang out one after another.

"Clear!"

"Room 5D clear!"

"Same for 5E."

Taft walked over to the edge of the stairwell. His chin dipped. He looked into the opening there, his gaze diving all the way down to the lobby. Some wave of vertigo grabbed him for a second and then released him almost as quickly.

"Is the basement clear?" he called down.

The silence hung for a second.

"Yes, sir. All clear. Bunch of garbage down there, but that's about it."

Impossible.

He just vanished?

No fucking way.

Another involuntary breath heaved out of Taft. The sound reminded him of a bulldog.

"Well, we'll start double-checking every room. He's gotta be here somewhere."

CHAPTER 95

Putnam squats like a backwards gargoyle on the concrete ledge outside the apartment window. Wind flapping the back of his t-shirt.

He tries to stop himself from looking down. Can't.

His gaze flits over the lip of the concrete. Spears the nothingness leading down and down and down.

Five floors of emptiness stretch all the way to the grass and brambles below. The sight of it makes his stomach lurch and ball itself up. It feels like he has two fistfuls of wadded-up ham for guts.

He leans closer to the building. Turns his face sideways and presses his cheek right against the brick.

Closes his eyes. Breathes.

There's a shadowy spot maybe ten feet to his left where the building forms a corner. The perfect place to hide. But he'd frozen where he was when the sounds started — suspended in a catcher's crouch.

Even now someone stirs just inside the unit, their feet scuffing over worn carpet. The floorboards whine in steady pulses.

At least he'd picked the right side of the building — he isn't facing the parking lot or the street from here. He might be able to stay hidden for a few minutes if need be. Maybe more, if he has to.

The footsteps inside the apartment cut out suddenly. The silence seems to bloat into something huge.

Putnam opens his eyes. Almost flinches at what he sees framed in the open window. Instead he holds his breath.

He can just make out a cop out of the corner of his eye. The side of his face — a big blockheaded guy with piggy features.

He doesn't see me.

The uniformed officer stands at the window, eyebrows creased. He faces straight out, his gaze fixed on the next building over.

He shakes his head and mutters to himself, but the wind picks up and Putnam can't make out the words.

The cop stands there a few more seconds. Blinking those piggy eyes. Then he turns and heads back inside.

Putnam breathes. Quiet breaths. Deep. Light-headedness prickles in his skull.

The wind exhales on his back. Hot and sticky, but the motion of the air feels kind of good, at least.

He looks around again. Eyes daring to venture to the next floor down — or what he can see of it, which isn't much.

Then his mind skips ahead. Tries to plot out his next move.

He knows that if he could make his way to the opposite side of the house, he could jump to the roof of the neighboring building and make his escape. But there are two problems with the plan.

First of all, he can't balance beam his way around. The ledge doesn't run all the way around the perimeter.

And even if he could reach it from the ledge he was on now, the roof over there is only three floors high. If he jumps from up here, the fifth floor, he'd probably break his leg or some shit.

So he needs to get back inside. Needs to get down at least one flight of steps, too. Make the jump to the lower roof from one of the fourth-floor windows, and he'll be free.

Have to wait for them to clear out.

Have to hope nobody looks up here in the meantime, too.

He adjusts his hands on the brick, fingers clawing into the mortar lines. Then he toes up a little closer to the wall. The soles of his shoes scuff out sand-papery sounds against the cement.

And he can vividly picture himself tipping backward. Pitching over the edge and falling forever.

Voices inside start calling out again.

"Clear!"

"All clear here, too."

"The top floor is clear, Taft. Double-checked and all. So what the hell do we do now?"

There's a huffing breath. The voices go on, but they're too low for Putnam to make out after a second.

Taft. Yeah, the name seems familiar from the scanner.

Heavy footsteps thud, and wood groans in counterpoint. He can hear the cops climbing down the steps, their voices trailing down and down and down.

Putnam waits. Breathes. The wind whips around him.

The footsteps trail away. Shrink. Vanish.

Quiet.

Quiet.

He edges back toward the open window. Feet gritting whisper-soft on the concrete. Hands perching and bouncing like spiders on the brickwork.

Just at the lip of the windowsill, his balance lurches. Shoulders rocking backward. Hips bucking, unable to right him.

His head whirls. Vision pitching out over the chasm. The ground lurches for him.

His hand shoots out like a snake and latches onto the window sash. The tension seems to shoot through him like a wire being pulled taut.

And then he's steady again.

He swings into the window like a monkey. Soundless as he steps down onto the half-rotten floor.

He squats there a second. Watches the doorway. Listens.

Nothing moves.

He licks his lips.

Just have to be careful now.

Take it slow.

That's all.

Then he stands. Legs extending. Pushing him upright in slow motion.

The shadows twitch to his right. Something swinging for

him out of the bathroom doorway.

Detective Taft steps out of the gloom and shatters the killer's nose with the butt of his gun.

CHAPTER 96

The Hyundai rocketed north on the highway, a silvery blur with a damn near full tank of gas. They chewed up asphalt, mile markers strobing in the corner of Ellie's eye.

She felt in control. Even with the police lights twirling in the mirror, she felt in command now.

Somehow, someway, only three cruisers had followed them out of Durango Beach and onto the freeway. They hadn't shaken them, but so far, the cops seemed satisfied to keep them in sight, lying back.

Ellie didn't know what to make of that, but for now she didn't care.

Sparse traffic dotted the way, minivans and sedans easily navigated around. Ellie worked the lanes without losing speed, mostly passing on the left but swooping into the right to get around a slow-ass if need be.

And the ride stretched out like that. The cops keeping their distance. The mile markers ticking off the progress.

The craggy gray road turned to fresh black tar, and then that charcoal strip of road widened as they entered the next county. Something almost luxurious about the new width, in Ellie's opinion. On the other hand, the traffic did start picking up too.

"Ah shit," Jimmy said.

Ellie's eyes flashed to the mirror, but she saw only the twirling cop lights some ten or so car lengths back. The same as it had been for miles now.

"What?" Scarlet asked.

"I know what they're doing. I know exactly what they're doing. We're driving right into their, uh, hands… or whatever."

Scarlet sounded more forceful this time.

"What?"

"They wanted us to do this. Take the highway and head for the big city. Why else would all those cruisers drop back like that? State po-lice got a big outpost here. Shit-ton-a cops probably headed out to skullfuck us even now. Roadblocks. Spike strips. Probably even deploying choppers and shit. We drove right into the trap. Hey, Ellie, get off at the next exit."

Ellie's eyes flicked from the road to the mirror and back again.

"Don't do that," Scarlet said. "Stay on the freeway. We're flying now. When we leave the interstate, it should be on our terms."

"Look, if they get the chopper on us, we're toast, OK? We're done. Already dead."

He paused a second before he went on.

"We gotta get off the freeway and get lost in town. Like now. Take the next exit, Ellie."

"Don't listen to him."

"Right here. Exit 191. Quarter mile. Do it."

"Don't."

The road signs whooshed past. The exit ramp zoomed closer.

Ellie froze. Arms rigid. Legs numb.

She wasn't sure who to listen to.

Scarlet had been the leader all along, brave and shrewd. Ellie trusted her.

But in this case, she found Jimmy's reasoning compelling. The highway locked them onto one path, drew a line on the map that law enforcement could use to thwart them.

Her eyes flicked to the exit ramp. Traced the white lines guiding the lane around a loop leading off the interstate.

She swallowed hard. Her palms suddenly felt slick against the steering wheel.

The exit zoomed closer. The time running out.

Ellie couldn't think. Couldn't decide.

The mouth of the exit came and went.

The backseat exploded with noise. Jimmy was yelling at

Ellie. Scarlet was yelling at Jimmy.

Ellie couldn't pick out enough of the words to understand complete sentences, but she got the gist.

Doesn't matter.

Tune it out.

She focused. Watched the police in the rearview. Blocked out the yelling and let her mind go blank except for the image in the mirror.

Two of the cruisers rode side by side up front, a third hanging back. They'd moved up a hair, shortening the distance to just five or so car lengths between them now.

Ellie watched as the front two cars pulled even with the exit ramp. Then she jerked the wheel hard to the right.

The Hyundai veered. Crossed the diagonal white lines cordoning the exit ramp from the highway.

The tires whirred over the rumble strip there. Vibrations thrumming through the car, quieting the yelling in the backseat all at once.

Ellie managed to dart neatly between a couple of yellow crash barrels set there. She cut off a minivan shuttling onto the ramp.

The driver honked. Ellie didn't hear it, not really.

Her eyes locked onto the rearview again.

The two cop cars in the front row tried to cut into the exit lane at the last minute and collided. The two front ends bashed into each other, fenders hugging and meshing, seeming stuck together right away.

Holy shit.

They clogged the exit lane. Slid into the mouth of it together, a skid that reminded Ellie of watching the rocks collide in an Olympic curling match. She heard the pop of a tire bursting, though she couldn't tell which car it came from.

The third cruiser fanned out onto the shoulder to the right. Skirted around the collision between the first two cars.

But at the last minute, one of the original cruisers pulled out that way, managing to detach its fender from the other. It jerked right in front of the third cop car.

The dodging cruiser veered into a skid, but it was too late. Another collision.

His front end hammered into the center of the sedan, the hood crumpling as it punched an imprint into the front and back doors.

Holy shit, again.

The noise inside the vehicle faded back in for Ellie then.

Scarlet and Jimmy were cheering. Jimmy thumped his hand against the roof in celebration.

A silent giggle vented between Ellie's teeth, but then she focused on the road again.

They coiled around the ramp, and then they couldn't see the police in the rearview anymore.

Gone.

Free.

Maybe.

Gotta press the advantage.

Now or never.

She jammed the accelerator harder. The Hyundai sat up straighter and did its best to growl.

At the bottom of the ramp, they ran a red light. Zipped through another intersection without slowing at all.

Cars honked all around them. Outraged drivers yelling behind their windshields. Teeth gnashing. Red faces shaking.

But Ellie knifed through the traffic unperturbed. Aggressive. Focused.

Buildings rose up from the ground ahead of them, and trees soon joined them. A thousand places to get lost. Ellie raced toward the cover.

Unseen, they disappeared into the city.

CHAPTER 97

Taft smashed the gun into Putnam's face again and again. The detective's cheek twitched like it did before, some knot of muscle pulsing under his left eye.

And his face went hot, some fever seeping into his blood, into his flesh, into his skull. The heat clouded his thoughts, sharpened his senses, gave the moment a hallucinatory feel.

His arm pulled back behind his ear. He swung.

The butt of the gun smacked into that splintered nose. Felt like mashing something mushy. A rotten apple with a hard core of bone at the center.

The killer sank to his knees. Legs folded up like a lawn chair.

And Taft stepped toward him. Weight forward on his toes. Hot breath on the back of his teeth. He stepped into the next swing.

He hammered the butt of the gun downward again. Heard the wind whistle around his descending arm.

The metal struck down. Pounded flesh.

Putnam moaned. The blood spattered and gushed. A steady flow weeping from the nostrils.

Taft could see the tears in the killer's eyes. Water leaking from the corners.

He lifted the gun and swung again.

The slap of the impact sounded wet now. Sharp. The sound of a chicken breast pounded flat to the cutting board. It echoed funny in the empty room.

Putnam squirmed. Tried to shield his face with his arms, with his hands, but it was no use.

Taft threaded his swing right between the raised palms. Slammed it home.

And something clean burned in the rage as he pounded

down on the broken nose once more. Something pure.

This is the guy who killed Stinson.

Taft coughed as the words played in his head. Like the idea was choking him.

This is the guy who killed Stinson.

It couldn't be real, but it was. It was all real.

He raised his arm. Swung again.

But this time, Putnam moved. Dodged. His shoulders swooped left.

Taft waved the gun through empty space. A hammer blow striking air.

And then Putnam lifted his own arm. His hand chopped down onto Taft's wrist.

The joint jolted. Pain shot up into the elbow. Then his whole arm went numb.

Putnam chopped again. A shorter stroke this time. The side of his palm a blade striking the back of Taft's hand.

The gun raked out of Taft's numb fingers. Tumbled between them.

Skimming down the front of Taft's shirt. Bouncing off his knee.

He flailed for it.

Too late.

The Glock skittered over the bare wood floor and melted into the shadows.

CHAPTER 98

Putnam rises. On his feet. Fists up. He circles to Taft's left like a boxer working the ring.

Blood weeps from the killer's nose. He can taste the salt of it at the corners of his lips, feel the heaviness of it. A viscous mustache running down from the corners of his mouth to form a patchy red goatee.

He moves for the gun. Shuffling steps drawing him into the murky corner where it had slid. Feet thunking on the planks.

There. The gun takes shape a few paces before him.

He closes on it. Reaches out a hand.

But as he goes to bend down, Taft surges at him. The big lug is light on his toes, quick, kicking out like the Karate Kid or some shit.

Putnam stutter-steps back. Dodges the detective's foot.

And some fresh rage flares in the killer's skull.

Angry.

Angry at this pudgy cop for coming at him. Angry that he'd gotten so close to Scarlet only to have her ripped away again.

He strides forward and kicks the gun away. Sends it spinning over into the opposite corner, the black matte thing disappearing under a dresser there.

You wanna settle this hand to hand? No sweat off my sack. Flabby piece of shit.

He mops a hand over his top lip. It comes away covered in blood.

Doesn't matter now. Worry about it later.

Putnam stalks straight for Taft. Fists ready. Chin tucked. He feels much taller than the detective as he gets to within an arm's length.

Big bad cop doesn't have his gun.

You're mine now.

The detective scurries back. His shoulders square toward the open apartment door, and his mouth twitches.

Shit. He's about to yell for the other police, most of them downstairs now.

Putnam throws a straight right hand into the guy's throat. Feels his knuckles punch the Adam's apple back into the neck meat there.

Taft gags. Chokes like a cat with a hairball. Eyes bugging.

That'll shut him up.

Putnam's feet shuffle under him. Scuffing and swishing over the exposed planks of the subflooring with faint scritching sounds.

He closes in. Feints toward the cop's jaw and then delivers a body blow. His big fist pounds into Taft's gut.

The detective's white dress shirt indents at the point of impact. It reminds Putnam of the Pillsbury Dough Boy getting poked in the belly.

The detective gags some more. Still choking.

But then he turns nimble. He evades the next body shot and the next.

Quick on his feet for a heavy guy.

Putnam mops his wrist over his lip again. Blood smears over the back of his hand.

When he goes in for the next shot, the detective gets him in a bear hug. Holds him tight.

Heat swelters off the big cop like his body is a space heater.

Even locked together as they are, Putnam keeps working that flabby body. He patters shots at Taft's beer belly.

Up close, he can't get much leverage into the punches. But he can hear the detective's mouth up against his neck, sucking wind. He's wearing him down.

Time to finish him.

He wrenches back. Throws his arms down to free himself of Taft's clutches.

And in the same fluid motion, he rocks forward into a big right hook. Hears it land with a crack. Whips that fat head around.

The big cop whimpers involuntarily and starts coughing again. He shuffles back into the corner.

Got you.

Got you now.

Putnam moves to cut the cop off. If he corners him, it's over.

But Taft turns agile again. Choppy steps going soundless on the floorboards.

He lurches left and slides past Putnam somehow. His chest scraping right against the killer's shoulder. Outmaneuvering. Quicker.

Putnam clenches his jaw and whirls, still trying to give chase.

And suddenly the cop hurls himself into the killer. Flings his body in one motion and then jerks his head after like he's cracking a whip. Something strange in the motion. Unnatural.

The big forehead fills the killer's field of vision. Its shadow darkening everything as it closes in.

Putnam tries to get his fists up. Tries to move his feet, to dart backward.

Too slow.

The word "headbutt" occurs to him a fraction of a second before impact.

Taft's forehead pounds Putnam right in the broken nose, the cop's skull cracking home with a wet slap.

Putnam can feel the broken shards of cartilage pushing deeper into his flesh, like a flathead screwdriver under the fingernail.

The pain detonates. An explosion of bright motes popping everywhere in his head.

Putnam sees the blood bursting everywhere, bits of red flung from his face, and then everything goes black.

CHAPTER 99

Taft nudged the lifeless form on the floor with his toe and watched. Watched Putnam's torso rise and fall. Watched the man's face to make sure he was really out.

When the detective was certain, he lowered himself, knees planting on the floor. Then he cupped his hands under Putnam's ribcage and lifted.

The big brute rose in slow motion, shaking, then hit the tipping point all at once and slapped down like a sack of potatoes. Rolled onto his belly.

Yep. He was out alright.

Taft went to work slapping the cuffs on. Pulling limp arms. Cinching the loops shut. Nice and tight.

The detective stood. Admired his handiwork.

With his arms pinned behind him, Shane Putnam looked trussed like a turkey ready to be dipped into a deep fryer. He wasn't moving. It wouldn't matter if he did.

Only then did Taft take a deep breath and feel the pins and needles prickling in his head. The effects of the fight seemed to catch up with him all at once.

He staggered backward a step. Sucked wind. Felt the tender places along his ribs and gut already starting to bruise, the pain blooming anew with every inward breath.

He stood over the fallen body of Putnam. Heaved for breath, chest quivering.

Then he turned his shoulders toward the doorway. Ready, finally, to call for the others.

His lips parted. His throat tightened.

But he couldn't speak. Not at first.

Neck tight. Hands trembling, icy at the ends of his arms. Some crazy electric current spitting behind his eyes, like all the circuits inside were overloaded.

But he swallowed, and then his voice came out, loud and strong.

"Up here."

He listened as the rest of the building went dead quiet. Something charged in the silence.

"Up here," he repeated, projecting his voice into something sharp. "I've got him."

And then the footsteps came. Mounting the steps. Pounding the treads. Louder and louder.

Uniformed cops spilled into the doorway, a whole flood of them. Wolfish smiles splitting their faces.

They formed a semicircle around Putnam, and they held still like that for a second. Watching and waiting.

An airiness seemed to waft into the room. The sunshine piercing the open window grew brighter.

Then someone moved, and everyone else followed. They picked the killer up, hoisting him from his belly to his knees and then tilting him back to carry him by the arms and legs.

He was a limp thing, all stretched out. His slack form bent at the waist, his hips dangling lower than the rest.

The whole troop worked in unison. The individual pieces coalescing into one for this moment. A team of sled dogs pulling together.

They carried him down the stairs like that, with Taft on their heels, following that spiraling handrail down, down, down.

Taft struggled to keep up. His lungs felt wet, heavy with sputum, but he almost didn't notice.

He watched the bob and sway of Putnam's elongated form, swinging in the center of all those arms carrying him. He looked childish, somehow, in this flimsy state.

At the bottom of the stairs, one of the uniformed officers, a rookie named Duckworth, confronted the detective.

"Are you bleeding?"

The rookie's eyes looked big and clear. Baby face drawn with concern.

The detective patted at his mouth and nose. Looked down at his hand. No blood.

He glared at the rookie for a second. Confused.

Some kind of joke?

But the kid's face held sincere, almost comically so. Maybe Duckworth just looked that way because he couldn't grow facial hair yet, but…

Taft swiped two fingers at his forehead, and they came away red.

"Nah. This? This is his blood."

CHAPTER 100

Ellie sat in the backseat now, face pointed out the window. Rural scrub washed past, green growth creeping over everything. Swampy pools still pocked the flatter land, black water reflecting patches of white sunlight.

The air-conditioning vents hissed full blast, strange mouths breathing cold in an endless exhale. It added white noise — a sibilance — to the atmosphere inside the car.

The Hyundai was gone. Dumped some miles back in the ditch along the edge of a cornfield. There'd been some talk, at the time, about covering it with pine boughs or something, but the potential time investment was deemed unworthy. Poor ROI. They'd guided it down into the muck below the shoulder and rushed off in an ancient Subaru they'd found parked outside a small ranch-style house up the road.

Judging by the pile of mail clogging the mailbox, the owner of the Subaru was out of town, some kind of extended vacation. With a little luck he or she wouldn't know the car was gone until Jimmy and Scarlet were in Mexico and probably onto the next vehicle or even the next.

Jimmy spoke from the passenger seat as though reading Ellie's thoughts.

"Should have a clear shot to the border from here. I mean, you never know, but..."

He tapped a finger at the road map sprawled over his lap. Traced his fingernail up one of the blue veins traversing the page.

"We'll stay off the interstate from here on out, I think. Take the US highways and shit. The back roads. I don't want to jinx it or nothin', but I think we're good."

Scarlet nodded in the driver's seat. She turned her head and glanced at her partner, and for just a second Ellie could see the faint smile playing at her lips.

Then Ellie's gaze trickled past the front seat, speared through the windshield at the tangle of green rushing toward them, the ribbon of road stretching out into the distance.

A splash of bright colors — red and yellow — pulled her eyes up above the tree line. A Shell logo rose up in the distance, looming over the swamp and scrub, the long metal pole like an exaggerated giraffe neck running up to the thing.

Ellie licked her lips. It felt funny, knowing she was about to talk, and she realized she hadn't in a while.

"You can drop me up here," she said. "At the gas station."

The car held quiet then. Those hissing vents seemed to get louder.

Scarlet looked at Jimmy again, that smile erased from her expression this time, something grave etched on her face instead. When she spoke, the words came out slowly.

"Are you sure? You could wait until we're somewhere less… middle of fucking nowhere."

"No. This is good."

Something new flickered over Scarlet's face — a sadness, Ellie thought. Maybe something like grief. She leaned over the center console and muttered something to Jimmy that Ellie couldn't make out.

Then Jimmy reached down toward the floorboard. He pulled the duffel bag up from between his feet, rested it on his lap. The zippered mouth sighed as its teeth parted, and then he stuck his hand into the opening.

He came away with a fistful of bills. Thrust them toward Ellie.

"We'll drop you here then," Scarlet said, her eyes watching in the rearview mirror. "But you have to take some money. It's the only way we can say thank you and make up for… well, everything."

Jimmy still held the wadded-up bills toward her. Ellie just stared.

"Take it," he said.

Ellie squirmed in her seat. She couldn't take the money. For her, it was probably the price of a textbook. For Jimmy and Scarlet it was time, freedom. Another three days of food. Another tank of gas. Something that actually mattered. Something real.

But before Ellie could talk, Scarlet went on.

"It's not up for negotiation. We're not leaving you out here in the sticks with nothing. If you want to stop here, you'll take it."

Ellie hesitated. Then she took the money and shoved the whole wad into the pocket of the purple scrubs.

The blinker clicked in the silence that followed. Then the car slowed and tucked into the Shell station lot, crossing a swath of asphalt, cruising along the backside of the building.

"You see any cameras here?" Scarlet asked just above a whisper.

"Nah," Jimmy said. "We're good."

The car snugged right up next to the side of the building and stopped there. It felt strange, almost queasy, to stop that forward momentum.

Ellie climbed out to face a wall of concrete blocks painted a glossy beige. The wind whipped at her hair, tickled against her neck and ears which still felt newly exposed after her haircut.

She turned back as though to wave at Jimmy and Scarlet, but they were already out of the car.

Scarlet pulled Ellie in for a hug. Jimmy clapped her on the shoulder.

"Thanks for everything," Scarlet said. "You saved us. You really did."

Ellie didn't know what to say, so she just nodded.

Scarlet held her at arm's length and fixed her with a hard stare.

"You know what to do, right? You tell the cops it was me. I made you do it. All of it."

"Yeah, I know," Ellie said, holding her gaze.

The idea of throwing them under the bus now that she

knew their whole story felt wrong to Ellie, but as Scarlet had pointed out, kidnapping Ellie and forcing her to act as their accomplice was kind of the least of their crimes. If the law caught up with them, they'd have plenty to answer to whether Ellie talked or not.

But there was one last way Ellie could try to help them out. She'd been thinking of it ever since they ditched the Hyundai.

"So… Canada, right?"

Scarlet squinted.

"What?"

"That's where you said you're headed," Ellie said. "To Canada."

Scarlet looked confused until Ellie winked.

"Oh! Yeah. I mean, Mexico would be too obvious, right?" Scarlet smirked. "Plus, Jimmy's got an old friend up there in… where was it? Vancouver?"

Jimmy's mouth hung open.

"Me?"

Scarlet elbowed him.

"What? I don't have no friends in Canada."

"Ding-dong! Are you serious?"

Jimmy shook his head.

"Babe, Mexico is way easier to—"

"I know that. And she knows that." Scarlet sighed and rolled her eyes.

Jimmy's mouth stretched even wider now, a cartoonish display of understanding.

"Ohhh." He reached up and scratched the top of his head. "Oh, shit yeah. I got a real good friend in Canada. Uh… Sam."

Scarlet hugged her again, tighter this time. A true goodbye.

"Remember everything I told you. Your life belongs to you. No one else," she murmured in Ellie's ear.

"I'll remember," Ellie promised.

"And don't tell any of our other victims this, but you're my favorite," Scarlet said, planting a kiss on Ellie's cheek, making her laugh.

And then Jimmy and Scarlet were back in the car, rolling away. The station wagon peeled around the corner, scuttled back out onto the road, disappeared over the next hill.

Ellie stared at the spot where they'd fallen out of sight for several seconds. And she felt some sense of loss she didn't understand. A hollowness that manifested physically as a pit in her gut — a kind of emptiness she couldn't fully explain to herself.

A semi rolled past, diesel engine grinding, and the oversized truck carried a big whoosh of wind along with it. The humid air skimmed over the parking lot and buffeted Ellie, warm and heavy against her body. Muggy.

The rush of air seemed to wave that forlorn feeling away somehow. Like the breeze was pushing time itself along toward the next moment and the next, reminding the seconds and minutes and hours that they were never allowed to hold still.

Ellie's eyes traced the lip of the hill one more time. Nothing moved there now. Whatever had happened here was already past.

Finally, she dug in her pocket and pulled out her phone.

CHAPTER 101

Heat radiated up from the concrete as Courtney paced along the edge of the motel parking lot. She kept to the sliver of shade along the hulking structure of the motel. This kept it tolerable to be outside, if barely.

She and John had seen the breaking news reports about the apprehension of a suspect at the Burdick Murder House. And while they knew it had to be related to the Jimmy and Scarlet thing and whatever had happened to Ellie and Wes, they hadn't heard any specifics yet.

Courtney's eyes flicked over to where John stood near the door of his room. His phone was pressed to his ear.

"Yeah. OK. Thanks, then," he muttered before ending the call.

Courtney stopped pacing.

"Anything?" she asked.

He sighed and shook his head.

"She said it doesn't matter how many times we call — they *still* can't release any information to anyone right now. She promised that Detective Taft would return our call at his earliest convenience." John scoffed and kicked at a crinkled beer can someone had left behind on the sidewalk. "Might as well be never."

Something about the stress of the situation seemed to finally be wearing on John. His usual good-natured demeanor was cracking.

Courtney walked over to him and pressed her face into his chest.

"This sucks," she said.

"I know."

They fell into an embrace, and Courtney felt relieved that at least she wasn't going through it alone. They pulled apart when they heard a vehicle wheeling into the motel parking lot.

The black and white police car turned into the lot.

Courtney reached out and grabbed John's arm. Clung to him.

Finally.

But will it be good news or bad?

Courtney peered through the glare on the windshield and studied the driver's face. His jaw was set, his mouth a hard, straight line.

Oh no.

CHAPTER 102

Ellie climbed out first, and the afternoon heat blasted her bare skin. Courtney and John were there in the lot, almost like they'd been waiting.

The look on Courtney's face reminded Ellie of a slot machine the way it cycled through a variety of emotions — fear, confusion, shock — before finally landing on joy.

Ellie was barely out of the car fully when Courtney collided with her, knocking her backward. Wes had been in the process of stepping out behind her so the three of them fell into a jumbled heap onto the backseat.

"Oh my God, Ellie! We've been so worried! What happened? Where were you? Are you OK? And look at your hair!"

Not knowing how to answer all of these questions at once, Ellie chose the last.

"I'm good. But you're crushing me."

Courtney released her, stepping back to make room. Ellie actually saw tears in her friend's eyes.

Damn, she must have been really worried.

Officer Perez, the one who'd been tasked with driving them back to the motel, hooked his fingers around his utility belt.

"Detective Taft will be wanting to talk with you two more down at the station, but not 'til sometime tomorrow. I suggest you rest up for now."

After giving their solemn promises not to leave town, Officer Perez got back into the cruiser and drove away. They filed into Ellie and Courtney's room to escape the heat, and then the questions began.

Ellie went first. Explaining everything with Scarlet. As condensed as she could, which was difficult, given all that had taken place.

There was a lot of gasping from Courtney, and John kept adding sound effects to the dramatic parts with his mouth.

Then Wes told his part.

More gasping. More sound effects.

When they'd finished, Courtney looked at them solemnly.

"Well, what do you guys need? Are you thirsty? Do you want to eat something?"

Ellie and Wes responded in unison.

"Sleep."

CHAPTER 103

Taft walked down a silent hallway toward the interrogation room. The night inked the windows of the county jail, black pressing right up to the glass. Only one streetlight glinted against the gloom from the detective's vantage point — a distant shard of brightness tinged yellow.

Then he turned a corner, and there were no more windows, just a tunnel of beige interrupted now and again by thick steel doors. His eyes skipped down the hall to the last one on the left — his destination.

The air-conditioning was absolutely blasting on this side of the building, chilling the ring of faint sweat around Taft's collar. But a paper cup of fresh coffee radiated against his palm, hot enough to make his fingers tingle.

He took a sip, and it scalded all the way down, the bright bolt of pain dying back to a steady flare in his stomach. He didn't figure he'd be able to sleep, so what the hell. He might as well get some caffeine in his system, try to get his thoughts clear before he talked to this scumfuck — if Putnam was even willing to talk.

Taft's gut told him a hardcore criminal like Shane Putnam would lawyer up, but he'd been wrong on this kind of thing before. Being honest with himself, he could never really tell who would talk and who wouldn't. Might as well see it through.

He could hear footsteps somewhere behind him, a swish and clap echoing funny through the long corridors. When he turned back no one was there. The Durango County jail was funny like that in Taft's experience, somehow hushed all the time like a church service. Sounds seemed to bounce around it like a vast cavern.

At the end of the hall, he twisted the doorknob and pounded a shoulder into the heavy door. The steel stuck in the frame for a second, and then it popped out with a rubbery sucking sound. Taft braced his cup hand throughout the process, careful not to spill any of the molten brew.

Somehow it was even colder in the little cinder block cube of a room. The chilly air whooshed at him as soon as the door swung free. Frigid.

Taft crossed into the new space. Felt that icy touch reach right through his sports jacket to wrap itself around his chest and belly.

And there he was.

Putnam was shackled to the interrogation table, a loop of chain running through the clasp there, the line of links leading to his wrists and ankles. He looked smaller, somehow, in the orange jail uniform, the puffed-up body language of earlier sagging into something tired and defeated. His busted nose had been cleaned up, but the flesh still shone a violent red shade and looked all rumpled. It reminded Taft of the blown-out tip of an exploding prank cigar.

The killer's dark eyes met Taft's and held steady. But the detective didn't read any real malice in the eye contact. The dude just seemed blank now. Hollow. Some whipped dog air wafted off of him.

Taft set his cup of coffee on the table, and he sat down in the chair opposite Putnam. The inmate adjusted in his seat, and the chain tinkled and scraped against the tabletop.

"How ya doin'?" the detective asked, trying so hard to sound casual that he was almost doing a Chris Farley impression.

Putnam slow-blinked. His eyes shifted to the door and then back to Taft.

"I've been better."

Well… he answered the first question. Talking so far.

Gotta get him comfortable, get him loose. Ease into it.

"Long day, huh? Same here. Guess you already know all about that."

Putnam shrugged. Stared down at the tabletop. One of his

hands looked to be cradling his belly.

"So… can I get you something to eat? Something to drink? Coffee ain't necessarily great, but it's fresh. And hot."

Taft took another sip as though to punctuate the point. Once again, the brew blistered the length of his esophagus.

Putnam shook his meaty head.

Refusing food and drink. Don't like that.

Taft took another sip. He could feel the caffeine burning bright in his eyes now, liquid energy gushing through his bloodstream.

"You sure? You don't want anything?"

The big head shook again.

"My stomach hurts."

His eyes narrowed then. He lifted his chin.

"Actually, I could use an Alka-Seltzer. You got that?"

"Sure. Yeah. Plop plop. I can get you that."

"None of that Pepcid or Zantac shit or anything, either. Alka-Seltzer. That's the one that works for me."

"Hey. You got it."

Taft padded back out into the hall and made his way three doors down. The little first aid station there held a menagerie of meds and bandages. He picked through until he found the little packets of Alka-Seltzer. Then he filled a small plastic cup at the water cooler and headed back.

Putnam opened the foil sleeve and dropped one of the tablets into the water. The white disc sank to the bottom. They sat in silence watching it fizz.

After what felt like a long time, Putnam drank, taking down half of it in one go. Popping bubbles tapped along the side of the plastic cup.

"Me? I'm a Pepto guy," Taft said, trying to get the conversational ball rolling.

He rested his forearms on the lip of the table. Tried to make his body language as relaxed as he could.

"Never tried it," Putnam said. "That pink shit actually work?"

Taft pumped his head.

"Yeah. Feels like you're putting out a fire in your gut. Most of the time, anyhow."

"I always wondered what it tasted like. Bright pink goo. They flavor it, like, strawberry or something?"

"Nah. It's like... you know that sort of birch taste that Pepsi has? It's like that, but stronger. All birch. No cola."

Putnam's lip curled.

"Sounds nasty."

"Hell, I can pour you a shot if you want to try it for yourself. Got a big bottle of extra strength a few doors down the hall."

"No thanks."

Putnam downed the last of his antacid fizz water. Then he sat back in his chair. Taft noted that he was no longer cupping his gut.

Time to go for it.

"You want to know what I'm wondering?" Taft asked.

"Not really."

Taft chortled.

"Funny. But no, I'm wondering what drives a man to trail a girl all the way down the coast, stopping at nothing to get to her, even killing the cop who got in his way. I assume this — all of this — is for the girl, right? For Scarlet?"

When he said nothing, Taft went on.

"And after all that, chasing her all the way down here, she still gets away. I mean, that's gotta piss you off, right?"

Putnam played with the Alka-Seltzer sleeve as he answered. Something like a smile twitched at the corners of his mouth.

"No, for real. My lawyer is flying in tomorrow morning. He already told one of the other suits to schedule an interview for then. So I ain't answering any questions or anything like that."

Fuck.

Think.

"So you're saying it wasn't for Scarlet?"

"No. I'm saying 'lawyer.'"

Taft pushed back from the table. Staring at nothing. He didn't know what to say.

Putnam watched him, not quite smiling all the while.

"So… can I go back to my cell now?"

Taft felt like he was waking up from a daze.

"Yeah. Yeah. I'll buzz one of the guards to take you back."

Taft did. The guard came some minute and a half later. He unhooked the inmate from the table, and then led him, chains jangling, back down the hall.

Taft sat and stared for another few seconds. Then he got to his feet, grabbed his coffee cup, and scooped Putnam's little plastic water cup, depositing the latter in the trash can as he swooped back down the long hall.

Something felt off to Taft. Incomplete. He couldn't figure out what.

They'd try the interrogation again tomorrow. No real surprise there. He'd known getting Putnam to talk on his own would be something of a long shot.

But if Putnam was this evasive now, there was almost zero chance he'd be willing to talk once his lawyer was present.

Taft didn't think that was what was bothering him, though. It was something else. Something he couldn't quite call to the surface of his mind.

So… what?

He ran his tongue along the roof of his mouth and tried to think. Listened to his own footsteps do that bat flutter up and down the halls.

The suspicious feeling passed as he neared the exit of the building and pushed through two sets of doors to reach the parking lot. Whatever it had been, he'd lost it.

CHAPTER 104

Courtney's flip flops made a slapping sound as she bustled around the room, gathering up her things.

"I'm *so* sorry I'm taking so long," she said while she tossed her sunglasses into her purse. "I know you guys are tired."

"It's fine," Ellie assured her.

Courtney hoisted the bag onto her shoulder and headed for the door. She paused with the door half-open, and the early evening dark streamed through the doorway.

"OK, you guys get some rest now. Don't forget, we'll be right next door, so if you need anything—"

Ellie smiled, amused at Courtney's sudden motherly turn.

"We'll let you know."

Courtney nodded her head and pulled the door closed behind herself. Shutting out the light and the noise, and then Ellie and Wes were alone in the room.

They looked at each other awkwardly.

"Hi," Wes said.

"Hi," Ellie said.

He took a step toward her, his eyes on her mouth. She tilted her head back, and just as their lips were about to touch, the door was flung open again.

"Me again," Courtney said, whizzing past them. "Sorry!"

She began rifling around her suitcase, flinging various garments to and fro.

"It's just that John mentioned that after we pick up the cars from the police station, maybe we'd grab dinner, so I want to make sure I have something nicer to wear. I wouldn't want to have to wake you guys up, not after everything you've been through."

She stuffed more items into her bag and snagged a pair of heels from next to the door.

"OK, bye. For real this time."

The door closed again. Ellie's eyes flicked over to Wes. That old awkwardness had returned, but it was lighter now, and they both burst out laughing.

"Did you want to use the bathroom?" Ellie asked. "I've been dying to brush my teeth, for some reason. Like, I've actually been looking forward to it to a ridiculous degree. But you should go first."

"Oh. Yeah. Good idea."

He disappeared inside, coming out a minute later. Ellie took her turn, brushing her teeth and delighting in the clean feeling and the lingering tingle of the mint.

When she exited the bathroom, Wes was pretending to study one of the generic artsy photographs on the wall. She realized he didn't know where to lie down, unsure if they would share a bed or not.

Ellie jumped onto her bed and patted the empty place next to her.

Wes, looking pleased with this invitation, flopped onto the mattress.

"Hi again," he said.

"Hello."

They stared at one another, and then Wes reached out and plucked at a strand of her dyed hair.

"This is new."

"You like it?" Ellie asked.

"I do," he said, tucking it behind her ear.

"I still can't believe you ended up with Putnam," Ellie said. "Didn't he give you bad vibes? The way Scarlet talked about him, the guy sounds like a total sociopath."

Wes shook his head.

"He did seem kind of weird, but I was so desperate at that point. I guess I just ignored it. The only thing I could think of was finding out what happened to you, and this guy was offering to help. So yeah… I just went with it."

Ellie tilted her head to one side.

"That's kind of sweet, actually."

He waved his hand dismissively.

"Ehh, some hero I ended up being. Turns out you're tougher than you look. You didn't need rescuing."

"It was still sweet," Ellie said, and she pulled him into a kiss.

CHAPTER 105

Randy Henson sat at the AdSeg security console, reading a Stephen King paperback. *Duma Key*. While the surrounding cell block had gone dark, his little cinder block office glowed with fluorescent brightness. Something about the light here reminded him of a dentist's office. Harsh.

He finished a chapter, kept his thumb in the pages as a bookmark, and then scanned the monitors. Grainy night vision images filled the three screens, everything tinted pale green and nothing moving.

He went back to the book. A hundred pages left, and it was getting good. He knew the atmosphere here at night had a way of enhancing a suspense novel, sharpening the imagery, making all the shocks and twists punch harder.

The jail was quiet at night. Eerie. Henson had only worked as a guard full time for six months now, and he still wasn't used to the late shift.

He'd applied to be a deputy at the county Sheriff's office, and technically he was one. But as far as the job duties actually went, working the night shift at the jail basically only had the brown and beige uniform in common with what Henson thought he'd be doing. Instead of busting drunk drivers or breaking up parties and bar fights, he sat in an office all night while the few inmates in solitary or protective custody slept — the emptiest, quietest cell block of them all. It was a pretty laid-back gig for a 26-year-old who'd been looking for some action.

Still, he could think of worse jobs. His reading habit had picked up greatly on the late shift. He'd finished three or four fat Stephen King novels a week of late. He only had about five books left until he'd have polished off the complete King bibliography. He was thinking about going for John Sandford next. Thirty-some books and counting in the Lucas Davenport series. It'd give him a lot to chew through.

Like always, the pages turned deep into the night. His eyes kept swiveling, now and then, to the darkness outside the porthole window on his office door. The bars were just vaguely visible from his vantage point, gray lines discernible against the black, a grid of meshed segments like spiderwebs.

The microwave dinged, and he jumped. The reminder ding. It must have gone off thirty seconds earlier when he was engrossed in a good chase scene.

He wheeled his office chair across the room and pulled a Tupperware bowl of chili out of the glowing box. Steam still coiled from the craggy red surface. Lines of shredded cheddar had gone soft and supple on top. Still too hot to eat, but his mouth was watering.

He set the bowl on the counter next to the microwave and went back to the book while he waited. The chili smell filled the room slowly but surely, some earthy blend of spice and beef and tomato.

This time, he found he couldn't concentrate on the novel. His eyes took in the words, reread the same paragraph a couple times, but the scene wouldn't come to life in his mind.

Instead, the hairs on the back of his neck pricked up. He whirled the chair around to stare out that porthole again.

Nothing there. Just the dark.

Still, he felt exposed. His little room glowed, one spot of light surrounded by the long dark of the cell block. Anyone out there could look in and see him, and all he could see in return was vague and mostly shapeless, outlines in the shadows.

For a second, he felt embarrassed. But hell, this wasn't like a normal night. There was an honest-to-God murderer out there in one of the cells.

He wheeled back to the console. Checked the monitors.

Shane Putnam lay still in his bed. Shrouded in blankets. Sleeping.

A nervous laugh puffed out of Henson's nostrils at the sight. He'd spooked himself over a sleeping guy locked in a cage.

Jesus. Real wound up tonight.

The truth was, he always felt weird when he got the Administrative Segregation assignment. A lot of nights, there was no such assignment — this wing of jail held empty. On a usual shift, there were only one or two inmates at a time confined to Protective Custody, maybe another couple in solitary, and at night all they did was sleep. Logically, this put him in less danger than the typical guard shift — less inmates to deal with equaled less risk, and the sleep factor pushed it over the top.

He was a babysitter dressed as a deputy, more or less.

But something about the stillness of the cell block at night, the aloneness of the little office, set him on edge. Maybe the darkness was a factor, too, if he was being honest with himself.

With a creep like Shane Putnam out there, the skittish feeling had only strengthened. Henson had seen the pictures of what Putnam had done to Detective Stinson. Nightmarish.

And Putnam was the only one assigned to AdSeg for the night. It was just the two of them. Henson half-wondered if Putnam's segregation was for the safety of the other inmates as much as anything. Did a drunk and disorderly or shoplifter really deserve to share a cell with a killer?

Henson picked up the chili. Took a test bite.

It stung his mouth. Good, though. Good as hell. Hot cheese slid down his throat.

He dug in then. Slowed by the sheer heat rolling off the food. It made his spoon all hot and steamy, too.

He adjusted in his seat and realized that his guard uniform had grown tight around his middle, the brown fabric pulled taut. Shit. Maybe the night shift made him snacky. It probably did. Too much downtime. Too many late-night stops at the vending machines when he got bored and restless.

A moan rang down the long hall, muffled by the office door.

Henson jerked and dropped a wad of hot chili onto his

belly. Watched it ooze down his shirt. The maroon smear looked thick, viscous. He could feel the heat of it leach through the fabric and prickle on his skin.

Shit.

He swiped a panel of paper towel at the splotch. The chili spot thinned, but it covered a silver dollar size of his shirt. He could clean it up later.

He moved to the monitor. Peered into the second screen. Half of him expected to find the image empty, the cell somehow vacated.

But Putnam was there. Lying in bed. It looked like the killer was moving under the blanket, but that was about all Henson could say for sure.

Then the guard walked to his window, stuck his nose up to the glass, and peered down the darkened corridor. The gloom seemed to bloom before his eyes, as though the darkness was filling in the empty space as he watched. He couldn't see anything.

By then the groaning had cut out anyway. Silence filled the cell block. The buzzing lights in the office and the whir of a computer fan were the only sounds.

Psycho is probably having a nightmare about going to the state pen.

Getting back to his chair — and his chili — Henson checked the monitors again. Putnam looked to be holding still now.

He went back to reading. Spooned chili into his face between pages. No longer molten, the chili had cooled into something palatable.

The night settled into that endless sprawl of dark and quiet again. A motionless hush that seemed to speed up the time.

Henson finished the chili and knocked out three longish chapters. He found himself fully drawn into the scenes now, a mind movie playing in his skull.

He heard a thump from somewhere on the other side of the door. Heavy. Loud.

Henson's head snapped up. Peered through that tiny circle of glass.

Then he wheeled over and checked the monitors. Breath catching in his throat. Eyes going wide.

The covers had been thrown back into a rumple on Putnam's bed. The mattress lay empty.

Holy shit.

But then movement drew his eye to the bottom edge of the screen. Something writhing on the floor.

His eyes swiveled to the buttons along the security console. For two seconds, he thought about clicking on the lights. He stopped himself shy of that. He'd have to fill out paperwork if he put the lights on during the off hours. Pain in the ass. Better to check first.

He stood, legs half-numb beneath him from sitting so long. He opened a desk drawer. Took out a flashlight the size of a cigar.

Then he elbowed through the door. Stepped into the dark.

The silence seemed bigger on the main floor of the cell block, like he could hear and feel the empty space stretching out in front of him. Vast darkness that made him feel small.

He thumbed the button on the flashlight. The beam leapt to life.

He swung the shaft of light left and then right, watched the shadows pitch and bend as the gleam slid over the bars. He tried to get a glimpse at Putnam's cell, but from this far out, he couldn't make out much.

So he strode down the darkened hallway. The flashlight beam swept along the smooth concrete floor, a glowing circle pushing ahead of him, something smooth in the way it rolled along.

Two empty cells scrolled past on his left. Putnam's was the fourth cell down.

He found himself wanting to speak before he reached Putnam's cell. Instinct telling him to call out, to telegraph his arrival. A vocal warning of some kind.

Scared of startling him.

"Everything all right in there?" he asked, the words occurring to him right as he said them. His voice sounded strong in his ears, more confident than he felt.

He stepped in front of the bars. Plunged his light into the killer's chamber.

Half of him expected the cell to be empty, for the killer to have vanished like Ted Bundy or Freddy Krueger. His heart jumped up into his throat and fluttered there like dove wings.

The flashlight beam touched the mattress. Empty, as expected.

He angled the circle of light lower. Brushed it along the floor.

Putnam was there.

On the floor in the fetal position. Something of a crumpled spider look to his body language. Sure looked like he'd fallen out of bed.

And now he was shaking. Core rocking. Limbs pulled taut.

Henson stepped forward. Swiped the beam up the length of the body and reached the face.

Putnam's eyes were rolled back in his head. Eyelids fluttering around blank whites.

A mound of froth protruded from his open lips. Bubbles and fluid drizzling down from the sides.

Little choking sounds stuttered out of the hollow of his throat. Awful.

Holy shit.

Seizure?

Suicide?

Henson ran back to the office. Leaned over the console. Threw the switch to open the gate.

He tried to talk himself through the emergency protocol as he ran back to the cell.

Gotta... clear the air passages.

That's first.

For sure.

And then...

The cell door stood a couple inches open. His fingers found the edge and he peeled it the rest of the way.

As soon as he stepped into the cell, Putnam was on him.

One thick arm coiled under Henson's armpit and reached up to grab him by the back of the neck. A death grip squashing the muscles there.

The other hand grabbed a fistful of hair and pulled. Pain screamed along the crown of Henson's scalp. Wrenched his head sideways. Tears flooded his eyes.

The guard fought. Tried to lurch.

But Putnam was too strong.

The killer forced the guard forward. Maneuvered him deeper into the darkened cell.

Henson swung his elbows backward, one and then the other. But the blows just barely grazed Putnam, who had the superior reach of the two.

And then the guard found himself lifted off his feet. Slung forward as though thrown.

He saw the metal corner of the bed frame rushing for him. Finding him.

The first impact burst bright orange sparks inside his skull like they were lifting off a campfire. The hurt arrived on a half-second delay, reverberated through like his skull was a struck bell.

The second impact with the steel put some distance between him and reality. Numbing. Confusing.

The dimmer switch turned lower. The darkness grew. His senses pulled back from the moment.

Henson saw the bed frame coming for him again and again. Angular metal zooming in.

And then he saw stars slowly blot that reality out. Black nothing pricked with shards of light.

The emptiness swelled and left the light behind.

After that he didn't see anything.

CHAPTER 106

The motel room door thunked shut.

Ellie shot upright, confused, her eyes squinted down to slits.

The room was still around her. Wes lay asleep beside her.

She'd sworn she'd heard the door close, but apparently not.

She vaguely remembered reading something about this. It was called "exploding head syndrome" and was a common auditory hallucination people experienced just as they were falling asleep or waking up. If she recalled correctly, it was more likely to occur during times of stress.

Well, that checks out, she thought.

They'd passed out — they must have — without remembering to turn the lights off. The dusk outside had gone full dark in the meantime. With only the sheer part of the curtains drawn across the window, they were on full display to the parking lot.

Ellie slid off the bed and padded to the window, tugging the blackout curtains closed. She worried turning out the lights might rouse Wes, so she left them on for now.

Then she spied the paper bag on the table next to the door. There was a bottle of Gatorade, too. And a sticky note.

She yanked the note from the bag.

Didn't want to wake you, but thought you'd be hungry at some point

-C&J

There were two paper-wrapped subs inside the bag along with some chips. Ellie got a whiff of briny dill pickle smell, and her stomach growled.

She glanced over at Wes again. Still asleep.

She wondered if she should wake him. Decided against it.

Ellie snagged one of the little disposable cups from the bathroom and sat down on the unoccupied bed with the food Courtney and John had left. She poured herself a wee shot of Gatorade and drank it. Usually, she thought sports drinks tasted like vaguely flavored sweat, but just now, it tasted pretty damn good.

She poured herself three more cups and downed them before slowly unwrapping one of the subs. She was trying to be quiet about it, not wanting the crinkle of the paper to interrupt Wes from his slumber.

While she unwrapped, she thought of her adventure with Scarlet. Because that is what it had been, ultimately, hadn't it? Certain parts were, without a doubt, dangerous. Illegal, even. But she couldn't deny that quite a bit of it had been kind of… fun. Sort of like breaking into the Burdick Murder House.

She smiled now as she thought of all the people who'd doubted she had enough backbone to be a lawyer. People like her parents, who were always doubting her about everything. Thinking she was weak and fragile and naive and needing to be told what to do. Well, she'd shown them, hadn't she?

With the sub finally free from its papery shackles, she took a bite. And froze.

Ellie closed her eyes, overwhelmed by a sudden flood of food-fueled endorphins.

This shitty fast-food sub was the most glorious thing she'd tasted, maybe ever.

CHAPTER 107

Putnam stops just shy of the fence running the perimeter of the trail grounds. He breathes a second.

Harsh lights angle down in all directions. Cameras are everywhere. He's partially hidden by the dumpster to his right, he thinks, but even with the skeleton crew running a podunk county jail like this, someone will see him out here if he takes too long.

Then he grunts and heaves. The rubber floor mat, swiped from the guard's office, soars from his hands.

He flings the rug up over his head, aiming for the line of barbed wire at the top of the fence. Tries to get it to drape over the top.

The first toss doesn't work.

The mat is big and awkward — probably three feet by five. It kind of flutters toward the fence, comes up short, slaps into the top, and crumples up against the chain-links before falling back to the asphalt.

He swallows. He can still taste the Alka-Seltzer foam coating his tongue. Smiles a little at the memory of using it.

Then he kneels and gathers the rug. Feels the ridged treads scrubbing at his palms and wrists.

The guard's keys dig at his ankle — an irregular bulge protruding from the side of his sock.

Maybe I should have taken his uniform. Probably should have.

Would have been small. A real tight fit.

Covered in fucking blood, too.

Maybe better that I didn't bother.

Some blind panic had filled Putnam as soon as the guard was dead and still. An overwhelming flight response had told him to take the keys and go, and so he had.

He can see the border just a few feet beyond the chain-link where the glow of the lights gives out, and the darkness strengthens. So close. Maybe fifteen feet, at most. He just needs to get over the fence and dissolve into that gloom.

The night seems to go still as he observes it. Nothing stirring. Crickets chirp somewhere out in the dark, but they seem far away.

He stands. The rug lies limp in his arms. He adjusts his grip along the edges, trying to figure out how best to magic carpet the thing up and over the twelve-foot fence.

If he couldn't do it in the next minute or so, he was going to have to do without it. He'd cut the shit out of himself for sure, but he'd dealt with worse than that before.

He shuffles back a couple steps. Whips the rug up at the top of the fence again.

The mat sprawls. Floats. Sinks toward the top of the barrier.

It lands crooked. Not fully draping the top of the fence as he'd hoped.

But this time the barbs spike the rubber backing and grip it there. He gives it a tug to test it. The rug will hold. It will work.

Yes.

He rolls the dumpster a couple feet over until it's just under the mat, and then he scrabbles up onto the lid. His feet skitter on the molded plastic.

He flops forward onto the mat. The Brillo pad texture of the ridges scours the skin on his cheek, his hands, the insides of his arms.

And he feels the coil of barbed wire sag under his weight. Bending. Reclining and shimmying like a hammock. It won't keep still.

He pushes off from the lid of the dumpster. Body fully resting on the mat, on the buckling wire.

He seems to hover a second, body surfing atop those straining cords. Then he pitches forward. Dumped. Roughly spilling onto the other side face-first.

He reaches out, makes contact, grips reflexively. The metal

barb gashes his palm, that little star hooking and tearing, the pain bright and sharp.

But he manages to roll into the fall. Toppling. Feet swinging over his head. Laying him out flat in the dewy grass. Sliding him a few inches down the gentle slope there.

And he stares up at the night sky. Tiny stars glittering against all that endless black.

The moisture from the grass seeps right through the orange jail uniform. Wetness pressing itself into his back.

He picks himself up and runs into the dark.

Putnam sprints the first three blocks. Arms pumping. Legs churning. Feet chewing up ground, putting distance between himself and the jail.

Muggy wind floods his lungs. Humidity slicking his insides the same way the sweat lacquers his outside.

A nest of gas stations seems to occupy the land just around the jail grounds. He gives the bright lights a wide berth. Sticks to the dark side of the road. Ready to jump into the copse of woods to his left if any cars come by.

He runs past a stoplight, a four-lane intersection thankfully barren of traffic. Looks both ways. Crosses the swath of asphalt.

And then, finally, the residential creep starts. A web of cul-de-sacs, their lanes like wide-open mouths waiting to swallow him. He picks one. Hurtles for it.

And he feels bolder as soon as he moves in the shadows of those suburban homes. His spine straightens. His chest opens up. Shoulders back.

The night feels cooler here, too. Dank like a basement.

Putnam runs and breathes. Breathes and runs.

The jail-issue rubber slippers clap on the asphalt — too loud now that houses are close by — so he steps up onto the curb and drifts onto the grass. The sound cuts out. He glides.

And his eyes see everything. Pierce the murk to take in the

details of the passing homes.

Pleated garage doors. Darkened windows. Cars parked in most of the driveways.

He's not seeing what he wanted to see. Not yet.

The land slopes downward again as he nears the end of the cul-de-sac, his footsteps going choppy when they hit the incline.

He slips on a dewy patch of sod, arms splaying to his sides for balance. He wobbles into a skid, knees shaking, hips shimmying.

But he rides it out. Doesn't fall.

At the bottom of the hill, his balance evens out, and he runs on. Eyes still crawling over every house.

Finally, he finds one that looks right, feels right. A yellow split level. No lights. No car in the driveway. It has a very still look about it.

He zags hard to the left and cuts through the yard. Hurdles a small bed of pea gravel with plants jutting out of it.

He gets quiet as he steps onto the front stoop. Holds his breath. Angles his ear toward the front door.

Waits. Listens.

Something hums inside. Low-pitched and throbbing. A wetness to the sound. A gurgle.

The noise cuts out, and he places it finally. A dishwasher, running the night cycle.

No good.

Someone is here.

He jogs over to the next lot and the next. Keeps close to the houses now. The shadows are thicker as he gets away from the streetlights.

The third stoop from the dishwasher finally displays what he wanted to see all along. Three newspapers bundled with rubber bands sit at odd angles from each other, each of them touching a different part of the welcome mat. No car in the driveway, either.

He sets his ear about an inch from the front door and

listens. No hum and gurgle this time. Nothing.

He steps back. Cranes his neck to take in the house in detail. Vinyl siding swaddles most of the structure, with a band of bricks running just along the ground.

He scans each window, locking on every single one for several seconds before his gaze moves on. All the panes of glass hold dark. Motionless.

Putnam's heart beats faster. Hope blossoming in his chest now. But he wants to be sure.

He rounds the side of the house. Cups a hand over his brow to try to see through the black glass on the door leading into the side of the garage there. He can't be sure — it's dark — but no sedan or SUV shape leaps out at him. So far, so good.

He starts working his way around the perimeter of the house. The backyard lies darker than the rest. He realizes he can't see his own hands in front of his face unless he holds them up in front of the stars above.

He moves just along that brick rim of the structure. Scratchy bushes reach out of the gloom and claw at his orange jumpsuit. He ignores them and keeps going, mentally measuring, sizing things up.

Finally his eyes adjust to the murkiness. Darker boxes blot basement windows into the facade. He can even make out the rough impression of the mortar lines running pale between the bricks.

He finds the dryer vent poking out of the siding, and the slatted metal sides of the central AC unit catch his eye not more than three feet from that. Giving his best guess at the house's layout, he selects one of the windows near those two landmarks. He's pretty sure he's beneath the kitchen — better to be noisy there instead of under a bedroom, just in case someone is home after all.

He kneels and runs his fingers over the window in question. The glass blocks feel cool and smooth. Heavy, too. Substantial.

But he can make it work.

He stands again. Gives the window a stomping kick, foot

knifing down at a slightly inward angle.

The thump reverberates. The impact jolts up into his calf and knee. But the blocks hold.

He kicks it again. And again.

On the third blow, something crackles like plaster. He can feel the caulk and thin bead of mortar giving now.

The next kick knocks the window free. The whole thing wrenches out of the wall, plunks down onto the floor below. It sounds loud and oddly musical, like something heavy thumping down on a single xylophone bar.

But Putnam is already retreating. Feet swishing through dewy grass, socks going soggy.

He creeps deeper into the backyard, moves for the darkest corner. Crouches in one of the bushes there. Waits.

He stays like that, squatted in a shrub, hands flat to the ground, for two full minutes. He watches the house, eyes flicking from window to window.

Waiting for a light to come on. Waiting for any sign of movement or life.

Nothing stirs save for the soft flutter of his own breath.

He licks his lips. Scuttles back to that open socket where the basement window had been. Hesitates there at the edge of the hole.

He wishes he had a lighter, a match, a phone flashlight, anything to light the way.

Instead he climbs down into the dark.

CHAPTER 108

Ellie had wolfed down half of the sub before she even remembered to open one of the bags of chips. She crunched down on the first one, forgetting in her gluttonous fervor that she was trying to be quiet.

Wes rolled over and cracked one eyelid. Sniffed.

"Do I smell… pickles?"

Ellie nodded.

His eyes snapped open.

"Is that a sub?"

Ellie nodded again.

He practically leaped out of the bed. She chuckled, handing over the bag with the other sandwich and chips. He tore into it, evidently just as hungry as she had been.

He moaned after the first bite.

"I usually think their subs suck, but it's good, right?" Ellie asked.

He shook his head, looking almost disgusted.

"So fucking good."

His mouth was so full, the words bordered on unintelligible.

When they'd finished the food, they toasted each other with mini cups of Gatorade, and then Ellie went into the bathroom to brush her teeth again. She was never going to take brushing her teeth for granted, not for as long as she lived.

While she brushed, she considered Wes. Considered what he'd think of the New Ellie. What if he only liked the Old Ellie? The shy, awkward version of herself that for all intents and purposes might as well be dead now.

She blinked at her reflection.

"Only one way to find out," she said to herself.

Her robe hung from a hook on the back of the bathroom

door. A Christmas gift from Courtney.

Ellie plucked it from the hook and fingered the smooth fabric. It was a very Courtney garment. Deep teal satin with lace trim. The kind of borderline inappropriate thing Courtney regularly strutted around the house in, but Ellie only ever wore hers for a few minutes after a shower.

Back in the room, she slunk back over to her bed. Crawled in next to Wes.

"I was just trying to remember where we were before we got so rudely interrupted."

He looked at her quizzically.

"At the lifeguard hut," she explained.

"Ah. Yes," he said, smiling. "I think I can refresh your memory."

His mouth was warm against hers, his tongue probing but soft.

After a moment, Wes pulled away.

"Thinking back, I'm pretty sure we were wearing way less clothes than this, though."

"That can be corrected," Ellie said.

She reached for the light and then stopped herself. Old Ellie would be too shy to leave the lights on. But New Ellie? She didn't want to hide.

Ellie tugged at the tie on her robe, letting the silky fabric slide away from her body to reveal that she was wearing absolutely nothing underneath.

Wes stared at her with a whole new kind of hunger.

"Oh."

CHAPTER 109

Putnam eases down through the open window, sliding in on his belly, body unfurling. His fingers hook onto the lip of the window frame, arms extending to lower the rest of him into nothingness.

His shoulder blades scrape the top of the window frame, and then his chest presses into the cool wall. He kicks his legs into empty space, toes pointing, reaching for anything.

One of his rubber sandals slips off. Slaps the floor not so far below.

And then he touches down, one foot and then the other. It takes a second to trust that the floor will hold him, and then he unlatches his fingers from the frame.

He steps back. Staggers into the open. Feels strangely exposed, even shrouded in dark.

He stands still then. Waits and listens.

There's no sound here but his own heartbeat. Nothing is moving in the house.

Still, he waits. He lets his eyes adjust to the deeper blacks here. Watches all the forms around him slowly take shape in the void.

A couch winnows into focus — a sectional wrapping around a corner. The rectangular dark blur of the flat screen across the room somehow shines different than the blackness around it, catching the half-light.

Hockey jerseys hang in frames on the wall. Sports-related knickknacks fill a pair of bookshelves. He thinks a strange coil on one wall might be a neon light of a famous beer logo.

The puzzle pieces snap together quickly. He's dropped down into some kind of man cave.

Some jock-sniffing loser sits down here and yells at the TV night after night. Hilarious.

He stalks from room to room then. Peeking into grayscale versions of a guest room, laundry room, and some kind of storage space crowded with dusty exercise equipment. He finds the lower level, unsurprisingly, vacant.

Then he mounts the staircase leading up and out, wraps around the landing near the front door and up another flight of steps. He still moves slowly, keeps his feet light, quiet.

The top of the stairs looks into a vast kitchen. Stainless steel appliances. Gleaming quartz island catching the moonlight glinting in the window.

He cuts left. Clears the pair of bedrooms there, as expected.

As soon as he lays eyes on the empty bed in the master, he finds the tightness in his chest releasing. The bedspread sprawls smoothed out, untouched.

He peers into the en suite. Finds a blank shower stall.

Then he marches back through the house one more time, checks the living space off the kitchen. The sofas facing off there, too, hold empty.

That makes it official.

Nobody home.

He strides back for the master bedroom. Flips on a bedside lamp there.

A trickle of yellow light pools over Berber carpet and modern-looking furnishings. It looks like a hotel room. Soulless.

He kicks off the remaining sandal and strips out of his jumpsuit. Lets the orange fabric rumple at his feet.

Then he sits on the edge of the bed and sheds socks heavy with dew. He bunches and unbunches his toes a few times. God, it feels good to get that soggy cotton away from his skin.

He walks barefoot to the closet. The bunched texture of the carpet like soft toothbrush bristles scrubbing at his heels and tickling at his arches.

He opens the closet doorway. Gapes into the darkness there.

Fishing a hand just inside, he finds the switch. Flips it.

Let there be light.

A walk-in closet appears as the bulbs overhead wink to life. Putnam squints his eyes to slits and steps into the space.

The racks to the left and right hold a variety of generic dad fashion ranging from casual to formal. T-shirts. Polos. Button-ups. Sports jackets. Full suits. Even an actual tuxedo.

The clothes look about the right size — he can tell that even at a distance. Maybe not perfect, but he can make it work.

Sneakers fill the built-in shelf climbing up the far wall. Wooden cubes of brightly colored shoes from floor to ceiling. This fits, Putnam thinks, with the man cave he'd kicked his way into downstairs.

Jerkoff has to wear all the same shoes as the jocks he worships.

He puts on a pair of jeans and a black t-shirt. Both seem near new.

He checks himself in the mirror angled in one corner. Not bad. It feels good to be back in normal clothes.

The socks he pulls on are brand-new. Never worn. He can tell, somehow, by the way the fabric stretches around his foot, the little zipping sound the elastic makes as the tube reaches up over his ankle.

Finally, he starts trying on shoes. Shoving his way into Nikes worth as much as a used Toyota that, also, clearly haven't been worn. He knows enough to know that these older or limited-edition shoes are collected and highly valuable, though he can't understand why.

In any case, these are too small. Narrow as well as short. They pinch his toes together.

But digging through the shoe pile for a couple minutes, he finds a pair of tie-dye Crocs that, although ridiculous, are bigger than the rest. He paws at the clogs for a second, prodding a finger at the holes above the toe, at the strap meant to run behind the heel.

Finally, he slides the rubbery things over his socked feet. Surprisingly comfortable. He bounces on them a few times, bending the toes, flexing his feet. They will work.

He walks back through the house then, flipping on a few more lights along the way. A glass fixture burns bright over the hallway. Pendant lights light the foyer and stretch their glow into the kitchen.

As soon as the house is more or less fully lit, his eyes flick to the windows. He peers out through gauzy material at the darkened neighborhood beyond the glass — what little he can see of it, anyway. It occurs to him that maybe someone — one of the neighbors — will see the lights in the middle of the night and wonder what's going on, especially if they know the owner is on vacation or some such.

A tightness enters his abdomen, pulling the muscles along his flat stomach taut. But he takes a deep breath, and the rigidity flees just as quickly.

Oh well.

I'll be out of here within minutes.

I doubt anyone is calling the police the second they see some lights on.

Anyway, out in the McRichy suburbs like this? They're all probably in deep Ambien-fueled sleep shortly after nine P.M.

He eyes the kitchen. The stainless steel fridge looks to be about a man and a half wide. Saliva fills his mouth at the thought of eating, but there's something he needs to check first.

He pounds down the steps. Crosses the ridiculous man cave. Lets himself into the garage.

He sweeps his hand along the wall for several seconds before he locates the light switch.

The glow flicks over the space, reaching out to the walls, up to the exposed joists above.

Another set of steps lifts him back up to ground level, and he finds the front half of the cement slab there empty. That makes sense. The owner's car is probably sitting in long-term parking outside an airport somewhere.

Nevertheless, he takes a second to take this part of the garage in. Two bikes hang on the wall. A fridge huddles in the corner — smaller and older than the one upstairs.

Finally, he turns toward the rest of the space.

A bulk occupies the back half of the slab, concealed by a tarp. The gray mesh material snugs around the bottom edge like a fitted bed sheet.

He steps closer. Observes. He's pretty sure he knows exactly what this is even before he hooks his hands around the bottom of the tarp and pulls.

He works his way around the perimeter, loosening the tarp. Once the edges are free, he gives it a good hard tug.

The sheet billows up and tears away like a yanked tablecloth. Floats out of the way. Drifts to the barren cement toward the front of the garage.

The purple enamel beneath glitters as soon as the light touches it. Curves plump the fenders and taper the middle of the car, something feminine, exciting about the shape.

Putnam's breath catches in his throat.

OK. Fuck yeah.

A 1984 Corvette lies before him. Custom painted a metallic purple with tiny glittery flecks in it.

Back inside, Putnam finds the keys to the 'vette hung on a peg just inside the garage door. Funny.

He stomps back up the stairs and heads for the kitchen. A smile curls his lips as he closes on the stainless steel box there.

He stands over the open refrigerator for what feels like a long time. That harsh fridge light washing over his face.

Grabbing and eating.

First he takes to a block of cheddar. Bites off a big hunk of cheese. Examines the perfect mold of his teeth left behind in the gelatinous orange. He'll make sure not to leave those imprints behind, though he doesn't know how much it might matter in the long run.

He tests out some kind of pickles in a fancy jar. Moves on to a drawer full of deli meat wrapped in plastic sheaths. Turkey. Salami. Roast beef. He feeds the slices into his mouth one at a time.

He cracks and chugs down two Dr. Peppers as he works. The acidic drink seems to bring the other flavors to life, harsh fizz that he can feel in his sinuses.

Then he works the cupboards. Wolfs down a whole row of Oreos, washes them down literally with mouthfuls of milk straight out of the jug. Eats some crackers. Dips his finger into a jar of peanut butter a few times.

Fullness seems to arrive all at once, a leaden bloom in his gut catching him off guard. He looks over the mess left behind, the torn-open packages strewn over floor and counter, the gaping fridge door leaking that white light over everything, and a momentary regret brims in him. Some feeling of loss. He wishes he could just keep eating, wishes he could never stop. It seems unfair, somehow, to get full, for the feasting to end.

But the feeling passes quickly enough. He has another idea. A way to make things right. Scarlet might have escaped his grasp, but that doesn't mean he can't even the score another way.

Another quick search of the house turns up more tools he could use. A certain spray can in a cabinet in the garage. A flashlight and a lighter from a kitchen junk drawer. Something big and cold and mean from a wooden box on one of the closet shelves. It's all better than he could have hoped for. More than one kind of hunger will be sated tonight.

He grabs the keys on his way back out to the car. Needs to check that second fridge in the garage.

Again, pale light reaches up under his chin to light his face from below as he stands over the open refrigerator.

This one is barren compared to the spread he'd found upstairs. But that doesn't matter.

A lonely item sits in the middle of the top row, shadowed in the front as it's lit from behind. He reaches in, hooks his fingers into the cardboard handle, plucks the six pack from the gloom and pulls it into the light — only then does the Budweiser logo come clear.

Perfect fuel for the road. Like it was meant to be.

He piles into the Corvette. Twists his wrist to crack the first long neck. Ready to go.

He just has one stop to make first. One loop to close.

The Sea Spray Motel.

CHAPTER 110

Wes climbed to his knees on the bed and tugged off his shirt. Ellie expected him to waste no time stripping down completely, figured that he'd be eager to get this show on the road. But after removing his shirt, he crawled to the edge of the bed and pulled her into a kiss. Long and slow and not at all in a rush.

He ran his fingers down the length of her back, pausing to cup her buttocks. Goosebumps rippled on her flesh.

Part of her wanted to shy away from his touch, still a little frightened of this ultimate vulnerability. But the New Ellie resisted. Cast aside the urge to tense her body, to put up a wall. Instead, she let go. Relinquished herself to the sensation of his hands on her bare skin. Caressing. Stroking.

It stirred a deep wanting within her. A hammering in her heart and a throbbing between her legs. She suddenly remembered how much she'd wanted him that night on the beach.

When he brought his mouth to one of her nipples, she surprised herself by letting out a moan of pleasure. Wes took that as a sign to guide her onto the bed. He removed the rest of his clothes, and she readied herself.

But he was only getting started. He returned to his task of exploring her body with both hands and lips. Kissing and fondling until she was practically dizzy with longing, begging him to enter her.

Ellie cried out with ecstasy when he finally thrust inside her. She expected it would be over soon. That was how it had always been before.

But Wes started slow, taking his time even now, finding a rhythm until they moved together as one.

The countless sensations threatened to overwhelm her. The sweet friction of his sweat-slicked skin against hers. The hard swelling of him moving deep inside her.

The intensity and momentum built to a crescendo until she felt like she might explode. And then she did, losing herself in the climax.

When it was over, when her heartbeat had finally begun to slow again, she laughed.

Because Courtney had been right, again.

Sex really was different when you did it with someone who knew what they were doing.

♥

They lay in the darkened room after, their bodies tangled up in a lazy embrace.

Ellie couldn't believe what she'd been missing all this time. And not *just* the sex. All of it. The pleasant warmth of their mutual affection. The contentment of feeling accepted by another person. The thrill of vulnerability.

And then all the old worries began to swarm.

What would they do now? Was Wes actually interested in her, or was this just a fling? If he was interested, would they try to do some kind of long-distance thing, despite the fact that relationships like that rarely seemed to work out? Was she doomed to have her heart broken one way or another?

Shut up, Old Ellie, a cooler, calmer voice in her head said.

New Ellie.

Ellie made herself listen to the voice. Thrust the anxious thoughts away and refocused her attention on the present moment. The sensations of lying here with Wes's arms around her. The heat and smell of his skin. The slight sheen of sweat adhering them together.

The only thing that matters is Right Now, the New Ellie voice said.

Ellie's head rested on Wes's chest, her ear pressed against his sternum. She listened to the steady *lub-dub* of his heartbeat. It was like a lopsided metronome, and it lulled her into a trance-like state.

Lub-dub.

Lub-dub.

Lub-dub.

Thump.

Ellie lifted her head and blinked in the half-light. That last sound hadn't been Wes's heart.

"What is it?" Wes sounded groggy, like he'd already been drifting back to sleep.

"Thought I heard something."

"Where?"

"Outside."

They both held still, listening.

Other than the white noise of the air-conditioning, there was nothing.

"What did it sound like?" Wes asked, breaking the silence.

"I don't know. Like a thud?"

They listened for a few more seconds, and then Wes tucked one arm behind his head.

"Probably just a car door or something."

The Old Ellie probably would have left it at that. Allowed herself to be reassured. But the New Ellie wanted to know.

She rolled off the bed, sliding a t-shirt over her head. She only made it a few more steps toward the window before she paused again to slide on a pair of shorts.

Just as she got them up over her hips, there was a terrible crash.

The window beyond the curtain shattered, and glass exploded into the room.

CHAPTER 111

The curtains flapped back over the broken window. Everything went still.

Screaming, awful quiet filled the motel room. Strange after the shock of the glassy explosion.

Wes's skin crawled. A million prickles creeping over the surface of his chest, arms, the scruff of his neck. Every follicle bristling.

Out of instinct, he hooked a hand under the lampshade, found the switch and twisted. The room plunged to darkness save for that rim of light leaking around the curtains.

His eyes found Ellie's silhouette in the dark, confirmed she was still there a few feet shy of the window. She moved for the bed, for him, nestled herself close.

Then they waited in the quiet. Frozen to the mattress. Eyes glued to the half-billowed curtain blocking out the broken window.

Wes's vision adjusted to the gloom in increments. The blacks faded to grays. The shards of glass slowly formed under the window — flat, shiny spots forming a mosaic on the otherwise soft carpet — icy and brittle where the trickle of light touched them.

Wes's mind reeled.

Maybe it was some kind of an accident.

Like a baseball bashing the window or…

But no.

No.

He knew who it was. He didn't know how, but he knew.

He could feel it.

He brushed his hand across the mattress, grabbed Ellie's hand. Waited for her face to turn away from the window, for her eyes to find his.

When they did, he shook his head. He mouthed "don't move." The room was so quiet, he could hear his lips parting. Tiny pops of skin on skin.

After a second, Ellie nodded. Gave his hand a squeeze. She understood.

Then he slid off the edge of the bed. Careful. Quiet.

The carpet seemed to reach up for him. Soft for just a second before going solid.

He squatted there on hands and knees. Waiting again. Watching and listening.

He kept expecting movement at the window, but the curtains lay still. Eerie in their motionlessness.

Wes breathed. Quiet breaths. Shallow.

Nothing in the room seemed to move. A streetlight buzzed somewhere outside, a tiny mosquito sound in the distance.

The air-conditioning blasted his bare chest. He wished he had a t-shirt. A jacket. Something.

And then he felt stupid for thinking that.

A thin sheath of cotton over his torso would do him no good here. With all the glass, what he needed was shoes. But those were gone in the dark somewhere. Maybe over by the bathroom door. He couldn't remember.

Still in a squat, he lifted himself from his knees onto his feet. Flexed his toes on the carpet and felt the pile squish between them.

He eyed the flat shards of glass again, glittering under the window. He'd need to give those a wide berth.

Then his jaw muscles contracted, and he revised his internal list again. Forget a t-shirt. Forget shoes, too.

He needed a weapon.

He reached out in the dark. Patted his hands over the floor. Bobbing his arms. Touching that sprawling sheet of coarse fiber.

Empty. Nothing.

He squat-walked forward a few steps. Kept feeling along. Fingertips brushing, brushing.

He tried to picture some blunt object there on the floor — a baseball bat or a tire iron — though he knew it made little sense. But there had to be something here.

He found the edge of the nightstand. Touched his way around the perimeter with one hand. Fished his hand all the way into the corner between the mattress and the wooden leg.

Nothing.

But as he withdrew the limb, his wrist brushed something cold. He backtracked.

His fingers swept over metal. Rounded.

He rocked forward and searched the dome with both hands. Found a protrusion at the top. A nozzle.

And then he knew what it was.

He hoisted the fire extinguisher out into the open. Felt its cold metal brush against his chest.

He turned back to the drapes. A couple paces closer now, the rectangle of fabric looked bigger, the light seeping in around the edges brighter.

The curtain bulged like a pregnant belly then. Pushed into the room in slow motion.

Cold feelings rippled over Wes's body again. Icy fingernails spearing his skin.

Wind?

No.

Glass crunched, and then quiet again.

It was him. Putnam.

He was creeping into the room.

The curtain kept pluming. Growing angular at one point. Maybe an elbow.

He's right there. Just on the other side of this thin fabric barrier.

Wes stood. Raised the fire extinguisher and strode forward two steps.

The flap of curtain peeled back. Fresh moonlight spilled into the wedge where it lay open. The silvery glow stretched over the floor, a finger of light slowly broadening, reaching to expose Wes.

A blacker shape stood out from the brightness. Part of Putnam made visible for a second. Maybe a leg.

Wes took that last step forward. Hurled himself. Ripped his arms downward like he was swinging an axe.

The fire extinguisher arced toward the place where he estimated Putnam's head would be.

But then Putnam's silhouette flexed. Not a leg.

The muzzle flared. Fire snorting a burst of orange brightness.

The glitter laid bare Putnam's hand, his arm, part of his shoulder.

The gun popped and jerked. The whole arm bunched just a little.

Then he fired again. And again.

The bullets took Wes in the belly. All three. Stabbed into his guts.

Pain exploded from the points of impact. Surged outward.

His naked torso pounded into the carpet. Woofed the breath out of him.

He blinked. Felt his eyelashes brush against the shag. Felt the blood gushing out of him. Felt his body going frigid all at once.

He writhed. Tried to piston his legs, get his feet back under him.

But it hurt too much. Too much.

The dark got bigger. Flickered.

A blackout rolling through him. Taking him away from here little by little.

Expiration happened too fast for him to even be scared of death, too fast for the initial shock to give way to realization. He went under confused, face cold and sweaty, panting those final breaths.

All he could think about was the sense of loss, the sensation of the fire extinguisher twirling away. He'd needed that. Needed that weapon.

And then the light inside went out for good.

CHAPTER 112

Ellie flinched at the first gunshot. A loud pop that filled the motel room, rang in her head, and shoved long strands of cotton into her ears.

She flinched again and again as two more shots were fired. The sounds were muffled this time but still jarring.

She scooted toward the edge of the bed out of instinct. Put one foot down to the carpet and then the other. Shoved off the mattress to get herself upright. Top half still angled toward the window.

And she could see the orange flicker jetting out of the gun, the muzzle laid bare in the glow of miniature fireworks. A black hole in the center that dealt death, strobing and spitting like stop-motion animation.

Wes's silhouette stood up straighter, spine elongated, shoulders stooping at the top. He seemed to freeze like that for perhaps a full second. Hunched like a raccoon.

Then he dropped straight down onto his belly — a felled tree smashing into the carpet. Even with her hearing blown out, the thud was audible.

The fire extinguisher he'd been hoisting drooped out of his hands as he fell. Tumbled over the floor into the murk near the bathroom door.

And then Wes didn't move at all. No twitch of the limbs. No expansion of the ribcage for breathing.

A voice inside interrupted Ellie's thoughts:

Dead weight.

His pose looked wrong. *Was* wrong.

He'd landed on one of his arms, legs bent a little. Face down and motionless.

Just planted there. A tossed toy. Something ragdoll about it all.

No one would mistake him for sleeping. Not for a second.

The position told the story. Showed how his final action had been interrupted. Cut off all at once.

Dead weight.

And Ellie was gasping. Heaving for breath. Throat scraping.

She found herself shuffling backward. Realizing there was nowhere to go — not this way.

Putnam came for her.

He pushed through the curtains — those dark flaps folding and stirring around his shoulders like wings. His broad torso looked angular along the edges, chiseled into a capital V.

With the light streaming into the gap behind him, the gloom blotted out his front. A walking shadow pressing for her.

He stepped over Wes's fallen form, striding over the carpet. Arms splayed. Posture rigid. His face a black smear slowly tightening into detail.

And then a smile appeared there, the soft gray glow of teeth splitting the bottom half of his head. Wet and wolfish.

Ellie tried to run. Darting and juking to his right. Eyes locked on the glowing rim of light leaking around the window frame.

She could jump out the window. It was the only way.

But his free arm shot out like a striking copperhead. He grabbed her by the hair. Fingers like claws raking against her scalp and then cinching tight.

He yanked her head hard to the side. Stopped her all at once. Cranked her neck far enough that her cheek bounced off the point of her shoulder, and then he pulled her close.

He jammed the muzzle of the gun into the side of her neck. The metal was still warm.

And words interrupted Ellie's mind again, forcing themselves to the surface. A song title this time:

Happiness Is a Warm Gun.

When Putnam spoke, his voice was a low growl. Deep and surprisingly soft. She could hear the smile behind the words.

"Hey now. Don't go running off. The party is just getting

started."

He let go of her hair, and she stumbled forward. Tottering off balance. Legs stabbing at the carpet to try to keep her upright.

Then he was on her again, one arm wrapping around her, the other shoving something over her face. Something wet. Something that smelled like vodka with something sickly sweet in it.

Don't breathe.

Ellie held her breath and squirmed against him. The rag reached up over the bridge of her nose and covered part of her field of vision, but she could still see that glowing rectangle of the window over the top of it. Maybe ten feet away. Escape was so close.

His arm felt like a python cinching around her chest, crushing her ribcage. A tube of all hard muscle slithering over her.

She threw her arms back, one then the other. Tried to elbow him. The pointy bones got him in the flank.

But the shots had no power. No leverage.

And then he squeezed her tighter. Tighter. Their bodies pressed close. She felt something in her chest pop.

And she gasped. Sucked in a big breath.

That sweet vodka smell rushed into her mouth, her throat. Its heaviness spiraled into her lungs, coated her windpipe, lacquered her tongue with its chemical test.

Her head got lighter. The room swirled around her, throbbing gently at first. Everything getting fuzzy along the edges.

And the dark seemed to press in on the sides of her field of vision. Gelatinous black closing in on her, runny like egg whites along the edges.

She found herself breathing deeply now. Involuntary. Her chest working on its own. Heaving.

The chemical taste seemed to pervade all of her being. She could feel the fumes trembling in her skull like shimmering heat distortion.

She felt separate from the moment, apart from physical reality. The motel room receding. Her consciousness funneled into some deeper inward place.

All the fight fled her body. Muscles going slack. Eyelids drooping. Shoulders hunching.

And the poison sucked down the drain of her windpipe. More and more. Great clouds of it. It spread itself all through her bloodstream.

Her consciousness cut out abruptly. The black nothing flipped her off like a switch.

CHAPTER 113

John woke to the crack of gunfire. Sat up in bed. Listened over the throaty strain of the air-conditioning unit in the corner.

One shot first. He knew it was a gunshot, no doubt in his mind, even though it'd come while he was sleeping, wrenched him out of a recurring dream about hiding in his old apartment as the new tenants walked in.

He blinked and listened. Felt the cool breeze touch him where the blanket had slid down from his chest. Felt the dark like strange cobwebs stretched over the room.

No other sounds came at first. No yelling. No footsteps. No distant sirens answering the gunshot's call.

The silence stretched out. Fought the rumble and churn of the window unit.

John got up and glided toward the air conditioner. The cold wrapped itself around him as soon as he was out of bed, made his skin feel tight.

His fingers found the dial in the dark. He cranked hard to the left, a rattling sound stuttering out.

The blower cut off, but the unit still made a wet sucking sound, water trickling somewhere in the metal folds of the thing. It slowed to a *drip drip drip*.

John focused his ears past that sound, tried to orient himself toward the direction the shot had come from. He thought it'd been off to the left, toward Wes and Ellie's room, but he wasn't certain. Not yet.

He sidled along the front wall and flipped on the lights. Slitted his eyes against the harshness.

He was moving toward the door when fresh noise made him jump back. His fists came up. His feet knifed apart to put him in something like a karate stance.

Two more shots rang out, right together, almost on top of

each other. Something thudded down a second after that. Something heavy.

And close.

Too close.

Courtney spoke up from across the room. She'd pulled the covers up over the bottom half of her face and talked through the blanket.

"Was that…?"

John bobbed his head once.

"Gunshots."

They listened for a beat. That slow-motion drip still plinked inside the AC unit. The silence beyond the room screamed its endless note.

"Were they… next door?"

John clenched his jaw. Then he bobbed his head again. His voice came out small.

"I think so."

"Turn off the lights," Courtney said, her voice suddenly flat, suddenly urgent.

John's jaw tightened again. It felt like his mouth had become a clenched fist.

"I have to go out there," he said.

"You can't."

"I have to."

"No. Don't be an idiot. It's not safe. Turn off the lights, and call the police."

He moved for the door again. Stopped there with his hand on the knob as he processed what she was saying.

"That'll take… I mean, they could be…"

A soft patter played out from the other side of the wall. The crunch of someone walking over broken glass. Heavy footfalls. Slow.

John stared at the wall. Knew that he was listening to something just on the other side, though he wasn't sure what or who.

The slow footsteps kept going. They walked deeper into the

room. John's head swiveled to follow their path.

Then the steps turned around. Went back.

At the front of the room, that sound ended, and the silence beat in its place. The sucking void, an awful nothingness. John could hear its emptiness in his heartbeat, in his breath.

He finally pried his eyes away from Courtney's, turned back toward the door. He knew that whatever would happen next lay just beyond this flimsy expanse of wood.

A car door thumped shut somewhere in the lot. The sound made John's shoulders do that marionette jump again. The noise somehow reminiscent of the gunshots.

He glanced over at Courtney. Her eyes twitched and met his. Their gazes fastened like that, held.

An engine whinnied to life and revved. Then the tires squealed as the thing tore away.

John rushed to the window and flipped back the curtains just in time to see a flash of taillights. Red circles glowing like eyes, smearing out of view.

He closed his own eyes. Told himself to encode the image, the few details he could pick out about the car.

Some kind of sports car.

Curvy. Like a Corvette or Dodge Viper or something like that.

Older. Like 90s or maybe even 80s.

Purple. I think.

And then his eyes were open again, and he was running for the door. Peeling it open. Stepping into the dark.

The humid air swirled around him. Felt strange after all that time in the air-conditioning. Tacky and warm against his taut skin.

His feet pushed off of lukewarm concrete. He wheeled toward the next room over.

And right away the vacancy gaped back at him.

An empty socket where the window should be. Tiny triangles of glass still clung to the rim of the frame like jagged claws.

Movement fluttered in the corner of John's eye, wrenched his head to the right.

A dark blur smeared over the sidewalk. A heat-seeking missile surging for him.

John stopped. He blinked. The image tightened into focus.

It was Dan, jogging over. Tanya trailing behind.

"You guys all right?" Dan called, his voice honking funny, still heavy with sleep.

"Yeah," John said. "Er... well... I am."

Dan slowed as he padded the last few paces. His bare feet clapped against the concrete.

"What the hell was that? Were those gunshots?"

"Yeah."

John tilted his head toward the room where Ellie and Wes had been sleeping.

Dan's eyes went wide when he saw the broken window.

"Oh shit."

John lurched to life again, half-jogging toward the room.

The door hung a couple inches open — a mouth with parted lips — and darkness seeped through the crack between the door and frame. John swallowed hard when he saw it. He could feel wetness in his eyes.

He pushed through the doorway. Stepped into the room. Stopped just inside.

The broken glass looked like pockmarks in the dark, a moonscape denting the carpet. But the half-light streaming through the door only reached a couple feet into the room. He couldn't see much else.

Dan jogged up behind him and bumped into his back.

"Careful. There's broken glass everywhere in here," John said.

Dan took a step back.

"Damn. Sorry."

Then John felt around for the switch and flipped on the lights. There was a fraction of a second between the snap of the switch flipping and the bulbs flicking on.

The brightness punctured his eyes. He squinted.

And then he saw the bulk on the floor, and his mind went blank. Vacant.

He froze like that in the doorway. Staring. Mouth a little bit open.

That vacancy yawned wider inside. Nothing. Dazed.

Wes lay face down on the carpet. Something rumpled and awkward about his back, limbs jutting out of him funny.

And blood.

There was blood.

Dark red stained the beige carpet. A puddle of it forming an uneven circle around Wes's torso.

Dan shouldered his way into the doorway. He hissed something John couldn't understand.

Tanya spoke up from somewhere behind them.

"What is it?"

"Stay back, baby," Dan said. "Just keep back."

John could only watch now. Staring and blinking. Some icy wind rushing through him inside.

Dan stormed into the room. Edged right up to Wes, his toes dipping into that red puddle.

Then he got down on one knee. Put his hand to Wes's neck.

He recoiled right away.

"What is it?" Tanya said. She peeked into the edge of the doorway, Courtney too.

"Cold," Dan said.

He brought his hand back to Wes's throat. Two fingers sliding under his jaw, finding the vein there. Waiting.

And the whole scene held still like that. Hushed. Reverent.

Dan kept his fingers there for what felt like a long time. Probably just a few seconds.

He blinked a few times. Licked his lips.

When he finally spoke, his voice came out small, almost under his breath.

"No heartbeat."

He let his hand slide away from Wes's neck.

"What?" John said, his own voice getting hard, accusatory. "What'd you say?"

Dan licked his lips again. Shifted his eyes from face to face. At last, he spoke.

"He's dead."

CHAPTER 114

Putnam grips the steering wheel. Flexes his fingers against the cold plastic slowly going warm at his touch.

He stares into the dark strip of road laid out before the car. The Corvette slices through endless swampland now, headlights shining down a straight stretch of road.

The night sprawls everywhere, reaches up into eternity. A dark so vast it's hard to fathom.

But Putnam feels at home in the endless night. He likes that lonely feeling the big dark seems to arouse in him. The void makes a certain kind of sense to him, feels natural.

The girl sleeps next to him, her slack body folded funny in the bucket seat. Something floppy in the pose.

She's a frail thing. Small. Fragile like an injured bird.

The sad expression on her face says as much. The downward curling bottom lip bulges just a little, cheeks pulled taut. A frown etched there by the ether.

He dips his hand into the cup holder. Comes away with a sweaty bottle of Bud.

He tips his head back and drains the amber liquid down his throat. That clean beer smell flushes into his sinuses, crisp, just a faint touch of bitterness to it, and the carbonation leaves a subtle sting tingling up and down his throat.

Damn. Half the six pack is gone already, spinning just that first wave of a beer buzz into his head.

He needs to pace himself now. Savor those last three beers. He wants this night to last a while.

Or maybe he should chug 'em now and be done with it. Is there a right answer here?

That's a funny thing about life, he thinks. The push and pull of wanting to enjoy it now and wanting to preserve it is everywhere, a tension that never really fades.

From the outside looking in, life looks like a road map. Endless possible routes intertwining.

Your path branches with every choice you make. Infinite possibilities.

There's something paralyzing about the options, when you look at it from afar. Something that makes most people kind of coast, numbed, never really going for anything. No purpose.

But in real life, all those possibilities fold up into nothin'. Illusions.

You only get to pick the one course. You barrel down the road you chose, for better or worse.

Life is a singular path. You only get to live it the one time, the one way. No do-overs.

At some point you have to commit to something. Stand for something. Live your life. Here and now.

He reaches down into the shadows along the floorboard. Finds the cardboard handle of the six pack and then palms another bottle. The brown glass pulls up into the glow of the dashboard, and he twists the top off.

Life is for livin'.

Better to drink it while it's still cold.

Nothing lasts forever.

He glances over at the girl again. Eyes climbing up the length of her thigh.

She sure won't live forever.

Something about her nearness excites him. He can feel her presence there — a soft, warm energy just an arm's length away.

She's a young one. He likes 'em young.

He imagined keeping her. Pictures her kept in a windowless room, perpetually dark. The two of them could be together there, whenever he wants. He licks his lips.

But he knows he can't be greedy. Not now.

The cops will be pissed about the deputy in the jail. They always went apeshit when one of their own got taken out, and now he'd downed two of 'em.

The heat will intensify now. No doubt.

Trying to keep a hostage in the midst of a manhunt just isn't smart. Oh, it seems easy enough from afar, but the up-close reality is something more complicated.

You gotta keep 'em detained. Gotta keep 'em watered. Gotta let 'em go to the bathroom. It's a whole lot more than laying out newspaper in the bottom of a birdcage. Babysitting. Total fucking headache.

Better to get some use out of her and dump her soon.

Keep things uncomplicated.

Keep things clean.

If I'm smart, I can still get out of this. Go on my merry way.

Hell, maybe Scarlet is long gone. Out of reach.

But maybe not.

His gaze dwells on her thigh again. Follows the gentle curve to where the skin disappears under her shorts.

His jaw muscles bunch. Goddamn it. In different circumstances, she'd be a keeper. For sure.

Then he smiles. A little puff of laughter comes out of his nostrils.

He won't be stupid. He still has his whole life ahead of him. So much living to do.

Not to worry. Not a bit.

See, the world is full of girls just like her. They're endless.

♥

Ellie's consciousness bobbed to the surface in spurts, not able to hold. The feelings came first, even before she knew where she was.

Wes.

Wes is gone.

The sense of loss felt like a tooth torn out roughly. A violent vacancy. A missing piece.

Grief and guilt intertwined in her chest. Misery pumping through her with every heartbeat.

She remembered that final image of him. Face mashed into the carpet. Blood pooling around him.

None of this would have happened if it weren't for me, if I'd never stuck out my neck, if I'd never lied and crept down here on vacation.

Putnam never would have heard of me. Or Wes.

How things were before still seemed so close. Right there. It seemed like she should be able to rewind, to go back, to undo this catastrophe, but she knew she never could.

Unconsciousness stilled her mind now and again, pulled her out into the deep, but the sharp ache of grief always brought her back to the surface.

Wes.

For once, it had felt like life was starting to make sense. She had seemingly taken control of her own destiny, seemingly found someone worth getting closer to, someone worth falling in love with.

Now it was all gone. Dead.

It's just like he said about life. None of it adds up to anything. It doesn't mean anything at all.

Ellie had never felt so lost.

♥

When she woke again, she tried to focus on her surroundings. Flashes of sights, sounds, and feelings came and went in the brief periods she could stay awake.

The headlights glinted on a country road. Hollowed out the darkness.

The dotted yellow line sliced down the middle of the asphalt. Gleaming where the headlights touched the reflective paint. Watching the yellow dashes rush for them and get swallowed under the car made Ellie think of that ancient arcade game Pac-Man.

The leather seat held her, reflected its cool into her.

And underneath it all, the engine purred. It revved louder

now and then. A wild thing trapped beneath the hood and angry about it.

The dark persisted in pulling her under, erasing the world around her. Sleep dulled the chemical taste in her mouth, but it couldn't touch the pain in her skull. A headache stabbed an ice pick in her frontal lobe over and over.

This time when she woke, she swiveled her eyes toward the driver's seat. Saw the dark figure perched there, one hand gripping the bottom rim of the steering wheel, the other picking at a scab on his cheekbone.

The dash lights lit Putnam's face from below, caught on the hard line of his jaw. Shadows pitted the hollows of his cheeks and cupped the arch of his brow.

His focus stayed locked on the windshield, flicked over the strip of road endlessly scrolling before them. He didn't know she was awake.

She closed her eyes. Tried to think.

She needed to do something while his guard was down. Needed to…

Sleep hugged new warmth around her. Numbed her mind. Slowed her thoughts.

The next time she woke, her tongue felt huge. Swollen. Stuck to the roof of her mouth. That chemical taste like a glaze coating the surface.

This time she was only able to keep her eyes open long enough to realize that they were riding very low to the ground, the seats angled funny.

A sports car or something?

It must be.

Her eyelids were already heavy again. She managed to see the chrome Corvette logo on the steering wheel as they passed under a streetlight.

A Corvette.

Never rode in one of those before.

Before she could contemplate the notion further, the dark reached up with open arms and pulled her back under.

She drifted. Weightless and dreamless.

Time passed. The seat slowly warmed against her, a development only half-sensed. Her sleep deepened.

The ride stretched out. Ellie floated through it, those bouts of consciousness coming less and less frequently.

She dreamed of Wes, still in motion, still alive. Walking on the beach, right along the shore. Waves crashing to his right.

Then the car slowed. Inertia shifted.

Ellie tensed. Leaned forward in her seat. Not quite asleep and not quite awake.

She listened. Felt.

The Corvette curled off the road, holding steady at a lower speed. Gravel crunched under the tires, plinked at the fenders.

The car shook over the rough terrain, jostled Ellie in her seat. She opened her eyes.

The headlights speared a cinder block building. White cracking paint shot up the walls of the windowless structure. A blue door was set toward the middle, slightly off center.

They drove straight toward it. Closer and closer.

Her eyes flicked to the mirror. It wasn't until she saw the brake lights blushing red in the glass that the reality occurred to her.

They were parking.

CHAPTER 115

Ellie watched through slitted eyes as Putnam wrangled the gearshift into park. The engine changed pitch, its grunt going a couple tones lower, the new rumble felt as a faint vibration through the seats.

He twisted the key in the ignition and killed the engine. The motor knocked a couple times, soft pings babbling under the hood, and then the quiet rose up.

Ellie closed her eyes. Feigned unconsciousness. Fought to keep her breathing even.

You're not scared, she told herself.

You're having fun. That's all.

Putnam cracked his door and climbed out of the car. She could feel his weight leave the vehicle, the shocks shifting, the whole thing lifting a fraction of an inch upward. The door thumped shut behind him.

And then she heard his footsteps rounding the front end. A muffled cadence trailing away and then coiling back. The dirt scraped against the soles of his shoes. Maybe a little gravel mixed in.

He peeled open her door, and she could feel the open night just there to her right, cool and vast. Escape felt close. Tangible, somehow, in that thick Florida air. Just go. Any direction from here. But she couldn't.

He leaned in. Loomed over her. A heavy breath rolled out of him, steam released from a vent. She didn't know what to make of it.

And then one hand looped around her shoulders, the other cupped under her knees. He lifted her like that, brought her in to his chest.

This isn't scary. It's fun.

She found herself nestled against him. Cheek resting on his

pectoral.

A wave of revulsion surged through her. A nest of ants roiling where her cheekbone touched his chest.

The disgust balled up her stomach. Lifted some bile up her gorge that tasted like sour spaghetti sauce on the back of her tongue.

But she had to keep still, had to keep still. Had to.

Fun.

Exciting.

You're having fun.

He was hot to the touch, some fiery swelter rolling off of his body in waves. A furnace of a man.

He smelled vaguely of sweat — the sharp scent of fresh perspiration. Some leathery musk note was detectable underneath that. It was like Wes's smell turned inside out and made repellent. Revolting.

And she realized she could hear his heart beating through the wall of his chest. A squishing, pounding, angry thing that hammered at the center of him.

He turned. Strode forward.

She kept her eyes clenched tight. It felt like she was swooping through the dark, empty space, out of control. A package clutched in front of him. Like he'd set her down on a doorstep somewhere and mark her as delivered.

His footsteps crunched over the gravel, beat at the sand. And then he stopped. Hitched her up a little higher on his chest.

He lurched funny then, lower body bucking. A fraction of a second later, the wood of the door thumped.

The impact of the kick jolted through him, somehow reminding Ellie of the jerk of a fired crossbow.

He readied himself again. She felt his body harden and twitch into another kick. His torso seemed to broaden, grow more powerful, as he tensed.

He kicked like that again and again.

The wood splintered. The thuds grew louder. On the fourth

kick, the door busted open.

She could hear it. The wood-on-wood *shunk* of the plank bursting through the frame. The squawk of the hinges like angry gulls.

He pressed forward again. Turned himself sideways to finagle her into the darkened space.

She sensed the darkness growing deeper, even through eyelids clamped shut. The scent of dust was heavy here, mixed with something else, a grease smell that reminded Ellie of tools.

Two steps in, a faint whiff of death joined the other odors. The putrid rot of long dead rodents that had gone earthy in time.

Ellie's nose wrinkled. She forced it smooth again and hoped he hadn't noticed.

He leaned forward then. Tilted. She could feel his arms extending. The heat of his chest peeled away from her all at once.

He laid her down on her back on the cold concrete slab of the floor. Surprisingly gentle in how he nestled the back of her head down.

She could hear his feet stutter backward. The scritch of his shoes echoed funny in the enclosed space, whispering everywhere.

And she felt empty somehow. Exposed. Laid out like a body at the morgue.

The icy cement sheet pressed its chill into her back. The cold seeped through her clothes, saturated her flesh. Within seconds, she was already going numb.

He didn't move. Didn't make a sound.

She slit her eyelids. Just a little. Looked up through thatched eyelashes.

And he stood over her, the frame of light from the doorway cutting a rectangle of brightness behind his broad silhouette. He loomed there, motionless for another couple seconds. She couldn't see the details of his face, but she could tell by the angle of his jaw's shadow that he was staring down at her.

Her stomach leaped again, tried to force itself up her throat.

But she kept her breathing steady. Even. She waited.

And then he turned and walked out into the light outside. Disappeared through the doorway.

Ellie resisted the urge to bolt right away. She lay still. Made herself count to five.

One.

Run.

No.

This is your chance.

Two.

No.

You have to wait.

Three.

Fun. It's fun. It's a game.

Four.

Hide and seek.

Five.

Ready or not…

Ellie sat up and started patting the concrete around her. Her fingers bounced back and forth in front of her, brushed dusty cement.

She crawled deeper into the shadows. Hands still bobbing out in front.

She found something smooth then. Enamel coating cold metal.

She knew what it was. Popped the clasp. Peeled it open.

Time to have some real fun.

CHAPTER 116

Putnam strides back through the doorway toward the 'vette. He'd left the last of his six pack out there.

A cool breeze slides over his chest and brushes at his shoulders as he moves. The chill of the deep night offers relief from the blistering day. It feels good, especially out here away from the city blocks that soak up the sun all day and radiate that heat all night.

He stalks out by the Corvette's flank. Then he swings himself the other way and unzips.

May as well take a quick piss while he's out here.

She's out now anyway. Deep in the ditch of unconsciousness. He could see it in the way she breathed, that slow rise and fall of her chest. She's way down in the hole.

Shoot, maybe she won't wake up at all. That'd be a pity.

Not as much fun without 'em squirmin' and screamin'.

He likes it when they're scared.

But hell, he can't worry about all that now. He has to get going.

The more he thinks about it, the more he thinks Mexico is the only way forward for him now. Too much heat here.

They have his name and face now. Even have fresh mugshots courtesy of the Durango County jail, for shit's sake. He needs to get gone — somewhere way, way away from here.

His piss slaps against the ground for what feels like a long time. He takes a deep breath. Leans his head back and looks up at the stars.

The heavens above are endless. Gazing into that vast black of the night sky, it's hard to believe that just earlier tonight he'd been locked up in a cell. Penned into maybe fifty square feet. Caged like an animal.

And now he's free again. On the move. Taking what he

wants.

Headed down Meh-hico way. Heh.

And it occurs to him out of nowhere that Jimmy and Scarlet are probably going to Mexico, too. Where else?

Jesus. It ain't over. It's just getting started.

He pictures Scarlet. A flash of images riffling through his head.

First he sees her as he'd last seen her, just a flash of her in the backseat of that car as it drove away, hair cut short and dyed a dingy blond, brow wrinkled in concern. He pictures the way she'd turned back. The rear windshield framing her heart-shaped face like a movie screen. And then she was gone.

Then he remembers her as he'd first known her. Fresh-faced. Different. That gleam in her eye that let you know she was a fighter right from the start. But all smooth skin, too. Creamy.

That girl he threw his life away for, ultimately. And he'd throw it away ten more times to have her, if he could.

We'll meet again, you and me. I promise.

Finished, he zips up and turns back to the Corvette. Pops the door. Leans over the driver's seat to grab the beers.

Just as he turns around, he sees the blur of the girl running out of the shed.

CHAPTER 117

Ellie darted through the doorway. Stepped into the silvery light. Her right foot planted into the ground, and she veered hard to the left, going from zero to full sprint within three paces.

For just a second, she could sense the outbuilding to her left, the white paint catching moonlight, glowing purple splotches flickering. Then she rocketed past the edge of the building, and that glow was left behind.

The dark swelled and became total. Filled her field of vision.

And she didn't flinch. She ran into the blackness. Face-first.

Some soaring feeling lifted her stomach, a weightless sensation like tipping over that first hill on a roller coaster. Airy.

Her eyes adjusted second by second. Focusing. Texture and details gradually populated the gloom.

She found herself drawn to the darkest places. Running for the safety of the murk. She avoided the strips of darkest black that represented tree trunks, running between them like goalposts.

Plants clawed at her. A thousand green tendrils trying to rip at the skin of her arms and legs.

But the space felt open and huge. She sprinted into it, picked up her knees. Free.

The night enfolded her. So many times in her life, the dark had been a scary thing, vast and unknowable. But now it was her only ally, concealing her, keeping her safe.

Bugs screeched everywhere, a choir of insect life singing some awful one-note song. Throaty voices lifted in some primordial worship. Some of them cut off as she ran closer, the individual bug sounds winking out as she passed, but the choir itself never really wavered.

She ran through a patchwork of moonlight shining through the leaves. Caught just a glint of the dark shape in her right hand. The pointy thing pumped up and down with her arm.

And something cold coursed through her at the sight. Adrenaline like ice water mainlined into every vein.

Her palm shifted. Fingers squeezing the handle tight. Maybe she wouldn't need to use it.

Hide and seek, she reminded herself. *Fun.*

And something about it *was* fun. A little.

The wind in her hair. The night's chill hung up everywhere here under the trees. The cold swoosh of running through it all.

Fun.

But a twig snapped somewhere behind her. The crack rang out over the droning bug sounds.

Heavy footfalls followed a beat later. He ran through the brush, leaves and branches swishing out of the way.

The steps grew louder. He was gaining on her already. She could tell.

And turning back over her shoulder, she saw something worse.

Branches trembled and parted. And a beam of light shoved into the leafy cleft as though splitting it wide.

A flashlight.

He has a flashlight.

The beam shattered the darkness. Speared it. Obliterated it.

The dark around her suddenly wasn't safe. Or wouldn't be, soon enough.

The fear welled up in her. She clenched her jaw and tried to fight it.

She ran harder. Cut to her right.

Thicker brush blotted out the flashlight again here. The way behind her inked black once more.

But the beam reappeared almost as quickly. It rose up over a gentle hill and lanced the shadows.

Then the beam swung around. Gliding like a blade, left and then right. It swept over the ground. Reached for her.

Hide and seek, she thought again. *Hide and seek.*

She dropped down onto hands and knees. And she moved again for the darkest of the dark.

That the night might see her through was her only hope, her only chance. She had to embrace it.

She scrabbled into it, ducked and speared the top of her head into a thick bush, arms and legs working together to propel herself through the surface tension. The branches fought her at first, prodding and resisting, and then they seemed to give, to relax. The going got easier.

She crawled deep into the needled branches of the thing, swaddled herself in darkness, and held her breath.

CHAPTER 118

The girl lopes like a gazelle. She disappears into the gloom, like the tree line at the edge of the woods just swallowed her up.

Putnam gives chase before he's even fully processed what he's seeing.

How the fuck?

She was out. Sleeping like a dead baby. Or she had been. He'd monitored her breathing himself.

He clenches his jaw then, realizing.

Faking.

She was fucking faking.

Little bitch.

Rage surges through him, makes his face hot, his breath hotter.

He bashes through the edge of the woods, broad body mowing down saplings, heavy feet crushing the greenery along the ground.

The side of his neck twitches where the fury touched it. He wants to run her down, run her over, run her through. And he will. He will.

He churns his legs, pumps his arms, hands bladed at the ends. And he tears ass some fifty feet into the dark.

Then he catches himself. Stops.

He takes a breath. Shakes his head. He can't let the anger blind him. Not now.

He digs into his pocket. Fishes out the little flashlight he'd taken from the Corvette house. Remembers finding it there in the wooden cigar box on top of the dresser.

Thank Christ I thought to grab it.

He turns the black metal cylinder over in his hands. Searches for the switch. Finds it.

Better fucking work.

He touches the button. The glow shoots out of the end of the flashlight, alive all at once.

His nostrils flare.

Yes.

You're mine now.

Mine.

He stabs the light before him like a sword and runs again. She won't get far.

But he swings the beam around and sees only blank woods. Fat tree trunks squat every few feet, lichen coating the bark like tooth plaque. A sea of dead leaves surrounds islands of green moss. Stalks and stems poke out of the ground and hang down from the sky alike, limbs reaching out for each other. It all holds still, keeps its secrets.

No sign of her. No white flash of her t-shirt. No trembling branches signifying she'd been there.

His nostrils flare again. Breath hot against his parted lips.

Keep it together.

Instinct tells him to press forward at roughly two o'clock. He trusts it. Keeps moving that way. A little slower now.

He brushes the flashlight back and forth. Watches the glow flit over all the scrub, shadows twitching everywhere.

He stays focused. Stays patient.

Finally, a bush flaps its many arms in the distance, tattling on her. He bursts into a sprint.

The movement of the branches dies before he gets there, but it doesn't matter now.

He throws his hips to the side and dodges around the shrub. Brings his light up.

There.

His light catches on her, reflects off her, that white t-shirt practically glowing in the dark. The beam holds her for just a second like a tractor beam.

Yes.

He wants to reel her in like a fish. Pull that line of light connecting them. Draw her to him.

Instead she comes unglued from the beam. Veers right and disappears behind a wall of foliage.

He sweeps his light that way, tries to stab it through the brush. The glow can't pierce those tight snarls of green.

Fuck.

But it's OK. It's OK.

He has her now.

He presses toward the place where she disappeared. Wheels around the corner. Brandishes his flashlight.

Nothing.

Gone.

Nothing.

The flashlight cuts out all at once, and his skin pulls all the way taut.

No.

The dark closes around him, blankets him. He gasps, air sucking and rasping deep in his throat.

What the fuck?

He jabs the flashlight button a few times. The clicks ring out over the empty space between the trees. No light.

He whaps the tube against his palm four times. Tries to bring the flashlight back to life that way, a rough kind of CPR.

He tries the button after. Still nothing.

His hand fishes into his pocket again. The object that he withdraws this time is smaller.

He flicks the lighter four times before the flame finally holds. Then he hoists it over his head, wields it like a torch. Swings it to the left and then to the right.

The little sphere of light glides over tree branches, ferns, various bushes and shrubs.

He can't see her. Can't really see shit compared to the flashlight.

He stomps forward a few paces, frustrated. An urge tells him to run. Sprint. Catch up with her.

Instead, he stops. Breathes. Two deep breaths. Three.

Stay calm. Just think.

He turns in a full circle. Slowly lets the light fall in all directions. It doesn't reveal much, but it's better than running blind.

Deep in.

The light seems to dance where it touches leaves flicking in the wind, the white undersides reflective. He keeps going.

Deep out.

On the second go round, he finds himself drawn to a big ass bush some five or ten paces back. It looks empty, but he stalks closer anyway.

Deep in.

When he gets to within two or three feet out from the bush, he squats lower. Snakes his arm into the branches. Thrusts the lighter out in front.

Deep out.

Yes. There's something there.

CHAPTER 119

Ellie's chest ached. She could feel her blood beating in her face, a hot thrumming under her skin.

Still, she didn't breathe. Didn't move.

His flashlight had gone out, the whole woods plunging to black for a few seconds before the moonlight seemed to turn back up. The dark had made Ellie's chest and shoulders tense. It seemed to her a gift and a curse. He couldn't see her now, perhaps, but she couldn't see him either.

And then a moment later he'd streaked past, hoisting what looked like a lighter or maybe a match.

She'd only seen that little spear of orange, the flame itself, gliding by. It flickered past the weave of branches and needles between her and the world.

Now, she breathed. Twice. Three times. Slow breaths. Quiet.

She counted ten such inhales, and then she held it again.

The beat of his steps had been quiet for some time. She lowered her head and tried to peer through the gaps in the bush, the bars of her cage, but the flame still wouldn't show.

He wasn't far off, though. Something told her that. Some animal instinct.

And that same gut feeling told her to stay put. To wait it out.

This bush would be the place where she'd make her stand. Right here. For better or worse.

The endless shriek of the bugs sounded different from inside the bush. Dampened. The treble sliced out of the sound, leaving a dull chorus of insect voices. Almost sounded like radio static sizzling inside her skull.

A stick snapped somewhere not so far off. Her head rotated that way.

She sucked in five more quick breaths. Held it again.

The flame reappeared. Definitely a lighter. A match couldn't burn this long, this steadily.

The brightness crested the top of a small hill and stepped between the black crinkles of foliage there. A floating thing disembodied for the moment — she couldn't see the arm holding it, just that glowing sphere drifting some six or so feet off the ground.

The orange spike stabbed the darkness, pointed up. The orb of light around it seemed to gently morph, its edges shrinking and then expanding. Flexing and warping as it caught on leaves and branches. Shifting shapes.

It floated closer. Closer.

And she could see him then. The light shone down on the L-shape of his arm leading into his shoulder, lit half of his jaw. Dark stubble clouded one side of his chin, and shadow shrouded the rest. His mouth was a grim hard line in between.

He strode closer. Roughly aimed for her.

Two more breaths. Then she held again.

The ball of light glided, something so smooth about its progress. Fluid. It seemed to drift right up on her like a wave lapping up on the beach.

The foliage swallowed him up then, blocked out most of the view, and she could see only the light again — that disembodied sphere once more drifting alone.

It bobbed a second as he stepped over something. The flame shot sideways and then straightened back up.

And the glowing orb was above her now. Very close. She had to crane her neck to see it as it drew to within an arm's length of the bush concealing her.

The flame flickered again. Danced a little on the wind.

She fought the urge to shuffle back, to try to disappear deeper into the shadows. Instead she kept herself still, kept herself quiet.

And she focused on the tightness in her chest. The emptiness formed a vacuum there where the air should be. This held breath had been her longest so far.

She could feel the veins in her face pulsing in time with her heart, blood beating in her cheeks again. Little panicky feelings begged her to inhale, but she ignored them. Held on. Leaned into the empty feeling in her chest.

The orange spike of flame passed right by her hiding spot. Drifted on. Kept going.

When it got to about fifteen feet beyond, she breathed again. Shallow. Quiet. Some relief touched her face, a coolness swirling in the flesh.

Ten breaths, and then she held it again. Watching. Waiting.

The flame stopped its forward progression. Held steady for a few seconds.

All at once, it floated back the way it had come. Then it cut out.

The footsteps continued. Crunched closer. Three more steps. Four.

They drew up close to where she cowered, and then they, too, stopped.

The quiet got bigger. Bigger.

Nothingness spiraled in Ellie's chest. Made the muscles squirm along the flanks of her ribcage.

The lighter flicked out that gritty snapping sound. Sparks flew, glittered, caught.

When the flame shot up this time, it was lower. Eye level to where she sat.

A hiccup motion quaked in Ellie's chest. She kept it quiet. Her hand choked up on the octagonal handle in her hand, thumb and index finger squeezing the grooved bit.

He's crouching down.

He's right there.

The flame pushed forward, shoved into the branches, into her space. That awful glowing sphere reached out and touched her.

And then his other arm was there all at once. Reaching into the hollow under the bush. Hand outstretched. Fingers splayed.

A big arm coming in from the darkness beyond the flame, a big hand sliding over her, fingers hooking at the elastic waist of her shorts.

She jumped back. Squirming to disentangle herself from his grip.

Branches and needles clawed her neck and arms. Thorns ripping at her flesh.

He crawled in after her, lighter still burning in one clinched fist. Shoulders somehow looking thicker as he wriggled in on hands and knees.

His head crossed the threshold. Angled up toward her.

A smile split his face. Shiny teeth gleaming in the wound. Something bestial in the grin, in his eyes.

And he grew at her feet. Swelled into the underbrush like he was forming right here and now.

Ellie's back butted up into a tree trunk. Shoulder blades planted against rough bark.

She flailed. Tried to shove out to the left, but the branches of the bush were knitted too tightly. They caught her. Held her back.

He was close now. Still growing. Rising up onto his knees.

His mouth quirked and words oozed out of his smile.

"Didn't know you were the outdoorsy type. Hell, we can seal the deal out here in the bush if you want. All rustic like."

Ellie hurled herself face-first into the meshwork of branches.

Nubby sticks ripped at her skin. Prickles scratched for her eyes. The bush wouldn't give, wouldn't budge. It tore at her face like dozens of buzzard beaks.

There was no place to go. No way out of here.

She turned back. Lifted a shaky arm.

The tool felt tiny in her hand now. Not much of a weapon after all. Her arm felt weak, quivering.

He loomed over her. Still on his knees. Edging over the grainy dirt.

Closer than an arm's length. Closer.

Fun.

Fun.

That's all it is.

She lurched forward now. Swung her arm. Swung the tool.

The flathead screwdriver arced for his face. Slammed into skin. Stabbed him in the eye.

Not scared.

She felt the gelatinous eyeball give. Felt the metal rod penetrate it. Soft. Wet. A feeling like pricking a hardboiled egg with a knitting needle.

Not scared.

She shoved harder. Threw herself into it. Pressed the metal deeper into his eye.

She almost couldn't believe that it worked, that nothing stopped her, blocked her. That the eyeball just took it. All of it.

Not scared.

With the flathead shoved in to the hilt, she tumbled back against the tree trunk again. Mouth breathing funny. Breaths fluttering out. She realized she was laughing.

Fun?

His hands fluttered to the eye socket like two birds. Cupped the injury. The screwdriver handle jutted through the small gap between his palms.

Blood sheeted down that side of his face. He fingered the broken place, hands coated red.

A little suction sound emitted somewhere deep in his throat. A breath. A rasp. A pop.

And then he screamed like a dying cat.

CHAPTER 120

The rim of moonlight glowed around the edges of him, marking the way out of here. He rocked backward, sat up on his knees.

Ellie threw herself for him. Upper body flung. Arms open. Legs driving.

Everything flashed red and then blackened as they slammed together. The darkness engulfing them.

And then they were tangled together. Pressed close. All four arms fighting for the screwdriver.

His hands felt cold, skin dry and a little scratchy. Her fingers crawled over the backs of them, climbed toward the jutting silhouette of the handle she could just make out there.

She got a thumb on it. Felt it tilt at her touch. Some faint sucking sound emitting from deep in his eye socket.

He hissed and wrenched away. Twisted himself to the side and threw her down.

She slammed down on her belly. Got a mouthful of dust. The rolling cloud aiming itself into her lips.

The sand gritted on her teeth, pasted grains to her tongue. She grimaced and tried to spit it out.

And then she scrabbled back up. Climbed the side of him.

And he was whispering, spitting, urgent words pouring out of him.

"Don't pull it out. Don't pull it out. You're not supposed to pull it out."

He hiccupped. Kept going.

"You're not supposed to do that. Not supposed to."

He wasn't all the way here anymore, she realized. The shock of the injury had spiraled some madness into his thoughts.

Pull it out, he says.

I like his idea better.

She launched herself at him again, one shoulder getting higher than the other. Her collarbone got him in the throat.

He choked. Tongue bulging out between his lips.

Again, he turned sideways. Tried to shield himself from her with his elbow, both hands still cupping the injured eye.

"No," he said, weak whimpers stuttering out of him. "Stop. You'll knock it out."

She draped herself over his tilted form. Dipped her hand under his elbow to strike from below. She had him now.

Her hand knifed right between his. Her grip closed around the screwdriver handle. She pulled.

The shaft slurped again as it eased out. Squelched. Wet sucking somewhere in that soft, deep socket.

And then the sword came free of the stone.

CHAPTER 121

With the screwdriver out, blood squirted out of Putnam's eye socket. The red sheet sluiced over most of his face, ripples of it glittering in the moonlight, the flow visible wherever the light touched it, fluttering darkly.

His lips popped once and stayed open. Bottom teeth exposed. Breath wheezing out of him.

Then he stumbled back, scrabbled out of the bush like a crab. Hands chopping at the foliage. Knees pointed at the sky.

He pushed himself up to his feet. Momentum carried him backward another step and a half, and he stumbled again before he got his footing.

Then he turned and sprinted into the dark. His moans and footsteps quickly trailed away.

Ellie watched it all through the semicircle opening in the shrubbery — the domed boughs forming the edges of her screen. He exited stage left, really moving.

She blinked when he was gone. Listened for a second.

Nothing.

The woods had absorbed his footsteps already, taking the stream of whimpers with them. Now the bug noises seemed to wash everything else out.

Ellie waited another second, confirming the silence. She wiped the screwdriver in some ferns and tucked it in the waistband of her shorts. Then she crawled through that bright circle into the open, wriggling the last bit flat on her belly.

Out in the open, she laid still for a second. Breathing.

The air felt fresher, cleaner somehow, as soon as she was free of the clutching branches. She could feel the sky overhead, that vast emptiness always hung up above. Usually it was something she took for granted, barely noticed even, but just now, it seemed a great comfort.

She lay there for eight or ten seconds, the front of her body mashed to the weeds and the dirt. Then she took a couple deep breaths and stood.

She scanned the full panorama around her, oriented herself the best she could. The woods looked basically indistinguishable in all directions — copied and pasted chunks of trees and thicket repeated over and over — but she was pretty sure she knew the way to the road.

She pointed her arm that way for a second, let it fall. Then she started walking.

She found herself surprisingly calm as she set out. Heartbeat steady. Breathing even. Everything under control.

Maybe she had faith that the worst was over, at least for now.

She walked. Kept her head down. Tried to see where she was stepping.

Grass and brush scrolled under her feet, all of it smeared with the charcoal of the shadows, which were thickest right along the ground. Some of the fronds tickled against her calves.

And images came to her as she stared into the dark places. Interrupting thoughts overwriting the pictures inside.

She saw Wes. Face down on the motel carpet. The dark pool spreading outward from his shape.

Part of her wanted to believe he might make it, that somehow he might still be OK.

But she couldn't hold onto the hope for long. He'd looked dead, that was for sure.

She remembered watching his chest, seeing that it wasn't moving, that he wasn't breathing. Already gone. Just like that.

She chewed her lip. Wiped at the wetness rimming her eyes.

He couldn't really be gone. It was impossible.

But it was real. Somehow, it was real. Somehow, the world really could be that awful, really *was* that awful.

It brought the pain, the suffering, the death.

It snuffed people out like they were nothing. Plucked them from this plane of existence.

Daily. Hourly. Second by second.

Wes.

It didn't seem right. It would never seem right.

Her footsteps crunched out that steady beat underfoot. She kept going. Maybe that was all anyone could do.

Because she was still here. With no help from anyone, she'd lived. Fought. Won.

She'd survived. She wouldn't feel guilty for that. Not now. Not later. Not ever. Wes wouldn't want her to.

She swallowed, and her throat felt funny. Tight.

A car engine roared to life somewhere in front of her. Something almost frantic about the whinny and growl of it.

The Corvette.

Ellie lifted her head. Tried to see through the thicket.

The diffuse red glow of the taillights puddled over the woods, tiny shards of it flitting where the branches swayed. A second later the headlights flicked on — two spears of light thrusting through the foliage, pointed off to Ellie's left.

The lights shot up the sides of the cinder block building, making the structure seem to appear there all at once where only shadows existed a second before.

All of this was only a hundred feet or so from where Ellie stood, much closer than she'd realized.

Some instinct told her to jog that way, and she did. She hurtled a rotting log, wove around some birch trunks that gleamed a few shades paler than the other trees.

The Corvette ripped backward. Jounced over the craggy makeshift driveway. The headlights bobbled up and down, slowly shrinking back from the cinder block wall of the shed.

Ellie reached the clearing around the building just as the car screeched out onto the road. The headlights wheeled away from her, pointed down the long strip of road ahead, the shaft of open space gashed into the trees.

Something thunked under the hood as it shifted from reverse to drive, and then the vehicle lurched forward, accelerating quickly, tearing over the asphalt. The rear end shimmied for a second and then straightened out.

The darkness swelled around Ellie.

Looks like I'm on my own from here on out.

Red flared out on the road. Taillights.

Ellie lifted her head. Squinted to see the vehicle between the trees.

The Corvette was only a few hundred yards down the road.

It fishtailed. The rear end wagging back and forth like an excited cocker spaniel.

Then it jerked hard to the left and even harder to the right. All over the road. The tires squawked, wondering what the fuck.

That shimmy in the back tires seemed to spread into the front. Tremors overwhelming the thing.

The whole car shook now. Uneven. Like something about to explode.

The Corvette jerked like that again. Skittered all the way to the left shoulder. Overcorrected all the way back to the right.

But this time it kept going. Careened off the road.

The headlights pointed out into the woods. Flickered over the tall weeds along the shoulder.

The sports car dipped down into the ditch. Raced up the other side.

Ellie sucked in a short breath. Mouth open. She could only stare.

When the inevitable bang came, she shuddered. Shoulders inching up into a hunch.

The front end of the Corvette wrapped around a thick tree trunk. The car stopped dead. All that momentum killed at once. Metal sheared, crushed, bent into impossible angles.

The engine snuffled a few times — its death rattle grunted into the exposed pulp of the tree — and then it, too, died.

The sudden quiet sprawled in all directions. Stark. Empty. The tension reached out to weave itself around Ellie, pulled her skin into goosebumps.

She didn't care what happened to Putnam. She knew that,

reminded herself of it now.

Kinda hope he's dead, so…

But, care or not, the sheer violence of the wreck made her adrenal gland pump anyway. The iciness coursed through her veins, surged into her cheeks, chilled the tip of her nose.

She padded down the beaten path toward the road, the subtle decline making her steps choppy in the dark. She found herself conscious of her breathing as she walked, the night air curling down her throat and into her lungs. She felt better when she thought about the flow of it.

At the bottom of the hill, the trees gave way to the open road. Ellie stepped that way.

She padded down the lane. Let her eyes drift to the wrecked Corvette in the distance from this new vantage point.

The impact had snuffed out both headlights, but the taillights still stared back at Ellie. Glowing scarlet eyes turned slightly crooked on the uneven land.

She dug the lighter out of her pocket. She didn't light it yet — she could see well enough to keep on the road, which was all she needed for the moment — but she wanted it ready.

She closed in on the Corvette. Toed up to the edge of the pavement and stopped when the gravel of the shoulder crunched underfoot.

The car was maybe twenty-five feet off the road. It seemed to have picked the biggest tree trunk of the lot here.

Ellie flicked the lighter. Held the spear of flame out in front of her.

The glittery purple enamel of the car came clear first. Then she could see the wounded front end, a shredded mess, rumpled metal where half of the sports car's curves used to be.

She lowered the torch. Held it toward the ground at her feet.

The ditch fell away below her, a bathtub-wide divot in the land with mucky slop occupying the bottom. She could hop it easily enough, but she didn't see why she should.

Putnam hadn't leapt out of the car so far. He could be dead

or maybe unconscious. Either way, the information did her no good. And the car itself was worthless to her now.

If he came at her again, he'd get it in the other eye.

She released the button, and the lighter winked out. Then she started walking down the road again, trawling into the murk.

Her eyes slowly readjusted to the darkness, and porch lights came to life in the distance. Ellie squared her shoulders toward what she thought was the closest one and kept moving.

CHAPTER 122

Ellie stared dead-eyed at the TV mounted to the wall of her hospital room, which was currently playing one of those home renovation shows. This one was hosted by twin brothers who were only distinguishable to her as Beard and No Beard.

No Beard was babbling about "giving the space a modern feel with a vintage touch," which was something he seemed to say in practically every episode.

She snatched up the remote and turned the TV off. The constant babble of the renovation jargon was replaced by the muted sounds of the hallway beyond her door. Rubber soles squeaking on the tile floor. An automatic door swooshing open. The bump and rattle of some kind of cart or perhaps a gurney or wheelchair. The voice of one nurse asking another for a bag of Lactated Ringer's.

Ellie closed her eyes, thinking she'd just nap until the doctor came. She scooched a little to the left. And then a little to the right. But no matter what she did, she couldn't get comfortable in the stupid bed. All she'd done for the last two days was lie around, and she was sick of it.

She glanced at the clock, wondering how much longer she'd have to wait. She picked up the remote and was about to turn the TV back on when there was a peppy knock at the door, and Dr. Nemec breezed in with Ellie's nurse in tow.

"OK, Thelma and/or Louise. How are we this morning?" the doctor asked.

He'd been making jokes like that ever since he found out that Ellie had been part of the effort to sneak Jimmy Maddox out of the hospital. At one point, he'd called her Patty Hearst, which made Ellie squirm a little when she thought about how close to the truth it really was.

"Good. Great. Ready to be discharged," Ellie said.

Dr. Nemec smirked while paging through Ellie's chart.

"I think that can be arranged. But you're going to have to empty your pockets first."

Ellie stared at him in confusion.

"My pockets?"

Dr. Nemec looked serious now.

"That's right. Gotta make sure you're not trying to make off with a bunch of gauze and gloves and whatnot."

Another moment passed before Ellie realized the doctor was teasing her again. He scribbled something in her chart, chuckling to himself.

"Everything looks good." He closed the chart and handed it to the nurse. "If you'll put the orders in, we can get our outlaw here discharged."

He turned back to Ellie.

"All joking aside, you went through some serious trauma. You remember what we discussed about seeking counseling once you get back home?"

Ellie nodded.

"I know. I will."

As soon as Ellie was alone again, she hopped out of bed. She couldn't wait to get dressed. Then she remembered the police had taken her clothes as evidence, and now all she had was this gown that showed her entire ass no matter how she tied the little strings. What the hell was she going to wear? Would they let her borrow a pair of scrubs?

There was another knock at the door. Ellie had a sudden irrational worry that it was Dr. Nemec, coming to tell her that he'd changed his mind and wanted to keep her here another day.

But it was Courtney's face that peeked through, followed by John.

Courtney had a clear plastic clamshell with a single cupcake inside.

"Happy discharge day!"

Ellie smiled at the cupcake.

"How did you know?"

"Oh, the nurse told us yesterday you'd be ready to leave today."

Ellie found it annoying that no one had told *her* that. Everyone she'd talked to just kept saying, "We have to wait and see what the doctor says."

John wheeled in her suitcase.

"We brought your stuff, too. Since we had to check out of the motel and everything."

Ellie was delighted to see her luggage. Now she had clothes. She dropped the suitcase on its side and unzipped it.

"Here, let me help you," Courtney said, shooing John out of the room.

"Help me what?"

"Get dressed."

"I think I can dress myself," Ellie protested. "I'm not an invalid."

"The nurse said you'd need help, and I really think they're the experts here, don't you?"

"Isn't that a HIPAA violation? I feel like that should be a HIPAA violation."

Courtney pulled out an outfit that looked appropriate for a day at the beach. Ellie nudged her aside and picked out a pair of joggers and a t-shirt.

The first thing Ellie donned was a pair of real underwear, which was a delightful experience after what the hospital had provided. Some kind of weird baggy mesh things that felt like wearing a hairnet on her nether region.

When she bent to put on her pants, she realized how sore she was. Every movement sent a jolt of pain through her muscles.

Courtney stooped to help her and then recoiled when she saw the bruises all over Ellie's body.

"Are you sure you're ready to be discharged?" she asked, her eyes bugging out.

"I'm fine."

The shirt was another ordeal, since she could barely raise her arms high enough to get the sleeves on. In the end, she only managed with Courtney's assistance.

By the time she was finished getting dressed — which took about ten times longer than usual — her discharge papers were ready. She was free.

In the hallway, John insisted on taking her suitcase. As they proceeded through the various corridors and waiting rooms, Ellie recognized some parts of the hospital from when she had been here with Scarlet. It gave her an odd sense of déjà vu. Memories of Scarlet's giant gauze-wrapped head gliding out in front of her in that wheelchair kept coming to her.

John wheeled her suitcase up to her car and deposited it in the trunk.

"You're sure about this?" Courtney asked, handing her the keys.

Ellie shoved them in the pocket of her pants and nodded.

"Classes start in two days, though. Aren't your parents going to flip out if you're not back by then?"

"Oh, they definitely will." Ellie shrugged. "But that's their problem."

Courtney squinted at her.

"Wait a minute. Did you finally grow a pair?"

Ellie snorted.

"What about you? Are you sure you don't want to take my car back? I could always fly back later or take a bus."

Courtney linked her arm through John's.

"Nah. I'm going to ride back to Detroit with John and take the train back to school from there."

They hugged and said their goodbyes, and then she watched Courtney and John drive away in his car.

She made sure her car was locked and then headed back inside, turned down a hallway that smelled inexplicably like French fries, and pushed through the door that led to the ICU. She passed the spot where she'd spilled that cop's coffee all over the floor and found herself smirking.

She turned again, gliding past rooms with Plexiglass windows set into the walls. Some were blocked by curtains, others were left open.

That was how, before she'd even reached the door of the room, she saw that the bed inside was empty.

She let out a panicked gasp and quickened her pace.

Don't panic, she thought. *There's surely an explanation. There are a thousand reasons an ICU patient might not be in their bed. A CT scan. An MRI.*

She halted on the threshold, staring at the various monitors, their screens black. The stripped bed. This patient clearly wasn't coming back.

No.

Ellie spun away from the door and ran farther down the hall, nearly colliding with a nurse as she rounded a corner.

"Excuse me!" The nurse glared at her. "There's no running in here."

"What happened to the patient in room 8?"

"Room 8?" The nurse blinked, and her face turned thoughtful. "Oh, he was transferred up to 4 this morning. Room 457, I think it was."

"Transferred," Ellie repeated. The rush of relief was so intense she almost felt dizzy.

"That's right."

"You said the fourth floor?" Ellie said, already backpedaling.

"Yes. And there's no running up there, either, just so you know."

There was a sour note in the nurse's voice, but Ellie didn't care. She grinned.

"Thank you!"

She walked as fast as she could to the elevator, bouncing on her heels as she waited for the door to open. It was only three floors up, but the ride felt like it took an eternity to Ellie.

"Should have taken the stairs," she murmured to herself.

When the doors finally slid open with a ding, she consulted

a sign with arrows indicating which rooms were left and which were right. She went right, counting down as she went.

459.

458.

457.

This was it.

The door was slightly ajar, and Ellie poked her head in to make sure it was the right room.

The patient was lying on the bed. Face turned slightly away. But even so, she knew it was him.

Wes.

She slipped inside, tiptoeing closer to the bed. His eyes were closed. The rise and fall of his chest was slow and steady.

Ellie was slightly disappointed that he was sleeping. Every time she'd visited him in the ICU, he'd been so heavily sedated it was as if he was sleeping then too, so she had yet to be able to talk to him.

But even so, it was enough to simply sit by his bed and hold his hand.

There was a chair against the wall, and Ellie dragged it closer to him. At the sound of the chair legs scooting and scuffing over the floor, his eyelids fluttered open.

"Oh!" Ellie said, startled. "You're awake!"

Wes grimaced and swallowed.

"Yep."

She felt suddenly unsure of herself. What if getting shot had changed how he felt about her? This whole thing was her fault, after all. If she hadn't gotten mixed up with Jimmy and Scarlet in the first place, none of this would have happened. Putnam wouldn't have come after her, and Wes never would have gotten shot.

His mother had even said as much, the first time she'd had Courtney and John wheel her up to the ICU to visit Wes.

"Wes, I'm so sorry."

He frowned.

"You're *sorry*?"

He sounded indignant. Oh God, he *did* blame her.

"I never meant for you to get hurt, I—"

"Ellie, will you stop?" Wes said, shaking his head. "None of this was your fault."

She took a breath.

"You don't blame me for what happened?"

"Of course not."

"It's just... your mom..."

She winced, remembering the way his mother had glared at her. The words she'd hissed. "I already lost one son, and you almost cost me another."

Wes let out a dismissive puff of breath.

"Oh. Her. The thing you have to understand about my mom is that she's certifiable. Total whack job."

"But she said..."

"Who cares what she said? She's gone anyway."

"Gone?"

"Yeah. She left last night, as soon as they approved my transfer out of the ICU. Said I'd already cost her at least five thousand dollars between the plane ticket and missing work, and that I was old enough to kiss my own boo-boos now."

"Wow."

"Yeah. See? Whack job."

"I'm sorry."

Wes rolled his eyes.

"Stop apologizing, and come here."

Ellie didn't need to hear anything more than that. She threw herself into his arms.

He pulled her close, and she inhaled. There was a faint odor of alcohol wipes, but underneath that, it was Wes. Her Wes.

"So what exactly happened?" Wes asked. "After I got shot, I mean. I don't really remember."

Ellie explained the encounter with Putnam. Escaping the shed. The chase through the woods. The screwdriver.

"Jesus," Wes said, holding her tighter. "I can't believe that happened to you. I'm glad you're OK."

"Sorry, but I win on that front. I thought you were dead."

Wes scoffed.

"'It takes more than that to kill a Bull Moose.'"

Ellie squinted her eyes at him in confusion.

"That's what Teddy Roosevelt said after he got shot," Wes explained.

"Oh. My God," Ellie said.

"What?"

"You're a nerd," she went on in mock horror. "Like a *huge* nerd. This changes everything. I'm out."

She pretended to pull away from him in disgust.

Wes started to laugh and then grabbed his stomach.

"Ow! Don't make me laugh."

"Sorry," Ellie said. "Should I call a nurse? Do you need more pain meds?"

"No, I'm good," Wes said, settling back against the pillow. "They did some kind of nerve block apparently, so it's hasn't been too bad. I don't really feel pain so much as it sometimes just feels… weird and wrong. Like there are staples on my insides, and something's pulling on them."

Ellie shuddered at the description.

"Could be worse," he went on. "Could have gotten stabbed in the eyeball."

Ellie's jaw hardened. She'd been dismayed to learn that Putnam was, despite the stabbing and the car crash, still alive. He'd been on the opposite end of the ICU from Wes, but she'd seen the police hanging around the floor often enough over the last few days that it was a near-constant reminder that she'd failed to truly finish the job. After all, he'd escaped prison twice now — once through the means of a legal technicality, another by his own guile. If he made a full recovery, what was to stop him from trying for a third time? She doubted he'd forgotten his vendetta against Scarlet, and Ellie didn't think he'd be so quick to forgive the girl who'd taken his eye either.

"I should have stabbed both his eyes out."

Wes opened his mouth to speak but was interrupted by

Ellie's phone ringing.

She pulled it from her pocket and glanced at the screen.

"My parents. Again."

She hit the ignore button and slid the phone back in her pocket.

"I mean, they're probably worried about you, right?" Wes said.

She rolled her eyes.

"They were at first. But pretty much the second they found out I was OK, the concern seemed to evaporate, and then it was, 'You've got some explaining to do,' and 'How is this going to look to people?' and 'We're going to have to rethink paying for your education if this is the kind of thing you're doing behind our backs.'"

Wes clicked his tongue.

"They sound about as nuts as my parents."

"Yeah."

After a moment, he asked, "Do you really think they'll cut you off?"

Ellie shrugged.

"I told my dad to go ahead. That I wasn't interested in his money if it meant not getting to make my own choices."

Wes raised one eyebrow, and Ellie smiled.

"I'm making some changes."

CHAPTER 123

Taft strode the grounds of the cemetery long after the others at Stinson's funeral had come and gone. He walked down endless rows of headstones, trudged up and down grassy hills with thick tree trunks shooting up here and there among the graves.

The sun glared down on him all the while, but no one else was there. He was thankful to be alone. Thankful, too, for the sunglasses that dimmed the brightness some.

The grief seemed to ebb and flow in waves. A heaviness in his chest that strengthened in intervals and tried to choke him.

It felt better, somehow, to keep moving, keep walking. Momentum.

Memories flitted through his head as he walked. Little slices of Stinson's life captured in short films. Some older and some more recent.

Stinson picking up her daughter from school, scooping the little one up in her arms and carrying her across the parking lot.

Stinson driving her knee into the back of a meth dealer laid out prone beneath her, winding the cuffs around his wrists and cinching them tight.

Stinson's face growing serious as she contemplated the mess of clues in the Putnam case, what would ultimately become their final case together.

His mind grew still at the thought. No more words inside.

He climbed the biggest hill in the graveyard now. Feet digging into the gravel of the footpath, attacking the slope.

And he remembered Shane Putnam as he'd last seen him. Laid out in a hospital bed, a mess of gauze wound around his head, swaddling the pit where his eye used to be.

Putnam would live, they said. Behind bars, Taft supposed.

Or who knows?

Maybe he'll live exactly long enough to sit in the electric chair.

Ride the lightning.

Jimmy and Scarlet had gotten away, seemingly. Drove off into oblivion. No sightings since the chase when they fled the hospital.

Maybe that fit somehow.

The hostage or possible accomplice, Ellie, had said they'd been headed to Canada, that Jimmy had family there or some such.

Taft didn't buy it.

But it was out of his hands now, wasn't it? Out of his jurisdiction. Another piece of his life relegated to the past, where he couldn't touch it.

At the top of the hill, Taft stopped and looked down.

The cemetery sprawled below in all directions. A green field pocked with gray blocks in various sizes.

He turned to take it all in. Found Stinson's grave way in the back.

He could feel it still, even if he couldn't make out the details from here. The socket of open dirt where her casket lay. It seemed to radiate an energy still, some kind of current that connected it to him.

And he wondered how anyone ever really moved on. The people were gone, yes, but the memories never let go, did they?

Again, his mind went still. His eyes traced that rectangular vacancy in the earth.

It came as no comfort to think that time would erase some of these feelings. Like all his new memories would record over the old ones, slowly dulling everything to a gray smear.

It came as no comfort at all.

EPILOGUE

Scarlet sits in the driver's seat. One hand loops over the bottom half of the steering wheel.

Through the windshield, the waves lap at the beach in the distance. Cars and asphalt occupy the place between them and the water.

And people.

Beach-goers teem on the sand. Walking. Lounging. Lifting various alcoholic beverages to their mouths. A group of kids toss a Frisbee back and forth.

The sun descends as they linger there by the waterfront. The pink ball sinking into the ocean, the rosy hue slowly going darker and darker.

They've made it, she reminds herself.

The last few days have carried them from one coast to another. Flipping their perspective from the Atlantic coast of Florida to the Pacific coast of Sinoloa.

"Are we waiting for something?" a voice says from the passenger seat.

It's Jimmy, of course. She'd assumed he was asleep.

He's still recovering, stitches still holding his middle together, but he isn't in pain anymore that she can tell.

"Better to wait for dark, I think," she says after a second.

He nods.

It shouldn't matter. Nobody here will recognize them, more than likely. All that is 2,000 miles behind them now. And extradition generally only becomes a factor for serious criminals, like rapists and murderers, from what Scarlet has read. Maybe drug trafficking.

Still, it's better to lie low, at least for a while. Better to ease into it.

The sun disappears at last, dipping under the lip of the

horizon, but a half-light still occupies the sky. The full dark won't hit for a while yet.

They wait.

The crowd on the beach begins to wane as the dark thickens, and the people gather their beach towels and coolers, reeled back into the parking lot as though by some magnetic force flipped on by the dark.

Eventually a couple strides up the gentle slope of the sand and enters the parking lot just next to Jimmy and Scarlet. The woman's voice sharp and angry. The man's face twisted into a grimace.

The foreign language flows in fast speed. Sounds like backwards music to Scarlet's ears. She doesn't understand any of it, but she knows what's being said just the same.

"What did you say before?" she asks Jimmy. "That being miserable and hating each other is all part of the vacation fun?"

He smiles, his teeth bright in the gathering gloom.

"Not like us, right?"

"No. Not like us."

When the darkness settles, they climb out of the car and pad barefoot down to the water's edge.

It feels good to be moving again.

COME PARTY WITH US

We're loners. Rebels. But much to our surprise, the most kickass part of writing has been connecting with our readers. From time to time, we send out newsletters with giveaways, special offers, and juicy details on new releases.

Sign up for our mailing list at:
http://ltvargus.com/mailing-list

SPREAD THE WORD

Thank you for reading! We'd be very grateful if you could take a few minutes to leave a review on Amazon.com.

How grateful? Eternally. Even when we are old and dead and have turned into ghosts, we will be thinking fondly of you and your kind words. The most powerful way to bring our books to the attention of other people is through the honest reviews from readers like you.

ABOUT THE AUTHORS

Tim McBain writes because life is short, and he wants to make something awesome before he dies. Additionally, he likes to move it, move it.

You can connect with Tim via email at tim@timmcbain.com.

L.T. Vargus grew up in Hell, Michigan, which is a lot smaller, quieter, and less fiery than one might imagine. When not click-clacking away at the keyboard, she can be found sewing, fantasizing about food, and rotting her brain in front of the TV.

If you want to wax poetic about pizza or cats, you can contact L.T. (the L is for Lex) at ltvargus9@gmail.

LTVargus.com

www.ingramcontent.com/pod-product-compliance
Lightning Source LLC
Chambersburg PA
CBHW020616310726
48979CB00008B/1507/J

* 9 7 8 1 9 5 4 2 0 3 1 3 6 *